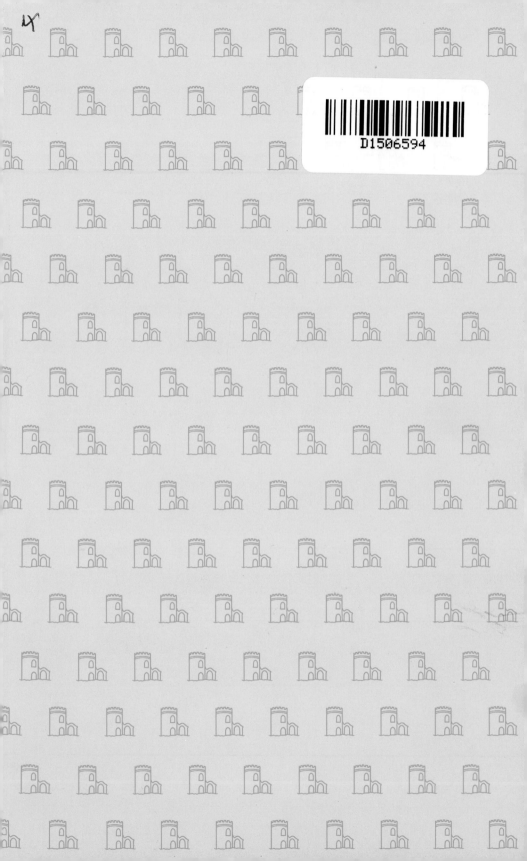

SPECIAL MESSAGE TO READERS

This book is published under the auspices of
THE ULVERSCROFT FOUNDATION
(registered charity No. 264873 UK)

Established in 1972 to provide funds for research, diagnosis and treatment of eye diseases. Examples of contributions made are: —

A new Children's Assessment Unit at Moorfield's Hospital, London.
•
Twin operating theatres at the Western Ophthalmic Hospital, London.
•
A Chair of Ophthalmology at the University of Leicester.
•
The establishment of a Royal Australian College of Ophthalmologists "Fellowship".

You can help further the work of the Foundation by making a donation or leaving a legacy. Every contribution, no matter how small, is received with gratitude. Please write for details to:

THE ULVERSCROFT FOUNDATION,
The Green, Bradgate Road, Anstey,
Leicester LE7 7FU, England.
Telephone: (0116) 236 4325

In Australia write to:
THE ULVERSCROFT FOUNDATION,
c/o The Royal Australian College of
Ophthalmologists,
27, Commonwealth Street, Sydney,
N.S.W. 2010.

I've travelled the world twice over,
Met the famous: saints and sinners,
Poets and artists, kings and queens,
Old stars and hopeful beginners,
I've been where no-one's been before,
Learned secrets from writers and cooks
All with one library ticket
To the wonderful world of books.

© JANICE JAMES.

TAMARISK

Tamarisk, daughter of a French Vicomte and the exquisite Mavreen, had inherited her mother's beauty — and her reckless, sensuous nature. It was almost inevitable that she would be drawn in a passionate attachment to Mavreen's former lover. But Sir Peregrine thought of Tamarisk only as a child. Humiliated at his rejection, Tamarisk offered herself to a notorious poet. Throughout the disgrace that followed, her love still burned for Peregrine, the man whose dangerous secret she had uncovered — the secret he shared with her rival — Mavreen.

CLAIRE LORRIMER

TAMARISK

Complete and Unabridged

CHARNWOOD
Leicester

First published in Great Britain in 1978

First Charnwood Edition
published 1996

British Library CIP Data

Lorrimer, Claire, *1921* –
Tamarisk.—Large print ed.—
Charnwood library series
1. English fiction—20th century
I. Title
823.9′14 [F]

ISBN 0–7089–8903–9

Published by
F. A. Thorpe (Publishing) Ltd.
Anstey, Leicestershire
Set by Words & Graphics Ltd.
Anstey, Leicestershire
Printed and bound in Great Britain by
T. J. Press (Padstow) Ltd., Padstow, Cornwall

This book is printed on acid-free paper

FOR JOY

Foreword

Whilst the historical facts are accurate to the best of my knowledge, as are the descriptions and movements of historical characters, licence has obviously been taken when the latter are in conversation with fictitious characters.

For readers who may be interested, the story of Mavreen, covering the years 1779 – 1812, precedes this story of her daughter, Tamarisk. *Tamarisk* is nevertheless complete in itself and covers the exciting years from 1812 – 1822 when, despite declarations of peace between England and her enemies, America and France, the world was undergoing great change and hovered on the brink of social revolution.

Cast of Characters

Mavreen (*Tamarisk's mother*)

Gerard (*Vicomte de Valle, Tamarisk's natural father*)

Sir John Danesfield (*Tamarisk's grandfather*)

Clarissa (*Sir John's mistress and second wife*)

Gilbert, Lord Barre (deceased) (*Tamarisk's legal father and Mavreen's first husband*)

Gideon Morris alias Sir Peregrine Waite (*Mavreen's ex-lover*)

Dickon Sale (*Mavreen's childhood friend and servant*)

Rose Sale (*wife of above*)

Patty and Anna Sale (*Dickon's sisters*)

Sale Family (*Sussex farmers, Mavreen's foster parents*)

Elsie (*Tamarisk's personal maid*)

Dorcas (*Mavreen's personal maid*)

William (*Mavreen's butler*)

Frederick (*Gideon's footman*)

Edward Crowhurst (*a young blood*)

Nikolai Kuragin (*Gerard's Russian servant*)

Baroness Helga Von Heissen (*Gerard's former mistress*)

Baroness Lisa Von Eburhard (*family friend*)

Charles Von Eburhard (*nephew of above*)

Herr Mehler (*Austrian music teacher*)

Hon. James Pettigrew (deceased) (*Mavreen's second husband*)

Anne Lade (*sister of above*)

Faustina, Vicomtesse De Valle (deceased) (*Gerard's first wife*)
Mistress Tyeson (*Lake Country farmer's wife*)
John Tyeson (*son of above*)
Leigh Darton (*actor*)
Blanche Merlin (*French farmer's daughter*)
Antoine Merlin (*Gerard's natural son by above*)
Monsieur Corot (*French innkeeper*)
Monsieur Mougin (*French lawyer*)
Rev. Cripps (*Sussex parson*)
Davinia Gurney (*Tamarisk's governess*)
Alfred Mumford (*Antoine's tutor*)
Princess Camille Faloise (*Gerard's friend and neighbour in Compiègne*)
Signor Galvanti (*Italian merchant*)
Signora Galvanti (*wife of above*)
Guiseppe (*servant of Signor Galvanti*)
Yonesti (*Gipsy tribe*)
Kako (*the Gipsy chief*)

Miarka
Zorka
Michel
Mara } (*gipsies*)
Torina
Tamara

Leonardo Conte Dell'Alba (*Gerard's Italian cousin*)
Contessa Dell'Alba (*wife of above*)
Maria Dell'Alba (*daughter of above*)
Pietro (*member of the Carbonari*)
Lord and Lady Greensmythe (*friends of the British Consul in Naples*)
Sir Robert Wilson (*member of London Society*)
Marquis de Guéridon (*friend of Gerard's mother*)

1

January 1813

TWILIGHT had given way to dusk as Tamarisk rode swiftly out of the woods and onto the road. Now she was not far from Richmond Bridge, on the far side of which there would be night watchmen and passersby to safeguard her.

But her relief was short-lived as her horse suddenly whinnied, shied, and all but unseated her.

"Who goes there?" a voice cut the silence. "Halt, I say!"

Tamarisk chilled with fear. Only two days ago on her fifteenth birthday, Aunt Clarrie had chosen the occasion to warn her yet again of the dangers besetting those who went out alone at night — pickpockets, murderers, drunken men who molested females, cutthroats. She had no weapon but her whip, and her horse was far too exhausted to be spurred to a gallop that might outpace the danger.

Her heart jolted and her chest pounded as a tall, dark figure stepped from the shadows and caught her horse's bridle.

"Why, 'pon my soul!" the man said, his speech sounding cultured but slurred to the anxious young girl staring down at him. "If 'tis not a female! What in the name of heaven

1

do you out here alone in the dark?"

"Unhand my horse!" Tamarisk ordered in what she intended to be a tone of authority but which quavered annoyingly. "Stand aside!"

The man laughed and moved a step nearer so that she could see his face. He was young and not unhandsome, but she could detect brandy fumes on his breath. Her body stiffened. Instinctively she raised her whip to protect herself, but a sudden laugh from her unknown companion bewildered her.

"Would you strike a wounded man, my fair lady?" he inquired in mocking tones. "Why, I had begun to hope for an Angel of Mercy when you came galloping into view. My phaeton overturned, throwing me onto the road, and only by God's mercy have I not sustained a broken neck!"

With a sigh of relief and an expression of contrition on her face, Tamarisk sprang gracefully to the ground and stepped forward. She was near enough now to see the blood trickling from a cut on the man's hand. His white frilled shirtfront and cuffs were stained red and his fashionable, cutaway jacket was mud-bespattered. He was hatless and his light brown curls were in disarray.

"You are not seriously injured, Sir?" she inquired as she removed her gloves and, taking her stock from about her neck, began nimbly to bandage the cut on his hand.

"My dignity more than my person, I think!" he replied.

He surveyed the girl with intense curiosity. Her

2

speech and appearance were those of a young lady of quality, yet he could not reconcile this supposition with the extraordinary circumstances in which he had encountered her. No young girl of good family would have been permitted to ride out alone, far less after dark. She was pretty too, with large green eyes, shining gold curls, and a temptingly curved mouth. Youthful and unprotected as she was, she would make an easy target for a man with fewer scruples than himself.

By the time Tamarisk had finished her ministrations, darkness had fallen and a bitterly cold wind was blowing around them. The first heavy drops of icy rain began to fall.

"I have righted my phaeton and we could shelter within it," he said, shivering. "Hopefully, 'twill be but a shower."

Tamarisk hesitated. To shelter from the rain was clearly desirable, but she would be even later home to face her aunt's wrath.

Aunt Clarrie would have every reason to punish her, she thought. In the first place she should never have gone out riding in Richmond Woods with only the stableboy for escort. But Aunt Clarrie had needed the head groom to drive her to her milliners, and Tamarisk, tediously bored with her embroidery, had been tempted out by the bright December sunshine. Sam, the stableboy, had had to be bullied into complying with her wishes. He had made no secret of his fear that his employer would heartily disapprove of Tamarisk's escapade. He had been even more fearful when his horse had cast a shoe.

3

By this time they had tarried overlong, and with this unexpected mishap, it would greatly delay their return.

"'Twill soon be dark, Milady!" he had muttered uneasily as an owl hooted from one of the shadowy trees surrounding them.

"Then I shall ride home alone," Tamarisk had replied, thinking of Aunt Clarrie's reactions were she not back by nightfall. But the boy protested that this was far too dangerous.

"What possible harm could befall me?" she had mocked him for his fears. "I shall be home in half an hour. 'Tis you who will have to brave the witches and ghosts and werewolves!" And she had laughed as she had galloped away through the woods.

But now her concern with the plight of this stranger had made it unlikely she would reach home before Aunt Clarrie's return, and she could but hope that she might avoid a great deal of her aunt's anger by explaining her part in coming to the aid of this unfortunate gentleman.

As if reading her mind he now said:

"Pray allow me to introduce myself. My name is Edward Crowhurst, and I am a secretary in the household of the Princess of Wales."

Supposing that her aunt would approve such an acquaintance, Tamarisk allowed her companion to tether her horse and lead her to the shelter of the phaeton. Within the comparative warmth of its confines, he peered more closely at her shadowy countenance.

"Now may I know your name?" he asked curiously.

4

"I am Tamarisk Barre," she said. "I am presently living with my aunt, Mistress Manton, at Orchid House in Richmond, because my mother is abroad. Usually I live with her in London."

Edward Crowhurst, despite his pleasant afternoon's drinking at a card game with some contemporaries in Richmond, was sober enough to be able to control his gasp of surprise, for he now knew exactly who this girl was. Daughter of the late Gilbert Barre, she was also the offspring of that fabulously beautiful woman Mavreen, who not so long ago was known to London Society as the Barre Diamond. His own mother — who was a lady-in-waiting to the Queen — had told him all about old Gilbert's widow: how she had taken one lover after another, treating them with cold indifference and apparently loving none of them until finally she married a rather dull, worthy gentleman by the name of Pettigrew — James Pettigrew. Nobody had understood how he had managed to tame the wild beauty. 'Unscrupulous and totally immoral' his mother had called her. And if but half she had related were true, then one could scarce be surprised that her daughter was equally unconventional.

With a stab of excitement lending fire to his blood, Edward Crowhurst put an arm tentatively around the girl's shoulders. She did not stiffen but leaned her head back with apparent innocence and smiled up at him. His arm tightened imperceptibly as in a small,

5

excited voice she told him of her afternoon's impulsive sortie.

"I shall be punished doubtless," she ended her story, her green eyes twinkling with merriment. "But I do not care! You can have no idea, Sir, how tedious life is, living with an elderly aunt, dearly as I love her, and had I remained stitching my embroidery — why, I would never have met you, would I?"

He was momentarily confused by the childlike artlessness of her compliment and wondered how old she was. But by the gentle swelling of her breasts beneath the confines of her riding habit, he judged her to be woman rather than child. Her words and the relaxed way in which she leaned against him misled him to consider that she might welcome a furtherance of this 'adventure'.

"Indeed, 'tis my good fortune," he said softly. "And now, since your young groom will soon be upon us, let us not waste further time in talk but use the moments to get to know one another better."

Until then Tamarisk had felt only pleasure and excitement in this strange, romantic encounter with the wounded young man beside her. She knew from Aunt Clarrie's warnings that it was not gentlemen who molested ladies but uncouth men who had no manners or education and must therefore never be spoken to in familiar fashion. Mr. Crowhurst, she considered, was a man of breeding and courtesy and she knew no fear of him. When suddenly, without preamble, he not only put his lips to hers but actually placed his

6

hand over her breast, she was both frightened and angry.

Struggling free, green eyes blazing, she faced him furiously.

"You take advantage, Sir!" she said. "I had not thought you capable of such despicable behavior!"

The young man's thoughts were still mildly befuddled by brandy and were now further confused. Was the girl genuine or was she pretending unwillingness for a little dalliance in order not to seem too easy a conquest?

"Come now," he said. "Do not trifle with me. I am scarce likely to be taken in by this pretended innocence. Would you have me believe you have never been kissed or fondled before?"

"Indeed I have not!" Tamarisk cried, her cheeks flushed with indignation. "And you have no right to assume otherwise!"

She made as if to leave the phaeton, but the man caught hold of her arm.

"So it amuses you to lead a man on and then reject him!" he said angrily. "Like mother, like daughter, eh?"

Tamarisk, whose intention it had been to leave without further preamble, paused as his words penetrated her consciousness.

"And what might that mean?" she asked. "What has my mother to do with this . . . this affair?"

She sounded so genuinely unknowing that for a moment her companion hesitated. But the desire to justify himself overcame caution.

7

"Since your mother was renowned for trifling with men's deepest feelings and taking pleasure in humiliating them, 'tis no surprise to me to find her daughter behaving likewise!"

Tamarisk's astonishment was so obviously unassumed that the young man instantly regretted his jibe. But it was too late to retract, and now the girl was forcing him into further explanations. His words so shocked Tamarisk that she took in only part of all he had to say. Her own mother — the Barre Diamond, cruel, immoral, heartless . . . ?

She could bear no more. She wrenched open the door of the phaeton. Disregarding the cold, lashing rain, unaware of the feeble cries of the stableboy who had just emerged from the woods and espied her, she swung herself onto her horse, dealt the animal a swift cut with her whip, and galloped away into the darkness without a backward glance at the man she had befriended.

Although it had been Clarissa Manton's intention to punish her young charge most severely when she returned home, her feeling of relief at finding the girl unharmed but in such distress swept all thoughts of punishment from her mind. She herself helped the maid to strip Tamarisk of her wet clothes and put her to bed with several warming pans. The servant girl was sent to the kitchen to fetch a hot toddy, and only when Tamarisk had drunk it and was lying white-faced against her pillows did the elderly woman question her more closely on the afternoon's events.

8

When the story was told, Clarissa remained silent as she pondered how best she could restore the girl's confidence in her mother. She sighed deeply. So much had happened that had contributed to this unhappy situation! Her mind winged back seventeen years to the time when Mavreen had been Tamarisk's age. She, Clarissa, was then, as now, Sir John Danesfield's mistress. Despite the love they shared, they could not marry because his cold, austere wife was still living. Her beloved John had not known of the existence of his illegitimate daughter Mavreen until she was eight years old. But discovering her living with the Sale family on a farm in Sussex and becoming quite enchanted with her, he had taken her under his wing — educated her, brought her to London to live with Clarissa — and eventually launched her in Society.

Until Mavreen was grown, it had all been easy and happy, Clarissa reflected. But then the girl had fallen in love with John's ward, a young French aristocrat whose family had lost their fortunes. Gerard, Vicomte de Valle, had returned Mavreen's love but had felt obliged to put duty before happiness and ultimately married a girl of wealth and good family as was expected of him by his widowed mother. Heartbroken, Mavreen had rushed wildly into marriage with a man even older than her father. Despite her genuine affection for Gilbert Barre, she and Gerard had become lovers when Gerard had returned from a visit to France. Tamarisk was the result of that union although none

9

knew of it but Clarissa, and the world believed Tamarisk to be Gilbert's posthumous daughter.

"Aunt Clarrie!" Tamarisk's small, persistent voice dragged Clarissa back to the present. "Why did Mr. Crowhurst call Mama the Barre Diamond? It cannot be true that she behaved so badly — not Mama!"

Clarissa drew a deep breath.

"Your mother was a very lonely and unhappy young woman in those days," she said. "The man she loved had disappeared without word, and when next she heard of him, he had married someone else. I fear the hurt was such that she hated all men for a while; and since she was very beautiful, young, and a widow, her suitors were many. It was only natural that other women in Society resented her, for the men they wanted had eyes for none but your Mama. Doubtless Mr. Crowhurst's mother, Lady Esme, was among them. She is known for her vicious tongue!"

The color was returning to Tamarisk's cheeks.

"Am I really like Mama in appearance?" she asked. "Will men find *me* irresistible, Aunt Clarrie?"

Clarissa frowned.

"Vanity is not becoming to a young girl, Tamarisk — but yes, you are like your mother — very like!" She did not add that Tamarisk also resembled her true father. She had no intention of revealing to the girl that she, like Mavreen, was a love child, even although she had been born in wedlock and legally bore the title of Lady Tamarisk Barre.

The elderly woman felt a new wave of anxiety. Tamarisk was growing up fast and was far too like the tempestuous Mavreen for heart's ease.

Clarissa, now nearly seventy, felt herself too old to be responsible for this volatile child if her mother did not return from Russia. Many were the terrible stories that were filtering back to England of the awesome retreat of Napoleon's army from Moscow; of the battles fought and the thousands who had perished from disease and starvation.

If her mother had not survived, Tamarisk would undoubtedly need a stronger hand to guide her; and although she and dear John would soon marry, now that his unfortunate wife had died, he was too doting a grandfather ever to deal with Tamarisk as firmly as Clarissa anticipated might be necessary.

It was typical of Mavreen that she should have rushed off to war-torn Europe on a wild, impetuous search for her beloved Gerard the instant she learned that he was alive and fighting in Napoleon's army. With none but her faithful manservant, Dickon, to accompany her, she had departed seven months ago and no word had been heard of them since. It was to be hoped that her lover, Gideon Morris, who had gone to look for Mavreen, would bring her safely home. Tamarisk, who doted upon him, believed that he would do so.

As if aware of the object of Clarissa's thoughts, Tamarisk said suddenly:

"Oh! I do wish Uncle Perry were here!"

Clarissa remained silent. Sir Peregrine Waite

was Gideon Morris's alias, the name by which all but a handful of people knew him. A wild, fearless, lawless man, he had spent his early years as a highway robber amassing riches with which he set himself up in London Society. He had adopted the name of Sir Peregrine Waite and with it the rôle of a dandy. He played the fop so skillfully that none would have guessed him to be a highwayman with a price upon his head.

By some trick of Fate, Gideon Morris bore a marked physical resemblance to Gerard de Valle. Mavreen had been captivated by this likeness and had become his lover, even joining him upon some of his escapades. He had encouraged that daredevil streak in Mavreen which this very afternoon Clarissa, to her disquiet, had discovered Tamarisk also to possess.

The girl was fortunate to have suffered no worse misfortune at the hands of the young man she had encountered and soon, if Mavreen did not come back, would have to be told more explicitly the dangers lying in wait for her if she went out unchaperoned. But Tamarisk seemed as fearless in character as her mother and listened to no caution unless it were given by Sir Peregrine. Clarissa had never understood why the girl so adored her 'Uncle Perry', more especially as the child had no inkling of his illicit escapades which doubtless she would consider romantic.

"Aunt Clarrie!" Tamarisk's voice, carefully soft and appealing, aroused the old woman from her reverie. "You won't punish poor Sam, will you?" she went on in an effort to protect the young stableboy. "He did not wish to go with me but I made him. The fault was entirely mine."

"That I do not doubt," Clarissa said. "We will say no more about this misdemeanor as I hope you have learned your lesson. 'Tis best forgotten."

But Tamarisk could not stop herself from pondering the strange story her aunt had related about her mother's past. Beautiful although her mother was, Tamarisk had never before considered her as a woman men might find irresistible. She had always known that Uncle Perry had a great fondness for Mama, but now, strangely uneasy, she wondered if he, like those past lovers, found her desirable.

"Aunt Clarrie, *where is Mama*?" she asked suddenly. "And if she is in danger, why did she not take Uncle Perry with her? How will he ever find her whereabouts in so large a place as Europe? And why will no one tell me what they are about?"

"Because it is none of your business, young lady!" Clarissa replied. "I have answered quite enough questions this evening and I do not intend to answer anymore." And without more ado she left the room.

And with that Tamarisk was obliged for the time being to be content.

She had much to think upon as she lay in drowsy warmth in her comfortable bed watching the flickering light of the log fire dancing on the patterned wallpaper. She wondered why Aunt Clarrie always seemed so reluctant to talk about

Uncle Perry. She sighed, wishing he had not made her promise never to reveal the secret she shared with him. Aunt Clarrie might have a far better opinion of him — and Grandpapa too — if they knew that the bejeweled Sir Peregrine Waite was only a façade for a very different character hidden beneath the foolish words and dandified airs. Alone with her, Tamarisk, he would cease his nonsensical babbling and talk to her of the countryside, of Nature and animals; of which he seemed to know even more than dear Dickon. He talked too of the poor people and their struggle to survive; of the cruelties and injustices of life where children like herself lived in safety and luxury whilst others died in rat-infested prisons or starved to death because their parents had no money to feed them.

Always, whenever they walked or rode or talked together as they did most often at Finchcocks, Mavreen's country home in Kingston, he made her renew her promise to keep their conversations secret. It was a request she found exciting but which aroused her curiosity since he would never explain why he must keep his real, most admirable self hidden from the world; why he preferred folk to laugh at him and never take him seriously.

Tamarisk's heart thudded painfully as it was wont to do when she thought of Sir Peregrine Waite. No one in the world — least of all Uncle Perry himself — knew how greatly she loved him. It needed but one word of approval from him to make her whole day golden with delight. It took but one word of disapprobation for her to cry the night hours away in shame and despair.

Only her dear friend, Princess Charlotte, knew there was someone she secretly adored, but not even Charlotte knew *who* he was! Many was the hour she and Charlotte had wiled away in talk of love. Charlotte was two years older and, at seventeen, was far more enlightened upon the subject. Although her father, the Prince Regent, had sought to prevent her seeing her mother, he had been unable to withhold permission for fortnightly visits to Princess Caroline. There were many who criticized the Regent's open dislike of his Hanoverian wife, yet others were sympathetic to his attitude that the coarse, vulgar woman he had been forced to marry was unfit to have the care of their young daughter. It was certainly the case that Charlotte had learned far more from her mother than was proper for a young girl to know.

Poor Charlotte was in torment because there was talk of marrying her to Prince William of Orange, a sallowfaced, frail, bumptious young man whose nickname, 'Young Frog', well suited him. She desired, as did Tamarisk, to be married romantically to the man of her choice, someone with whom she would find pleasure in the marital bed — someone she could love.

Both girls appreciated that it was unlikely such happiness could be Charlotte's. As heir to the throne after her father, she must marry suitably and advantageously for her country. But Tamarisk had no such impediment. There was only her mother to say yea or nay to her choice

15

of husband, and *she* had disappeared, perhaps never to be seen again. In the event of her death, Tamarisk's grandfather would become her guardian, but she knew, none better, how easily she could twist him round her little finger! Her love for Sir John was equalled only by his for her, and he seldom denied her any wish.

Tamarisk sighed. Life was not always as simple as it sometimes seemed. At fifteen, she was not always taken seriously by adults, and it vexed her beyond bearing that Uncle Perry, who normally addressed her as an equal, should nonetheless treat her as a child in the matter of love.

"No one will ever love you as much as I do," she had declared last summer when he was about to depart for Europe. "And I am advanced for my years — you have said so many times! Will you marry me when I am a little older?"

He had put his hand beneath her chin, turning her face toward him so that she was looking directly into his laughing brown eyes.

"I have no doubt that you will one day make some man an excellent wife," he said, his tone gentle even whilst he mocked her. "But you know already, my sweet wild rose, that I love another."

Tamarisk pulled free of his hand, pouting as she stamped her foot.

"You are talking of Mama," she said, "yet you know very well you may never find her. Europe is a vast continent and you have said yourself you know not where to begin searching. Besides, Mama does not love you as I do."

16

The expression that came over the man's face was unfamiliar and frightening to her.

"Your mother loves me as you never could," he said harshly, cruelly. "Moreover, she is the only woman I will ever love! And never again let me hear you say your mother may not return. I shall bring her safely home and then I shall marry her."

Tamarisk's eyes had filled with tears of mortification.

"You are cruel . . . hurting me . . . when all I wished was to tell you I love you!" she had choked on her tears. Instantly he became gentle and kindly again.

"Dry those eyes, my sweeting, for they do of a certainty spoil that pretty face," he said, handing her his 'kerchief. "I would not hurt you for the world, my darling. How could I, when I love you second only to your Mama, whom you so resemble?"

He wiped her tear-streaked face before kissing her cheek.

"You can best prove your love for me by supporting my cause with your Mama," he said. "For she *is* alive, Tamarisk. I know it here!" He had touched his heart.

Tamarisk had been disappointed but not surprised. Uncle Perry, like everyone else, seemed intent upon keeping her a child. In any event, since his heart was set upon marrying Mama, he would become part of her family and she could enjoy his company every day instead of at infrequent intervals.

If only Uncle Perry would come home, she

17

thought. He would have understood the strange feelings of guilt she was now experiencing when she recalled her encounter with Edward Crowhurst. She could have told Uncle Perry — but never Aunt Clarrie — that she had actually liked being kissed; and had it not been for the further liberties the young man had taken, she might even have returned his kisses. As for the horrible accusations he had made about Mama — why Uncle Perry would doubtless have challenged him to a duel if he had been unwilling to retract the falsehoods.

As it happened, Edward Crowhurst was only too ready to make amends. Upon the following day a vast bouquet of Christmas roses was delivered to the house together with a letter of abject apology and a request that he might call upon Tamarisk to make his apologies in person.

"Under no circumstances!" said Aunt Clarrie, who was well aware that Mavreen had never cared for Esme Crowhurst and would certainly discourage an association between Tamarisk and her son. Tamarisk was immensely flattered when, despite her silence, the young man continued his efforts to renew their acquaintance and during the next few weeks could sometimes be seen waiting in his carriage at the end of the street. As they rode past he raised his hat, but Aunt Clarrie feigned ignorance of his presence and bade Tamarisk do likewise. By the end of January he must have tired of waiting, for they saw him no more.

Tamarisk might have regretted the loss of

excitement her distant admirer lent to the otherwise monotonous routine of life at Orchid House but for an event of far greater import. One cold afternoon early in February, Clarissa's manservant opened the door to a messenger sent from Barre House — Mavreen's residence in Piccadilly — with a note for Clarissa.

The elderly woman broke the seal. She was trembling as her eyes scanned Dickon's semiliterate scrawl. He, Mavreen, and Sir Peregrine were in England. Dickon had this day ridden ahead to London to prepare the house for Mavreen's arrival and to announce their homecoming. Mavreen and Sir Peregrine would arrive by post chaise later that evening. Would Mistress Manton, Sir John, and Tamarisk await them at Barre House.

The news so affected Clarissa that she subsided on the sofa with an attack of the vapors. Whilst her maid brought smelling salts, Tamarisk glanced at the note. With cheeks aflame with excitement she sent for the messenger and plied him with questions. He could say little to enlighten her further but related with an ill-concealed grin that Dickon had grown a beard — the same carrotty red as his hair!

In the midst of this confusion Charles Eburhard arrived. Charles was the eighteen-year-old midshipman with whom Tamarisk was permitted, upon occasion, to go out riding. His elderly aunt, Baroness Lisa von Eburhard, was a lifelong friend of Clarissa's, so he was considered a suitable companion for Tamarisk.

19

Freckle-faced, with a short, stubby nose and sandy hair, he was unlikely to set a young girl's heart on fire.

Nevertheless Tamarisk enjoyed riding with him and found a good deal of harmless amusement from the knowledge that Charles believed himself in love with her. His shy, stuttered compliments, his blushes whenever he addressed her, the way he trembled if she put her hand upon his arm were delightful novelties and made her feel that he considered her to be a grown woman.

Tamarisk ran to greet him, ladylike behavior forgotten as she hung on his arm, dancing excitedly from one foot to the other.

"We have news of Mama, Charles!" she cried. "She is safe and well and even now upon her way from Dover. Dickon has sent word from Barre House. Is it not exciting? We are all quite overcome! Sir Peregrine is with her and has brought her safely home, just as he vouchsafed."

The young man looked at Tamarisk's glowing face and smiled. Fond as he was of her — and immensely attracted by her — her extrovert nature was a frequent embarrassment to him.

"'Tis excellent news if it be the truth," he said shyly, blushing as was his wont.

"Why should you doubt it, Charles? Oh, just to think that I shall see dearest Mama and Uncle Perry in but a few hours!"

Clarissa was at last reviving. Sensing that he was *de trop*, the young man made polite excuses to the radiant girl at his side and, with a bow

20

to the semiconscious Clarissa, took his leave without further ado.

"How inconsiderate of Charles to depart so precipitately," Tamarisk protested. "I was hoping he would invite me to go riding in the park, and there was no reason why we should not go just because Mama is coming home. Dickon says she will not be arriving until this evening."

Tears of disappointment filled her eyes.

Clarissa, now fully herself, looked at the girl reproachfully.

"You must not always think first of yourself, my dear," she chided. "It was both tactful and considerate of young Charles to leave us. We have much to do. I shall repair to Barre House this afternoon to assist in the preparations for your Mama's return. And if you can overcome your sulks, you shall accompany me."

It was not in Tamarisk's character to retain any mood for long. Volatile by nature, capricious by virtue of her adolescence, the barometer of her emotions changed from minute to minute. Her disappointment forgotten, she hastened upstairs to change into her new lilac cambric daydress. Her elbow-length gloves matched her dress as did the round-toed, low-heeled shoes. With the assistance of Clarissa's maid, she smoothed her pink angora stockings free of wrinkles and selected a gray cloth mantle to don if the spring air should become chilly later. Her reflection in the mirror revealed her excitement at the prospect of seeing her mother again; and she was positively radiant at the thought of her reunion with her Uncle Perry.

Tamarisk's relationship with Mavreen had always been deeply affectionate at such times as they were together. But since Tamarisk's birth, events had frequently parted mother from daughter. And even upon those occasions when the two might have sojourned together at The Grange, Mavreen's house in Sussex, Tamarisk had elected to holiday at the seaside in Bognor in the jolly company of the five children of family friends, the Lades — a convenience for Mavreen who spent the summer in Sussex with her lover.

Mavreen therefore was a romantic, fascinating, somewhat fairy-tale figure in the background of Tamarisk's life, dominant only in the remote control she exerted over her daughter's education and well-being.

Tamarisk's adoration, therefore, was whole-hearted except for her secret resentment that Mama would not come to her senses and marry dearest Uncle Perry so that they could all live happily together.

Wanting more than anything in the world for Uncle Perry to be happy, as she drove to Barre House with Clarissa later that afternoon Tamarisk said dreamily:

"Would it not be perfect, Aunt Clarrie, if Mama and Uncle Perry were now to become betrothed?"

Clarissa did not reply. If Mavreen had found Gerard alive, she would have thought for no other. In this, John's daughter had been steadfast since the day the young French émigré had seduced her when she was but a girl of fifteen,

22

no older than the child sitting beside her in the carriage.

Clarissa found herself wishing that John was even now with her to give his wise counsel. But Sir John Danesfield was in Yorkshire attending to some business affairs of his late wife's.

He would, she knew, be happy enough for Mavreen to marry Gerard; but if Gerard was dead, John would never be reconciled to the foppish Sir Peregrine as a son-in-law. With a certain wry humor Clarissa mused that John, not knowing they were one and the same man, would prefer highwayman Gideon Morris as husband for his daughter. John was ever a man to admire adventure and daring.

"I trust we will not have too long to await your Mama's arrival," she said now to Tamarisk, "for I declare I am in a fever of impatience to see her."

But their patience was untried, for none other than Mavreen herself greeted them at the door of Barre House.

As Tamarisk dropped instantly into the curtsy politeness demanded, Mavreen ran forward and drew her daughter unceremoniously into her arms.

"Oh, my darling child!" she cried. "How you have grown!"

"And you, dear Mama — how thin you have become!" Tamarisk rejoined, surveying her mother's finely boned face in some alarm.

"'Tis naught to worry over," Mavreen said, laughing as she kissed Clarissa warmly and drew both inside the great doorway into the hall. "I

23

am safe and well, I do assure you. And very, very happy to be with you both once more!"

Tamarisk was not listening. She was glancing eagerly over Mavreen's shoulder into the shadows beyond.

"Uncle Perry?" she asked. "Is he not here with you, Mama?"

Mavreen linked her arm through Tamarisk's, smiling in her pleasure at being with the child again.

"He returned to his house in Harley Street but an hour since." She saw the look of disappointment on Tamarisk's face and laughed. "You shall pay him a visit on the morrow, my love. Meanwhile, I have wonderful news to tell you."

She saw the question in Clarissa's eyes and her own sparkled.

"But first, let us make ourselves as comfortable as we may in the morning room. The servants are not yet all returned from Finchcocks, and only in the morning room have the dust covers been removed."

"You should have come to Orchid House until all was prepared here for your return," Clarissa remonstrated. "'Twill be damp and chill in this great house, empty this last winter."

"I will be well enough here," Mavreen rejoined. "Thank you, nonetheless, dear Aunt Clarrie. I fear you have no idea as yet how warm even a damp, chill house can seem after the rigors of a Russian winter! Come, be seated by the fireside and I will tell you of my adventures."

Obediently Tamarisk reposed upon a green hide Chippendale chair facing the mantel, her hands neatly folded upon her lap. Wide-eyed, she listened as her mother related a story that was so astonishing she could scarce believe her ears. No one, she thought with angry resentment, had told her that Mama had gone in search of a man — a Frenchman, at that! The Frenchies were enemies! As for a soldier of Napoleon's army . . . why, no self-respecting Englishman would do less than cut his throat on sight! Yet here was Mama stating that she had faced death many times as she followed in the mysterious Vicomte's wake even to the very outskirts of Moscow!

How pretty Mama looked whenever she spoke the Frenchman's name! How pretty she looked, even though she had not yet had time to change from her crumpled habit in which she had traveled. The swansdown trimmings were mud-bespattered and her hair was in disarray — anything but fashionably coiffed! Yet somehow, Tamarisk mused, Mama still looked elegant. She found herself comparing this beautiful, comely woman with Aunt Anne. Though the same age as her mother, Mistress Lade at thirty-three was a plump, matronly figure. She had lost her delicate blonde beauty. Her white skin was now florid and her figure amorphous, whereas Mama's figure was upright and shapely despite the fact that she was corsetless, as Tamarisk's sharp eyes had quickly discerned.

Even Mama's voice sounded like that of a

25

young girl as she reached the end of her saga.

"So, Aunt Clarrie, I finally found my darling Gerard, albeit at death's door. As I entered his bedchamber and saw him lying there, it was like entering the Gates of Paradise. Oh, if you could have seen how frail and ill he looked — but so happy to see me! The kindly Countess von Heissen and I nursed him with the greatest care, but even four weeks later he was not strong enough to undertake the journey to England. However, the doctor said that in another week or so he should be well enough to travel. Is it not wonderful news? Now, at long last, Gerard and I can be married!"

Proudly she lifted her hand so that all could see Gerard's signet ring on her third finger.

It was Clarissa who was smiling at the happy ending to Mavreen's story; Clarissa who hurried forward to kiss Mavreen and congratulate her upon her courage and fortitude, to express her pleasure at Mavreen's betrothal. Tamarisk remained perfectly still in her chair, her face white, her eyes wide and dangerously bright. It was a minute or so before Mavreen noticed her daughter's silence.

"Have you nothing to say, my love?" she inquired of the child. "Are you not happy to hear of this miracle of my good fortune?"

Tamarisk's mouth tightened.

"I cannot be happy, Mama, since your betrothal to this strange Vicomte will surely break the heart of the man who loves you."

Mavreen's finely drawn brows lifted in genuine astonishment.

"What nonsense is this, Tamarisk? Of whom are you speaking?"

"I speak of Uncle Perry," Tamarisk replied in a hard, tight voice. "If to any man, should you not be betrothed to him?"

"To Gid . . . to Sir Peregrine!" Mavreen gasped. "But of course not, my love. What gave you such nonsensical a notion? Did he speak of it? Why, Tamarisk, you should know better than to take any word of his in aught but jest!"

"*He was not jesting!*" Tamarisk contradicted, entirely forgetful of her manners. "He is deadly earnest in his wish to marry you. Moreover, he has told me many times that you love him."

Now it was Mavreen's cheeks that burned; whose eyes were flashing as she replied sternly:

"You speak of matters of which you know nothing. I wish there to be no more talk of Sir Peregrine, Tamarisk. Do I make myself clear? I am in no way committed to him."

Although Tamarisk lowered her eyes submissively, there was no mistaking the obstinate set of her red mouth. Glancing at her, Mavreen's annoyance changed abruptly to approval. Quite suddenly she loved her daughter very dearly for her loyalty to poor Gideon. It proved she was no changecoat in her affections.

"Come now, my sweeting," she addressed her with a new tenderness. "We must not mar our reunion with cross words. Besides, I do assure you that you will come to love the Vicomte very greatly once you have made his acquaintance. Do you not agree it will be so, Aunt Clarrie?"

Clarissa looked doubtful. Mavreen too was strangely uneasy.

Mayhap she could convince Tamarisk with some pertinent facts, Mavreen thought, at the same time unsure of the wisdom of revealing too much to a child of such tender years. And yet, she reasoned, Tamarisk was clearly more woman than child and could not be protected much longer from the ways of the world.

"Come sit beside me, my dearest," she said impulsively. "For I have made up my mind to tell you a truth that will doubtless reconcile you to my forthcoming marriage . . . "

"Mavreen!" Aunt Clarrie interrupted, her face suddenly wary. "Do you think it wise to speak of the past to so young a person?"

"I am not so young! And is it ever unwise to tell the truth?" Tamarisk interposed before Mavreen could speak. She was now agog with curiosity as to what her mother might have to say.

"Since Gerard and I are to marry, she has a right to know," Mavreen said quietly. "The fact is, my love, the Vicomte de Valle is your real father!"

Tamarisk, who had resolved not to show any emotion but to appear coolly adult no matter what her mother revealed, was now shocked out of her poise. With a directness that was all child she cried:

"I do not believe you! My father was Lord Barre! My name is Tamarisk Barre."

"Legally that is so," Mavreen agreed. "You need have no fear that any can call you bastard,

28

for you were born in wedlock."

Tamarisk's eyes narrowed.

"Now I understand what Edward Crowhurst was implying." She turned to Clarissa. "Why did you lie to me about the past?"

"I told you nothing but the truth!" Clarissa cried, her plump face scarlet with distress.

"But not all of it, 'twould seem," Tamarisk said bitterly.

"Tamarisk, your good name cannot be questioned," Mavreen broke in.

"But yours can — and bastard I am, if you speak the truth!" Tamarisk's accusing voice stabbed the air.

Mavreen turned deathly pale.

"Tamarisk, apologize to your Mama this instant!" Clarissa remonstrated.

"And for what must I beg Mama's pardon?" Tamarisk asked, the insolence in her tone ill-concealed.

Mavreen was suddenly painfully reminded of her shocked reaction on discovering her own bastardy. Too late now, she recalled how determinedly she had rejected her father when he confessed his paternity. How unhappy she had been, feeling as if the very foundations of her existence had crumbled beneath her. Now filled with sudden understanding and sympathy, it seemed impossible that she had allowed such memories to escape her. She went to her daughter and tried to put her arms around her. But Tamarisk stiffened, so obviously rejecting the embrace that Mavreen's hands fell to her sides.

29

For a moment neither spoke to break the painful silence that had befallen. Then Mavreen said softly:

"You will come to love your father, as I do. At least reserve your judgment of him, and of me, until you have made his acquaintance," she pleaded.

"I want Uncle Perry for my stepfather, and I shall never forgive you if you hurt him by marrying another!" Tamarisk cried. "As for your Vicomte . . . I shall not love him, now or ever. I hate him . . . I shall always hate him, and you cannot make me do otherwise!"

With which pronouncement she sprang to her feet, lips and hands clenched. Manners and dignity abandoned, she ran past her mother and out of the room.

Mavreen made as if to follow her, but Clarissa lay a restraining hand upon her arm.

"She will be back," she said. "Tamarisk's moods never endure for long. You'll see, my dear, she will soon reconcile herself to acceptance of your wishes. 'Tis but a momentary tantrum."

Neither Clarissa nor Mavreen realized that Tamarisk had departed not just from the room but that her intention was to leave her mother's house forever.

2

February 1813

GIDEON MORRIS, alias Sir Peregrine Waite, lived at Chiswell House — a charming, terraced residence in Harley Street which he had rented on a long lease from a serving naval commander.

Although it was essentially a bachelor establishment, Gideon had adorned the rooms with the most fashionable fripperies. He had gone so far as to emulate the Prince Regent by having the drawing room redecorated *à la Chinoise* with the draperies in yellow silk. He believed his house lent authenticity to his chosen rôle of Sir Peregrine.

Only four people in the world knew of his exploits as Gideon Morris: Dickon, Clarissa, Mavreen, and her Quaker friend, Mistress Elizabeth Fry, to whom he gave the spoils of his highway robberies to benefit her charities. But long ago he had kept the proceeds for himself to enable him to acquire the prerequisites of a gentleman, his right by birth but denied him by virtue of his bastardy.

Now a man of considerable means, he was established in Society and made his secret forays upon the highways only for adventure and excitement. He had long since amassed sufficient fortune and invested it wisely enough to keep him in moderate luxury. He had been prepared — if Mavreen so desired him — to give up his gentleman-of-the-road escapades. In any event he felt little inclination for any such derring-do without her.

Mavreen was the first and only woman he had loved. Now that it seemed as if his last hope of persuading her to marry him had vanished, he wanted no second best. Despite his increasing awareness of the purposelessness and loneliness of his life, he could not bring himself to contemplate marriage with any other woman but Mavreen.

He had set off in pursuit of her to Russia, convinced that even were she to find her former lover alive, the virtues with which she had endowed Gerard's memory over the years of separation would turn out to be no more real than a youthful dream; that the French Vicomte, by now in his mid-thirties, would in no way resemble the romantic boy Mavreen had once adored with the blind passion of a young girl enslaved by her first love.

None knew better than Gideon Morris the depth and complexities of emotion of which the now mature Mavreen was capable. As her lover he had explored with her all the heights and depths of which the senses were capable. In a harmony that had increased with the years, they had matched one another as perfect equals, sharing not only the secrets of their bedchamber, but the dangerous delights of highway robbery; risking their lives, their reputations, for no more than the sheer amusement of it. He alone understood the wild streak in her nature that precluded physical or mental confinement, that demanded recognition of her intellectual equality, and that steadfastly refused to accept conformity for Society's sake.

But by the time Gideon had caught up with Mavreen on the frozen outskirts of Vilna, she was already on her way back to England. She had found Gerard de Valle alive but seriously ill. As soon as he was out of danger she had decided to return home, both to reassure her child and family as to her safety and to prepare for Gerard's arrival.

In vain Gideon had sought to persuade her that her happiness lay with him, that he loved her with a passion that Gerard de Valle could never equal. But Mavreen remained steadfast in her insistence that the years had not diminished her love for Gerard, and all doubts as to the extent of that love had gone forever now that she had been reunited with him.

Throughout the long journey to England she remained adamant in her avowal that she would marry Gerard as soon as he joined her in London. Not even the shared dangers of the journey, so reminiscent of their highway companionship, could move her from her resolve.

Gideon stretched his long legs toward the fire. He had eaten not an hour since and now reclined on the yellow-and-white brocade settee, a decanter of cognac on the Chippendale table beside him.

He was deeply depressed by his thoughts. For

the past five years his life had revolved around Mavreen. Now he had to face the fact that if his love for her was as great as he professed, and therefore selfless, he must in future avoid her; cease his pursuit of her and leave her free to follow the path she believed would bring her happiness.

Lost in such meditations, Gideon's astonishment knew no bounds when his butler, Frederick, announced a young lady visitor. None of his acquaintances knew yet of his return to London. He had wished to spend this evening alone coming to terms with his parting from Mavreen. He needed time to reconcile himself to the knowledge that his association with her was finally ended; time to nurse his wounds in private, to decide what now he would do with his life.

"And who might this caller be?" he asked, irritated by this interruption.

"The young lady refused to give her name, Sir," the butler replied. "But I think you do know her, Sir, if I may presume to say so. I think she has visited here before."

Still no wiser but resigned to the fact that the easiest way to satisfy curiosity was to see his visitor for himself, Gideon instructed his servant to show her in.

He had barely given this command before Tamarisk came bursting into the room, only just avoiding a collision with Frederick as with all decorum forgotten she flung herself into Gideon's arms. Tears were streaming down her face and Gideon could make no sense of her admixture of sobs and strangled outpourings.

Gently he led her to a chair. With a tenderness which might have surprised other ladies of his acquaintance, he drew out a 'kerchief and wiped away the girl's tears.

He was deeply attached to this child, not only because she was Mavreen's daughter and quite extraordinarily like her mother in features and manner, but because he had no children of his own and Tamarisk had always adored him with a child's uncritical devotion.

"Now, my pretty Princess, my little weeping willow," he said, greatly concerned by her positive storm of tears. "Dry those sea-green eyes of yours else I declare we shall both be drowned ere long in the flood!"

He was pleased to see her lower lip tremble in the most fleeting of smiles.

"Tell your old Uncle Perry all that is the cause of such distress," he said, seating himself beside her and stroking the damp ringlets away from her flushed face.

Now her eyes flashed, the brighter for her tears, in a way that reminded Gideon painfully of her mother.

"You are *not* old!" she cried. "And I have to tell you of a great disaster . . . " Her voice broke as she added, "Oh, Uncle Perry . . . Mama is to be married — *and not to you* — and my Papa who I thought was my Papa is not my father at all — and I HATE my mother! I wish she had never come home. I wish . . . "

"*I forbid such comment in my house!*"

The sternness of his voice silenced Tamarisk

instantly. The anger in her eyes now gave place to uncertainty. She said hesitantly:

"Did you not hear me correctly, Uncle Perry? Mama is to marry a Frenchman — the one she says is my father. I hate all Frenchmen and oh, I so dearly wanted *you* for my stepfather! Oh, Uncle Perry, is your heart not breaking as mine most surely is?"

Despite the gravity of this emotional storm and the unpleasant facts Tamarisk was stating, Gideon smiled.

He could not reveal to the child that he already knew the truth as to her parentage.

"'Tis not the end of the world, my sweeting. You may find you will care very much for the Vicomte de Valle when you come to know him." With an effort he added, "He must be a fine man for your mother to love him well enough to want to marry him! Indeed, a very fine fellow to deserve such a love as hers!"

Tamarisk stared back at Gideon indignantly.

"But I shall never love him — not as I love you! And *you*, Uncle Perry, what is to become of you if you are not to marry Mama after all?"

Gideon Morris turned away. The child's question was too near the bone for comfort and he did not wish her to remark the pain that must be revealed in his eyes.

"I shall do well enough." He forced the words to sound light and carefree. "After all, my Princess, the world is full of beautiful women. I shall simply have to find myself another to love, shall I not?"

Tamarisk flung her arms around him and hugged him.

"*I love you!*" she cried. Her desire was at first only to comfort him, but her quick mind pursued another train of thought. "Why, you could love *me* instead of Mama!" she cried, her tears ceasing as she warmed to her idea. "Everyone tells me how like I am to Mama — and I am no longer a child, Uncle Perry. I am *fifteen*! And that is quite old enough for marriage!"

Gideon took care to hide his amusement. He was touched by Tamarisk's concern for his happiness.

"You are a very sweet girl, Tamarisk, and I thank you most warmly for your solicitude. But you know, my love, fifteen cannot marry with thirty-five!"

"And pray tell me who made such a law?" Tamarisk argued, quite undaunted. "Why, Mama married Papa — I mean Lord Barre — when she was fifteen and he was fifty-six, and they were well matched. Mama has often told me how happy they were until he died."

Gideon drew in his breath.

"Let us not continue with this dispute over ages," he said carefully. "Suffice it to say that for the time being I wish to remain unmarried. What is far more important is that we discuss what reason has brought you here. The hour is late and it is most improper for you to visit a bachelor establishment alone. Have you your mother's permission?"

Suddenly very young again, Tamarisk pouted, her eyes sullen.

"I did not seek Mama's permission," she said haughtily. "Nor shall I do so ever again. I have run away, Uncle Perry! I have come to live with you . . . that is, if you will have me," she ended, her voice quavering as the first doubt assailed her. "I *may* stay here with you, may I not?"

"Indeed, you may not!" Gideon said, drawing Tamarisk to her feet and depositing her bonnet upon her head as if, Tamarisk thought indignantly, she were still in the nursery. "You will go straight home to your Mama — and I shall escort you."

"I will not! *I will not!*" Tamarisk cried, the tears flowing again. "Not even although you wish it, Uncle Perry! Not even if you beg me!"

"I see. Then I shall not beg," Gideon replied sternly. And before the girl could anticipate his movements, he scooped her up in his arms, her petticoats flying as he marched with her into the hall. He drowned her protests with shouted orders to his butler to have the coachman bring the phaeton to the door within two minutes, lest he desire instant dismissal, he added.

"You do not love me!" Tamarisk wept, struggling feebly in the viselike grip of his arms. "If you loved me, you would not make me go home."

"I love you very much indeed," Gideon replied angrily. "Too much to permit you to behave in such outrageous fashion. Have you no thought for your poor Mama? She will be quite out of her mind with concern, not knowing what has become of you."

"I do not care," Tamarisk muttered defiantly, two angry spots of color reddening her cheeks.

"But I do," Gideon retorted coldly. "And it is clear to me that it is high time you did have a stepfather to enforce a little discipline upon you."

"I do not need discipline enforced upon me," Tamarisk argued. Suddenly she was pleading with him again, all woman as she wound her arms around his neck and pressed her soft wet mouth against his cheek. "If *you* were my Papa, I would do anything you said. I'd want only to please you. Pray do not be angry with me. I cannot bear your displeasure."

Gideon set her down upon her feet, entirely won over by this display of docility. Despite himself he smiled.

"Then do you begin showing a little of that great affection for me this very instant," he said, "and return home with no further argument. Moreover, I desire you to apologize to your Mama for the distress you have caused her. What kind of homecoming is this?"

"If I apologize to Mama, it will be only to prove my love for you," Tamarisk answered as he led her out to the waiting phaeton. "And not because I am sorry."

She glanced sideways at Gideon as he followed her into the carriage.

How handsome he looked, she reflected, in his sage-green kerseymere breeches and matching superfine coat. Over this he had draped his Polish greatcoat, leaving the loops and frogs

39

unfastened. He wore no hat. His brown hair curled naturally to his neck and outlined his cheeks in the manner the Prince Regent had recently made fashionable.

He was not in the least old, fat, and debauched like the Prince Regent, she thought. Uncle Perry had the taut, muscular frame of a soldier; the upright bearing of a man far younger in years. There were, indisputably, lines about his eyes and mouth, but these, in her opinion, lent interest to his face, enhancing his good looks rather than detracting from them.

She laid her head against his arm with the easy familiarity of a child with a favorite uncle. But as Gideon's arm moved to encircle her shoulders so that she was nestled comfortably against his chest, her heart began to pound in the strangest way. Every nerve in the parts of her body which were in contact with him seemed to have become hypersensitive.

Suddenly the very essence of her love for him changed. The vague, unchanneled longings that had had no better explanation than romantic dreams were now in one miraculous instant given meaning and form. They crystallized into a brilliant, glowing understanding. The childish adoration she had always had for her Uncle Perry must all the time have been but the dawning of that most wonderful of adult emotions — love. How often had she spoken that magical word and yet never until now understood its true meaning!

Tamarisk drew a deep breath, scarce able to contain the forces of feeling within her. Her heart seemed to be bursting. If only she could tell Charlotte this very instant of the revelation that had come to her! But no sooner had the idea materialized than she rejected it. This strange new excitement was too great, too important, too new to be shared with anyone. It was her secret; and the miracle of it not yet fully comprehended even by herself, the one transformed.

Gideon, meanwhile, was lost in thought and was only vaguely aware of the girl beside him. Had he realized what thoughts were milling in her mind, he would have been greatly perturbed. But he was as unmoved by the slight contact of Tamarisk's golden head nestling against his shoulder as she was vividly conscious of her proximity to him.

Such was her confusion of thought and feeling that Tamarisk was relieved Gideon was staring ahead, his attention far removed from her. With an effort she forced herself to breathe more calmly, but her pulses would not steady.

All senses heightened, Tamarisk became aware of the fresh sweet smell of spring grass carried by the strong breeze blowing from the direction of the Marylebone Gardens. Wanting only to find beauty in this extraordinary metamorphosis she was undergoing, she tried not to see the dirty ragged vagrants huddled in the doorways nor hear the whining voices of the beggars as they ran perilously near to their coach wheels pleading for alms. Instead she closed her eyes, feeling the warmth of Gideon's body beside her. If only he would kiss her as Edward Crowhurst had done, she thought, wistfully. She would

41

have no misgivings if he were to fondle her, and her very last desire would be to run away. She wished that this coach ride might continue forever.

She made no move that might draw his attention to her, having no wish for him to remark how the blood had rushed to her cheeks or that she was trembling with the torrent of emotions engulfing her — all new and the more alarming because of their unexpectedness. She was both excited and afraid at one and the same time.

Amidst the tumult in her bursting heart, only one fact was clear in her mind — that the love she felt for her Uncle Perry had changed, deepened into a totally new dimension. She loved him now not as a devoted niece but passionately as a woman. Her body was alive with new and extraordinary sensations.

As the phaeton lurched over a rut in the roadway, throwing her even closer against him, she was aware of such intense excitement and sweetness rising through her veins that her whole being seemed to be on fire with longing.

I love him! I love him! The words echoed round her mind, flowed down through her bursting heart, and settled in the pit of her stomach.

Now she wanted him to understand what had transpired; to realize that she was transformed from child to woman. More than anything in the world she desired that he should turn his head and embrace her — not in the kindly manner of an affectionate uncle, but with the fierce, passionate embraces of a lover. He was *not* her uncle, nor ever had been. He was Perry, *Perry* — the man she loved.

She made no effort to control her imagination as her thoughts raced beyond the mere romance of kisses. She would, she decided, offer no resistance if Perry's passion demanded the surrender of her body. Her virginity now had meaning for her. This gift which she had been cautioned to keep sacrosanct for her future husband she could and would offer to Perry, thereby convincing him of the depth and maturity of her love for him.

In her naïveté, it did not occur to Tamarisk that her very youth and innocence would protect her from despoilment; for Gideon Morris was a man of honor who would forbear to take such advantage even were Tamarisk other than the daughter of the woman he loved.

They were now nearing Barre House. The phaeton had turned into Piccadilly. Rudely Tamarisk was wakened from her dreaming as Gideon withdrew his arm and said sternly:

"Remember, Tamarisk, you have given me your promise that you will apologize to your mother and that you will accede in future to her wishes!"

With a shock Tamarisk realized bitterly that whilst *her* mind and body had awakened to sensations she had never before experienced, the man who had evoked this miracle remained unmoved, unchanged.

Despite the intensity of her newfound love for him, she came near to hating him at this

43

moment for his cold indifference.

But quickly she reassured herself that he was not to blame. Perry knew nothing of her love for him nor, in all probability, would wish to know whilst he remained enslaved by her Mama. She felt a fierce renewal of resentment toward her mother. How could she bear to make this wonderful man so unhappy? How could she prefer another? What kind of man was this French Vicomte that he could hold so tight a rein upon her mother's heart? Despite Perry's attempts to defend him, she, Tamarisk, knew he was no paragon. No true gentleman would have seduced her mother and got her with child, or, having done so, failed to marry her.

This thought had barely crossed her mind before another followed. Her mother was already married to Lord Barre when she, Tamarisk, was begotten. So she was conceived in adultery! Mama was the one without honor!

How could Perry love and respect such a woman? Tamarisk longed to ask him but dared not voice such a question. He had made it completely clear to her that he would not tolerate any criticism of her mother, and she dared not risk antagonizing him. Reluctantly she removed her head from his shoulder and sat up, her eyes filled with tears of hopeless frustration. Unable to remain silent she cried bitterly:

"You care only about Mama! You do not care one jot about me!"

"You know that I love you very much," Gideon replied with a calmness the young girl found as infuriating as it was hurtful. "But I will not have your Mama distressed because you choose to throw a tantrum, young lady."

He looked down into the flushed young face and his expression softened.

"Come now," he said more gently. "What is so terrible in the acquisition of a new stepfather? Doubtless the Vicomte will take pains to win your approbation and will spoil you quite shamelessly. Mark my words, within a week or two you will be running to me all smiles with tales of his virtues and your happiness."

Tamarisk was silent, her mind in a positive whirl of perplexity. Not a few hours since, she had been insistent that it was Perry she desired for her stepfather and not the Vicomte de Valle. Now the very last thing she wished was for her Mama to marry Perry. Indeed, the mere thought of her mother in his arms, receiving his embraces, consumed her with a jealousy that was beyond bearing; and even more tormenting was the knowledge that Perry still loved her Mama.

There was but one hope left to her — that he might in time recover from his broken heart. There was consolation to be drawn from her belief that even the greatest passions in a man's life did not endure forever. Since leaving London to live in Richmond, Tamarisk had seen little of her childhood friend, the seventeen-year-old Princess Charlotte. But they corresponded regularly, and Charlotte's letters this past year had contained many stories of the handsome, romantic young poet, Lord Byron. Recently made famous by the immense success following the publication of his poem *Childe Harold*, all London was at his feet. Lord Byron had chosen the lovely Lady Caroline Lamb from among his many female admirers, and their passionate love for one another had seemed to be without parallel. Yet Charlotte's last letter stated that the poet had ceased to love his *amorata*. If Lord Byron could fall out of love, so too could Perry.

She had but to bide her time, Tamarisk consoled herself.

As Gideon assisted her out of the phaeton she said anxiously:

"You will not leave me to go in alone? You will accompany me, will you not?"

"I have every intention of so doing!" Gideon's voice was uncomfortably sharp. "I wish to be present when you make your apology, Tamarisk." He was addressing her once more as if she were a child, she thought. She looked at him reproachfully, her mouth trembling. But he was unaware of her as he hurried up the steps of the house and pulled the heavy bell handle.

Mavreen was standing in the hallway. Tamarisk watched as Perry's arm reached out to rest reassuringly upon her mother's shoulder. She could hear the murmur of his voice and saw her mother's anxious glance in her direction. How beautiful Mama's face looked in the candle-light! How tender was Perry's expression! How kind!

Jealously consumed her.

I hate her, I hate her! Tamarisk thought. Her mother had betrayed Perry and betrayed her, Tamarisk, in the nature of her birth. She would never love her Mama again!

Slowly she walked up the steps and curtsied to Mavreen. Eyes lowered, she took care to keep all expression from her voice when she made her promised apology. Conscious of Perry's scrutiny, she made no protest when her mother dispatched her instantly to her room like some miscreant child. For the moment anger at Mavreen was a stronger emotion than her newfound love.

Mavreen led Gideon into the morning room. She looked exhausted.

"I have been beside myself with anxiety," she told him. "Dickon has been searching the streets and I have been imagining . . . " She broke off as tears of relief engulfed her.

Gideon, who had remained by the door, now covered the distance between them in two quick strides and took her in his arms. For a few moments Mavreen allowed herself the luxury of tears, forgetting momentarily that when she and Gideon had parted company earlier in the day, it was intended as a permanent farewell — a final ending to their long years of friendship. The decision, although mutually agreed, had been of Mavreen's making. She feared that the continuation of their friendship, albeit on a platonic basis, might put at risk her relationship with Gerard.

" 'Tis true I can never be indifferent to you, Gideon," she had admitted, "but it was always Gerard that I loved. What I felt for you these past years was nothing but a passion of the senses."

"I remain unconvinced that you never loved

47

me, but I have no alternative but to accede to your wishes," Gideon had replied. "I will keep myself apart from you, Mavreen, but you will never be out of my heart or my thoughts."

Neither had known that in less than the passing of a day Gideon would be drawn back into Mavreen's company, and in circumstances so distressing for Mavreen that her need for his counsel and consolation outweighed her intention to debar him from her life.

Content to find himself back in her orbit, no matter the reason, Gideon sought only to comfort the woman he loved.

"There is naught to cry about," he said, gently wiping her tears with his 'kerchief. "No harm has come about. 'Twas but a storm in a teacup," he added with more conviction than he felt. "Tamarisk is at an awkward age and, I fear, had a trifle too lenient a guardian in Aunt Clarrie whilst we have been on our journeying."

"Mayhap I have not been the best of mothers," Mavreen said unhappily. "How could my own daughter run from me as if I were an ogre?"

Despite the gravity of Mavreen's expression Gideon smiled.

"You are far too beautiful ever to be thought an ogre," he remarked tenderly.

Mavreen too smiled. But tears still trembled on her eyelids.

"'Twould seem as if Tamarisk is determined to reject her real father," she murmured. "If she persists, Gerard will be so hurt, and all the while I have been certain they would love one another. I was determined upon it."

Once again Gideon smiled.

"One cannot, alas, demand that people should love one another," he said gently. The tone of his voice was not without a tinge of bitterness as he added softly, "Were that possible, my love, I should long since have demanded that *you* love *me*."

Mavreen looked up at him, only now aware that she had been far too self-absorbed to give thought to Gideon's feelings. Conscious now of his arms still encircling her, she withdrew from his embrace as if she had not heard his last remark. She turned the conversation back to her daughter.

"I have always known of Tamarisk's devotion to you," she said, sighing. "But I must confess it did not cross my mind that she might have come to you this evening. I am sorry that the girl should have involved you, Gideon."

Gideon shrugged.

"'Twas no great inconvenience, I assure you. But much as I am loth to worry you, Mavreen, I feel I should caution you. Tamarisk's mood is rebellious, to say the least. Do not be misled by her apparent docility. Her apology to you was made only at my insistence."

Mavreen's eyes flashed in sudden anger.

"She is but a child, Gideon, and I will not have her upsetting me and my household in a fit of the tantrums. It is time she learned to do as she is told, whether it pleases her or not!"

Gideon's eyes now held a glint of amusement.

"Your daughter, my dear, is not only alike you in looks, she has your independent spirit and your courage. I would recommend most earnestly a light rein, for a heavy hand will not curb this filly."

"Then 'tis a pity *you* are not at hand to control her since you seem to understand her better than I."

Mavreen spoke without first considering her words. The silence that followed her unguarded comment was embarrassing for them both.

Gideon stood up, saying quietly:

"You well know that I would be happy to assist you with Tamarisk were circumstances otherwise. But 'tis better for us both that I should not become further involved in your affairs. Tamarisk has promised me she will do no more to distress you. Methinks her precipitate behavior was but an expression of mistaken loyalty to me."

Mavreen nodded.

"So Aunt Clarrie opined. Maybe I should take her advice and look about for a suitable husband for Tamarisk. She is young, I know, yet she has matured far more this past year than I had thought possible."

"In this respect I can assure you she will not go unnoticed," Gideon said. "There is a combination of passion, wildness, and innocence about her which I predict will turn many a man's head."

Mavreen glanced at him curiously. It was the first time he had voiced an opinion of her daughter as if she were a grown woman rather than a child. The fulsomeness of his compliment surprised her.

"Then it must be my duty as her mother to put her on her guard since she is clearly too young to foresee the dangers into which her beauty might lead her," she spoke her thoughts aloud. "And first of the lessons Tamarisk must learn is to refrain from hiring hackney cabs to take her to lonely bachelor apartments in the nocturnal hours! 'Twas most improper!"

Gideon's face broke into a smile.

"Be not too hard upon her, Mavreen," he said meaningfully, "for 'twould be hypocritical, would it not, for you and I to preach strict observance of the proprieties! Believe me, I find it easy to forgive Tamarisk. Your madcap, pretty, improper daughter, Mavreen, bears marked resemblance to her Mama!"

Mavreen's eyes now lit with laughter as she recalled the wild, dangerous sorties she had made with Gideon upon the highways.

It was all Gideon could do not to take her in his arms again as she said with a certain wistful longing:

"We made the most of every minute, did we not, Gideon? How happy we were! And never more so than when we were engaged upon our misdemeanors."

The hour was late and Gideon was tired. His control over his emotions was consequently at a low ebb and further weakened by Mavreen's sentimental references to the past. Cupping her face with his hands, he stared down into her eyes and said hoarsely:

"Mavreen, it is not too late! You admit how truly happy we were. *We can be so again.* No

51

man could love you more than I. You *must* reconsider your decision!"

Although his words were but a renewed protestation of his love for her, now suddenly she was perturbed by them. As she drew his hands away from her face, she was trembling. It frightened her strangely when he spoke with such conviction — as if he were about to prove that he knew better what she wanted than she did herself. Were he to succeed in convincing her, it would not be the first time she had surrendered to his will against her better judgment.

She shivered, remembering inopportunely the superstitions implanted in her early childhood by the simple country folk. Gideon's mother had once been branded a witch by such unenlightened people. It would be but a step further to imagine now that Gideon himself had some supernatural power over her; that if he so desired, he could jeopardize her future happiness with the man she loved.

But even as the thought of witchcraft crossed her mind, she rejected such a notion as total absurdity.

"I am sorry, Gideon, but my heart's intent cannot be changed," she said firmly. "So long as Gerard lives, I can do naught else but love him. I am sorry, truly sorry that I have hurt you. But you always knew Gerard came first in my affections. In this I never deceived you."

Gideon's face looked weary, lined with disappointment as his brief moment of hope was dashed.

"Then 'tis farewell a second time," he said.

"I wish you well, Mavreen, even whilst my heart denies the possibility of your happiness with another. Do not forget that I love you — now and always."

Without consideration for her wishes he pulled her to him, put his arms around her, and kissed her fiercely. She stood silent and unresponsive in his embrace. His arms dropped to his sides. His face now impassive, he made her an elaborate bow.

"Your servant, Ma'am!" he said, and turning on his heel walked quickly from the room.

As the door closed behind him, Mavreen felt the tension leave her body. Only now that he was gone did she dare relax the iron control she had imposed upon herself. She felt both triumphant and weak with relief that she had somehow succeeded in hiding from him her inexplicable desire to surrender herself to him.

Gideon had departed in the mistaken belief that her love for Gerard was absolute; that his ardent kisses had left her unmoved.

But she could neither explain nor hide the truth from herself.

3

March 1813

SIR JOHN DANESFIELD sat on the settee in the withdrawing room at Barre House, one arm about the plump shoulders of Clarissa, the other around his daughter Mavreen. Opposite him sat his future son-in-law, Gerard, Vicomte de Valle, whom he now regarded with affection and approval. Gerard had this very morning arrived in London. At Sir John's suggestion he had taken up residence with him at his London home, Wyfold House.

"'Twould be most improper for Gerard to reside in Barre House before your wedding," Sir John pointed out to Mavreen who had prepared a room for Gerard in her own home. "Despite the irregularities of the past, nay, even because of them, 'tis all the more necessary that you and Gerard should now most strictly observe the conventions."

Mavreen would have protested but Clarissa said wisely:

"'Tis not only your reputation that is your father's concern, Mavreen, but that of Tamarisk. If she is to be well married you cannot disregard the opinions of Society."

Now, two hours later, bathed, changed, and refreshed, Gerard looked with affection upon his former patron, Sir John. He was equally attached to Clarissa who had befriended him since his youth and supported him when he and Mavreen had first fallen so passionately in love. He was delighted to learn that after forty years Sir John and Clarissa were to be married. Although the old gentleman was now in his seventies and Clarissa only a little younger, their devotion to one another was evident.

It was only by an effort of concentration, however, that Gerard could pay attention to Sir John's conversation, for Mavreen had crossed the room to seat herself beside him. His beloved's hand was clasped in his and she sat so close to him that he could feel the warmth of her body through the light muslin of her dress. They had had time for but one short fierce embrace upon his arrival before Sir John had carried him off to Wyfold House, perhaps fearing, Gerard now thought with a smile, that were he to leave them long together, they might there and then succumb to the physical passions aroused by their reunion.

It never ceased to astonish Gerard that each time he saw Mavreen after a separation she appeared even younger and more beautiful than the picture he retained of her in his memory. He was finding it hard to believe that the slender, radiant young woman beside him was in her thirty-third year and the mother of their fifteen-year-old daughter whom at any moment he was going to meet for the first time.

But not even his pleasurable anticipation of this prospect could divert his thoughts for more than a moment. He was too aware of the proximity of the woman he loved; too conscious of her awareness of him. Her full, firm breasts were rising and falling with the swiftness of her breathing, and the hand he held in his seemed to throb as his own heart was throbbing. A tendril of hair, escaping from her coiffure, lay tantalizingly close to his lips. The loving smile curving and widening her mouth was an unbelievable temptation. His desire mounted until it became a dull ache of longing.

If Sir John were to continue to insist upon them observing the proprieties, he thought, how long might he and Mavreen have to wait before they could lie together and appease their longing? When Mavreen had sat at his bedside for so many long hours in the Countess's villa in Zagret, he had been too weak and ill to give more than verbal expression of his love. Now that his health was all but fully restored, his body was once more in urgent need of her. Mavreen always evoked this response in him. Her body seemed fashioned to arouse a man's desire, her fascination made the more overwhelming by the unconscious sensuousness of her nature.

But he need not fret with impatience too long, he told himself. Mavreen would find some way for them to be alone together! Nothing had ever daunted his love, his *petit écureuil*.

"You smile, my boy, yet I do assure you the matter is serious!" Sir John was saying reproachfully, mistaking Gerard's expression to be reaction to his comments. "Another war with

America is the last thing England needs, and it goes far from well."

"I received no intelligence on the matter whilst in Russia," Gerard admitted, forcing himself now to pay attention.

"Then I will give you the latest news," Sir John replied. "In *The Times* yesterday it was stated that upwards of five hundred British vessels have been captured by the Americans. Think on it, Gerard! Five hundred merchantmen and three frigates! Anyone who had predicted this a year ago would have been called a madman or a traitor!"

"'Tis said our ships are undergunned and the masts defective," Mavreen explained. "And moreover that our sailors are no match for the Americans."

"Pah!" said Sir John irritably. "'Tis that our navy lacks experienced seamen and the Admiralty has been obliged to make up the crews with raw landsmen."

Clarissa, who had remained silent until now, sighed deeply.

"If only the peoples of the world could live in peace," she murmured. "War brings misery to everyone."

But politics could never hold Clarissa's interest for long, and now her thoughts turned happily to romance as she looked fondly at Gerard.

"Pray tell us, Gerard, of your journey home. Were you in peril?" she asked.

Gerard shook his head.

"It must be Fate's intention that I survive all mishaps," he said, looking with tenderness at

Mavreen. "When I left Russia," he went on, "the weather was improving and the prospect of a safe and uneventful journey to England seemed excellent."

He took Mavreen's hand and held it tightly imprisoned within his own.

"I did, however, hear rumors at our stopping places of a massive Prusso-Russian Army gathering to defend the southern Prussian borders against an attack threatened by Napoleon."

"But I thought the Emperor was in Paris visiting his new Empress Marie Louise and their baby son!" Mavreen interposed.

"Of this I was unaware, but I have no doubt that Napoleon was in Prussia, for I came within a few miles of the armies not far from the River Oder. And Napoleon had his enemies on the run. 'Tis scarce to be credited, for 'tis but a few months since his crushing defeat in Moscow."

"Let us not talk of war," Clarissa pleaded. "Let us talk of happier things — such as your wedding, Gerard. No doubt you will be arranging a day for it in the not too distant future."

Gerard smiled at her.

"I am happy to fall in with Mavreen's wishes, whatever they may be. So far as I . . . "

But he was interrupted by the entrance of his daughter.

Unaware of Gerard's arrival that morning at Dover, Tamarisk had accepted an invitation to luncheon with Princess Charlotte at Warwick House. She knew nothing, therefore, of the presence of her father until Dickon called to collect her and informed her that the Vicomte de Valle was with her mother and grandfather at Barre House.

During the ride home with Dickon, Tamarisk plied him with questions. Dickon had known the Vicomte since Gerard had arrived in England at the age of fourteen — a refugee from the French Revolution. To her surprise Dickon was voluble in defense of her mother's lover.

"The Vicomte be a fine gentleman, surelye!" he said. "There's none as could speak a word to his dishonor. He be a kind man and unaccountable brave. 'Tis my opinion you'll find no fault with him whatsumdever!"

Until Mavreen's father, Sir John, had first discovered her existence in Sussex, Mavreen had looked upon the Sale family as her own and upon Dickon as her devoted brother. When eventually she became Lady Barre, she did not forget Dickon, and he became her head groom. Despite her elevated status, Mavreen many times declared that he was not just her servant but her friend. He was therefore privileged to speak his mind as he pleased.

So Tamarisk bore no resentment when Dickon advised her now to stop "your nonsense" and "do you put a good face on't, whatsumdever you be feeling in your heart!"

"I'll try," she promised. "But I fear I shall never feel toward the Vicomte as a daughter!"

Consequently it was with well-concealed but intense curiosity that Tamarisk now made her curtsy to the stranger, stealing a swift glance at him through half-lowered lids.

Her first reaction was one of shock. He so resembled Perry as to take her breath away. Although the Vicomte was more delicately built and his features and stature finer, he and Perry might be related, so alike were they one to the other.

Gerard rose to his feet. With natural gallantry he took Tamarisk's hand and raised her from her curtsy.

"It is my great pleasure to make your acquaintance," he said formally. "'Tis a moment I have thought on many times."

Suddenly shy beneath his scrutiny Tamarisk moved away to greet her grandfather and Aunt Clarrie. But her curtsies were automatic and her mind whirled with speculation. She tried, mentally, to give the stranger the name of 'Papa' but could not do so. It was somehow easier to think of him as 'the Frenchman' and in so doing reignite her feelings of antipathy to him. She felt this to be necessary because, despite all contrary intentions, she was impressed by his proud bearing and undoubted good looks. His hair was thick and styled to be very much *á la mode*. His eyes, dark as an Italian's and fringed with black lashes, were full of beauty and intelligence. There was too a gentleness in their expression that softened the hard core of her dislike and made her unwilling to hurt him with a direct rebuff.

But she would not embrace him, Tamarisk thought, stealing a quick glance at her mother lest it should be her intention to give such a command. Mavreen, however, wisely remained silent. Cautioned earlier by Clarissa, she had resolved not to make any attempt to force her willful daughter to acknowledge her father at this first meeting.

"Let it come about naturally," Clarissa had said. "For I am certain Gerard is well capable of winning the girl's affections if that is his wish. I know no one with more charm than he!"

Gerard was now unconsciously exerting that charm.

"Come sit beside me, Mademoiselle," he said, speaking with a formality which made Tamarisk feel adult rather than child. "I cannot tell you what happiness it gives me to be in your company. You must forgive me if I appear overwhelmed, but I had expected to find a child and am now disconcerted to find myself in the presence of a singularly beautiful young lady."

"Don't flatter the girl lest you turn her head," Sir John said, smiling as Tamarisk kissed him warmly on both cheeks. "She has quite enough spoiling from her old grandfather as it is!"

"And from her many beaux too, I'll wager," Gerard added, enchanted by his daughter's prettiness.

Tamarisk tossed her head.

"I am not yet permitted to have a beau," she told him, pouting. "At least, only Midshipman Charles Eburhard, and he's too dull and plain to be a feather in any girl's cap!"

"So you are fancy free!" Gerard laughed, gently teasing her.

To Tamarisk's consternation she felt the hot,

betraying color rush to her cheeks. Furiously she bit her lower lip, trying to conceal her perturbation. No one present must know of her secret love for Perry! Far from abating since that ride home in the carriage, her love had intensified with every moment she had spent thinking of him; with every word she had spoken to Charlotte, her only confidante, about him. Deliberately, when she went out in the carriage, Tamarisk ordered the coachman to drive past Perry's house in the vain hope that she might catch a glimpse of him. The previous day she had ridden for long hours in the park in the hope that Perry too might be riding there. On two occasions she had gathered courage enough to ask her mother if she could invite him to take tea with them, but infuriatingly Mama had refused and Tamarisk had dared not persist lest her mother should suspect how desperately Tamarisk longed to see him again, to be near him even for an hour.

If Gerard, who was close enough to note Tamarisk's blushes, did in fact do so, he was too tactful to draw attention to them.

Watching Tamarisk, Mavreen was well content with her daughter's behaviour. She had feared Tamarisk might be as openly resistant to Gerard as she had professed was her intention. Now it seemed as if the child was quite prepared to accept her father. In fact Tamarisk appeared to have settled down very well at Barre House, showing a dreamy docility that was quite at variance with the wild behavior she had evinced on Mavreen's homecoming.

How pretty she is! Mavreen thought, suddenly immensely proud of the child she was now, at long last, able to present to Gerard — their child, the living proof of their love!

She looked fondly from father to daughter and knew herself perfectly satisfied. There was nothing more she needed for total happiness. Gerard was in good health, and it was only a matter of weeks before they would be married and would become lovers again.

Seeing Gerard's hand, white, beautifully shaped, cuping his knee, she imagined it caressing her breast, re-awakening all the well-remembered fires of their shared passion. As her eyes wandered to his mouth, finely drawn but full lipped, she could almost feel the touch of those lips on her neck, her shoulder, on the soft crease of her inner arm. Was it really eight years since they had last lain together in the act of love? So long! Yet so vivid was the memory, it was as yesterday they had submitted to one another in hungry abandon, limbs entwined, mouth to mouth, body to body, in one great conflagration of desire.

Suddenly Gerard looked up and his eyes met Mavreen's across the room. He caught his breath, marveling at the strange, exotic beauty of this woman who, since the day he had first set eyes upon her, had captured his imagination and set his blood on fire. It seemed little short of a miracle that after more than twenty years she could still excite him with a mere glance from those flashing green eyes.

Catching Tamarisk's curious gaze concentrated

upon him, Gerard speculated as to her thoughts. It must be disturbing for the child to discover that he, a stranger, was her natural father.

Unhappily his beautiful young daughter was conceived whilst Mavreen was still married to Lord Barre and could never be acknowledged as a de Valle. Nor could he expect a son as a result of his forthcoming marriage to Mavreen. Many years ago Mistress Sale, who had assisted at Tamarisk's birth, had foretold that Mavreen would be unlikely to produce another child.

Gerard's sadness was but momentary. No man, least of all his unworthy self, could expect *le bon Dieu* to provide all the good things of life. He was reunited with the woman he loved; he had regained his health; he had a delightful daughter. What more could he ask from Providence?

"And what news have you to tell us, *ma petite*? Did you enjoy your luncheon with the young Princess?" he asked his daughter.

Tamarisk seated herself gracefully upon a footstool at her grandfather's feet and tossed her ringlets, frowning.

"None that is good," she replied. "Her Papa has refused to allow her to have her own establishment although she attained the age of seventeen two months past. Poor Charlotte is compelled to suffer the indignities of her governesses, Miss Knight and the Duchess of Leeds who is ignorant and ill mannered and a dreadful bore."

"You would be advised not to voice such opinions beyond these walls, Tamarisk!" Mavreen cautioned. "If it were to come to the Prince Regent's ears that you supported his daughter in views contrary to his own, he might well forbid your visits to the Princess."

"I think your Mama is right." Sir John spoke before Gerard could comment. "Do you guard your tongue, Miss, lest it lead you *and* your Princess into trouble!"

With the total confidence of one who knows herself too greatly loved to be in any danger, Tamarisk jumped up and twined her arms around her grandfather's neck, her eyes alight with laughter.

"And if I hold my tongue, from whom will you hear the latest gossip?" she said, twinkling. "You know you hugely enjoy all my tittle-tattle, Grandpapa! And there is still one choice morsel I have not yet told you. Would you have me relate it?"

"You little minx!" Sir John said, drawing Tamarisk onto his lap as if she were but five years old. "Tell me, then, since your mind is obviously set upon it!"

Tamarisk's voice dropped to a whisper.

"Charlotte was impelled to go riding in the park last week so that she might reveal to the people that she is not *enceinte*. Society has been saying that she was with child through an affair with her cousin, Captain Fitz-Clarence. Can you imagine poor Charlotte's humiliation! 'Tis not her fault she has put on weight and so lent credence to such unkind suggestions."

Mavreen frowned.

"If you value your friendship with the

Princess, never speak politics with her, Tamarisk, although . . . " she added, "doubtless the Prince Regent would think you too young and unimportant to hold any sway over his daughter."

"You may rest assured, Mama, that we never talk of such dull matters!" Tamarisk cried impulsively. "We greatly perfer to discuss . . . "

She bit off her words, her cheeks once again coloring a deep pink, a fact which did not go unnoticed or unremarked this time by her grandfather.

" . . . affairs of the heart?" he chuckled, finishing her sentence for her. "Though I'll wager the Princess talks whilst you listen, for you cannot have much to say upon the subject."

With an effort Tamarisk held her tongue although she longed to declare to the entire company that contrary to Sir John's opinion, she knew very well indeed what it was to love, even if she did not know how it felt to have her love returned. Skillfully she diverted everyone's thoughts to her one admitted admirer.

"You may laugh at my limited experience, Grandpapa," she said reproachfully, "but my one brief encounter with love is not a matter for hilarity. *You* would not care to receive, as I have, *billets doux* from someone as tiresome and persistent as Charles Eburhard. There is little romance in it, I can assure you."

"There, there, child, I was only teasing," Sir John said, taking the bait. "And whilst I most certainly would not welcome love letters from young Charles, I like him well enough. He has courage and a determination to succeed." His eyes twinkled again. "I'll wager no girl ever had a more tenacious admirer in the face of such discouragement!"

Tamarisk smiled back.

"Well, at least I am free of his pestering for a while, Grandpapa. He called upon me yesterday to bid me farewell for he is leaving to fight the war in America!"

"Is he, indeed?" said Sir John. "Well, I wish him good luck, and you should remember him in your prayers, Tamarisk, for doubtless he'll need them aboard one of *our* frigates!"

Gerard looked questioningly at Mavreen.

"That name — Eburhard!" he said. "It kindles a memory . . . "

Mavreen's eyes were radiant as Gerard's question transported her back eighteen years to the Eburhard's soirée at which Gerard had first fallen in love with her.

"Indeed yes, Gerard. Charles is the nephew of Lisa von Eburhard and her late husband, the Baron. Lisa had no children, you will remember, so Charles is the heir."

Tamarisk, watching them, wondered at the intimacy of the glances they exchanged and guessed intuitively that somehow the elderly Eburhards had been involved in their love affair. The thought was disturbing. She did not want to think of her mother and this man passionately embracing. They were too old for love! Yet the Prince Regent was in his mid-fifties and everyone knew he had affairs with ladies. Love, she was discovering, recognized no boundaries of age, yet she had fondly imagined, from her perusal of Jane Austen's delightful novels, that this emotion was for the most part the prerogative of the young.

Her thoughts returned once more to her mother and the Vicomte. They were now holding hands quite unashamedly. She stole a glance at Gerard from beneath her lashes. He was undoubtedly a comely man. His clothes were not modish by London standards, but Tamarisk was willing to concede that his attire might be considered fashionable in Russia.

Despite her resolve not to approve of Gerard, Tamarisk now had to admit — at least to herself if not to her mother — that the Vicomte seemed a very likable man. It was plain to see that he adored her mother! But would he look upon Mama with such devotion if he knew of her past reputation as the Barre Diamond? For all Aunt Clarrie had inferred that Mama's behavior had been impeccable after her marriage to Uncle James, on reflection Tamarisk was far from convinced. There had been all those long summer months Mama had sojourned alone at their country house, The Grange, in Sussex. But had Mama been alone? In retrospect it seemed unlikely since she had not even taken Aunt Clarrie and Grandpapa for company.

But if her mother had had a lover, which seemed more than probable, who was he? She had many admirers, the most persistent being Perry.

Perry! *He* had been the most constant, the most frequent visitor in London and the country.

Moreover, he had openly declared his love for Mama.

With a new heightened sensitivity to adult emotions, Tamarisk was struck suddenly by the suspicion that Perry's masquerade as a nincompoop had been adopted to conceal the fact that he was Mama's lover. If it were so, a most successful deception it had proved to be, for no one had considered Mama's reputation in the least endangered when she was found alone in Perry's company. Not even the most jealous of husbands bothered their heads about the popinjay who paid attention to their wives!

She longed to cross the room to her mother and ask if her guesses were correct. She had always known Perry was no fool. But had Mama known it? *Had* they been lovers? Although she recoiled at the mere thought, Tamarisk knew instinctively that the answer was 'yes'.

4

April 1813

TAMARISK dismissed her maid Elsie and turned to the gray-haired Rose who had been assisting with her toilette.

"Well, Rose," she said, pirouetting in her new muslin gown. "Am I as pretty as Mama when she was my age?"

Rose had once been Clarissa's maid and worked at Orchid House when Mavreen first went there to live. Later she became Mavreen's personal maid and remained in her service until her own marriage to Dickon five years ago. It was not surprising, therefore, that Rose had received an invitation to Sir John's and Clarissa's wedding along with the upper servants from Wyfold House.

"You be almost as pretty as your Mama," Rose replied, pinning a loose tendril of hair more securely beneath the sprigged muslin bonnet covering Tamarisk's golden curls. She stood back to admire her handiwork. Her eyes were dreamy as she recalled aloud her memories of Mavreen at fifteen, setting out for a secret assignation with the young Vicomte whom Rose had heard about but not then met.

"Why were they meeting secretly?" Tamarisk asked curiously. This was a story she had not as yet heard.

Rose sighed.

"Because the Vicomte was penniless after that there Frenchy Revolution," she said. "And there were plans for him to be wed with a rich furriner. Sir John meant as for your Mama to marry well too, so he and Mistress Clarissa were a-busying theirselves trying to keep the two young'uns apart."

"So they met in secret!" Tamarisk prompted as Rose paused.

"That they did — on Richmond Bridge. Your Mama was unaccountable calm when we slipped out of Orchid House, but I was that flustered I was all whichaways. Then I set eyes on the young man we was a-going to meet, standing on the bridge by his great black stallion, and I surelye never seed anyone more comely in all my born days! Like a fine Prince, he were! I dunna know as how your poor Mama could do aught else but fall for him."

"If the Vicomte loved Mama too, why did they not run away together?" Tamarisk asked, trying to make her voice sound casual in order to hide her deep interest in this romantic fragment from the past.

"'Cos, like I said, he had to have a rich wife. He went back to that there Frenchy country he come from. I never did see him again 'till after your Mama was married and he came a-visiting at The Grange down in Sussex. That was when he fell off'n his horse and suffered the concussion and was taken aboard a privateer by smugglers. After that he was 'pressed into the navy and served on Lord Nelson's own battleship *Vanguard*. He were nobbut a lad then, and now he do be back home again after all these years and handsomer than ever!"

It was obvious to Tamarisk that Rose was as blinded by her romantic memories of the Vicomte as was Mama herself. With no memories to confuse *her*, Tamarisk felt her view of him to be the more objective. In her opinion, though undeniably handsome, he could not even compare with Perry in looks!

Tamarisk had not had the good fortune to see Perry again recently, but her love for him had in no way abated these past two weeks. If anything, its intensity had increased. It was all too easy to belittle the obstacles that lay between her and her heart's desire. She convinced herself that she had only to make Perry aware that she was no longer a child for him to fall instantly in love with her.

Her hopes for the future were, however, somewhat diminished as her preparation completed to Rose's satisfaction, she went downstairs and saw her mother. She stood silently regarding her. How beautiful she looked in her new fur-trimmed green pelisse which so perfectly matched her eyes! What hope had she, Tamarisk, of attracting grown men such as Perry whilst Mama was there to turn all heads? The Vicomte, she saw, could scarce bear to take his eyes from her, although on seeing Tamarisk he did offer her his arm. He remarked with excessive gallantry that he was the most fortunate of men to have two such beautiful women to escort to the wedding.

Tamarisk disregarded such flattery. She knew instinctively that Gerard was seeking to gain her approval. In her opinion he was ever too ready to praise and please her. She was better used to Perry's frank criticism coupled with a praise given only if it were well deserved.

Perry was not invited to Sir John's wedding. Disappointed though she was, Tamarisk consoled herself with daydreams of romantic encounters with him and with memories of the many halcyon hours spent in his company. Sometimes he had told her stories of footpads and highwaymen, his descriptions of these rogues so vivid she could almost believe he knew them! And very occasionally he talked of the hopeless plight of the poor and how often they had no recourse but to resort to a life of crime merely to survive the daily threat of starvation. He talked of children being flogged; of young boys transported in heavy irons to the Colonies for theft; of women hanged outside Newgate Prison for no worse an offense than the passing of a forged pound note.

Mavreen was unaware of the true reason why her daughter was all too often closeted in her bedchamber. She could not know that Tamarisk was trying to express her unrequited love in poetry or merely staring out of the window, praying that the gods might be kind enough to allow her to meet Perry that day. Mavreen imagined she was still sulking because Gerard was to become her stepfather instead of Gideon; or else that Tamarisk was still smarting from the blow to her pride caused by the discovery that she was illegitimate.

That Tamarisk should feel angry and bitter toward her, Mavreen could understand. It was a reaction for which she could feel some tolerance. But that tolerance did not extend to Tamarisk's cold indifference to her father. Mavreen knew Gerard was deeply chagrined by his daughter's uncommunicative and unresponsive behavior.

"Does Tamarisk not like me?" he had asked Mavreen. "I have tried so hard to win her approval and yet . . ."

"You have been marvelously good and patient with her!" Mavreen attempted to reassure him. "She does not deserve your attentions, still less your generosity. The gold necklace you gave her yesterday was an unwarranted extravagance for a girl of her years!"

"But it is my pleasure to indulge my only child!" Gerard sighed. "Besides which I feel I must make up to her for my many years of neglect."

"Tamarisk is already overindulged," Mavreen argued. "Her grandfather and Aunt Clarrie give way to her every whim; and I fear that I too may have done the same in the past."

"Then do not ask me to do otherwise," was Gerard's rejoinder, "for I would dearly love to win her affection. She returns my embraces most dutifully, but never once has she proffered her cheek of her own accord."

Mavreen resolved to speak to Tamarisk; but an appropriate moment had not so far presented itself during the fortnight following

Gerard's return home. With her father's wedding imminent and her own to Gerard not four weeks hence, there were insufficient hours in every day for all that was needed by way of preparation. The problem of Tamarisk would have to wait, Mavreen decided, although she came close to issuing a strong reprimand when, in the carriage taking them to the wedding, her daughter gave only the most cursory of replies to Gerard's attempts at conversation and passed the journey to Kew staring out into the streets as if she had never traveled the route before.

The ceremony was performed in old St. Anne's Church at Kew Green. Since Sir John and Clarissa had determined upon a quiet wedding with only a few close friends and relatives present, the church was but half full this day. Aunt Clarrie, although nervous, looked charming and elegant in a dark blue-velvet pelisse buttoned down the front and cut short enough to reveal ten inches of a paler-toned blue bombazine dress beneath. Her blue-velvet slippers matched her pelisse and were prettily decorated with colored stones. Her gray hair was concealed by a net, on top of which she wore a wide-brimmed blue-velvet hat from which curved an ostrich feather.

Sir John, smiling happily, beamed with pride as he escorted his bride down the steps of the church and out into the early spring sunshine. As with all weddings, a crowd of passersby had gathered and now stood cheering lustily and calling out their congratulations. Despite the advanced years of the happy couple, some sprinkled sand in their path — a traditional rite believed to ensure that the marriage would be fruitful. Small boys ran behind the carriages as they rolled up to the church, and the ladies waved and smiled as one by one the elegant wedding guests were driven away to the reception at Orchid House.

Gerard squeezed Mavreen's hand as they awaited the arrival of Dickon with their carriage.

"Very soon now *you* will be the bride — my bride," he whispered.

Inevitably it was a nostalgic day for them both, steeped as they were in memories of the past. It was here, at Orchid House, that the nineteen-year-old Gerard had crept through the front door, left unlocked by Rose, and found his way to his beloved's bedchamber. There, in the soft, golden firelight, they had first become lovers, Mavreen as uninhibited as Gerard as she gave herself to the young man she loved.

Neither chose to recall on this happy moment of reminiscence that Mavreen had felt most cruelly betrayed when Gerard wrote three days later to tell her that he could not marry her.

Despite their outward observance of the conventions, Mavreen had found occasion for them to renew their relationship as lovers. The vastness of Barre House made a private rendezvous easily available, and whenever time permitted, whilst Tamarisk was out riding in the park, they repaired to the guest room in the east wing and there made love like conspirators.

"Soon we shall have legal sanction for our loving," Gerard said the day following upon

Sir John's wedding. They lay at ease, delighting as always in these stolen hours alone together. Gerard looked down at Mavreen tenderly, marveling anew at the beauty of her still youthful body. "Our marriage day cannot come soon enough for me, *mon amour*. I would be done with these clandestine assignations!"

Mavreen ran her hands over Gerard's naked body, delighting in the whiteness of his skin.

"You have no fear, then, that our loving will lack for excitement when we are wed? There will be no danger of discovery to lend piquancy to our situation!" she teased gently.

Gerard caught her wayward hand and pressed a kiss into her palm before replying:

"There is naught in this world I do with you that lacks excitement," he said. "But you, *ma petite*, will *you* feel differently once we are man and wife? Somehow I cannot see you settled to a tranquil life of domesticity!"

His question made her strangely uneasy. She sat up and began to dress herself.

Watching her graceful movements Gerard felt yet again the purest astonishment that this woman could still arouse him as quickly and easily as when they were in their teens. Though she had but a few minutes earlier satisfied his hunger to the full, yet he still desired her even knowing that he no longer had the power to take her.

"You have not replied to my question," he prompted gently.

"I can but remind you that I have been twice

married and am well used to domesticity," Mavreen said.

"But you cannot claim to have settled in either marriage!" Gerard pursued his unwelcome train of thought. "You were never without a lover, my Mavreen."

She paused, her dress remaining unbuttoned, her beautiful breasts swelling over the top of her chemise. Her eyes now flashed dangerously.

"That is unfair, Gerard! You were my only lover whilst I was wed to Gilbert or to James. Nor would I have lain with any other man had I not believed you dead. How can you, of all men, dare to reproach me?"

He held out his arms for her, but her anger had not yet abated and she stepped backward out of his reach, her cheeks flushed, her eyes stormy.

"Forgive me, my dearest. I was but teasing," Gerard said, anxiously attempting to mollify her.

Mavreen let go her breath, unaware until then how tense she had been. Her anger gave way to sadness.

"How is it possible that you of all people should doubt me? No other woman could have been more steadfast in her love than I in my love for you."

Gerard raised himself upon his elbow. He looked so woebegone, she at once relented and flung herself back into the safe circle of his arms.

"Upon my honor, I really meant no more than to tease you," he said, planting kisses between

78

each word upon her shoulders, neck, face, and arms. "Maybe my thoughts were prompted by my own feeling of inadequacy. I have never felt worthy of your love, my dearest. I shall never fully believe myself justified in claiming you for my own."

"Oh, Gerard, hush, I pray you!" Mavreen cried, trying to silence him with kisses. "I am no more perfect than you. I too have weakness of which you know nothing. I will now confess them to you, for I never again wish to hear you declare yourself unworthy of my love. *It is I, Gerard, who am unworthy of yours!* You know nothing of the years between our meetings in Austria and Russia."

She decided upon the impulse of the moment to make a full confession of her relationship with Gideon Morris. But on the point of speaking she found the words sticking in her throat. She was not afraid Gerard might condemn her for her unfaithfulness to him, since he knew very well she had had every reason to suppose him dead. Yet a relationship which should have been easy enough to explain to Gerard was suddenly proving too complicated to define even to herself. She could not with honesty speak of her friendship with Gideon as if it had been a matter of casual indifference to her. She had truly believed that, at its conception in the summer of 1808, the strange fascination Gideon held for her existed only because of his marked resemblance to Gerard. But as she came to know Gideon better and discovered him so opposite to Gerard by nature, the confusion of identity vanished.

There seemed no way now to describe to the man she loved the totality of her surrender to another. What began as the submission of her will to Gideon became, as the weeks, months, and years passed by, a voluntary exchange of shared passion. She and Gideon became friends — so close in spirit that they knew without the use of words what the other thought and felt. She and Gerard had never had sufficient time together to achieve this understanding.

Gerard was watching closely the changing expressions on Mavreen's face as, lost in thought, she pondered how to make her confession. As his uneasiness increased he found himself more and more reluctant to hear about the years they had lived apart. He said now:

"'Tis sometimes better not to speak of matters which are past. Is it not our future which is important now, Mavreen? I know all that I wish to know about you; and that you love me, I have not the slightest doubt. Unless you feel impelled to confess to me that you have had this man or that as a lover, unless such confession would ease your mind, then I pray you, *do not make it*. I would not expect or even wish for a woman of passion such as yourself to remain faithful to a memory. That would be a denial of all that I love in you — your vitality, your passion, your womanly beauty. You were fashioned to bring the greatest of joys to a man, my lovely Venus. Were I to have died I would have wept in my grave had I imagined you would continue forevermore in barren mourning for me."

80

"Oh, Gerard, you are far too generous to me!" Mavreen cried, her voice trembling upon the edge of tears. "You are right, my love — it is indeed only the future that matters. I love you so much, Gerard! I cannot remember a time in my life when I did not love you!"

"I would it were our wedding day today," Gerard said, kissing her tenderly. "Or better still, that it had been yesterday."

Mavreen stood up and with a sigh returned to her dressing.

"We have tarried over long," she cautioned. "Tamarisk will be returning shortly from her ride."

"I do believe you are afraid of our daughter," he commented as he pulled on his hose. "Is she really so innocent that it would shock her sensibilities to find us abed? There lack but two weeks to our wedding day. In the eyes of God we are already man and wife."

"I prefer to give Tamarisk no cause for criticism," Mavreen replied. "At her age we cannot preach morality to her whilst practising the opposite."

Gerard could not withhold his laughter.

"Forgive my merriment, my love, for what you say is true. But I am not yet reconciled to this new Mavreen. I have never before seen you in the rôle of a mother!"

"Perhaps because I have failed until now to behave like one!" Mavreen countered. She looked at Gerard anxiously.

"Does this aspect of my nature displease you?"

For answer he put his arms around her and kissed her.

"There is no aspect of your nature that displeases me," he said simply. "Or if there is, in twenty-three years I have not discovered it!"

Mavreen closed her eyes, permitting herself the luxury of a few more minutes in his embrace. She would not spoil the harmony of the moment by reminding him that throughout those twenty-three years they had spent less than one whole month together; that if the truth were to be admitted, neither knew the other very well.

5

April 1813

WHEN Tamarisk arrived back at Barre House, it was to find her mother and the Vicomte innocently occupied downstairs, inspecting the growing number of wedding gifts displayed in the Chinese salon. The presents were to remain there until after the wedding for all to see at the evening reception that was to follow the ceremony.

Still attired in her riding habit, her cheeks flushed from the exercise, Tamarisk looked unusually bright and animated as she approached her parents. Her radiance came as much from within as from her recent exertions for she had not only seen but, miracle of miracles, she had actually spoken to Perry in the Park! He too was out riding, enjoying the unusually warm April sunshine, and as far as she could ascertain, his pleasure in meeting with her was unfeigned.

For twenty minutes they walked their horses side by side whilst Tamarisk, her heart beating in delirious happiness, recounted the events of the past fortnight. She had even won his amused agreement that she was too old now to call him 'Uncle'. His manner, easy and unconstrained, remained so until Tamarisk took her courage in both hands and raised the topic of her mother's approaching marriage.

"I feel most fortunate in having this unexpected opportunity of talking to you, Perry," she said, choosing her words with care. "For I have a problem and I need your help. I fear I shall be in deep trouble with Mama unless I can count on you not to betray me. Please, dearest Perry, may I count on your complicity?"

"That I cannot promise until I know the problem and my part in the plot," Gideon had replied guardedly, although he was prepared to assist her if he could.

"I have been given the task of sending out the wedding invitations," she said, carefully keeping her eyes from his face. Her tone was one of childish appeal. "You should, of course, have recieved one long since."

She looked disarmingly woebegone.

"I was so busy selecting styles and materials for some new gowns, I quite lost count of the passage of time and have fallen vastly in arrears with my duties," she continued. "And you know how angry Mama would be if she were to learn that you, among all people, had not yet been advised of the wedding arrangements. So please, Perry, may I just mark your name on my list as having accepted and then Mama will never learn of my dilatoriness?"

The lies ran so easily off her tongue that Perry did not suspect his name had never been on Mama's list! Nor wished it so, she surmised, judging by his unwillingness to attend.

But Tamarisk had continued pleading with him until finally he gave his promise that he would be there. Hopeful that her mother would be too fully occupied on her wedding day even to notice Perry's presence, far less divine Tamarisk's ruse to get him there, she now beamed happily at her parents who were unwrapping the parcels delivered that afternoon.

"See, Gerard, this gift is from Madame de Staël!" Mavreen cried, holding up a leather-bound first edition of Sir Walter Scott's newest publication, *Bridal of Triermain*. "Is that not kind of her? Especially as I am so newly acquainted with her. Look, Tamarisk!" she added, handing her daughter another book. "'Tis a signed copy of *Childe Harold* — from the author himself!"

Tamarisk turned to Gerard and told him briefly of the young poet Lord Byron.

"Lady Oxford is bringing him to the wedding, so you, Sir, will be able to meet him in person and shake his hand."

Gerard laughed, well content to see Tamarisk so animated.

"If this poet is really so handsome, I would think you might prefer that he hold your hand rather than shake mine!"

Mavreen sighed happily.

"Is it not surprising, Gerard? We have already received over one hundred and fifty acceptances to our wedding celebrations despite having arranged our marriage at such short notice. Father will be delighted, for he was determined upon making the occasion important."

"It is a tribute to your charm and beauty," Gerard replied gallantly. "Not every woman could attract to her side such a long list of illustrious personages — especially if she was absent from Society for as long as you have been, my love."

"The list grows longer every day," Tamarisk said. "We shall be entertaining the Prince Regent, Princess Charlotte, and ... " she flicked an imaginary speck of dust from her shoulder in wicked imitation of the Prince's great friend and socialite " . . . and Beau Brummel. Then we are to be honored by the presence of the Prime Minister, Lord and Lady Jersey, the Melbournes, the Hollands, and, of course, Mama's great friend William Wilberforce."

"And have we heard nothing yet from *my* King?" Gerard inquired, for an invitation had been sent at his request to Hartwell in Buckinghamshire where Louis XVIII had spent the past seven years of his exile.

"Perhaps we shall receive a reply tomorrow," Tamarisk suggested. In her own present state of happiness she wanted everyone around her to be happy too. It was now her dearest wish that her mother should marry the Vicomte as speedily as possible and thereby put herself beyond Perry's reach forever. With Mama safely married, she had no competitor for Perry's love — or none that she knew of.

Already plans were formulating in her mind. Her parents would be departing to Sussex for their honeymonth and Tamarisk was not accompanying them. Alone in London with only Dorcas, Mavreen's maid, to chaperone her, she would be free to come and go as she pleased.

So Perry could visit her at Barre House without the presence of her mother to distract his attention from her. There would be ample time to present herself to him in a new light, for she would be mistress of Barre House in her mother's absence. He would discover how competent she was to run a large establishment; how adeptly she could play the part of hostess; how charming, entertaining, and attractive a wife she could make him if only he would give her the chance!

It was unfortunate for Tamarisk that Gideon's friendly manner and obvious pleasure in her company that afternoon in the park gave no indication of his true frame of mind. The sight of Mavreen's daughter, so greatly resembling her, had been both joy and pain. His common sense warned him clearly that he would more easily recover from his broken heart were he to forget Mavreen's very existence! But his hunger for news of her outweighed such caution. He had therefore greeted Tamarisk with a deal more warmth than sense, unaware that the child might build upon it to feed her hungry need for his love.

Ignorant of his true feelings Tamarisk never doubted that he would keep his promise and attend the marriage ceremony. But when, at last, her mother's wedding day arrived and the large church of St. James's quickly filled with guests, Tamarisk could not see Perry amongst them. Twice Clarissa was forced to tell her to stop fidgeting whilst the solemn vows were exchanged. When the triumphant notes of the organ gave way to the loud pealing of bells as the service ended, Tamarisk welcomed the moment, for it heralded her release from the confines of the church. Now she could seek Perry openly.

But a vast crowd had gathered outside the church to stare not only at the bridal couple and richly attired lords and ladies, but at the magnificently robed, corpulent Prince Regent and his no less flamboyant but more elegant companion Beau Brummel. In vain Tamarisk sought for a glimpse of the one man she wanted to see.

Later that day there was to be a lavish ball at Barre House. Tamarisk consoled herself that she would of a certainty see Perry there.

She had had a new white and silver gown especially made for the occasion, cut daringly low over her small pointed breasts. With the aid of a new corselet, her bosom could be pressed upward to appear more voluptuous. In her opinion, her dress was far more beautiful and seductive than her mother's creamy satin ball gown, and she was confident that she would not go unremarked or be compared unfavorably with her mother.

Tamarisk's personal maid, Elsie, newly appointed by Mavreen, was so nervous and excited that it took her twice as long as usual that evening to curl and dress her young mistress's hair. By the time Tamarisk was satisfied with her appearance, many of the guests had arrived.

Every room in Barre House was ablaze with candlelight — Mavreen having refused to install the new gas lamps which she considered gave too harsh a light. There were liveried footmen everywhere. The rooms filled rapidly as more and more carriages rolled up to the front door and discharged their richly clad, bejeweled occupants.

But as Tamarisk went from group to group there was no sign of the one face she desired to see. Perry was certainly not amongst those crowding around the bride and groom offering their congratulations nor amongst those encircling the Prince Regent. Once she thought she saw him in a corner of the Chinese salon in conversation with Princess Charlotte and went eagerly toward them only to discover that it was not he but the handsome Lord Byron, whom the Princess presented to her.

Charlotte smiled happily but apologetically.

"I trust your Mama will forgive me for monopolizing one of the most distinguished of your guests," she said. "But because you are my dear friend, I am prepared to share his company with you."

As the young man with the beautiful pale face and brooding gray eyes bowed over Tamarisk's hand and quizzed her curiously, she thought ironically that only a few weeks earlier she would have fallen instantly in love with the poet. But now it was too late! Her heart and mind were fully occupied with love for another.

Excusing herself, she curtsied to Charlotte and began once more to look for Perry, growing ever more frantic as she failed to find him.

The musicians struck up a waltz and the dancing began. Despite her anxiety to continue her search for Perry, her dance program filled rapidly. The young men who had known they must perform at least one duty dance with their hostess's daughter now clamored to be noticed by her. Those who were unlucky ribbed one another for not having suspected that the daughter of the beautiful Lady Barre might well have inherited her mother's looks.

Tamarisk, however, did not return their admiration. Their compliments were too effusive, their chatter meaningless, and their appearance so similar that she found it impossible to distinguish one from another. Whilst performing an obligatory dance with Lord Redesdale, one of her grandfather's Tory acquaintances, Tamarisk suddenly caught sight of Perry standing alone beneath one of the great chandeliers. His gaze was riveted upon her mother who was dancing with her new husband, oblivious to all around her. Across the heads of the whirling couples Tamarisk could not mistake the expression of bitter longing on Perry's face nor fail to see the despairing droop of his shoulders.

Her one thought and desire was to run to him and somehow comfort him, but etiquette demanded she wait until the music stopped. And although the dance continued no more than a minute or two longer, by the time Tamarisk had made her hurried excuses to her elderly partner, it was already too late — Perry was gone.

Heedless of decorum, she ran to the front hall. When one of the footmen in attendance by the door confirmed that Sir Peregrine Waite had departed "with some urgency," she was close to tears of disappointment and frustration.

"The gentleman left this," said the footman, his face impassive as he handed a small box to Tamarisk. "He asked that it should be presented to the Vicomtesse de Valle when the ball ended."

Unaccustomed to this new title, it was a second or two before Tamarisk realized the parcel was intended for her mother. Moving away from the footman's gaze she carefully opened the lid.

Inside the box lay a black mask, similar to those used by ladies at masked balls; and on top of this lay a silver bracelet from which hung two beautifully wrought tiny silver spurs and a pair of miniature silver pistols, each in its own perfectly fashioned holster.

For several minutes Tamarisk studied the contents curiously. She felt instinctively that the trinkets had some special meaning. Pretty although the bracelet was, it had no significant value. Nor was it a fashionable piece of jewelry to present to a woman who already possessed a priceless collection left to her by her first husband, Lord Barre.

'Tis but a meaningless bauble! she thought, dropping the bracelet back into its box which she returned to the footman with orders to put it in the Chinese salon with the other wedding gifts.

As she made her way back to the assembly her mind was in turmoil. Perry's abrupt departure had totally disrupted her composure. He had kept his promise to be there, but he had not stayed long enough to ask her for even one dance! It was unforgivable, cruel, heartless! But greater than her anger with him for so disappointing her was her determination to wipe that look of sorrow from his face. She quickly found excuses for his neglect of her. She had always known how greatly he had loved her Mama and should not, she now reprimanded herself, have expected him to arrive at the celebration of her wedding to another in a mood for rejoicing. And since he had no way of knowing Tamarisk's own intent to offer her love in compensation for his loss, there was every excuse for him to discount her presence and make an early departure. In her mind's eye she could picture him even now arriving at his lonely house in Harley Street, steeped in sorrow and despair. She, Tamarisk, was the cruel, heartless one demanding his presence when it could only bring him unhappiness.

"Not dancing, Tamarisk?" Her father's voice at her elbow startled her out of her reverie. "Then pray do your Papa the honor of standing up with him."

Obediently she followed him into the ballroom. The heat, the noise, and the heady smell of candlewax and perfume were overpowering. But Tamarisk was too deeply engrossed in her secret thoughts to be aware of the atmosphere, the festivities, or those enjoying them. Her feet followed automatically the pattern of the dance. Her ears heard only the cry of the violins. Later, they told her, later, when the ball is over and all are abed, then you can go to him, go to him, go to him . . .

I can slip quietly out of the garden door! a voice in her head responded. Find a hackney cab in Piccadilly; drive to Harley Street. Perry will be alone, Perry, *Perry!*

Gerard looked fondly into his daughter's rapt face. How sweet and young and virginal she looked! Her eyes starry, her cheeks flushed, she reminded him of her mother at this same age, half child, half woman. So had Mavreen looked on the night he had first fallen in love with her at Baroness von Eburhard's ball. Soon, doubtless some young man would initiate Tamarisk into the joys of loving. But not yet! he thought. Let her remain a child a little longer.

He felt saddened by the realization that he could never recover those lost years of her childhood.

"Do not grow up too quickly," he said. "There is no hurry to grow old, my little one."

But Tamarisk, remembering Perry's brooding gaze upon her mother, believed there was every need for haste.

6

April 1813

IT lacked but ten minutes to the morning hour of three of the clock when the hackney cab drew up outside the door of Chiswell House. Tamarisk paid the driver and pulled the bell handle. She was obliged to wait some time before a sleepy-eyed footman opened the door. He stared at the young girl with an astonishment he was unable to conceal despite his twenty years in service.

"Sir Peregrine is expecting me!"

Tamarisk's voice, intended to sound imperious, quavered with nervous excitement. She had had no difficulty in slipping out of Barre House via the garden, as she had planned, but it was many minutes before a hackney cab had come within hailing distance. In the cold, damp darkness of the predawn hour she knew there were dangers lying in wait for an unattended young lady abroad alone in the heart of London. Nor did she care for the appearance of the cab driver who leered at her with a knowing grin as if she were a woman of ill repute. She was convinced he asked double the normal fare for the journey to Harley Street but dared not dispute the matter with him lest he refuse to drive her at all.

Tamarisk's self-assurance took a further downward plunge when the footman, instead of opening the front door wider, made as if to close it whilst informing her that Sir Peregrine Waite was not at home.

Tamarisk shivered and pulled her cloak more closely around her. She longed to be safely back in her bed at home, but she was more afraid of a return journey alone in the hackney cab with its grinning driver than she was of confronting the footman.

She drew herself up to her full height.

"I am quite well aware that Sir Peregrine is out," she lied, surprising herself by the veracity of her tone. "Your master instructed me to await his return. Kindly show me in at once!"

Though by no means convinced that these were Sir Peregrine's orders — for he never brought ladies home — the servant knew better than to argue with a lady of quality, however young she might be.

To her great relief he showed Tamarisk into the salon and put a log on the dying embers of the fire.

As he hovered uncertainly at her elbow Tamarisk decided to be hung for a sheep as for a lamb. She had no wish for the footman to be present when Perry did return and find her there.

"You may go to bed now," she said in the most authoritative tone she could muster. "Sir Peregrine bade me instruct you that you were not to wait up for him."

The footman bowed. There was always a first time, he thought philosophically as he left the room. Maybe his master was changing his ways.

Maybe he was about to become a middle-aged rake! A seducer of innocent young females! He shrugged his shoulders as he made his way back to bed. It was not for him to question his employer's behavior.

Left to herself Tamarisk removed her cloak and bonnet and making use of the little mirror in her reticule tidied her hair as best she could. She then sat down upon the sofa, arranging the long folds of her white dress to their best advantage. She crossed one silver slippered foot over the other and rested her head gracefully against the cushions. Now carefully positioned in what she believed to be a nonchalant but elegant pose, she settled herself to await Perry's return.

She glanced continuously and impatiently at the hands of the ormolu clock upon the mantelshelf. They seemed barely to move. The careful pose she had assumed became impossible to retain and she was forced to change her position lest she arrest her circulation completely. If only she knew how long she might have to wait before Perry returned, she thought miserably. Her restlessness increased in proportion to her anxiety.

A half hour passed. Then an hour. Tears now trembled on her lashes. An idea had begun to form in her aching head. Suppose Perry were not to come back at all? Suppose he had chosen to spend the night elsewhere . . . with a friend . . . perhaps even with a woman? In her imagination she could envisage the servants appearing in the early hours of the morning to light the fire and clean the room. They would find her here . . . in her white and silver ball gown . . . still waiting . . .

The thought of such humiliation brought tears even closer. Forgetting her desire for Perry to discover her casually reclined upon his sofa, she jumped to her feet and began to pace around the room. He had to come home soon! He *must* come home! Soon it would be daylight. She could not remain here for the servants to find her and she could not possibly drive back to Barre House in such attire! What madness had possessed her to come in a ball gown? Why had she not considered such a contingency? If she were older, wiser, more experienced . . .

The tears of mortification spilled down her cheeks. Furiously she brushed them away. Perry must come soon. *He must!*

A cock crowed — from the kitchen gardens of Foley House in Chandos Street, she guessed. Dawn must be breaking.

Tamarisk's predominant fear now was of being found by the housemaids. Her eyes searched the room for somewhere to hide. But there was no adjoining anteroom. On the point of total despair a further possibility occurred to her — she could take refuge in Perry's bedchamber.

The idea seemed a good one. Since Perry's servants believed him to be out, they would not be likely to go to his bedchamber in the early morning. She would be safe enough there from prying eyes. Moreover, when he did return — and he must, he *must* — he would doubtless go directly to bed. In the meanwhile she could conceal herself there most effectively.

Tamarisk might have lacked for sense but not for courage. Having made up her mind she dried her eyes, took one of the candelabra, and tiptoed upstairs. The first room she entered was covered in dust sheets — a bedchamber for guests, she surmised. The second was a broom closet. The third was undoubtedly Perry's room. Her sharp eyes instantly recognized his gold repeater watch lying on the bedtable beside the silver candlestick.

Her fears and anxieties momentarily forgotten, Tamarisk closed the door softly and crossed to the big fourposter. Hung with thick crimson brocade drapes, shadowy in the light of her candle, the great bed looked like a dark cavern — a perfect place for concealment.

She put the candelabra down upon the bedtable and, kicking off her slippers, climbed onto the bed. It seemed to emit an inviting odor of tobacco and some special pomade that was instantly reminiscent of Perry. She lay her head upon the soft down pillow, her fear quickly evaporating as her excitement returned. In her imagination she pictured Perry's head beside her own, his lips closing upon hers, his arms reaching to enfold her.

She closed her eyes, feeling that same strange languor she had experienced in Perry's phaeton stealing over her and setting her pulses throbbing. All thoughts vanished save for the one overriding desire for him to come home, to find her, take her in his arms, and love her. She could not imagine how his loving would be, for she knew so little about such adult behavior.

In the novels she had read so avidly, the passion and sweetness of love was romantically but never factually described.

Nevertheless Tamarisk was certain that whatever was likely to occur, clothing would be a hindrance. And since it was her intention to abandon herself to passion and surrender her virginity for Perry's solace, then she must also abandon any thoughts of modesty. Besides which, she decided, suddenly wide awake again, Charlotte had told her that masculine passions were inflamed by the sight of a naked female body. If she rid herself of her clothing, she would ensure Perry's instant arousal.

Slowly Tamarisk began to disrobe. Her regret at the necessary removal of her beautiful white and silver gown was lessened when she caught sight of her naked body in the gilt mirror on the tallboy.

Viewing herself as she now imagined Perry would see her, she felt strangely excited. Her hands covered her small firm breasts which, though regretfully not as voluptuous as her mother's, were beautifully formed. The nipples looked like pink rosebuds against the whiteness of her skin. Below her tiny waist, her hips swelled in gentle curves. Her legs were long, her feet small and dainty . . .

The sound of footsteps outside on the landing brought Tamarisk's self-appraisal to a swift conclusion and sent her flying into the bed, the candles blowing out in the draught caused by her haste.

The door opened and Gideon staggered into the room.

He had been drinking heavily. But since no amount of brandy had effectively cured the ache in his heart brought about by the sight of Mavreen dancing in her husband's arms, he had finally given up the attempt to drown his depression and returned home.

Gideon Morris was no moralist and had ofttimes lived outside the law; but his wrongdoings had never included the sin of adultery. By her marriage to Gerard, Mavreen had put herself beyond his possession forever. It was this realization which he found so unbearable and which he had sought to obliterate from his mind with the aid of drink. But though indeed dulled, the ache and the longing for Mavreen remained.

In the almost total darkness of his bedchamber Gideon did not at first perceive the girl lying beneath the coverlet. He was about to stumble onto the bed when first he saw the pale glow of a face upon his pillow.

"In heaven's name, what is this?" he shouted, pulling back the coverlet and revealing the full nakedness of his unexpected visitor. His initial shock now gave way to amusement as he realized his uninvited guest was a female.

"A gift from the gods forsooth!" he declared. "Nay, I have indeed overimbibed!" And still totally unaware of Tamarisk's identity he fumbled for his tinderbox in an attempt to light the candles.

With his blundering arrival Tamarisk's self-confidence had speedily evaporated. Hurriedly she reached out a hand to prevent him illuminating the scene.

"No, please!" she begged. "No candle!"

Some vague recollection of her voice caused Gideon to peer more closely at his visitor.

"'Twould appear you know me, so pray name yourself!" he ordered. "I have a right to know with whom I am to share my bed this night!"

He sprawled across the coverlet and reached out his hand. It fell upon one of Tamarisk's bare shoulders. She cried out, shivering uncontrollably with nerves. She had never anticipated that Perry might be drunk and not even know her.

"Oh ho!" laughed Gideon, entirely mistaking her reactions as indeed he mistook her. "So my little whore desires to play the part of frightened virgin! I'll pay no more for it, I assure you. Though upon reflection," he added, his mood changing abruptly as his depression reasserted itself, "I have no appetite this night for whoredom. So dress yourself and be off, girl, by whatever magical means you gained entry to my house."

To be mistaken for a whore was bad enough, Tamarisk thought. But to be so peremptorily dismissed . . .

All caution now abandoned, she sat up and flung herself upon him, covering his face with kisses. In one long, incoherent rush of words she blurted out her identity, her love for him, her desire to give herself to him for his pleasuring. In vain Gideon sought to free himself from her frantic embrace, but she clung to him fiercely.

"You can see for yourself that I am no child!"

she cried. "I am a woman and I love you, I love you, *I love you!* My virginity has no importance for me. I want you to take me — to make me yours!"

Gideon was shocked into total sobriety. He was horrified by Tamarisk's indecorum, but most of all he was appalled by the thought that he had mistaken this child for a whore and might, had he been a trifle more drunk, have taken advantage of the extraordinary situation in which he found himself.

He was furiously angry — with her, and with himself.

"Dress yourself at once!" he commanded in a cold, hard voice. He wrenched himself free of her despairing grasp and walked quickly away from her. He crossed the room and stood by the window staring down into the street below.

The sound of Tamarisk's sobs increased his confusion. His little Tamarisk, Mavreen's daughter, here, naked, in his bed! What madness had overcome her? He was old enough to be her father. He was, to all intents and purposes, her Uncle Perry! Why, it was little better than incest!

Her quiet crying unnerved him. She had not moved from the bed.

"I will not speak with you until you are robed," he called over his shoulder. "Dress yourself this minute, Tamarisk!"

But as she obeyed him he found her silence even more disturbing than her sobs. Outside the window the dawn had broken. A few dark figures shuffled along the road on their way to work. A milk cart turned the corner at the top of the street, the horse's breath steaming in the cold morning air.

"What madness possessed you?" he said, turning in time to see the pale glimmer of Tamarisk's face as she pulled her cloak around her. Beyond tears now, she stared back at him, her eyes swollen, red-rimmed, and deeply shadowed with fatigue. Her pride in greater tatters than her hopes, she replied simply:

"I love you, Perry. I had thought to make you happy, not to anger you."

Gideon banged his fist down upon the windowsill.

"I have never heard such nonsense!" he shouted. "Heaven knows what has put such a ridiculous notion into your head!"

As his head cleared, so his anger abated and gave way to a deep consternation. It was morning and the silly child had compromised them both with her romantic folly. He dreaded the idea that he must now take her home and try to explain the inexplicable to Mavreen.

"I dare not think what your mother will have to say," he muttered. He remembered with a sickening shock that this night past was Mavreen's wedding night. Doubtless she would even now be abed with Gerard.

"I will not be held responsible!" he cried, more to himself than to the girl standing silently on the far side of the room. "I shall accompany you no further than your front door. You must make your own excuses for this night, for it is not of my doing. 'Tis time you learned to think before you act, Tamarisk, and mayhap this occasion will teach you the lesson you so clearly need."

"I am not ashamed."

Tamarisk's voice, though trembling, was not without dignity. "I cannot help it if you do not return my love. I came to console you . . . "

But she got no further, for Gideon, his face now white with renewed anger, broke in furiously:

"Did you believe that you — a mere chit of a girl but newly hatched from the nursery — could console me for the loss of a woman I have loved for many years? You are out of your depths, Tamarisk, and would do well to remember your age before you seek to attract the attention of grown men. You presume too much!"

He spoke on impulse and with no deliberate intention of cruelty. But his words struck deeper than he could have imagined.

Tamarisk, who until this moment was sustained by a love she believed big enough to withstand Perry's anger and even his rejection, was not proof against his ridicule. Her anguish, her shame, her disappointment, her pain were all obliterated by one overriding emotion — pride. *She would prove him wrong!* Somehow, in some way that was yet to be decided, she would show him that young though she was, she was quite as capable of attracting a man as her mother, no matter what age he might be. It was on the tip of Tamarisk's tongue to boast of her conquest of Edward Crowhurst, but instinct stayed the inclination. Aunt Clarrie had had so low opinion of the young man that she had forbidden his further acquaintance, and doubtless Perry would likewise disparage him. She must engage the attentions of a more impressive admirer, and when she had succeeded in finding such a lover, she would make certain that Perry knew of it. He would be someone of consequence; someone Perry could not belittle; someone, possibly, that he admired — even envied.

Gideon was already regretting that he might have spoken too harshly to Tamarisk. Now, too late, he judged her behavior more rationally, and what he had taken to be profligacy he realized was misplaced romanticism. He attempted to speak in a more kindly tone to her as he escorted her back to Barre House.

Tamarisk, huddled against one side of the carriage, as far apart from him as was possible, remained entirely mute. No matter how he tried, she spoke no word other than to refuse his help when he relented and offered to accompany her into the house and confront her mother with her. Despite his irritation, Gideon was forced to admire her courage when it became obvious she intended to face the consequences of her behavior all alone.

He was not to know, as did Tamarisk, that Mavreen and Gerard had planned a dawn departure to Sussex where they would be spending their honeymonth at The Grange. Barre House therefore did not hold the terrors Gideon imagined, and there was no one more formidable to face than a sleepy servant.

Ignoring the look of surprise on the face of the

footman who opened the door, Tamarisk went straight to her bedchamber. To the astonishment and delight of her goggle-eyed maid Elsie, she ordered the girl to remove the crumpled white and silver ball gown and dispose of it, since she had no wish to see it again.

"You may have it," she said curtly. "Now bring me some hot water and then you can go. I shall not need you again until this afternoon. And tell Dorcas I do not wish to be disturbed for any reason whatever. I will ring for you when I want you."

She climbed into bed, and too exhausted even to think, she slept without the slightest difficulty for the next six hours. Her slumbers were untroubled by dreams, but when she woke the shameful, humiliating memories of the preceding night returned in full force and washed over her in waves. She lay immobile, the linen sheet pulled up to her chin, her eyes closed as if by the absence of light she could shut out the reality of the day that must be faced.

For a brief while she thought of death. It held a strong fascination. Her fervid imagination could foresee the consequences of her demise . . . Perry overcome with remorse; her mother's deep sense of guilt that whilst she had been glorying in the delights of her honeymonth her only child had died of sorrow. Tamarisk preferred not to think for long of the unhappiness her death would cause her doting grandfather and poor, dear Aunt Clarrie. She preferred to dwell on the thought of the scandal that her suicide would evoke! What gossip there would be amongst the

106

hundreds of illustrious wedding guests who had seen her dancing last night and supposed her to be so carefree and happy! Maybe Lord Byron would write an elegy for her and so make her immortal . . .

At the thought of the handsome young poet, Tamarisk opened her eyes and sat bolt upright. Breathing deeply with excitement at the notion which had struck her, she recalled the curious and by no means unflattering glances he had given her last evening at the ball. Was it possible — however remotely so — that she might attract his serious interest in her? It was common knowledge that he was by no means immune to the attentions women were shamelessly forcing upon him since his rise to fame. It was said that some of these ladies went uninvited to his rooms in Bennet Street and were not all shown the door.

If she could by some miracle of good fortune cause Lord Byron to become enamored of her, what triumph this would be! What sweet revenge upon Perry who had scorned her as too young and callow to attract a grown man! How humbly Perry would have to retract that statement if Lord Byron were to pursue her! There was no more eligible man in London than he.

Tamarisk jumped out of bed and pulled the bell rope. Not waiting for the maid to arrive from the distant regions of the servants' quarters, she began quickly to dress herself, white lawn chemise, pantaloons trimmed with pale blue ribbons, silk hose held up by ribboned garters. She selected one of her new gowns, a yellow and white striped silk dress, and matching pelisse. By the time Elsie knocked upon her door, there was little for the girl to do but dress Tamarisk's hair and arrange her fine plaited straw bonnet with its trimmings of yellow flowers and white ribbons.

"Will you require luncheon, Milady?"

"No, I shall not," Tamarisk replied impatiently. "And you may go now and tell Dorcas that I wish to take a walk. She is to put on her cloak and bonnet immediately and accompany me."

The girl bobbed a curtsy and hurried away, agog to inform the other servants of Milady's new airs and graces!

"You'd think it was her as had just got wed," said Elsie, "that haughty she spoke!"

She longed to reveal that her young lady's bed had not been slept in that night, but Dorcas, anticipating this, had taken her on one side and cautioned her never, ever to gossip about what went on 'upstairs'.

"A lady's maid and a gentleman's valet are in a privileged position, Elsie!" the elder servant said. "There's trust put in us as isn't given to housemaids and footmen and the like. You keep your mouth shut if you want to keep your place — and take notice of my advice. You be a lucky girl to be employed by her Ladyship . . . I mean, the Vicomtesse. Unlike some as couldn't care, she teks good care of her servants if'n they serve her loyally, and you'd not find a better position elsewhere. Do you mind your tongue, girl!"

This caution to Tamarisk's maid in no way quelled Dorcas's curiosity, heightened now by her desire to know where the young lady intended walking. Tamarisk did not offer to satisfy Dorcas's wish for information and silently made her way along Piccadilly and into St. James's. From there she turned into Bennet Street and stopped outside number four, an unpretentious lodging house.

"You may ring the bell," she said to Dorcas. "Inquire if Lord Byron is at home and will receive me!"

Only Tamarisk's youth persuaded Dorcas that it was her duty to speak — respectfully to bring to Tamarisk's attention the fact that it would be more proper first to write a letter to his Lordship requesting an interview.

Tamarisk, who was well aware of the correct etiquette, had every intention of bypassing such a long-winded procedure and told Dorcas so. She gave the maid what she hoped was an admonitory look.

"You may have been instructed by Mama to act as my chaperone, Dorcas," she said coldly, "but I do not think it was Mama's intention that you should give me instruction upon my manners! As it happens, I have need of his Lordship's advice about my verse!" She held up the reticule she carried containing her poetry. "And I have no wish to let petty niceties of behavior delay my instruction."

Intimidated in the way Tamarisk hoped, Dorcas rang the bell.

The door was opened promptly by a manservant who glanced sideways at the pretty young girl standing a little apart from Dorcas. He was not in the least surprised to see yet another young woman calling upon his Lordship. Half the female quality in London seemed to be chasing his master. He would inquire if Lord Byron was 'at home' to visitors, he informed the maid.

Lord Byron, upon hearing his servant's description of Tamarisk, decided that he was 'at home'. He was both bored and worried. Caroline Lamb was pestering him with letters and was demanding a lock of his hair, pictures, letters, trinkets, and was threatening to ruin him. His affair with Lady Oxford had in all possibility met with the most awkward of consequences. He had left her but a few days ago, far from happy, at her country home, Eywood, in Wales. He was bored by the long speeches he had been forced to listen to when he attended parliamentary sessions. And he was extremely worried about money, or the lack of it; not least because he was unable to offer financial assistance to his half-sister Augusta, whose husband was busy gambling them further and further into debt. The mood all these concerns engendered was hardly propitious for work. These depressing reflections made him vulnerable to any relief the Fates offered and caused him to welcome Tamarisk with more interest than he might otherwise have felt.

He remembered the girl as soon as she entered his room. She was the one who had barely given him a second glance at her mother's ball last night. His pride had been momentarily piqued, for it rarely happened that a female ignored him.

Tamarisk, her eyes modestly downcast, dropped into a graceful curtsy. Her host approached her, the limp caused by his clubfoot barely perceptible as he crossed the room, arms outstretched, and raised her so that she stood facing him. She was but a few inches shorter than he and she found herself looking directly into his large gray eyes. So heavily fringed were they with thick dark lashes that they appeared almost black.

"You must forgive me, Sir, for intruding upon your time," she said. The steadiness of his gaze made her suddenly nervous and unaccountably shy. A blush colored her cheeks most becomingly.

Entranced by the girl's youth and prettiness, both qualities to which he was always susceptible, Lord Byron sought to put his visitor at her ease.

"Pray be seated," he said, pointing to his sofa. "And do not look so frightened. You are perfectly safe with me, whatever warnings you may have been given to the contrary!"

"I have heard nothing to your disrepute, Sir," Tamarisk replied. "In fact I hear only that which is complimentary and this includes your kindness to others. I have been hoping such kindness extends to advising yet another struggling would-be poet, namely, myself."

She was about to reach for the reticule containing her verses, but on a sudden impulse she changed her mind and replaced it on the sofa beside her. Seeing Lord Byron's curious gaze centered upon her, she smiled as she said guilelessly:

111

"Forgive me, Sir, but it would be wrong of me to waste your time giving an opinion on verse I already know lacks talent and beauty. At the risk of incurring your bad opinion of me, I must now confess I intended to deceive you. It was but pretense that I needed your literary opinion and that this was my reason for coming to see you. To be perfectly honest, Sir, and at the risk of shocking you, I came here for no other reason than that I desired to further our acquaintance!"

Tamarisk could not have chosen a better means of arousing her companion's interest. He found her frankness totally disarming.

He smiled at her and bowed as he replied:

"I am flattered! And if I may be equally honest, I must admit to being a little surprised. Last night at your house, you were too intent upon some secret mission to give me a second glance. Or even to notice that I noticed you."

At the memory of her desperate search for Perry a blush spread over Tamarisk's face, making her look even younger than her years. Lord Byron was captivated. Although Lady Oxford was his mistress, he was also a little in love with all her lovely young daughters, and the twelve-year-old Lady Charlotte Harley in particular. His romantic sentiments were invariably excited by the very young and Tamarisk's youth did as much to attract him as did her bright green eyes, her pretty Grecian nose, and her sensuous mouth.

Tamarisk had inherited her mother's single-mindedness of purpose. She had gone to Bennet

Street with the sole intent of being seduced by the poet. She permitted herself no last-minute qualms as he seated himself beside her and tentatively put one arm around her waist. When she made no resistance, he began to kiss her passionately. Tamarisk closed her eyes and forced herself to think of the kisses Perry had denied her.

This man, she thought with satisfaction, did not consider her a child, judging by his increasing ardor. His kisses grew more fervent, his caresses more intimate.

Tamarisk was momentarily aware of a sense of wrong-doing; paradoxically the sensations of her body were very pleasing. She had associated such sensations with her proximity to the man she loved and her conscience smote her that this stranger could as easily arouse her passions.

But these fleeting doubts as to the veracity of love were quickly outweighed by a far less philosophical consideration — curiosity. His Lordship was even now unbuttoning her dress and placing his hands upon her breasts. What next, she wondered.

As her nipples became suddenly erect, they seemed to develop a new sensitivity — a need of their own to be fondled, stroked, caressed to an ever increasing excitement. It spread downward through her body, causing her heart to race, her cheeks to flame, her breathing to come in short, quick gasps.

"Ah, my pretty, my sweeting, my lovely girl!" her lover murmured as he bent his head and kissed the firm, pointed breasts with

113

knowledgeable skill.

So he finds me desirable, Tamarisk thought with a satisfaction which added a further dimension to the new and startling sensations of her body. As if in answer her lover slowly unfastened the remaining buttons of her bodice until her breasts were free of the confines of her chemise.

A trifle embarrassed by this sight of her bosom exposed to his entranced gaze, Tamarisk closed her eyes, preferring to enjoy the pleasures of dalliance unhindered by propriety.

It was clear that her would-be lover was finding her clothes an impediment to the further exploration of her body.

But Lord Byron was from experience very well accomplished at such tasks as disrobing females. Within minutes Tamarisk's dress lay in a pool at her feet, along with her pantaloons and chemise. He was unaware that her nakedness would bring back to her the most painful of memories — her humiliation when Perry had ordered her out of his bed as if she were a naughty child.

Such thoughts gave Tamarisk fresh determination, for her courage was rapidly deserting her as her lover now stripped himself as naked as she. She realized now for the first time what was almost certainly about to happen to her. Quickly she closed her eyes so that she could not see this frightening evidence of manhood. It was the more shocking to her virginal gaze because the sight of her nudity had fully aroused her lover's ardor.

"Come now, my dearest," he cajoled softly.

"Have no fear! I shall be gentle with you. I promise you the greatest joy."

But for all his gentleness, it was not joy but pain Tamarisk felt as he lay her on the sofa and bore down upon her with singleminded purpose.

Pride alone silenced her cry and stayed her protest. Mutely she submitted to the invasion of her body, accepting that its violation was brought about by her will rather than his. She even allowed him to believe, since he seemed so anxious it should be so, that she enjoyed the experience.

When it was over he kissed her with genuine tenderness, assuring her that next time she would feel greater pleasure. He was both loving and gentle with her. Had Tamarisk realized it, she would have considered herself fortunate to lose her virginity to so kind a man. Seeing that her intent was to revenge herself upon Perry, she might as easily have chosen a man with far less sensitivity and natural affection than her poet.

The deed accomplished, Tamarisk began to dress herself. Her lover did likewise. He was now feeling a belated concern that his young temptress had proved to be a virgin. Despite her youth and background he had supposed her familiar with the delights of dalliance since no totally innocent young female would invite herself to a bachelor apartment unchaperoned. He now considered it not beyond the realms of possibility that she would suffer some aftermath of regret or remorse — perhaps even confess her escapade to her mother.

It was with the greatest relief, therefore, that he heard Tamarisk say:

"I may count upon your total discretion, Sir, may I not? I fear my mother would be angry beyond belief were she to discover my whereabouts this day."

"It shall be a most treasured secret between us," he replied, kissing her hand. "Will I have the pleasure of seeing you again?"

In fact, although quite enchanted by his unexpected visitor and the satisfactory ending to their romantic encounter, he was further relieved to be told by Tamarisk that she dared not risk another secret meeting.

"But it would be my pleasure if you would call upon me at Barre House," she added, her mind fully occupied once more with her plan to revenge herself upon Perry by the production of Lord Byron as her official beau.

He promised gallantly to do so, but privately he thought it questionable that he would have the time. Not only had he consented to an interview with Caroline Lamb, an event he dreaded, but he was also expecting a visit from Miss Annabella Milbanke to whom he had on a sudden impulse proposed marriage! And not to put a finer point upon his difficulties, he was expecting Lady Oxford to return to London shortly. He had no wish to add another to these romantic entanglements.

Tamarisk refused the refreshments he now offered her and bade him adieu. Lack of sleep the previous night, the emotional upheaval, and her mental confusion were taking their toll upon her nervous system. She wanted nothing but to return to the solitude and perfect privacy of her bedchamber. She longed now for the refuge of her pretty pink and white curtained bed; for the very adornments of the childhood she had so recently and irrevocably rejected. The plump, familiar figure of Dorcas waiting patiently for her in the hall was yet a further reminder of her lost innocence. It was only with the greatest of difficulties that she refrained from laying her head upon Dorcas's matronly bosom and bursting into tears.

If this was 'growing up', she thought, as she walked silently homeward a pace or two in front of the maid, then she wanted no part in it. Her brief encounter with physical passion this afternoon had proved as painful and disappointing in its conclusion as it had been pleasurable and exciting in its beginning. She did not regret it since she still believed the end justified the means, but she was now very deeply regretting her rash folly the night before.

Much as she might want to, she could not hate Perry — not even although he had shamed and rejected her. She realized that by her mistake last night she had forfeited his love. She wished desperately that she could set the clock back to a time when he had truly loved her, albeit as a child. He need never know about her lost innocence. Yet the very reason for it had been to prove him wrong in his estimation of her; to force him to acknowledge her womanhood.

Mayhap, she thought, it was not too late to reestablish the old relationship with him.

In her tiredness and confusion, it did not occur to her that because of her afternoon escapade there could be no going back.

7

May – July 1813

"I HAD forgotten that England was so beautiful in the spring," Gerard remarked as he and Mavreen strolled homeward one mid-May afternoon. She had chosen to take him back to The Grange by an unused lane so thickly overgrown with the green leafage of the uncut road-side bushes that the path allowed passage for only one at a time. Only a glimmer of sunshine filtered through the overhanging boscage as they walked knee-deep in fragrant grasses.

Mavreen, laughing, told Gerard that even the smugglers had abandoned this molelike passageway, having discovered a quicker road from the coast northward.

"It was once one of their most regular escape routes," she told him. "Mayhap Dickon brought you by this very road twenty-three years ago! How I longed then to be a boy so that I might have gone with you to France."

As they came out of the semidarkness into the full warmth of the sunshine, Gerard reached out and touched Mavreen's golden head. His eyes were filled with tenderness.

"That is a wish I cannot share," he said. "You are all woman — every woman! Just consider what loss were you to have been born boy and not girl!"

Mavreen's arms were full of the wild flowers she had gathered during their walk — woodruff, wood anemones, red and white campion, sorrel, buttercups, daisies. She smiled back at Gerard over the top of her bouquet to show that she appreciated his compliment.

Nevertheless his words unsettled her. Somehow they seemed to indicate that he did not fully understand her nature. There was that part of her which, however hard she might try to subdue it, demanded to be free. She had no wish to be a man but only to be as free as a man from the petty restrictions and conventions required of a woman. Even the skirts she wore hampered her walking; and never did she enjoy a ride in the sidesaddle as she did astride a horse. Gerard paid tribute to her femininity, but Mavreen found the womanly rôle comparatively insignificant — unless she were involved in the act of love! She herself was never happier than when she was engaged in masculine pursuits or, more importantly, was using her intelligence like a man.

But men, alas — and Gerard was proving no different from most — preferred women who were not too clever. He was not as liberal-minded as her father. At the house of Lady Jersey, Sir John had been much amused to hear a fellow guest, the great literary lady from the Continent, Madame de Staël, haranguing an important Whig politician, preaching politics, and talking the men into silence with great eloquence.

"She thinks like a man," Sir John had said

approvingly. "And although men like Byron and Sheridan, who were also present, were amazed at her talents, as was I, I fear there were many others who were quite put out."

Three of the four precious weeks of her honeymonth were now past during which Mavreen had several times noted and regretted the intellectual differences which divided her and Gerard. At times it seemed as if they had been happily married for years, their knowledge of each other as lovers deepening the intimacy they enjoyed within the nighttime privacy of their bedchamber. But their daily companionship held many strains and Mavreen was forced to accept that they knew very little of each other's taste in literature, music, the arts. The long years Gerard had spent fighting in the Peninsular War had involved him in experiences she had been unable to share with him. His opinions upon war and politics were foreign to her.

Perhaps more perplexing for Mavreen was the discovery of Gerard's disapproval of her intimacy with the Sale family. In vain she reminded him that she had grown up with Dickon and his brothers and sisters as one of the farm children; that Rose's eldest son, now four years old, was her godchild; and that Rose would have been mortally offended if she failed to kiss and cuddle the boy as was her custom when they visited Owlett's Farm. Gerard's upbringing as head of one of the big French aristocratic families had instilled in him a deep consciousness of class; and the division between rich and poor formed a line he could not bring himself to cross. Nor was it his wish that Mavreen should continue to do so.

"You are now the Vicomtesse de Valle," he reminded her. "And as such I cannot allow you to hitch up your skirts, remove your shoes, and run barefoot with the Sale urchins. *Ma foi!* You behave as one of them, Mavreen!"

She fought her irritation and tried to be tolerant of Gerard's attitude. She understood how intensely he felt about his family lineage, how deeply he had revered his mother, the Vicomtesse Marianne de Valle. But Gerard, she was discovering, was proving himself to be very intolerant. He deplored the vulgarity and dissipations of the Princess of Wales, wife of the Prince Regent, permitting no excuse for her behavior. Unlike those of the English people, his sympathies lay not with this poor, unhappy, neglected woman but with the Prince Regent.

"The man has every justification for trying to keep his daughter apart from the influence of this coarse, undignified woman!" Gerard declared. "She lacks every refinement required of a Royal personage and I am not in the least surprised that the Regent should find her so distasteful that he cannot tolerate her presence in his household."

"But *his* behavior is no better," Mavreen argued logically. "He is gross, boorish, unfaithful not only to his wife but to his mistresses. He is disloyal to his friends, hopelessly irresponsible with regard to his debts, and a political turncoat. Yet although you condemn these faults in a woman, you appear to condone them in a man. It is unfair!"

"It is the way of the world," Gerard said, shrugging away his indifference to the principle Mavreen wished to establish. When she would have pursued the argument, he turned her words aside with a kiss, telling her not to concern herself with a state of affairs she had no hope of rectifying.

Rather than quarrel with Gerard on their honeymonth, Mavreen tactfully let drop the subject of women's inequality with men. But it was not forgotten. She was strengthened in her resolve to spend more time in future assisting her friend Elizabeth Fry. Here was someone actively engaged in trying to improve the lot of women, albeit women of the lowest orders living in hopeless and degrading conditions in prisons.

Thoughts of Mistress Fry inevitably evoked memories of Gideon. She found herself wondering whether he had returned to his former way of life — if he was back upon the highways robbing the rich to assist the poor. Or had his wedding gift of mask and miniature pistols been intended as a declaration that his days of highway robbery were over for him — as they were for her. At least Gideon made no division between the sexes!

Mavreen quickly put such comparisons out of her mind. Fortunately such moments of discord between her and Gerard were rare and for the most part they walked and talked in great contentment, enjoying the unusually mild spring days, the countryside, and one another.

Gerard spoke often of his home in Compiègne and his longing to go there with Mavreen as soon as they could arrange their affairs in London.

"Just think, my darling," he said, as arm in arm they now approached the drive of The Grange. "We shall be able to show our daughter her French heritage!"

Mavreen nodded her head noncommittally. She was far from certain that Tamarisk was anxious to identify herself with her father and this foreign half of her parentage. The child could not remember a time when England had not been at war with France, and 'the Frenchys' were enemies in her mind. Napoleon was an 'ogre' who had been used as a threat by her nurses: "*If you don't behave yourself, Boney will get you!*" How then could she be expected to welcome Gerard, one of Bonaparte's officers? Nor could it be easy for Tamarisk to set aside the conviction that she was Gilbert Barre's child. She had grown up in the belief that the portraits of the Barre family hanging in the gallery were her ancestors.

In fact Gerard was not the only Royalist to accept Napoleon as Emperor of France. Many had returned from exile and obscurity and been made mayors and councillors. As for the sons of those same Royalists, the gap of twenty years since the outbreak of war was so great that most were now staunch Bonapartists.

Mavreen could but hope that Gerard's natural charm and his love for his only child would eventually win Tamarisk's affection. But she did not dwell on such considerations for long. Being married to Gerard was still too new and wonderful for her to take for granted even an hour spent in his company. There had been too many long lonely years without him; too many silent restless nights when she had wakened to find him no more than a memory. To wake now still brought a return of that old fear that Fate would take him from her in the dawning of a new day. On such occasions she would turn towards him and clasp him in her arms. He would hold her in the darkness, whispering soothing words of love until she became calmer.

"As if I would ever leave you again, my dearest!" he would murmur against her hot cheek. "We are now together for always!"

Sometimes she rebelled secretly against his complaisance. He seemed so certain nothing could ever separate them again and yet Fate had treated them so cruelly in the past she could not acquire his confidence in the future.

"You love me less than I love you," Mavreen accused him, "else you would fear losing me as greatly as I fear losing you!"

Gerard's imperturbability left Mavreen with a feeling of frustration. She would have preferred a more violent and emotional reaction in keeping with her own. She longed for Gerard to force her, by sheer strength of will, to overcome her nameless fears.

But Gerard's nature was very different from her own, she realized. It was as if he felt most impelled to retain his self-control whenever she was nearest to losing hers. Yet she could recall moments in their youth when he had given way so totally to his emotions that he had brought them both to the brink of disaster.

During the years since they had last been together, time and experience had tempered Gerard's youthful impetuosity. The privations he had suffered during the war had sapped a great deal of his stamina. Maturity had lent him a new calm whereas it had given Mavreen an added vigor.

It was not surprising, therefore, that Mavreen began to feel restless after three weeks of inactivity at The Grange. She could lose herself for an hour or two in reading, but she required physical exertion as well as mental stimulus. She longed to go riding on Firle Beacon, but Gerard was obviously content to give way to inertia and she did not want him to feel compelled to accompany her.

But such sacrifices were of minor significance, Mavreen reassured herself. Given time Gerard would recover his former vitality as rest, good food, and the better weather restored him to full health.

But not even the wholeheartedness of her desire to please Gerard in all matters could persuade her to neglect the Sale family. Their affection for her remained as deep-rooted as was hers for them. Not even for Gerard's sake could she bring herself to hurt them by suddenly allowing the difference of their social status to divide them. She would, in future, she decided, make her visits to them without him.

With little else to occupy their days, Mavreen and Gerard had time to discuss their future at length. Gerard was determined upon the restoration of his home, the once beautiful Château de Boulancourt. It had been partially razed by fire during the Revolution, and only a few rooms were made habitable for his mother during the remaining years of her lifetime. Since her death the ruins of the great house had stayed barred and shuttered against vandals, guarded only by the former tenants of the farms on the estate. Now owners of their own land, they were still loyal to the de Valle family.

Although Mavreen shared Gerard's desire to restore his home in Compiègne, she did not wish to spend her whole life in a foreign country. Her father and Clarissa were now so advanced in years that neither was really capable of undertaking long journeys abroad.

"It would be wrong for me to abandon them now they are old," she explained to Gerard.

There was also the problem of Tamarisk for whom they must soon find a suitable husband. In Compiègne this would be difficult despite the fact that Napoleon had restored the Palace for his Empress and was often in residence with his entourage.

"Then we must so arrange our lives that we share our time between our two countries," Gerard had replied agreeably. "You know that my first desire is to see you and Tamarisk happy."

Staring unashamedly at Gerard across the table where, hungry after their ramble in the

127

lanes, they were enjoying their evening repast, Mavreen wondered how she could fail to love such a generous-hearted man! How handsome and noble he looked, the first few silver-gray hairs at his temples lending him an added air of distinction. His loss of weight these past years had heightened the aristocratic curve of his forehead and nose. Only his mouth remained quite unchanged. It was gentle, almost wistful in expression and aroused in Mavreen a fierce desire to protect him from all life's brutalities. Looking back over the years, she knew this aspect of her love for him had always been dominant since she had first set eyes upon him — an unhappy, handsome, perplexed youth sent to a foreign land to escape the outrages of the Revolution.

Gratefully Mavreen recalled the promise Gerard had given her that he would go no more to war; that his fighting days were in the past. Within the safe circle of her love he would be guarded for the rest of his life from any dangers which might threaten him.

"How fiercely you regard me," Gerard said, smiling at her across the table. "Have I offended you, my darling?"

"Oh, Gerard, no," Mavreen cried, laughing. But for the presence of the footman serving them, she would have run round the table to hug him. "I was merely thinking how very well and handsome you look."

Her compliment did not go unrewarded. As soon as their repast was finished and they were alone in the salon, Gerard pulled her down onto

128

his lap and kissed her.

"That . . . " he said, " . . . is for being so beautiful. And that . . . " he planted another kiss upon her lips, " . . . is for being so flattering. And this . . . this is for giving me so much joy and happiness."

As always, Mavreen's response to his loving was full-hearted and passionate. With cheeks flushed and eyes sparkling, she returned his kisses with fervor, at the same time removing his cravat and placing her hand inside his frilled shirt so that it lay upon his heart.

She felt Gerard tense and saw him glance almost imperceptibly toward the door.

"I do believe you fear surprisal by the servants," she teased him. She was disconcerted to see no answering smile upon his face.

"And you do not likewise?" he countered. " 'Twould be an embarrassment for all were we to be discovered."

"Why, Gerard, methinks I am the greater surprised by your feelings in this matter," Mavreen replied, choosing her words with care. She was genuinely astonished at his reaction and a little incredulous. "In any event, Gerard, I see no wrong in man and wife fondling one another. If one of the servants were to see us so engaged, would this be cause for embarrassment?"

"We would do better to keep such intimacies for the privacy of our bedchamber," Gerard insisted, obviously ill at ease.

Mavreen removed herself from his lap and stood up, straightening her skirts.

"I am sorry to discover you so prudish,"

she said coldly. Although her astonishment was uppermost, she was also conscious of humiliation. It seemed as if Gerard were correcting her for a *faux pas* she was unaware she had committed.

Sensitive to her mood, Gerard sought to mollify her.

"I meant no prudery," he said. "You know how dearly I love your caresses and I . . . "

"Not dearly enough, 'twould seem, for you to chance being seen receiving them," Mavreen interrupted. "There was a time, Gerard, when I think your passions outweighed your caution."

Gerard now rose to his feet and tried to take Mavreen in his arms. But she twisted free of him, her face white, her eyes narrowed as she surveyed him bitterly:

"'Twas you who threatened I might find domesticity lacking in excitement," she said accusingly. "Yet 'tis you, Gerard, who seem to wish to enforce restraints upon us that did not exist previously. Now that we are married, is it your wish that our love should become but a dull routine?"

His look of bewilderment was such that Mavreen nearly relented.

"Let us retire now to our room," he pleaded. "I will show you how little I desire restraint and how deeply I desire your caresses!"

Mavreen's anger softened, for there was no denying the implications latent in Gerard's tone of voice. She turned and impulsively lifted her arms, entwining them about his neck.

"I want you now, Gerard, now!" she

whispered. "Take me here, in this room, upon that sofa! Please, Gerard!"

He could not know that the urgency was brought about by a sudden violent memory of another evening in this same room; a memory of a man so like Gerard as to seem his ghost, striding through the French windows as if he were owner of the house . . . and her. Mavreen was recalling how decisive *he* had been in his desire to possess her. *He* had given no thought to servants, to discovery, although his very life would have been forfeit if he were discovered forcing himself upon her. What madness had possessed Gideon! And her too, as they wrestled upon this very floor until he broke her resistance and made her as desirous of him as he was of her.

But for Gerard, her husband, there was no such urgency. It was Mavreen whose appetites were fiercest, most demanding, most frequent; Gerard who warmed to the fire in her veins. He seemed to derive a greater enjoyment from the tender caresses she showered upon him after their needs were satisfied than from the wild abandon with which she gave herself to him.

"We will do whatever you want, *mon petit écureuil!*" he said now, using the soothing voice he might have employed to a child. "If it is your wish, we . . . "

She broke away from him with a sudden bright laugh.

"Do not be so serious, Gerard," she said, smiling at him gaily. "Did you think I meant what I asked of you? Why, you should know

131

me well enough to be aware when I am merely teasing. 'Twas silly of me, no doubt, and I see now that it was wrong to pretend about such matters. Am I forgiven?"

Gerard gave a deep sigh of relief.

"I must confess I was a little worried," he admitted as he drew her down beside him on the sofa and put his arm around her in the friendliest of fashions. "As to my forgiving you, you know there is no need for that. I was at fault for imagining that you spoke in earnest. So all is now well between us, eh, my dearest?"

"Of course it is," she murmured, glad that he could not see her eyes and read therin the perfidy of her reply.

8

July 1813

"I AM more than a trifle concerned about Tamarisk," Mavreen said to Gerard. Her seamstress was fitting her for a new pelisse in which later in the month she would wear whilst traveling to Compiègne. Gerard sat in an armchair watching as the sewing woman made a final adjustment to the skirt before sitting back on her heels so that he could see the finished effect.

"Charming!" he commented, and with a smile at his wife he added, "But then you look ravishing in everything you wear, my love."

Mavreen returned his smile, then thanked the seamstress and dismissed her. She was more immediately concerned with her worries about Tamarisk than about her wardrobe.

"I am beginning to fear she is seriously unwell," she said to Gerard as she removed the pelisse and lay it on the bed ready for Dorcas to hang in her wardrobe. "The child looks so pale and listless!"

Gerard sighed. Were it not for their daughter, he thought, he and Mavreen would be blissfully happy together. Since their return from their honeymonth, they had settled to a life of quiet domesticity at Barre House, receiving occasional visitors, making preparations for their journey to France, attending the opera or a theater of an evening. They had decided against any formal entertaining, preferring to enjoy each other's company. It was, in Gerard's opinion, a delightful existence but marred by Tamarisk's pale, unsmiling face and marked preference for the privacy of her bedchamber to the company of her Mama and Papa.

Mavreen could not understand it. Her young daughter had seemed so impatient to grow up and enjoy the delights of dancing and soirées with a string of young men in attendance. Since the ball that followed their wedding, several young men had called on her receiving days with obvious intent to further their acquaintance with her pretty young daughter. But Tamarisk had excused herself on one pretext or another and evinced no interest whatever in them nor in those invitations from Mavreen's friends which included her. It was as if she were clinging to the childhood so nearly over for her.

"Let her remain a child a while longer if she so chooses," Gerard had said indulgently. "Our chrysallis will emerge a butterfly when she is ready."

But now he too was worried.

"You do not think she is unwilling for this sojourn in France?" he inquired now of Mavreen. "I would not wish to force her there against her will."

Mavreen shook her head.

"I wondered at first if that might be the case," she admitted. "But now I am convinced she is unwell. We depart in ten days time, Gerard, and I think it would be advisable to call in a physician to see her, lest she is on the point of contracting some serious illness."

She did not want to reveal to Gerard her innermost fear that Tamarisk might be sickening for typhoid or typhus fever. Gerard himself was looking so well and was in every way so much stronger and healthier that her last wish was to give him cause for serious anxiety. She realized her fears were in all probability unfounded, for although both diseases were rife in Europe, there was as yet no epidemic in England. But in Russia she had seen the outbreaks of these terrible fevers; seen the corpses piled in the streets of Vilna where the starving French soldiers of Napoleon's defeated army had died in their thousands and remained unburied. Many of the survivors who had eventually found their way home had brought the disease back with them and it was known to be spreading its virulence with fearful rapidity in Europe.

"By all means call a physician if you deem it necessary," Gerard replied with his usual prompt consideration for any wish she expressed. "It will relieve our minds." He gave Mavreen a quizzical smile. "You do not think she is pining for her young midshipman?"

"Alas, no!" Mavreen replied. "I fear Charles Eburhard has no pull upon her heartstrings."

"Yet she is even now engaged upon the composition of a letter to him," Gerard vouchsafed. "'Tis possible she is concealing from us both an inner regard for the young man."

But as Mavreen suspected, it was not from any feelings of devotion that Tamarisk was penning her letter. It was prompted by a despairing effort to keep her mind employed upon matters that were unimportant to her, so enabling her to forget for a little while those which were seeming to tear her apart.

Charles von Eburhard was in Bermuda. His most recent letter, dated the month of May, explained that his ship had had to call in for repairs following upon a minor skirmish with the enemy.

'The Yankees swarm here!' he wrote. *'When a frigate goes out to drive them off, by Jove they take her! Yankees fight well and are gentlemen in their mode of warfare. Though so much abused, 'tis my opinion they are really fine fellows!'*

If only she had been born a boy! Tamarisk thought wistfully. She could even now be a thousand miles from this unhappy house.

But it was not Barre House which was unhappy. It was Tamarisk herself. Nothing in her life was going the way she wished. Lord Byron had not called upon her. He was still in London but fully engaged escorting his half-sister Augusta Leigh to the theater, to balls, and assemblies. Moreover, all London buzzed with the scandal caused by his discarded mistress, Caroline Lamb. At a small waltzing party given by Lady Heathcote, Lady Caroline, seeing Lord Byron go in to supper with Lady Rancliffe, had in a fit of violent jealousy snatched up a knife intending to attack him. But the only damage sustained was to the young woman herself, for she had cut her hand. As Princess Charlotte remarked to Tamarisk, she had sustained far greater damage to her reputation by making such a public exhibition of herself.

But Tamarisk had no wish to discuss Lord Byron. Her deflowering at his hands had left her with such a confusion of emotions, she tried to push all memories of the occasion out of her mind. Shame, self-disgust, and a great sense of disappointment in the culminating act mingled with a strange yearning for a repetition of those earlier moments when the poet had kissed and caressed her and set her body tingling with new, sweet sensations that could not be forgotten no matter how hard she tried.

She wondered now in retrospect if it might all have seemed different had she lost her virginity to the man she loved. Would she have welcomed Perry's invasion of her body where she had resented and feared Lord Byron's? But her imagination refused to contemplate Perry in such undignified and pain-inducing an act. She was far from certain that the poet had treated her as romantically as the occasion surely demanded, yet she could think of no other way in which men and women could be conjoined except by the exchange of kisses within the mouth, and clearly this had been insufficient to satisfy her chosen lover's needs. He had wanted to behave in the same manner as the four-legged beasts of the fields and this, she was convinced, was not as it should be between humans.

Without confessing her own debasement Tamarisk had no way in which she could inquire the answers to her uncertainty. To try to forget the whole incident seemed the only solution to her unhappy state of mind.

If only she could see Perry again, she thought despairingly. But the ugly truth had to be acknowledged — Perry had no time for her, no interest in her, no real affection for her. He had not once called at Barre House, and Tamarisk's suggestion to her mother that they might invite him was met with an adamant refusal.

"You are quite old enough to appreciate the position," Mavreen said to her daughter. "Your Uncle Perry was very attached to me, and now that I am married it is understandable he should prefer to center his attentions elsewhere. I know that you are very fond of Uncle Perry, Tamarisk, but it is better that we should no longer consider him persona grata in this house!"

How easy it would have been, before she fell in love with him, to argue the point with her mother; to insist that she cared very deeply for 'Uncle' Perry and demand why she should lose *her* friend merely because Mama had chosen to marry. But now she could say nothing without fear of revealing the full extent of her love for Perry — an emotion Mama would doubtless ridicule. As had Perry himself, she thought bitterly. How well Shakespeare had defined love in *Romeo and Juliet* when he had used the words 'a choking gall' and 'a sea nourished with lovers' tears'! Only they were her tears and not Perry's . . .

It was not beyond the realms of possibility, Tamarisk reflected as her concentration veered away from her letter to Charles, that she might even die of love. Her looking glass revealed how thin and pale she had become. She had lost all appetite for food, and when she ate, she had difficulty in digesting her victuals. On more than one occasion she was unable to retain what she had eaten. That she might pine away entirely was not an unwelcome thought.

She greeted with indifference Mavreen's announcement that she was to be visited that afternoon by a physician. Her malady, she thought bitterly, was not visible to a medical eye. Broken hearts were not revealed to even the most practiced and renowned of specialists.

She made no demur when Dr. Willis arrived. She answered his preliminary questions and was surprised when, after a few minutes, he suggested that her mother should leave them alone together, with Dorcas hovering nearby for propriety's sake.

The ensuing questioning and examination were far more shocking to Tamarisk than her inquisitor suspected. When he announced his diagnosis she at first refused to believe it.

"As doubtless you suspected, you are with child!" he had stated bluntly.

"With child? You must be mistaken, Sir," she stammered.

He peered at her over the rim of his spectacles.

139

"I do not make mistakes, young lady!" he said sternly.

"It cannot be so!" she cried vehemently. "It *cannot* be!"

The physician stood back from the bed and regarded the young girl with a look that contained pity as well as irritation.

"I am afraid that you can expect little else, Lady Tamarisk, if you disregard the warnings I am sure your mother has given you. Contrary to the nursery tales, babies do not appear beneath gooseberry bushes, you know. You cannot be unaware of the risks you have been taking!"

White-faced, Tamarisk stared back at him.

"It was but once . . . " she faltered. "Upon my word, Sir, there was but one occasion when . . . "

"It is not for me to take you to task with regard to your morals," the doctor broke in sternly but not altogether unkindly. "Your mother will have to be informed, of course."

"Oh, no!" Tamarisk begged. "Please say nothing to her. I pray you, do not tell her! She knows nothing of . . . of my waywardness."

"I have no alternative but to make a truthful report to her, and when you are a little calmer you will see for yourself that your mother must know the facts. There will be arrangements to make, and the young man who is responsible must be brought to face his part in this unfortunate affair. Doubtless a marriage can be speedily effected. The child will not be born until January of next year. A seven-month pregnancy is not unknown, and 'tis unlikely

140

anyone will be the wiser."

He made the same reassurances to Mavreen who, he could see, was as deeply shocked as her daughter.

"Try not to be too severe with the girl," he said. "Unfortunately we live in shockingly dissolute times. Even the highest in the land, who should set those beneath them a good example, are profligates and reprobates. Young people today cannot help but be influenced by their elders' behavior, and whilst you, my dear Vicomtesse, are doubtless the most ethical of mothers, I daresay Tamarisk's young friends and associates . . . "

Mavreen was not listening. Her mind was in a whirl of mathematical speculation. Of one thing she was certain: Charles Eburhard could not be the man responsible! And if not he, then who, in the name of heaven, could be the father of Tamarisk's baby? As far as she, Mavreen, was aware, there was no man in her daughter's life.

Gerard was still happily ignorant of the doctor's diagnosis and Mavreen decided to leave him so until she had questioned her daughter. The bitter pill he must eventually swallow might be the sweeter if she could inform him that the father of this unwanted child was unmarried and eligible; that Tamarisk's reputation might yet be salvaged.

But Tamarisk, dry-eyed and tight-lipped, refused to confess the name of her lover.

"I will not tell you who he is," she repeated doggedly. "And it would make no difference

141

even were I to do so for I will never marry him. Moreover, I doubt he would consider marriage to me."

"He shall be made to do so!" Mavreen cried, her cheeks flushed and her eyes stormy. "Have you no idea of the import of this matter, Tamarisk? Your reputation will be in tatters and you will never make a respectable marriage. Oh, how could you do such a terrible thing?"

"Terrible?" Tamarisk repeated coldly, meeting her mother's eyes with a rebellious stare. "Are you, Mama, telling me that it is sinful to beget a child out of wedlock?"

Mavreen took a step toward the bed, her hand raised as if about to strike her daughter. Tamarisk did not flinch, and it was Mavreen who first looked away, her eyes so filled with distress that had Tamarisk seen them, she might have regretted the cruelty of her barb.

But she was aware only of Mavreen's censure.

"Whatever I may have done wrong," she added, "I do not think you, or dear Papa, are justified in any condemnation of my behavior."

Mavreen bit back the angry retort which rose to her lips. She suspected that Tamarisk was endeavoring to divert her from the fact she wished to discover, namely, who was the father of this child.

She sat down on the edge of the bed. Her anger now subsided, she would have put her arms around her daughter, but Tamarisk stiffened so obviously that she refrained from the impulse.

"Please, my darling, let us not be at enmity

142

over this unfortunate affair," Mavreen said, keeping her voice level and reasonable in its tone. "What is done cannot be undone, and what is of import now is that we put matters to right insofar as is possible. You understand, do you not, Tamarisk, that you must be married at once?"

"And to whom must I be wed?" Tamarisk rejoined bitterly. "To a man I do not love and who has no wish whatever to marry me?"

Mavreen caught her breath.

"Are you so sure of that?" she inquired. "If he has already taken you in love, he cannot be without regard for you."

"I was not taken in love!" Tamarisk replied coldly, factually. "I was bedded because I wished it and for no other sentiment!"

"But why? *Why*?" The words were wrung from Mavreen. "I do not understand you, Tamarisk."

Her daughter regarded her through narrowed lids.

"Because you know nothing about me, Mama!" she told Mavreen. "You have thought of nothing but *your* lover these past six months. So long as you could have your precious Gerard, you did not care about anything or anyone else."

"You go too far, Tamarisk!" Mavreen cried, now seriously angry. "Your happiness has been much upon my mind. It is now clear to me that I have failed in my intent — at least insofar as your moral welfare is concerned."

"'Tis true you preached innocence to me,

Mama," Tamarisk retorted. "Throughout my childhood I believed implicitly in everything you told me. I did not know then, as I know now, that it was all hypocrisy; that those who do wrong do not always suffer the consequences. *You* did not suffer, did you, Mama? Despite your infidelities, your first husband gave you his title and a fortune, did he not? And then you married Uncle James, and even though he was so ill and unhappy, *you* were not; you had Perry to console you. You . . . "

"That is enough!" Mavreen's voice was like a whiplash. She was trembling violently as she now gave way to her emotions and shook Tamarisk by the shoulders. "You forget yourself!" she cried. "And you forget your predicament, Tamarisk, in your concern for *my* morals. You would do well to remember that were your condition to become known to others, none would censure your Papa or me if we were to turn you out of this house. You have led too sheltered a life to begin to understand what it would mean for a girl of your age to birth a child and bring it up in an alien world without the support of a man or your parents. So I will hear no more about *my* past. We will discuss instead *your* future and you will tell me . . . and I do mean *will*, Tamarisk, the name of the child's father."

Already bitterly jealous of Perry's love for her mother, Tamarisk's resentment now reached a peak as she realized the full extent of her dependence upon Mavreen. On sudden impulse she sought revenge.

"The baby is Perry's!" she lied defiantly.

144

She could only suspect the success of her gambit to pierce Mavreen's armor at its weakest point. The angry color of her mother's face faded to a gray pallor.

"That is not the truth, Tamarisk, is it?" she said in a small flat voice. "You invent the falsehood, do you not?"

"'Tis no invention," Tamarisk replied, certain now that she had struck home. "You may inquire of Perry if you doubt me. Ask him whether or not I was in his rooms on the night of your wedding! Yes, Mama, whilst you were celebrating your marriage to your lover, I was with mine!"

"No!" Mavreen cried, unable to keep the horror from her voice but convinced now of the truth of Tamarisk's declaration. "No, it cannot be true! Not Gideon . . . not with my daughter . . . "

Tamarisk looked at her mother curiously.

"Gideon?" she repeated the name, for it was quite unknown to her. "I told you it was Perry who seduced me. And I will not pretend I was unwilling, for I love him. I love him as you never loved him. And no matter what he might tell you to the contrary, he loves me."

"It is not true, not *true!*" Mavreen said, shaking her head as if her thoughts were paining her unendurably.

"'Tis true enough! Why should he not love me? He loved you once, did he not? And I resemble you, or so Papa tells me. What could be more natural than that he should turn to me when you rejected him, for he *was* your lover, was he not, Mama?"

Only as her mother turned on her heel and walked silently out of the door did Tamarisk feel the first thrill of fear replace the hot satisfaction the past few minutes had given her. Her revenge upon Perry, upon her mother, had seemed sweet whilst she indulged in it. But now, alone in her room, she was reminded forcefully of a line from Milton's *Paradise Lost*; he might well have written for her the warning: "*Revenge, at first though sweet, bitter ere long upon itself recoils.*" She knew that it was only a matter of time before her mother elicited the truth from Perry — and with it the full extent of the humiliation she had suffered at his hands. Not least of all did she dread the further humiliation to come when Perry learned of her pregnancy.

Tears of mortification and despair filled Tamarisk's eyes and flooded down her cheeks. The last thing in the world she wanted was to have a baby. Not a year ago she had with her mother visited Mistress Fry and been quite horrified at this first sight of a woman heavy with child. Nor did Tamarisk care for the sight of infants dribbling and drooling and always, so it seemed, crying and needing attention of the most unsavory nature. She had long since decided that when she was required to produce an infant for her husband, she would engage a wet nurse to feed it and in no circumstances would she do as Rose did and put her baby to her breast.

"I fear I lack all maternal instinct!" she had

146

once confided to Princess Charlotte who had remarked how *her* mother was quite besotted with infants and nursery paraphernalia — even to the point of adopting the child 'Willikins' and trying to pass him off as her own, although everyone knew he was the son of a Deptford dock laborer, Samuel Austin, and his wife Sophia. Some years ago Tamarisk had accompanied Charlotte upon a visit to Princess Caroline at Montague House and been shocked to discover the withdrawing room in the style of a common nursery. The tables were covered with spoons, plates, feeding boats, and clothes. Around the fire napkins were hung to dry, and the Princess of Wales herself was putting one upon a puny-looking baby.

Tamarisk shuddered at the memory.

"I will not birth a child," she said fiercely to herself.

Perhaps, after all, the physician was mistaken, she thought. Apart from the sickness, which he had seemed to find so confirmatory of his diagnosis, and that she had twice been without the annoyance of the monthly female event, there was no indication whatever that she was *enciente*. She placed her hand over her small flat stomach and pressed hard upon it. She could feel nothing.

But in her heart Tamarisk did not really believe the doctor was wrong. She remembered too vividly the pain and discomfort that she had endured in her encounter with Lord Byron. As the doctor had just enlightened her, it needed no more than one such invasion to bring about the conception of a child. Yet never once had she considered such a risk! Her fear had been only of discovery of her wrong-doing, for it had been impressed upon her since her twelfth birthday how vitally important it was to remain a virgin. But no one had explained why! She had been left to presume the outcome of illicit liaisons. But she had given the matter no thought.

In retrospect her stupidity appalled her. She had known since childhood days spent in the country how spring was the time for animals to mate and bring forth their young. She had even observed their pairing. Yet it had never crossed her mind that the creating of a baby was the same for men and women as for animals.

How different everything might now be if Perry had possessed her the night she had gone to his rooms to offer herself to him! To be with child by *him* would not seem so terrible. And Perry would have married her. Perhaps, were she to reveal the true name of her lover, Lord Byron might be persuaded to marry her! But not even to legitimize her child would she agree to such a union. Handsome, notorious, talented, eligible the Poet might be, but she would wed no one if it could not be Perry.

"I will die first!" she cried into her pillow.

There was some small consolation in the thought of the distress Perry and her mother would feel were they to discover her dead.

★ ★ ★

"I will not wed your daughter now, next year, or ever!"

Gideon Morris stood with his back to the fireplace, his hands gripped behind him, facing the full fury of the woman he loved. As always, he found her anger exciting, for it brought the fire to her eyes and set the pulses throbbing in her throat. In such moods of opposition she reminded him of an angry tigress; and in the past when they had been lovers, it had exhilarated him to tame her into reluctant submission.

Gideon was still in total ignorance as to why Mavreen should demand his instant betrothal to Tamarisk. He could only assume that she had discovered her young daughter had been alone with him in his house at night and considered the child compromised.

When Dickon had arrived on horseback with a note from Mavreen asking if she might call upon him on a matter of great urgency, he had replied briefly that he was at home and would be delighted to receive her. He did not believe Mavreen would suggest reopening the gates of friendship and guessed she must in some way be in dire need of him. His imagination toyed briefly with the thought that her honeymonth with her new husband had ended in disaster. But he doubted this was the case, for he had espied them at Drury Lane, and to his chagrin the newlyweds appeared to dote upon one another.

He waited patiently for Mavreen to explain the true purpose of her visit. She remained standing, supporting herself by retaining her

149

hold upon the back of the settee. She found Gideon's calm reply to her demand unnerving.

Too angry with him to employ a tactful approach to the delicate matter in hand, she came directly to the point.

"It is useless to deny the facts, Gideon. I know everything. There is but one honorable course open to you. You must marry Tamarisk as soon as possible!"

"Never!" Gideon repeated emphatically.

His blunt refusal lessened her self-assurance. She stared back at him askance.

"How can you, of all men, ignore your responsibilities?" she cried. "You must realize what is at stake! Have you no honor?"

"And have you lost all sense of proportion?" Gideon countered. He was now sure he had guessed correctly the reason for Mavreen's demand. "What if the girl did come here! No one but my footman saw her, and I can count absolutely upon *his* discretion. Unless Tamarisk has spoken ill-advisedly to someone less discreet, there is no reason why anyone should ever know she was here!"

Mavreen drew in her breath.

"So you may think," she said icily. "But unfortunately for both of you, there has been a serious repercussion — no doubt one to which you paid little attention when you took advantage of her!"

Gideon took a pace toward Mavreen. He was now as angry as she.

"I took no 'advantage' as you presume to call it. Tamarisk came here of her own free will,

150

uninvited, and, to tell you the truth, unwanted. Whatever she may have told you to the contrary is complete falsehood, and I am surprised that you should even listen to such implications against my character."

Mavreen gave a small sarcastic laugh.

"*Your* character!" she said scornfully. "What, pray, is that if not reprehensible in the highest degree? You are a rake, Gideon Morris! A seducer, a debaucher . . . "

She got no further for Gideon now covered the distance between them and gripped her shoulders.

"Be silent!" he commanded. "Not even from you will I listen to such . . . such malediction — nay, vilification." He released her shoulders and took hold of her arms, forcing her to look directly into his face. His expression was now more incredulous than angry as he added:

"Mavreen, you *cannot* believe that I seduced your child!"

"And why not, pray? There was an occasion I have not forgot when you took me against my will!"

To her dismay Gideon stood back, his eyes dancing with laughter.

"Ah! Now this interview is beginning to make a little sense. You think, Mavreen, that I have had my way with Tamarisk as once I had my way with you! *And you are jealous!* You do not want me any longer yourself, but you do not wish your pretty little daughter to enjoy the delights that once were yours!"

He was unprepared for the swift flash of her

151

hand as she struck him a stinging blow across the face. The large emerald in her ring caught his cheekbone and a thin rivulet of blood spurted from the cut. Mavreen stared at it as if hypnotized. Gideon stared at Mavreen. For a moment neither spoke. Then Gideon, seeing the painful tremor of her lower lip, relaxed his rigid stance and led her to a chair.

"I should not have spoken as I did, Mavreen!" His voice was gentle but unrepentant. "But you must admit that you provoked me sorely. I can only repeat what I have already told you. I did not seduce Tamarisk. I did not even wish to do so. She left my house in the same state of innocence in which she arrived — but I hope a trifle the wiser since I reprimanded her severely for her rash behavior. As for my marrying the girl, you cannot seriously believe it necessary."

"Not necessary?" Mavreen repeated. "When she is carrying your child?"

"What crazed notion is this?" Gideon demanded. "The girl is indeed hysterical if she so informed you!"

"Then you deny it?" Mavreen asked, her voice becoming firmer as she regained her lost self-control.

"Absolutely!" He made one last attempt to reason with her. "Mavreen, forget whatever preconceived notions you held when you arrived here; make use of that intelligence I know you possess. Tamarisk is but fifteen years of age. I have known her since she was a child. She is and always has been like a daughter to me. Do you seriously imagine I would have despoiled the child, even were she not your daughter?"

His quiet compelling voice went far toward convincing Mavreen that Gideon might after all be innocent. Yet if not Gideon, who else could have fathered Tamarisk's child? She had closely questioned Dorcas and discovered that Tamarisk had barely absented herself from Barre House whilst she and Gerard were away in Sussex. There had been one afternoon visit to Lord Byron's house where the girl had called upon the poet to obtain his opinion of her verses. She was there but an hour and, as far as Mavreen knew, had not seen him since. With every woman in London at Lord Byron's feet, Mavreen considered it most improbable that *he* would have interested himself in a girl young enough to be one of the daughters of his current mistress, Lady Oxford. If in the unlikely event Lord Byron had forced his attentions upon Tamarisk, Dorcas waiting in the hall could not have failed to hear her call for assistance.

And Tamarisk herself had named Gideon as the culprit.

"Why should he not love me?" she had said. "He loved you once, did he not? And I resemble you, or so Papa tells me. What could be more natural than that he should turn to me when you rejected him, . . . "

What indeed could be more natural? And Tamarisk had always adored Gideon. What more natural than that she, a romantic, adolescent girl, should offer herself as consolation. Gideon's involvement offered the only possible explanation. As for his denial, that too was natural, for he would well know the extent of *her* wrath if he was forced to confess his guilt.

She stood up, her hands clenched tightly, her voice deeply accusing as she said:

"There was a time, Gideon Morris, when I was fool enough to believe I might love you; that we might even, in time, be wed. Were it not for the fact that I was convinced Gerard still lived, despite the years of silence, I think I would have married you. Now I believe myself the luckiest of women to have been saved such misfortune. You are a liar and a profligate and you are no gentleman despite all your attempts to appear one. Moreover, I would not permit my daughter to marry you even to salve what remains of her reputation, and not even to legitimize the child you have forced upon her. I rue the day I ever set eyes upon you. No doubt you think you can evade the consequences of your selfish pleasure. But one day, God willing, you'll pay the price — if not for this misdemeanor then for some other!"

Gideon made no move nor spoke any word as Mavreen left the room. He watched her go, his face immutable until he heard the sound of the front door closing and the clip-clop of the horses' hooves as her carriage bowled away down the street. Then only did he relax his countenance and allow his bitterness to show.

It was not Mavreen's accusation of his seduction of her daughter which caused him pain, for he knew himself innocent; it was her

154

lack of faith in him as a man. He had long since accepted that he must lead his life without her; but he believed he still had her respect. Now he had nothing left of her but her totally unjustified scorn.

9

July 1813

IT was nearly eight years since the painter Sir George Beaumont had brought with him upon a visit to Finchcocks his great friend, the poet William Wordsworth, and his sister Dorothy.

Mavreen was totally captivated by Dorothy Wordsworth although she was some eight years older than her. She was a fascinating and invigorating companion with a nature as indefatigable as Mavreen's own and a mental and physical energy that took no account of her age.

Within days Mavreen's friendship with Dorothy had deepened to a mutual respect and affection that was to endure despite the fact that they lived far apart and could meet but rarely. Dorothy, unmarried and childless, was enchanted by Mavreen's little daughter and became Tamarisk's unofficial godmother.

It was to this most sympathetic and understanding of friends that Mavreen wrote when faced with the impending disaster now threatening Tamarisk. She knew that Dorothy would be unlikely to condemn the child too harshly. Living as did the Wordsworths in the remote tranquillity of the Lake Country, Dorothy might perhaps offer a temporary haven where Tamarisk could remain concealed until a more permanent decision was made about her future.

Dorothy's reply, when it arrived a week later, was as unexpected as it was welcome for its content.

'*You have doubtless heard of our recent bereavement,*' she wrote. '*My poor sister-in-law Mary has been quite distraught with the sad loss of little Thomas following not half a year after the sudden passing of baby Catherine. We have talked at great length about your daughter's unfortunate situation and William, dear man, is in agreement that we offer to adopt the poor unwanted baby. It will, after all, be your grandchild and you will doubtless wish to be assured of its welfare. William says that with three little mouths already to feed, another will make small difference. No man is a more merciful judge of his fellow creatures than William, so Tamarisk need not fear his condemnation.*'

'*As for dear Mary, I need not tell you that all children are well loved and cared for under her roof.*'

Her good friend went on to vouchsafe her own particular fondness for Tamarisk and her desire to be of assistance in the most practical way. Not two months previously the whole Wordsworth family had removed from the Old Rectory in Grasmere to Rydal Mount, a farmhouse overlooking Rydal Water. They had rented

157

this new home from Lady le Fleming as a refuge, despite the dilapidated state of some of its rooms, since they were no longer able to endure the sight of the two little graves in the churchyard opposite the Rectory.

'*It is a paradise here and the nicest place in the world for children,*' Dorothy wrote. '*Which brings me to the second purpose of my letter . . .*'

There was, so it seemed, a charming house not half a mile distant whose owners were on the point of departing for Switzerland. They would be away from their home, Rothay House, for at least a year and would be only too delighted if it could be occupied during their absence by friends of the Wordsworths. Dorothy outlined the accommodations and ended her letter with a fond wish that her dear friend Mavreen would avail herself of this offer so that they might enjoy one another's company in the months to come.

The idea, as outlined by Dorothy Wordsworth, was perfect in every respect but one, namely, that it would necessitate the cancellation of the proposed visit to Compiègne.

Gerard had suggested that France might be the perfect retreat for Tamarisk, but Dr. Willis was afraid lest the long and arduous journey with its attendant dangers in wartime might prove injurious to Tamarisk's health. Mavreen, well accustomed to country ways and attitudes, believed that there was far too much ado made by the upper classes and their doctors over the matter of childbearing. Nature did not intend the reproduction of the species to be a matter for illness, she argued, and poor women took it as a matter of course, continuing to work until their time of birthing came. But Gerard reminded her that although she had kept wonderfully well whilst carrying Tamarisk, she had had a long and difficult birth, resulting in her subsequent childlessness. Had she been under a physician's care, this might not have happened. She could not, therefore, justifiably argue with the learned doctor on the matter of Tamarisk's well-being.

So it was decided to take full advantage of the Wordsworths' timely offer containing as it did the complete answer to all difficulties. Gerard's behavior, Mavreen opined, was exemplary. Far from condemning his daughter for her wayward behavior, he sought to find excuses for her whenever Mavreen made the slightest hint of criticism. He sacrificed his longed-for return to Compiègne without complaint and refused, with flattering promptness, to consider going there without Mavreen.

"Nothing shall part me from you, my dearest!" he said. "We will postpone our visit until after this unfortunate affair is safely behind us. My poor darling! I only wish I could ease this suffering both for you and for our little girl!"

"Tamarisk is not a little girl, Gerard, and not the innocent victim you may suppose," Mavreen felt forced to point out to him. "She admits quite freely that she invited her own seduction; indeed, intended it!"

159

"It is my belief she has told you this only in a spirit of bravado," Gerard argued. "Young girls do not invite their own despoilment unless they are deeply enamored, and we know there is no such amoretto in her life."

Mavreen remained silent. Gerard would never believe that Tamarisk was enamored of a dandified fop old enough to be her father. But to reveal Gideon's true name and character would entail explanations as to his past — a secret she had sworn never to betray since Gideon's very life depended upon his assumed rôle of Sir Peregrine. His good name, his credit, his financial stability were all at risk if rumors were ever to circulate that he was the highwayman wanted by the law throughout the country. If the facts were ever proved, he would be hung upon the gallows — a fate she could not wish upon him despite his perfidy.

It offended her sense of truth that she must deceive Gerard. In so doing she felt strangely uneasy. Her mental confusion was complicated by Gideon's cruel barb accusing her of jealousy of her young daughter. It was proving far more disturbing to her than she cared to admit. She wondered if her fierce objection to the idea that Gideon had taken Tamarisk to bed really sprang from the jealousy of a woman for a young girl, or if she was objecting on the grounds that an older man had taken advantage of an innocent child. The longer she considered the matter, the more uncertain Mavreen became. She had no wish to visualize her daughter as a woman, soft, sweet, rounded, seductive to a man's eye — to

160

Gideon's eye. Yet female instincts were inborn, and doubtless Tamarisk had known how to invite Gideon's attentions; and he had been tempted.

Had not she herself upon occasion chosen a pose she knew would enhance her curves? Placed a smooth, bare shoulder where Gideon could not fail to see and kiss it? Held his gaze longer than was seemly, knowing full well he would read the message in her eyes?

How many were the ways she and Gideon had devised to excite and arouse one another! How quickly Gideon fired to the very thought of the bodily delights they shared! How fiercely she resisted him when he had angered or teased her and then, resistance gone, still pretended it in order to provoke him to further extravagances! Tamarisk, so it seemed, was no less a coquette than her mother!

Try though she might, Mavreen was unable to prevent her mind from conjuring up the past. Guiltily she lay beside the sleeping body of the man she had married and whom she loved so devotedly, and hated herself for remembering another, her past lover, her daughter's lover.

There was no possibility of explaining her emotions to Gerard since she could not explain them to herself. He loved her and was goodness itself — tender, gentle, unselfish in his attentions to her. Every day he found some little gift with which to surprise her — a brooch, a miniature, a posy of flowers, a new book, a fine new quill, or even some special delicacy to eat. He made each day like a birthday, filling it with compliments and kisses, vouchsafing it was for his pleasure rather than for her indulgence that he did so.

She was delighted beyond words when he agreed so unhesitatingly to go with her to the Lake Country.

"'Tis said to be very beautiful in that part of England, and you will love the Wordsworths, my darling," she told him.

"I will be happy anywhere with you," was Gerard's simple reply.

He glanced at Mavreen's face anxiously. It seemed to him that she had lost weight recently, and because of her concern for Tamarisk she had also lost a deal of her natural ebullience.

"It is magnificently generous of these kind Wordsworths to offer a home to Tamarisk's child," he said thoughtfully. "But is Tamarisk willing to part with her infant? Perhaps she will finally confess to us the name of the father and can yet be married to him!"

Mavreen shook her head.

"She is but fifteen years old, Gerard, and too young to be burdened with the responsibilities of motherhood. Tamarisk abhors the very idea. I have spoken to her about this suggestion of Mistress Wordsworth's that they adopt the baby and she favors the plan. As for the father . . . " She paused. "Tamarisk tells me he is a man approaching forty, and I am sure you will agree with me that such a marriage, even were the man willing to enter into it, would be far from satisfactory. Do you not think, Gerard, that we shall be able to find a younger, far more

162

suitable husband for her when this episode is behind us?"

Gerard smiled wistfully.

"I seem to recall advising *you* against marriage to a man so many years older than yourself," he said. "But I shall leave the final decision regarding Tamarisk's future to your good judgment, my love."

So plans were made to remove to the Lake Country for the remainder of the year.

Tamarisk was vastly relieved by the thought that she would not be expected to keep the baby. At the same time she dreaded the removal to Cumbria. She knew the area was wild, bleak, and almost uninhabited except for the hill shepherds. She remembered little about the Wordsworth family, having met them last when she was a child of seven and they visited at Finchcocks. Mavreen had told her that there were three surviving children — John, Dora, and William, now aged ten, nine, and three; but that mainly on account of the deaths last year of two other children, Catherine and Thomas, the offer had been made to adopt Tamarisk's baby when it was born.

Try though Tamarisk might, she could not imagine any identity for the child within her. It seemed not to exist despite the discussions regarding the arrangements being made for her seclusion until its birth and for its future. Indeed she seemed incapable of any emotion other than distress at the thought of being away from London — and therefore from Perry — for the remainder of the year.

She was unaware that Mavreen had been to see him. She was too proud to ask if her mother had tried to verify her story. She lived in fear of Perry's anger should he learn of the accusation she had made against him. How desperately she wished now that she had held her tongue! But she had been afraid to name the true father lest her mother or father might try to persuade Lord Byron to marry her. It was not too late, even now, to exonerate Perry by confessing the truth, but she was reluctant to do so. Marriage to Lord Byron would put a final end to all her hopes of winning Perry's love; and slim though these might be, she could still cling to the belief that once he had time to grow accustomed to the idea, he might yet discover he loved her.

Tamarisk did not really believe in this happy ending to her unhappy sortie into the adult world of love. But equally she could not bear to relinquish the possibility, however remote, of ultimately becoming Perry's wife. She pondered upon his reaction if he were to learn that she was with child. Would he condemn her? At least he could no longer refer to *her* as a child too young to be worthy of a man's attention! As for the possible loss of his respect, she need hardly fear to lose what she had never possessed. Had Perry respected her as a woman, she thought misguidedly, he would never have sent her home so ignominiously the night she had gone to his house to console him.

But despite her suffering and contrary to her misgivings about Cumbria, Tamarisk was

164

entranced by the wild, panoramic beauty of the hills and lakes.

Rothay House lacked the grandeur of Finchcocks, and although larger than the Wordsworths' farmhouse, pleased Tamarisk by its homeliness. Built of lakeland stone with two gabled wings under a slate roof, it blended harmoniously with the surrounding mountainous countryside.

When Tamarisk forgot her condition, she was surprisingly happy in this new environment. In particular she enjoyed the company of Mr. Wordsworth who, although aware that she was with child, believed it a natural state permitting all normal healthy activity. Her parents fussed constantly lest she overexert herself and become tired, whereas Mr. Wordsworth was delighted when she took an interest in the garden he was creating around his new home.

In his company she learned to appreciate the beauty of her surroundings. Through his enchanted eyes she saw the view down to the water from the wild garden of birch trees, the wild flowers, the dark green of the lake water, the emerald green of the pastures, the azure blue sky.

Mr. Wordsworth reminded her of Perry because he too knew every facet of the countryside and was a veritable encyclopedia of knowledge where nature was concerned.

He seemed perfectly content at Rydal Mount despite the fact that the house needed a new roof, the back rooms were damp and uninhabitable even in the midsummer heat, and the ceilings of the rooms were too low. It was very much a family home, filled not only with the Wordsworths' children but with those of their friends — the Coleridges, the Southeys, and the Arnolds.

Tamarisk was a little in awe of Mr. Wordsworth's wife, who was quite clearly the mainstay of the household. She was tall, thin, with a beautiful complexion and a squint which strangely was not displeasing. Tamarisk respected Mary Wordsworth but loved the warmhearted, vibrant Dorothy, recognizing in her a kindred wild spirit. Secretly she envied the affectionate intimacy of this close-knit family. Simple in their ways, totally unpretentious and without social aspirations, they seemed to live for beauty, for love, for the sheer pleasure of life itself. Tamarisk deeply envied their contentment. The arrogance and hypocrisy of London Society now lost some of its glamorous appeal and she found herself wondering whether Perry could be happy in these simple surroundings without the gilded trappings of the rich and the well born. His nature was so paradoxical, she thought. He could be more dandified than Beau Brummel, taking unwanted pinches of snuff, paying meaningless compliments, exchanging pointless gossip, and appearing to enjoy the inanities of an 'At Home'. But equally she knew he gloried in a wild gallop across the countryside, his brown hair blowing in the wind, his face bright with joy as the horse's hooves bespattered him with mud; and when they slowed their sweating mounts to a walk,

166

he could talk to her quietly and meaningfully about life and his concern for the deprived.

He would, she was certain, like the Wordsworths and approve their way of life. She longed to be able to write to him, describing all she saw. But she herself had made the exchange of letters impossible by her thoughtless accusation. She could not expect him to forgive her for such treachery. She wrote, therefore, only in her journal and within the secrecy of its pages freely poured out her love and longing for him:

' . . . and if you are still nurturing a secret love for Mama, then you do waste your time, for she and Papa are every bit as close to one another as Mr. and Mrs. Wordsworth and do appear most happily suited.

'I pray you, my dearest love, to relinquish all thought of Mama and beg you to permit me some room in your heart; for I do love you as no other could, with all my being. Even my soul cries for you and I will never, never marry another. If you could but see into my heart you would pity me. The child I carry is my burden and my shame. How I wish it were truly your child!'

Unknown to her mother, Tamarisk's candle burned frequently into the late night hours as she wrote page after page, finding comfort in her outpourings. So the days and nights passed in midsummer idleness — until the last day of July.

When Tamarisk awoke, the sun was burning

167

fiercely through the open casement window. The great summit of Heron Pike shimmered in the early morning haze. She stretched her arms and legs in sleepy abandon, delighting in a feeling of healthy well-being.

But as consciousness gradually returned, so too did memory. Her hands went reluctantly to her thickened waistline and she thought with bitter resentment of the loss of her slender shapeliness. Her bosom too was fuller, and whilst she approved of this, the tenderness that accompanied the slight swelling of her breasts was yet another cruel reminder that she was burdened with the coming child.

She sat up abruptly, her happy smile turning to a scowl as she thought of the day ahead. Mama and Papa had planned yet another day in the company of the Wordsworth family. Today, she thought, with the first stirrings of excitement, she would not accompany them. She would plead a head pain; and once they had departed upon their way she would give Dorcas the slip and escape from the confines of the house and go up into the hills alone. She was heartily sick of being treated as if she were an invalid. The physician had prescribed short walks, plenty of rest in the afternoons, and nothing more exerting than a little sketching or work upon her tapestry in the evenings. It was of no avail to plead with her mother that she felt perfectly well and desired more than anything in the world to go riding upon horseback.

When Tamarisk reported that the head pain she suffered was too severe to permit of her going to Rydal Mount, Mavreen looked at her with alarm.

"'Tis of no consequence," Tamarisk hastened to reassure her mother. "Mayhap I was too long in the sun yesterday. When you and Papa return I shall doubtless be fully recovered."

Mavreen would have been severely annoyed had she been able to see her daughter, not an hour after their departure from Rothay House, skipping and dancing along the lane leading to the foothills.

Tamarisk's path followed the running waters of Rydal Beck and led her dangerously close to the Wordsworths' house. Delighting in a childish sense of adventure, she crept furtively around the perimeter of the grounds, peeping over the dry stone walls to reassure herself that Mr. Wordsworth was not at work in his garden from where he could espy her.

Alone, delighting in her freedom, she removed her bonnet and allowed the hot sun to beat down upon her golden curls. The scent of the wild honeysuckle was all around her and bees hummed busily amongst the creamy white flowers that were in full bloom. High above her head a lark hovered and shrilled its sweet song. She paused, looking up to Heron Pike and then down toward the receding woods and the lake in the valley.

How hot it was! How breathless the air! The climb became steeper. Oh, if only she were free as the lone lark and could soar upward into that brilliant azure blue sky! If only . . . if only she were free of the hateful burden inside her which, no matter how hard she tried, she could never forget for long.

Her thoughts veered suddenly away from herself as she approached the edge of a small ravine. Twenty feet or more below her, the white ribbon of a mountain stream curled downward toward the valley.

The wind was blowing the spray which rose from the heavy falls of water cascading over the rocks and Tamarisk was filled with a great desire to bathe her face and feet in the bright sparkling pool at the foot of one of the falls.

Cautiously she climbed downward, clinging to the rocks and tree roots as her feet slipped on the wet moss. Pausing to catch her breath, she was astonished at the extraordinary stillness which surrounded her. Far above her head she could still see the blue sky with its scurrying white clouds, but she could hear none of the sounds that had filled her ears a moment ago — the lark's song, the bleating of the sheep on the hillside, the distant bark of a shepherd's dog. She was conscious only of the singing torrent of water surging over the rocks and disappearing into the still, deep pool.

Her eye caught sight of a large flat rock bathed in a shaft of sunlight. Eagerly she made her way toward it and sat down upon the warm stone. It took but a minute to remove her shoes and stockings, and with a small cry of pleasure she plunged her hot feet into the icy mountain water.

The sound of the water must have deadened any noise Tamarisk made, for as she sat entranced, staring into the pool, a great red stag came to the water's edge. His massive antlers seemed almost too heavy a crown for his head as he bent to drink from the stream. There was no knowing how long he might have remained there, little more than ten feet from the girl watching him with fearful fascination; but a sudden flash of lightning followed almost at once by a heavy thunderclap sent the stag crashing back into the thicket. Tamarisk too jumped in alarm. So enrapt had she been that she had failed to note the heavy dark thunderclouds rolling in and obscuring the top of the mountain in a thick, cold mist.

With a cry of dismay Tamarisk jumped to her feet and began to scramble back up the steep slope. Within minutes the very skies seemed to open and great sheets of icy rain came slashing down upon her uncovered head and thinly clad body. The mossy banks became so slippery she could not keep a secure foothold. Clinging to the stubby birch trees Tamarisk peered down in increasing fear as she saw that the cheerful cascade of water that had fed her sparkling pool was now become a raging torrent, churning up great masses of dirty yellow froth and white spray as it bounded over the rocks.

With foolish haste brought on by her alarm, she renewed her precarious scramble upward. But her handhold upon a none too securely rooted sapling was ill chosen, and as her foot slipped on the sodden moss beneath her, the little tree uprooted and Tamarisk had no remaining purchase. Desperately she tried to grab at the roots and lower branches of nearby trees as she felt herself slipping downward, slowly at first, and then with increasing speed. Terrified, she screamed aloud, but her voice was drowned by the violent deluge of the rain and even fiercer maelstrom of water below her. Her foot caught in a crevasse of rock and she somersaulted with sickening rapidity toward the river. Then her head struck a tree and she knew only a second of pain before blackness engulfed her.

When Tamarisk recovered consciousness she was lying half submerged by the water of the now relatively quiescent stream. She had no idea how long she had been lying there. There was no feeling in her frozen body but her head ached from the blow she had suffered. Bemused she noticed that the rain had stopped, the dark clouds had vanished, and the sky was once more a brilliant blue far, far above her head.

For a moment she wondered if she had had a nightmare but soon she realized that she had not imagined the storm and her frightening experience. The skirt of her cambric dress, made heavy by the water, streamed downward, its wet folds clinging about her waist like hands trying to drag her in the direction of the current.

She tried to move but her legs seemed numb. Weakly she began to call for help, but although her voice echoed around the high walls of the ravine, she knew there was little chance that anyone could hear her.

"Help me! Someone please help me!" she cried. Tears coursed down her cheeks and her hair hung in soaked ringlets about her wet face.

She did not want to die — to drown here all alone on a strange mountainside. Her folly in going abroad by herself now struck her as little short of madness. She thought of Perry with a vast intensity of longing. If only he would come striding down and gather her up in his strong arms and take her to warmth and safety! She would not care how angry he was with her or how many times he called her a stupid, thoughtless child! She wanted to live . . . *to live* . . . even if living meant trials and tribulations and sadness.

She called again, thinking she had heard the faint barking of a dog. She shouted louder. But her last call for help ended in a gasp as a sudden shaft of pain shot through her body. It was as if a knife had been turned inside her stomach. She held her breath; but within minutes yet another cruel twist of the knife brought her teeth together in a moan of agony. Her eyes closed and she slipped back into unconsciousness.

When next she became aware of her surroundings, Tamarisk found herself out of the water, her shivering body partly covered by a piece of rough sacking. A lad in homespun woollen breeches and smock was kneeling beside her, peering anxiously into her face. Beside him, a small dog was feverishly licking the water from her arm.

"So ye's awake, a'ar ye, por little lass!"

The young shepherd stared at Tamarisk's

173

white skin and gold hair, at the delicate blue-veined hands that were clearly unused to labor of any kind. His concern deepened. This was no farm girl but a young lady of quality, and by the look of her she was in a bad way. He had seen sheep with the selfsame expression, lying mute and helpless beyond ability to fend for themselves. There was blood seeping from a cut on the girl's white forehead and her dress too was stained bright red.

His natural reluctance to lay a hand upon a young lady of such obvious high standing caused him to hesitate a while longer. But when she suddenly doubled up in pain, he decided that immediate action was required of him, whatever convention forbade. Reared in the hills and well accustomed to lifting a full grown ewe and her lamb when necessary, he had no difficulty in hoisting Tamarisk onto his shoulders.

He began talking to her in the same low, crooning voice he would have used to a sick animal.

"Is'll have 'ee home safe an' säound, nay däoubt on't," he muttered as he struggled upward with his burden. "Me Mam'll tek care o'ee, nay däoubt on't. Poor lass, ye be didderin wi't cold! Soaked to't buff. Ye'll seun get dry aside our fyrer!"

Tamarisk closed her eyes and drifted in and out of pain. She heard vaguely the shepherd boy praising his dog for having heard her cry for help and leading him to her.

"Else none might of thowt ta search for 'ee down t'ravine," he said as he reached level ground and began to stride forward in the direction of the stone farmhouse, not a mile distant.

As they neared the farm gate the boy stopped to put the fingers of one hand to his mouth and blew an urgent, piercing whistle. At once the farmhouse door opened and a plump, rosy-cheeked woman, forearms bare, stood shading her eyes with her hand as she gazed in the direction of the path leading to the house. Sighting the boy and his unknown burden, she hurriedly put down the bucket she carried, and shooing two dusty-looking chickens away from her feet, gathered up her gray wool skirt and ran forward to meet her son.

"Eee!" she shrilled when she caught sight of Tamarisk's blood-soaked dress. "Eee, näow, John, bring t'por lass inside, quick näow, and lay'er on t'bed."

The farmhouse was clean enough, though lacking any kind of luxury. Tamarisk was laid on a big four-foot-wide bed with a hair mattress covered by a clean wool blanket. There was little else in the room but a scrubbed table in one corner and in the other an oak chest on which stood a pewter candlestick.

The shepherd's wife took one careful look at Tamarisk and shooed her son out of the room.

"There'll not be time for 'ee to go däown to t'valley for Doctor!" she said dryly. "T'por lass is birthing afore 'er time. Fetch me my clean Sunday petticoat and some clean water from t'beck. Quick näow, lad!"

Hurriedly the woman stripped off Tamarisk's wet clothes and stockings and began her ministrations with the quiet, calm efficiency of a countrywoman used to nature's emergencies. To her there was little difference between females — human or animal — and she coped now with Tamarisk's miscarriage as she would assist one of her husband's ewes. Had there been more time to sit and think, she might have been overawed by the likelihood that Tamarisk was high born — a fact the fine fabric of her clothes and the delicate whiteness of her skin made easily apparent.

An hour later Tamarisk lay propped up in the bed, drinking a bowl of warm goat's milk and surveying her accoucheuse with shy gratitude.

"You have been very kind to me," she said. "May I know your name?"

The shepherd's wife bobbed a curtsy.

"I be Mistress Tyeson. And 'twere my son John as found 'ee. T'lad is waiting näow to go däown to t'valley to tek word to your folk as seun as tha'llt tell us their names."

Tamarisk put down the bowl of milk and said thoughtfully:

"My parents are away visiting this day. Could I not stay here a while longer?"

Tears filled her eyes and trickled down her cheeks. She looked even younger than her fifteen years. The shepherd's wife had noticed the absence of a wedding ring on Tamarisk's finger. She now abandoned the restraint she had felt was required of her, due to their different stations, and spoke to Tamarisk as she would to one of her own.

"Ye 'as lost t'bairn," she said gently, "and a fair deal o'yourn strength. And albeit was nobbut a meager kittling as I däoubt would have come ta term, ye've suffered from t'loss. Ye'll be needin' yourn Mam."

Through the mists of pain she had endured, Tamarisk was aware dimly that she had miscarried the baby. Now that she fully realized the fact, she felt an overwhelming relief of her spirits which far outweighed the physical weakness of her bruised body. She thought of her mother and wondered if indeed she did desire either her company or her comforting as the kindly Mistress Tyeson suggested. Would Mama be angry, she pondered. Or merely concerned for her health? Doubtless Papa would fuss a great deal in his gentle, concerned way. And the Wordsworths — would they be disappointed that there was now no baby for them to adopt as their own?

Suddenly her lethargy became so intense that Tamarisk longed only for sleep. She did not have the strength to argue with Mistress Tyeson when she insisted Tamarisk tell her where her Mama and Papa were living. She murmured her reply, closed her eyes, and relaxed into unconsciousness.

10

August 1813

TAMARISK lay on the basketwork bedchair beneath the great willow tree in the garden. Rothay House basked in the shimmering heat of the August afternoon. Swallows and housemartins wheeled overhead searching for insects in the cooler shadows cast by the trees. The air of somnolence and peace was broken only by the screaming of the gulls on Rydal Water and the harsh carping of the 'hoody' crows, the evil scavengers of the hills.

She shivered despite the warmth.

Mavreen glanced at her daughter's pale countenance anxiously. Since her miscarriage Tamarisk had been apathetic and listless.

"In Keswick yesterday I engaged a governess companion for you, Tamarisk. Her name is Davinia Gurney and she is a distant relative of Mistress Fry. She is twenty-two years of age, unmarried, and a staunch Quaker. Mayhap you will find her a little quiet and dull, but I am sure you understand why I feel it necessary for you to have a reliable chaperone in the future. Miss Gurney will also, I hope, be a companion to you when we return to London next week."

Tamarisk remained silent. She was secretely delighted by the thought that at long last, whatever the cost, they were to return to

178

London. At the same time she realized that the presence of Miss Gurney would mean a serious curtailment of her former freedom. It could only lessen the possibility of seeing Perry.

Desperate for some hope to cling to, Tamarisk took her courage in both hands and asked hesitantly:

"Will I be permitted to see Perry when we return home?"

A faint color stained Mavreen's cheeks. She had not been prepared for such a question. His name had not been mentioned between them since Tamarisk had admitted to her seduction by him.

"I see no reason for wishing to reestablish any connection with such a despicable man," she rejoined sharply. "It was my hope and belief, Tamarisk, that you had put all thought of Sir Peregrine Waite out of your mind forever — as indeed have I!"

Tamarisk raised herself upon her elbow and regarded her mother speculatively.

"Doubtless you are still blaming him for . . . for my former condition, Mama," she said softly. "And for that I can only apologize and say that I am truly repentant. It . . . it was very wrong of me, I know, to impart such a wicked lie to you. I can offer no excuse other than that I did not wish to reveal the true name of . . . of the man responsible."

Where Mavreen's face had been flushed, now it paled as she listened to her daughter.

"Do you now speak the truth, Tamarisk?"

she asked. "Or is this another falsehood to mislead me?"

"I swear it upon my oath, Mama!" Tamarisk said urgently. "I *did* go to Perry's house as I told you, but he would not permit me to remain. He . . . he called me a troublesome child. I was so piqued I wanted to prove to him I was sufficiently grown up to have a lover if I so willed. On the following day, when you and Papa left to go to Sussex, I called upon Lord Byron and . . . and . . . it happened!"

There was no doubting the sincerity of Tamarisk's confession. Mavreen stared at her daughter aghast.

"Have you no sense of responsibility whatever?" she cried. "Do you have no idea how . . . how embarrassing a situation you have imposed upon me? I called upon Perry — accused him, vilified him, refused to listen to his denials. I believed you implicitly, Tamarisk!"

"I am sorry, Mama," Tamarisk said in a small voice, genuinely contrite. "It is not too late, is it, to make amends? I will go to him as soon as we reach London and beg him to forgive me. I will explain that it was all my fault and that you were quite blameless in your accusation."

"If I were he, I would refuse ever again to receive any member of our family," Mavreen said, as much to herself as to Tamarisk. Her anger had abated and now she felt only relief that Gideon had not after all seduced her child.

"I will consider the matter," she added. "When I have decided what is to be done, I

180

will inform you. Meanwhile, I want no more trouble from you, Tamarisk. You have been the cause of a very great deal of anxiety to your father and to me and I will tolerate no more of it."

"Have you . . . told Miss Gurney . . . about . . . ?" Tamarisk asked.

"I have told her nothing!" Mavreen broke in, suddenly feeling sorry for her daughter. "It is not my intention to humiliate you before strangers, Tamarisk. Let us hope you have now learned your lesson and will behave more circumspectly in future."

Her mind went to the recent ugly rumors she had heard of Lord Byron's incestuous love for his half-sister Augusta. Tamarisk must not be associated with such a man.

"I take it Lord Byron did not force his attentions upon you since you called upon him with intent to arouse his interest?" she said.

"I offered myself to him," Tamarisk replied with an honesty Mavreen could not question. "I alone am to blame for what ensued."

"You do not love him?"

Tamarisk turned her face away.

"I love no one but Perry," she said in a small flat voice. "As for Lord Byron, I care not if I never see him again."

"And he knows nothing of the child you miscarried?"

"Nothing," Tamarisk said. "Nor ever will."

Mavreen drew a sigh of relief.

"Then I would prefer you see him no more," she said. "Have I your word on this, Tamarisk?"

The girl nodded, so obviously disinterested that Mavreen had no further misgivings.

"And you understand, do you not, that in future you will not venture outside the house unless accompanied by Miss Gurney?"

Once again Tamarisk nodded, but Mavreen was far from certain that she could count on her daughter's compliance. It would be better, she reflected, to rely upon the governess to see that her orders were obeyed.

★ ★ ★

Miss Davinia Gurney appeared to justify Mavreen's confidence in her. Although when she arrived at Barre House she wore the stiff drab-colored camlet gown and close-fitting linen cap of the Quaker, she was quite prepared to adopt more fashionable gowns at Mavreen's request. She dispensed with the ugly black silk, shovel-shaped hood bonnet and adopted more becoming colors and designs.

The new clothes did much to flatter her rather pale angular face. She had large, soft hazel eyes and straight raven black hair which she parted in the center and combed simply behind her head. Her quaint reposeful charm could not compare with the more volatile, colorful beauty of Mavreen and her daughter but was noticeable by its very contrast.

Although Davinia Gurney altered her way of dressing, she clung rigidly to her Quaker speech and to the observance of strict Quaker Sundays, attending at least one Meeting during the day.

182

If Tamarisk did not find anything in common with her new governess companion, at least there was nothing abrasive in Miss Gurney's nature to provoke active dislike. She was quiet and unobtrusive.

Gerard, in particular, welcomed the new arrival. The girl seemed to have some magical healing quality in her hands. He had previously derived little benefit from the physician's remedy of a thirty-grain dose of bromide of potassium mixed with Indian hemp. Clarissa's recommended application of chloroform and mustard only lessened his discomfort. Yet by the simplest of soothing strokes upon his forehead, Miss Gurney was able to relieve the intense pain he suffered from time to time in his head.

"It is quite extraordinary," he told Mavreen when Miss Gurney had succeeded in the removal of his pain for the first time. "She believes the movements of her hands are dictated by her silent prayers for Divine guidance. I myself feel nothing extraordinary in the lightness of her touch, yet within minutes the pain is gone and I am able to open my eyes and face the daylight without discomfort."

"It matters not from whence her power comes," Mavreen said practically. "What is important is that you should feel relief. In the meanwhile, 'twould perhaps be best if we do not speak of this to Dr. Willis. He might not care to think an inexperienced girl in her twenties has a cure more efficacious than his medicaments."

It did not occur to Mavreen that the girl could

give her cause for jealousy. Davinia lacked all the ingredients that might set a man's pulses racing. Her essential femininity was as subdued in her manner of speech and deportment as in her dressing. Mavreen was convinced that the girl's shy manner of lowering her eyelids and blushing whenever she was spoken to was prim rather than seductive. When summoned by Gerard to soothe his pain, her desire to be gone as speedily as possible was so ill concealed that even Tamarisk remarked it, saying:

"I do believe poor little Miss Gurney is frightened of you, Papa!"

Yet as the weeks passed Mavreen discovered herself resenting Gerard's growing dependence upon the young governess. It was fast becoming a habit for him to send for her each evening to stroke his forehead before he changed for the evening meal.

"'Tis not as if you have an attack of the megrims!" Mavreen commented when Gerard complained of Davinia's absence one Sunday whilst she was at her religious devotions.

"But nevertheless, the power in Miss Gurney's hands is such that it can prevent the occurrence of a migraine," Gerard argued. He looked at Mavreen's flushed cheeks in surprise. "You do not object, my darling? I am not preventing her from carrying out her duties, for I understand these are few enough."

Mavreen bit back a caustic rejoinder that this was not the point of her objection. Yet, strangely, she did not wish to give voice to the true reason — that it curtailed the time of

184

day she enjoyed best. Before the advent of Miss Gurney, Gerard had loved to sit upon the edge of their bed and watch Dorcas dress her hair, fasten her clothing and jewelry, and to share in the choice of costume and adornment as if it were of the utmost importance to him.

He had once told her laughingly:

"I do not expect you, a woman, to understand how seductive I find this little exhibition. A glimpse here and there is all Dorcas will permit me. I do believe she is quite shocked by my observation."

"But not so shocked as when I dismiss her so that you can undress me!" Mavreen had laughed delightedly.

She might have voiced her regret for the loss of so precious a time had it not been that they were soon to go to Compiègne and Mavreen was quite determined that Davinia would not go with them.

Meanwhile, she was content to be back in London where she could renew her association with her friends.

To Mavreen's delight they received a visit from Mistress Fry. Although her visitor's purpose in the main was to show a kindly interest in her young relative, Davinia, she had come also to enlist Mavreen's support for her 'unfortunates'. In February, she told Mavreen and Gerard, she had been permitted by the Governor to enter Newgate Prison so that she could distribute clothing to the prisoners.

"I cannot describe to thee the fearful scene of

squalor, vice, and misery which met my eyes!" she related.

Mavreen looked at her friend with affection. Though tall and sedate in bearing, Elizabeth Fry had become matronly since the birth of eight children; but the face beneath the fine flaxen hair was still as unlined and youthful as Mavreen's.

A staunch Quaker, Mistress Fry, like Davinia, used their mode of speech.

"Oh, Mavreen," she continued. "All I can tell thee is but a faint picture of the reality. The filth, the closeness of the rooms, the ferocious manners and expressions of the women toward each other, and the abundant wickedness which everything bespoke are quite indescribable. We must help them if we can."

"I fear I now have only a very few close contacts in political circles," Mavreen said ruefully. "Perhaps I could arouse some concern amongst those at Court. But you yourself will carry more weight than I in such quarters. I need not tell you that you may count upon me for such financial assistance as you require."

Elizabeth regarded Mavreen with a grateful smile upon her gentle countenance.

"Thou art already more than generous to the poor, my dear," she said.

Her departure was followed closely by the arrival of another visitor — the effervescent Lisa von Eburhard.

The Baroness settled herself comfortably on the settee and proceeded to relate the newest London gossip, pausing only to sip occasionally at the cool lemonade Mavreen had ordered, the August afternoon being hot and airless.

"I was not, of course, present at the Argyle Rooms on the occasion of the Dandy Ball last month," the Baroness said. "But all London is agog with details of the quarrel that took place between Prinny and his erstwhile favorite Beau Brummel. It was their host, Lord Alvanley himself, who told me that the Prince cut Brummel dead, having taken exception to his recent witty if tactless remarks about him." She laughed delightedly at the memory of what had ensued.

"Beau Brummel," she went on, "then inquired of Lord Alvanley in a loud voice: 'Who's your fat friend?' As you can imagine, my dears, the Prince has not spoken to him since! Not that Beau Brummel seems very perturbed."

The Baroness lowered her voice as she added:

"I fear the Prince of Wales is well gifted in only three particulars: the running up of vast debts, the offending of the populace by his treatment of his miserable wife, and the losing of his friends. He will never attain the popularity enjoyed by his father or by his daughter."

She turned to Tamarisk.

"Doubtless you have not had time to see the Princess since your return home. Although she is once again permitted to visit her mother, the poor girl is otherwise at frequent loggerheads with her Papa. 'Tis rumored she was having a flirtation with the young Duke of Devonshire. As you know, the Duke has been head of that powerful Whig family since his father's death, and Prinny took exception to the association on the grounds that he did not wish his daughter to be involved in politics. Such nonsense! The unhappy girl was doing no more than amusing herself with a personable young man who found her attractive! She has been banished to Windsor where she will have naught to distract her but the dull company of her unhappy aunts and the Queen."

The Baroness patted Tamarisk's hand.

"You should count your blessings, child, that you were not born to Royalty!" she said. "And that reminds me, Tamarisk, I have news for you. My young nephew Charles has been wounded and is even now on his way home from America. He fears he might lose his leg. His wound is not healing as it should."

Remembering how her second husband, James Pettigrew, had had to have his leg amputated in Vienna, Mavreen shuddered.

"At least if he must lose his leg, medical science has greatly improved since poor James's wounding," she said to Gerard. "Baron Domenique Larrey, the French surgeon, has perfected the amputation of the leg at the hip joint, making far less butchery of the operation."

"Our Emperor thinks most highly of the Baron," agreed Gerard. "During the freezing weather of the Russian campaign, it was Larrey who realized that ice packed about the limbs of the wounded made painless the surgery performed upon them."

"I have heard mention of this man Larrey,"

said Lisa. "Was it not he who organized that the wounded should be collected in ambulances during the battle rather than await the stretcher-bearers when the fighting abated?"

"You are well informed, my dear Baroness," Gerard said, smiling. He for one had hitherto supposed that this eccentric old lady was interested only in the most superficial of life's events.

Lisa twinkled at him from merry blue eyes, still as bright as forget-me-nots.

"I have my ears and eyes open," she admitted. "Which brings me to the latest morsel of gossip, namely, that Sir Walter Scott has refused the offer of the Poet Laureateship. 'Tis thought Robert Southey might be pleased to accept the honor should it be offered to him, though some say Lord Byron is next upon the list to be asked."

She was unaware of the swift glances exchanged by Mavreen and her daughter at the mention of Lord Byron's name, and continued:

"I hear our handsome poet is positively determined upon another long journey abroad." She leaned toward Mavreen, lowering her voice so that Tamarisk could not hear her. "Many are saying quite unrepeatable things about him and his 'affection' for his half-sister Augusta Leigh. No one knows if there be truth in the rumors, but a scandal is brewing in my opinion."

When finally she left, Mavreen and Gerard retired to the seclusion of their bedchamber.

"One cannot help but be fond of Lisa,

whatever her foibles," Mavreen said, laughing. "I challenge you to name me a fault in her other than that she is given to tittle-tattle."

Gerard sighed.

"I have no wish to disillusion you," he said. "But when I accompanied Lisa to her carriage, I saw, as you did not, her new footman — a handsome devil in a resplendent livery. The look the Baroness lavished upon him, and the manner in which he assisted her into her carriage, left no doubt that their relationship is other than that of mistress and servant. If it be so, then 'tis a most improper situation for a lady of her rank and, more particularly, of her advanced years."

Mavreen drew back, her expression more amused than shocked as she stared up at her husband.

"But Gerard, provided Lisa is discreet, does it matter so much if she finds happiness in such a manner? Do you object on the grounds of her rank? Or do you believe it wrong for a woman still to desire a man's attentions even although she is no longer young? A man may pay for the attentions of a pretty mistress and no wrong is attributed to him. Why, therefore, should a woman not do likewise?"

Gerard looked disconcerted.

"You know very well 'tis wrong! I am surprised that you should think otherwise. No respectable lady of Lisa's advanced age should continue to have an interest in the opposite sex."

For a long moment Mavreen was silent. Then no longer smiling she said quietly:

"Would you wish, then, that I should have

no further interest in you when I am as old as Lisa?"

Gerard looked annoyed.

"I said no such thing, Mavreen! Of course it is my hope that we shall both feel as deeply loving toward one another in our later life as we do now. But we will not be giving physical expression to our love, will we?"

"Then we shall no longer kiss? No longer sleep in each other's arms? No longer hold hands?"

They were on the point of a serious quarrel for which Gerard had no liking.

He said placatingly:

"Let us not waste further time arguing about the future. Happily we are still young enough to express our affection for one another in whatever way we please!"

He put his arms around her in a significant embrace, and unaware of her feelings, drew her down upon the bed.

But the conflict raging in Mavreen's mind, brought on by their opposite opinions, would not permit her to accept this diversion. She offered no resistance but neither did she assist Gerard as he began eagerly to disrobe her.

Unmoved by any emotion, she surrendered to his passionate demands.

It seemed as if she had become two separate people: the wife who lay silently submitting to her husband's needs, and Mavreen, the woman, who disagreed absolutely with her lover about the very nature and meaning of love itself.

11

October 1813

TAMARISK was in the music room with Davinia Gurney and Mavreen's old pianoforte teacher Herr Mehler. Recently returned from a year's visit to Vienna, the white-haired old man had written to Mavreen asking if he might call upon her to tell of his meeting with Ludwig van Beethoven. The Great Master, he subsequently informed Mavreen, tragically was growing more deaf with every passing day and yet still strived against this most terrible of handicaps to continue creating his magnificent music.

Mavreen decided to employ her former tutor to give weekly pianoforte instruction to her daughter.

Tamarisk was so engaged when Sir John and Clarissa paid an unexpected call at Barre House. They had cut short their sojourn to the grouse moors in Scotland because the weather had become too inclement to be good for Sir John's rheumatism.

"And where, pray, is my granddaughter?" he inquired, looking eagerly about him as he and Clarissa joined Mavreen and Gerard in the library where they were enjoying a game of backgammon.

"You will see your much adored granddaughter

as soon as her music lesson is over," Mavreen replied, smiling at Sir John as she led him to a comfortable leather chair by the fireside.

Although still young at heart and physically quite vigorous for a man of seventy, Sir John suffered upon occasions from painful bouts of rheumatism. His physician prescribed venesection and calomel, but Sir John professed that the former merely weakened him and the latter was ineffectual. Today, however, he was happily free of the complaint and in great good spirits as he spoke of the successes of Sir Arthur Wellesley.

"Have you heard the latest intelligence?" he asked, knowing very well that Mavreen and Gerard could not yet have received the most recent reports on the progress of the war. Proudly he announced: "The Allied armies, under the command of our illustrious Field Marshal, have inflicted an overwhelming defeat upon Napoleon at Leipzig. 'Tis rumored some fifteen thousand Frenchies were taken prisoner and a horrifying seventy-three thousand killed. Mark my words, this will be the end of Bonaparte and a good riddance too, begging your pardon, Gerard!" he added with an embarrassed cough as he remembered his son-in-law was a Frenchman.

"You have no need to apologize, Sir," Gerard replied sincerely. "Anything that will bring peace to our two countries is welcome news."

"Then 'tis the end of the war?" Mavreen asked.

"Not quite," admitted Sir John. "Wellington with his troops in the south of France has yet to defeat Marshal Soult. Doubtless he'll not be long about it. He more than proved his superiority in the field throughout the battles that ensued when he chased the French out of Spain and over the Pyrenees. A fine man, Sir Arthur, and more than deserving of his Field Marshal's baton!"

"But even if peace comes to Europe, we are still at war with America," Mavreen commented.

Her father nodded.

"For the present, as far as I am aware, the situation is stalemate with both British and Americans desperately short of food and supplies of all kinds."

Tamarisk's appearance put an end to further discussion of war. Sir John, still happily in ignorance of his granddaughter's unfortunate experiences, greeted her with his usual warmth.

"I am more than happy to see you looking so well recovered," he said. "Come sit by me and tell me what you have been about. Have you not yet found yourself a husband?" he teased.

Tamarisk sighed. Despite her mother's attempts to involve her in various social events, Tamarisk had steadfastly refused to be drawn into the circle of young girls in Society for whom suitable husbands were being sought by their parents. She surmised that Mavreen wished her to be safely married and out of harm's way and was intelligent enough to appreciate that she had given her mother good cause to mistrust her. But she herself had not the slightest interest in the titled young men hopefully presented to her by Mavreen whenever an occasion arose to do so. Their conversation bored her, their sheeplike insistence upon the scrupulous copying of Beau Brummel in fashion and apparent inability to act or think independently of one another made them appear ridiculous and immature in her eyes.

"I fear the young men I meet do not take my fancy, Grandpapa," she replied. "I find them vain and silly. They do not even have the gumption of poor Charles who has at least gone to prove himself in battle!"

"So that's the problem," Sir John said, rising stiffly to his feet as he prepared to take his leave. "But no matter — you are far too pretty to be left on the shelf, my sweeting! I'll warrant we will all be celebrating your marriage ere long!"

But marriage, Tamarisk decided firmly, was out of the question if it could not be with Perry. Although she had been back in London for over a month, she had not set eyes upon Perry and was unaware even if her mother had made the apology she had suggested.

Life in London was exceedingly dull, she reflected. Princess Charlotte was at Windsor where she had been quite unwell during the summer. So Tamarisk could not even visit her confidante. Charlotte wrote that her mother had been evicted by the Prince Regent from her apartments in Kensington Palace and was now forced to live on the north side of Hyde Park at Connaught House. Charlotte was forbidden to see her.

If Charlotte had heard the rumor that the unhappy Princess of Wales was now making wax effigies of her husband and sticking pins

195

in them before hurling them into the fire, she made no mention of it.

Comparing Charlotte's life with her own, Tamarisk felt a little less deprived and unhappy. She spent most of her days in the seclusion of her rooms writing verses and letters to Perry. But they remained undelivered. Her pride would not allow her to make the first approach to a reconciliation with him; and she was still painfully uncertain if he would ever forgive her for her malicious defamation of him in her mother's eyes.

On many occasions she pondered upon her mother's reaction to her accusations against Perry. Tamarisk was now no longer in doubt that at one time her Mama and Perry had been lovers. She deeply resented the thought; and whilst acknowledging her mother's kindness to her during the brief months of her pregnancy, she still felt alienated from and resentful of her. She made mockery to the prim Davinia Gurney of the affectionate behavior of her parents, likening them to two lovesick parakeets, and laughing at the shocked reproofs of her governess.

Instinctively Tamarisk knew that Davinia would never repeat such indiscretions. The young woman seemed very much in awe of her employers, and Tamarisk supposed that her state of dependence kept her in constant fear of losing her position. The fact remained that Miss Gurney exerted little control over her charge whose strength of character far exceeded her own, despite her seven years' seniority.

Tamarisk was not without a certain sympathy for her companion — not only because her governess was poor and insignificant, but because she sensed the older girl's silent suffering. Davinia, she guessed correctly, was fast falling in love with her Papa.

At first Tamarisk had been inclined to tease her young governess for her involuntary blushes whenever the Vicomte's name was mentioned. But when she saw the trembling of Davinia's hands and the fluster attending his summoning of her presence, she realized that she had stumbled upon something far more serious than mere shyness or fear of inadequacy. She noted Davinia's growing unease as the evening hour approached when she must attend her employer to soothe his head; her reluctance to leave the quiet seclusion of the nursery sitting room she shared with Tamarisk.

Only once did Tamarisk broach the subject with a tentative remark that her Papa was an exceedingly handsome man and must cause many female hearts to flutter — Davinia's too, perhaps?

To her consternation Davinia had burst into tears, her quiet calm changed to irrational hysteria as she told Tamarisk how wicked she was even to hint that she would entertain such a thought — an evil, adulterous, shameful thought regarding herself.

"Your Papa is a married man — a happily married man," she had gasped as she struggled for control. "Even to talk of such things is sinful!"

Contrite and not a little shocked at the depths of feeling she had stumbled upon, Tamarisk tried to make light of the moment, pretending she had meant nothing serious. She avoided speaking of her father from then on but, watching her governess, knew that Davinia suffered the same pangs of hopeless love as did she herself for Perry.

Her mother, she noted, seemed quite ignorant of Davinia's private feelings — indeed had little cause to be jealous, for her husband's dependence upon the Quaker girl was clearly confined to the healing power of her hands.

Fortunately, thought Tamarisk, her parents seemed entirely satisfied that her governess was exerting a good influence upon their daughter; so much so that when Tamarisk pleaded that she did not yet feel strong enough to undertake the journey to France and would be more than content to remain quietly at Barre House, they agreed to leave her behind in London in the care of Miss Gurney. Tamarisk felt not a little guilty at the lie about her state of health, for she was now as strong and full of energy as ever. But her desire to remain in England, in *London*, where she might yet hope to encounter the man she loved, far outweighed her sense of shame at the deception of her parents.

"I think we can be certain that Tamarisk will come to no further harm," Gerard remarked to Mavreen when they were finally upon their way. They were crossing the English Channel from Plymouth in the safety of a British naval supply ship.

"We must trust Miss Gurney in every respect," Mavreen agreed reassuringly. For her part she was pleased to be quite alone with Gerard. It was eight years since she had last made this journey to Compiègne, and her thoughts were filled with sentimental memories. She could feel the excitement contained within Gerard and understood how much it must mean to him to be going home at long last. No matter how many years he had spent away from France, Compiègne was the scene of his birth and his childhood — the place where his roots were deeply implanted — just as she herself would always feel she belonged to the countryside of Sussex.

Her homes in London and Kingston, much as she loved both houses and gardens, could never give her the same heart's ease as did The Grange with its wisteria-clad walls, its fir trees, its soft red bricks and clouds of pale yellow primroses and great shadowy oak trees. Sussex sights and smells, Sussex dialects, the great open sweep of the South Downs and the Weald were all part of her very being. And for Gerard, the Forest of Compiègne and the great stone walls of the Château de Boulancourt must bring the same sense of belonging.

Their entourage was small. Only Dickon and Mavreen's maid Dorcas accompanied them. Gerard was convinced they would have no difficulty engaging more servants from the village. He anticipated, also, that there would be craftsmen aplenty to employ, for since Napoleon had had the Palace of Compiègne restored for

199

his young Empress, the town had thrived with the return of the aristocracy.

Gerard's greatest fear was that bands of poachers and brigands might have pillaged what remained of his family's possessions. The previous summer in France had been so disastrous that a serious famine followed and armies of beggars were reputed to have besieged the more affluent farmers in search of work or food. Such rumors were to prove true. Deserters from the army abounded and crimes of theft and arson were the norm rather than isolated incidents. A smallholder, forced off his farm by debts, frequently set fire to his barn or even to his cottage in order to prevent it passing to a rival. Thieves, in their attempts to discover the whereabouts of some hidden source of wealth, sometimes set fire to their victim's dwelling and had derived the name of *chauffeurs* by using these means of smoking out information.

Jules, the de Valles' most faithful servant, was long since dead. Gerard believed Jules's son might be acting as caretaker, but he could not be certain whether he too had perished or perhaps been compelled to undertake compulsory military service.

But the homecoming to which Gerard had so greatly looked forward far exceeded their worst fears of disaster. The vandals had destroyed what had remained inside the burnt Château. Anything of value had been stolen and doubtless sold for whatever meager number of louis it might fetch. But not even Gerard had anticipated the extent of the desecration they found outside.

Stone and wood carvings, ornamental moldings, were crumbling or had been torn down. The lavishly carved tympanum of one of the great oak doors had been badly cracked and chipped when some heavy instrument had been used to break in. The other door was gone, leaving a gaping hole in the archway. Masonry lay in moss-covered heaps on the great flagstones.

Inside, the priceless and irreplaceable frescoes painted by Louis Lageurre a century ago were unrecognizable, the paint peeling from the walls which were gray-green with damp and mold.

"Oh, Gerard!" Mavreen whispered aghast. "It is a total ruin! Let us return here tomorrow morning when we are less tired."

Darkness was already falling and in the half-light the devastation of Gerard's old home looked appallingly grim and forbidding. It was bitterly cold, and despite their warm cloaks both were shivering. But Gerard was reluctant to leave as yet.

Mavreen turned to Dickon:

"Take Dorcas back to Compiègne and find us all lodgings for the night," she said. "Then return for us within the hour."

Dickon made no demur, although it was clear from his expression he was loth to leave them. He could tell by the dark shadows beneath Mavreen's eyes how exhausted she was after the long weary hours in the carriage. But he knew her too well to suppose she would refuse the Vicomte any desire if it were in her power to please him. Dickon could not understand how his master could abide the sight of his crumbling

201

Château and especially in the gray, cold damp of the autumn evening.

As soon as Dickon and Dorcas were gone, Mavreen slipped her hand in Gerard's and attempted to bring a smile to his grim countenance.

"See what I have here in my reticule!" she said. "A candle to light our way. Was that not thoughtful of me, my love?"

Gerard looked down at his wife, his eyes momentarily softened.

"Miraculously so," he agreed as he pulled her cloak more closely around her and touched her cold lips in a brief kiss. "I thank the good Lord that you are here beside me, my darling, for without you I doubt I would have the courage to pursue my inspection."

Hand in hand, like two children seeking comfort, they made their way upstairs, hoping with no real conviction that perhaps Marianne de Valle's salon which had been so painstakingly restored for her during the Revolution might yet be intact.

But the salon, lit by the single candle Gerard held aloft, was no less desolate than the hall below. Carpet, drapes, the *prie Dieu* — all were gone! Cobwebs hung from the hook that had once held a crystal chandelier. The peeling wallpaper was green with mold. The glass in the tall windows overlooking the garden was cracked and broken and the wind screamed in through the gaping holes like a howling banshee.

"It is like a tomb," Gerard said in a voice filled with pain and bitterness.

"Your mother is long since safe and happy in God's hands," Mavreen said comfortingly. "Come, dearest, let us not linger here."

Gerard turned in sudden weakness and buried his face in her hair.

"This is my home," he murmured. "The place of my birth — the house of my ancestors!"

"I know! I know!" she whispered, her hand stroking his head. "We will bring it back to life again, Gerard, I promise. We will work together to restore it. If you wish, we will make it exactly as it used to be when you were a child."

"Ah! If I could see it so!" Gerard cried. But at least his courage had been restored and he linked his arm through hers and led her out of the room.

Together they walked the length of the long gallery, their footsteps echoing on the uncarpeted floorboards. High above them in the nursery wing a door creaked and banged on its hinges and a bat flew silently, ghostlike, toward the attics.

Mavreen shivered.

"Let us go down," she said. "There is nothing to see here."

His face grim in the flickering light of the tallow candle, Gerard nodded.

"Dickon will not be long returning," he said as they retraced their steps along the gallery and went down the great staircase into the hall. "Perhaps there is still time for me to make a brief inspection of the reception rooms and servants' quarters."

"Then I will accompany you," Mavreen said

203

firmly, "for I have no desire to remain here alone in the darkness."

It was perhaps fortunate that Gerard kept a pace ahead of Mavreen, for it was he who first glimpsed the grisly sight awaiting them in the banqueting hall.

Pinioned to the floor by a sword was a man's corpse. By the position of the gleaming white bones, there was little doubt that he had been pierced through the heart, the sword buried to the hilt and stuck fast in the great oak floorboard beneath him.

"*Mon Dieu!*" Gerard gasped, and tried to shield Mavreen from the sight. But the tone of horror expressed in those two words left her in no doubt that a shock awaited her, and she was not so totally unprepared as Gerard when she caught sight of the fearful spectacle.

"There is one murderer abroad who will never be brought to justice," Gerard muttered as he moved slowly forward to take a closer look at the victim.

The man was doubtless a soldier and an officer, for the metal spurs and buttons were tarnished but undamaged by time. Only rags remained of his uniform.

Gerard said quietly:

"I fear the poor devil has been eaten by vermin, but at least we may take comfort from the fact that he was not alive to be aware of it."

"How can you be so sure?" Mavreen inquired, shivering. She had seen many corpses far more horrifying in death during the Russian campaign, but somehow this lone skeleton was more frightening by its very isolation.

"Had the man lived, he would surely have attempted to withdraw the sword that pierced him," Gerard said. "But his arms lie as he must have fallen. I imagine his own sword was removed by the murderer to replace this one."

"What is to be done with the body?" Mavreen asked.

"Nothing this night," Gerard replied practically. "Tomorrow we will arrange for him to be removed and decently buried. Come, my love, let us leave him. One more night alone will not hurt him, for he must of a certainty have lain here many years."

He put his hand to his head and shut his eyes. Glancing at him anxiously, it became obvious to Mavreen that not only was Gerard deeply distressed by all they had seen, but that he was suffering now from one of his intense headaches. No doubt it was aggravated by the fatigue of their long journey.

"Come, my darling," she said. "Let us see if Dickon has returned. We may rely upon him to have found an auberge where we shall be given a good meal and a comfortable bed."

"Which has been done," said Dickon, grinning as he joined them in the hall. He rubbed his scalp through his thinning red hair and added, "I never did see such a sorry sight as this place in all my born days, and there ain't no call as I can see to bide here no longer."

Gerard's head pains grew steadily worse

205

throughout the evening. Mavreen, with Dickon's help, undressed him and put him into the comfortable featherbed provided by the innkeeper at the Coq d'Or in the town. She tried not to feel hurt when he failed to thank her for her ministrations but groaned repeatedly his regret that they had not brought Miss Gurney with them.

"I should have anticipated my need of her," he said.

"You will feel better in the morning, my love!" Mavreen tried to soothe him but his pain seemed only to increase. Warming pans were brought up by the serving girl and Mavreen went downstairs and rejoined Dickon by the inglenook fireplace. The landlord had provided his titled guests with a small back room where they could enjoy privacy.

"We must do our best to relieve the Vicomte of too much strain upon his energies," she said thoughtfully to Dickon. "Despite what the physicians say, I do not believe my husband is yet fully recovered from his ordeal in Russia last year. What think you, Dickon?"

"He has never been overly valiant," said Dickon, using the Sussex dialect to describe his opinion of Gerard's physique. "He be too much a gentleman, doubtless, if you take my meaning. Delicate he be!"

Despite her concern for Gerard, Mavreen smiled.

"He's a deal primer-looking than what some others be," she responded, using the same dialect she had learned in her childhood and which had become her way of letting Dickon know that she was talking to him now as friend rather than servant.

"'Twill take a deal of time setting that there Château to rights," Dickon remarked thoughtfully. "Mayhap the landlord can recommend workmen as are needing employment immediately. We'll be wanting masons, carpenters, a smithy — the lot; and laborers aplenty to start cleaning up. I never did see such a larmentable heap o'ruins!"

It was not in Mavreen's nature to waste time. No sooner had Dickon made the suggestion that the landlord could help them, than she called the man in to question him.

The aubergiste, a Monsieur Corot, spoke no English, but Mavreen had never forgotten the French she had learned in her childhood. Monsieur Corot had already gleaned from Dickon that this English Milady was of some consequence and surmised that she had money aplenty. Rumor had it that the Vicomte de Valle had inherited a fortune on the death of the mad foreign girl he had married. The landlord respected the de Valles who had once owned a huge estate around Compiègne and part of the town itself. Now that the *aristos* were returning to France, he thought, it would be wise to keep on good terms with the family. He could see that if he managed his affairs intelligently, he might end up being the rich man he had almost despaired of becoming, things being the way they were in France. The war was not going well and many believed the Emperor was about to topple from his pedestal. Monsieur Corot himself did not think so, but who was he to judge in matters of politics?

As *le bon Dieu* would have it, he told Mavreen, his cousin Joseph Corot was *un maçon* of great aptitude. He had worked on the Palace of Compiègne itself not four years ago. And Joseph's wife's brother was a carpenter and *his* brother a *menusier* who could restore antique furniture so well that he defied anyone to know repairs had been effected . . .

So the list continued, Monsieur Corot volunteering to send a lad at daybreak to summon all these craftsmen to the Château. Not least of all his helpful suggestions, was the possible engagement of a French architect by the name of Augustin Pugin. This renowned gentleman, Monsieur Corot related, had actually worked in London under the architect John Nash so favored by the English Prince of Wales, and was now enjoying a pleasant holiday in Compiègne. If the Vicomtesse was fortunate, perhaps Monsieur Pugin would offer his services.

Gerard was asleep when Mavreen finally retired for the night. She therefore waited until morning to tell him the good news. When he awoke his head pains had vanished. On hearing that they might that selfsame day begin the restoration of his home his spirits too revived. After partaking of a hearty breakfast brought up to the room by no lesser personage than the landlord himself, Gerard turned to Mavreen with a contented smile.

"How fortunate a man I am to have a wife

who can work such miracles whilst her husband sleeps!" he said, kissing her warmly. "With you beside me, I have no doubt that the Château de Boulancourt will rise again to all its former magnificence!"

It was as if ten years had fallen from him. He lifted Mavreen by the waist and swung her round so that her transparent lawn nightgown billowed around her long slender legs, revealing her thighs. She laughed delightedly, thankful to see him happy again.

With sudden urgency Gerard carried his wife back to the bed. A pale, watery sun filtered through the heavy cotton drapes, but instead of pulling them more tightly across the mullioned casement, he drew them back so that the bedchamber was filled with a delicate gold light.

"*Ma chérie! Mon amour! Mon petit écureuil!*" he whispered as he hastily removed her nightgown.

Mavreen's heart quickened.

He flung himself upon her with a boyish impatience that brought back memories of the past when their desires were heightened by their consciousness of the brief duration of their time together.

She held out her arms and received him with a cry of joy.

"*Je t'aime! Je t'aime!*" she said in his language. And then in her own, "I love you, my Gerard!"

Gerard found her mouth and kissed her, full and soft and long. Tenderly he smoothed the tangle of gold hair from around one small pink ear and kissed her taut white neck. He could feel the pulse throbbing in her throat. He placed his hand over her beating heart.

Mavreen returned his caresses, feeling the heat of his body pressing against her breasts, her thighs. She was experiencing once more the half-forgotten ecstasy she had long ago shared with Gerard but had not known since his return from Russia.

Although common sense told her that his long and near fatal illness had taken its toll upon his health and strength and that this accounted absolutely for his more passive behavior as a lover, nevertheless she had been unable to rid herself of secret doubts. Was it, she had asked herself, *she* and not Gerard who had changed? Had her intoxicating affair with Gideon Morris altered her emotional responses and caused her to confuse passion and love? Believing that she lacked the former, she had felt cheated of the latter. She had even felt bitter regret for those years with Gideon, the memory of which seemed always to be haunting her.

Now as she and Gerard rode triumphantly in unison to an ecstatic climax, she knew that love and passion were once more totally united. She could forget Gideon's very existence; disregard the strange hold he seemed to have had upon her. She could think of him without fear or uneasiness. She could deny his importance in her life and relegate him finally and conclusively to her past.

Quiet now, she lay drowned in the floodtide

liberation of her mind and body. She was at peace. Gerard's arms cradled her, his beloved face, smiling in deepest satisfaction, reposed on the pillow beside her.

"I have never felt happier," he whispered.

"Nor I," answered Mavreen, knowing it to be the truth.

Mavreen had no way of foreseeing that by the end of the week her happiness would be in serious jeopardy.

News of the arrival of the Vicomte de Valle with his beautiful English wife swept quickly through Compiègne and spread to the farms, once part of the estate, that surrounded the Château de Boulancourt.

Although it was now eight years since Marianne de Valle had died, there were still a few villagers who remembered the remarkable old lady — one of the few *aristos* who had remained throughout the Revolution despite the privations, poverty, and antagonism meted out to her kind. Stories were still told about her handsome young son who had fought for France under Napoleon and married a foreigner who ended up insane in the Convent of St. Germain. The poor girl's mother and father had come to Compiègne to take her back to her own country; and rumor had it that the tragic young woman and her parents had all perished at the hands of brigands in Sicily.

Now that the young Vicomte was back home, these half-forgotten stories were revived and embellished by reports from the Coq d'Or of the richness of the new Vicomtesse's clothes and jewels — equal, it was said, to the finery of the Empress Marie Louise herself.

The gossip was late in reaching one particular farmstead whose inmates had little contact with their neighbors. Blanche Merlin, one-time kitchenmaid to the impoverished Marianne de Valle, heard it when she took the goats' milk cheeses to the weekly market in Compiègne.

Now in her thirties, the farmer's daughter had lost the fresh comeliness of her youth. Her strong peasant buxomness had been worn away by the long hours of toil upon her father's farm. Now thin, angular, and weather-beaten, she looked an old woman in her voluminous, shabby black peasant's dress and clogs. Only her huge eyes betrayed her former prettiness, their blackness sparkling like ebony as she half ran, half stumbled through the forest toward her homestead.

Monsieur Merlin, bent almost double with rheumatism and the privations of too much heavy work and too little food, barely troubled to glance at his daughter as she burst into the room. His three sons had long since been called away to serve in the army. God alone knew where they were now or even if they lived! He had long ago despaired of their return. Without them he could not hope to run his farm profitably, and every year had seen more acres left uncultivated, more weeds encroaching, less corn harvested.

As for his only daughter, hardworking though she was, the old man heartily disliked her. Her two years in service at the Château had, in his

212

opinion, given her airs and graces she had no right to assume. She was forever ordering him around, scolding him, chivvying him because he had not the strength to do what he had been used to doing in his younger days. Blanche, with her strong will, had taken over the management of the little money they earned and denied him even his weekly ration of tobacco if she thought that skinny little *métis* of hers was in need. Although the boy was his grandson, he disliked his daughter's bastard even more than he disliked Blanche herself.

"Pay attention!" she shouted at him, shaking his shoulders in an exasperated attempt to bring him out of his reverie. "I swear you are becoming more senile every day! Can you not understand what I am telling you? Antoine's father is home . . . back at the Château! My son's future is no longer in doubt! The de Valles have returned!"

She was almost incoherent with excitement. Not even her father's snort of derision could deter her.

"See how right I was to insist that Antoine be raised as a gentleman? Now when the Vicomte sees him, he will not doubt that Antoine is his son."

"You think he'll care about one bastard more or less?" the old man interrupted her spitefully. "Why should he interest himself in the boy?"

The woman's pale face flushed a dark, angry red.

"My Antoine's a little Prince!" she cried. "Not even if he had been raised by the Vicomte himself could any boy of his age be better mannered or more finely dressed! He is a son to be proud of!"

The old farmer spat into the fire in disgust. Since the boy was born, his daughter had been obsessed with the crazy notion of bringing him up as if he were a damned aristocrat. She thought nothing of depriving herself and her father of the bare necessities of life so that the miserable boy could have delicacies to eat and fine clothes to put upon his back. And for what purpose? None that he could see! The lad was never made to do a hand's turn around the farm. At five years of age he could have fed the hens, collected the eggs, herded the goats, helped with the threshing. But no! His mother sat him on the only comfortable chair nearest the fireside with a quill and costly writing paper to practice his letters; and paid good money to buy him secondhand books in the market; and once a week she took him to the nuns in Compiègne so that he could be taught to read. Whoever heard of a farmer's son reading and writing! But there was no arguing with Blanche nor disciplining the boy to give the respect due to his grandfather.

Fair haired, fair skinned, looking more girl than boy, Antoine Merlin had grown up believing himself someone special. He despised his grandfather, openly deriding him for his coarse speech and manners, knowing that his mother would not let the old man lay a hand upon him for his impertinence.

"And how will you convince your rich Vicomte the brat is *his* son?" the old man muttered in his thick peasant's argot.

His daughter, who had been wondering exactly the same, hid her faint misgivings.

"There'll be no need for any convincing!" she said firmly. "My Antoine will stand before the Vicomte who has only to take one look at him to recognize him instantly. *You* never saw the Vicomte like I did so you cannot see the family resemblance the way I do. Besides . . . " she added, her face suddenly lighting up with pride, " . . . anyone has only to see my son to know he is an aristocrat. You have only to compare him with those three great ugly sons of yours you are always talking about. They had no refinement, those big *rustres* of yours!"

It mattered not one whit to Blanche Merlin that her spiteful reminder of her absent clodhopping brothers reduced her father to maudlin tears.

"Silly old fool!" she muttered as she went to her bedroom to select her son's finest attire. At any moment Antoine would return from his lessons at the convent, and tonight she would wash his fine gold hair and dress it in curls. Then first thing in the morning she would take him up to the Château de Boulancourt.

Bastard the boy might be, but she would take him to his father looking like a Royal Prince.

12

October 1813

IT was not Gerard, however, but Mavreen who received Blanche Merlin and her son when they called at the Château de Boulancourt.

Gerard was absent somewhere in the region of the east wing of the house, engaged with the architect, Monsieur Pugin. Mavreen was supervising the work of two young servant girls who were scrubbing and polishing in the *petit salon*. It had been Marianne de Valle's favorite room and was now, beneath Mavreen's determined efforts, beginning to regain some pretensions to being habitable. The glass in the tall windows opening onto the balcony had been replaced and a huge log fire burned in the charred remnants of the once beautiful fireplace. The blackened ceiling portraying rosy cherubs, flowers, and white clouds had been cleaned as had the walls. Already Mavreen had purchased a fine tapestry from the convent to cover one side of the room.

She deeply regretted the absence of the portrait of Gerard's father, Antoine de Valle, which had hung over the mantelshelf. It had been stolen many years previously as had the two small sacred paintings of the Madonna and Child. But Mavreen had acquired two charming portraits of

216

the young sons of the Comte d'Artoise to hang in their place.

Further to enhance the beautiful proportions of the room, Mavreen had bought a magnificent Savonnerie carpet. There was nothing that was needed for the restoration of the Château that was not readily available provided one's purse was full, Mavreen declared to Gerard, and he informed her that she might purchase whatever she felt was necessary or desirable. It was most fortunate that Napoleon, when he became Emperor, gave such encouragement to all forms of art. The restoration of the Court had provided a market for France's many luxury craftsmen.

Mavreen was fully engaged on a task she was greatly enjoying. She was perfectly and wonderfully content as she hummed an amusing little French song called 'Vert-Vert,' which she had learned from the serving wench at the auberge. It told the story of a parrot, kept by the nuns in a convent, whose repertoire of holy words so impressed the sisters of a visiting convent that they begged to be allowed to borrow the bird. Unfortunately, on his journey down the River Loire by boat, the parrot was in the company of soldiers whose talk was of rape, loot, and bloodshed, so that it arrived at the new convent swearing like a trooper and had to be returned forthwith!

The song was reputed to be a favorite of the former Empress Josephine.

So it was without a care in the world that Mavreen instructed Dickon, who was acting as groom, valet, butler, and footman, to show the mysterious visitor up to the salon. She supposed that the woman Dickon described had come to the Château in search of work. Since word had got about that restoration had begun, there was a daily flood of starving villagers from around Compiègne desperate to find employment.

Mavreen's first impression of the woman who followed Dickon into the salon was far from favorable. Her curtsy as she introduced herself seemed grudgingly made and there was a hard, calculating look in her gaunt face which, was much at variance with the hopeful, anxious looks Mavreen was accustomed to seeing. The woman's black cloak gave her a sinister, witchlike appearance.

"Mademoiselle Merlin," Mavreen said kindly enough. "Please state your business!"

The woman did not reply but went to the door and called to whoever was left outside. To Mavreen's astonishment a young boy of about five years of age came into the room. His pale gold curls shone like silk; the white frills of his hand-embroidered shirtfront and cuffs were exquisitely laundered. His velvet breeches and cutaway coat were very much out of date but unquestionably in the mode of the French Court. He bowed to her in the most elaborate manner.

"Your servant, Madame la Vicomtesse," he murmured. He raised his head and gave Mavreen the most angelic smile from eyes so black they reminded her of . . . of . . . why, of Gerard's, she thought, enchanted.

"Dickon, go find some sweetmeats for the

218

child," she said as she waved her hand to indicate to her visitors that they might seat themselves on the only piece of furniture in the room — a workman's wooden bench. She turned back to the woman, supposing now that she was this boy's nurserymaid or governess.

"You have something you wish to say to me?" she inquired.

Blanche Merlin hesitated. She had so long determined in her imagination that her longed-for confrontation with the de Valle family should be with the Vicomte himself, that she was *bouleversé* to find herself instead in the presence of his beautiful and very aristocratic wife.

Though lacking any education, Blanche Merlin was not without a shrewd intelligence. She quickly decided that this woman might be sympathetic to her child and his interests. Women, no matter what their class, were often compassionate toward another female's misfortune. It was therefore possible that Mavreen might plead Antoine's case with his father even more forcibly than she herself could do.

"I have come to ask your assistance, Madame la Vicomtesse," she said in a voice so soft and appealing that her son glanced at her in surprise. "I am here in the interests of my son Antoine. I want nothing for myself — only what is due to him."

With an effort Mavreen concealed her surprise at learning that the delicate and refined young boy was in any way related to this peasant with her coarse, weather-beaten skin and rough

219

work-hardened hands. Even her speech betrayed her humble origins, whereas the boy had spoken with little trace of argot. He was sitting on the old bench, his pose strangely elegant, his white, delicate hands clasped together as if in prayer, his expression composed and most unchildlike as he listened to his mother with respectful attention.

Although Mavreen spoke French and understood the language perfectly, she had difficulty in deciphering the facts now pouring from the woman's pale, twisted lips. Words pierced her mind, flowed together to form a picture, and streamed away as her consciousness rejected their meaning. Blanche Merlin, kitchenmaid . . . Gerard, officer on leave . . . lonely, bereaved, seeking consolation . . . *les droits de seigneur* . . . the boy . . . Gerard's natural son . . .

"No, no! I do not believe one word of your story!" Mavreen burst out. "If it is money you want to help you educate your son, then have the courage to say so. But do not pretend your child is . . . is . . . "

"*Antoine is the son of the Vicomte de Valle!*" the woman broke in slowly and fiercely, her eyes blazing. Proudly she declared, "Look at him, Madame. See for yourself! He is no farm lad, no *mestizo*. Antoine is *distingué*. He has all the manners of a gentleman. He is his father's son!"

Aghast, Mavreen stared back at her visitors. The boy, seeing her gaze upon him, gave her his ravishing heart-melting smile. The gesture seemed at such a moment almost indecent. Once again his likeness to Gerard impressed itself upon Mavreen's consciousness, only this time she felt repulsed by the resemblance. As his mother said, there was no denying that this was Gerard's son. With an effort of will she forced herself to appear calm, even indifferent.

"We shall have to refer this matter to the Vicomte," she said coolly. "Personally I doubt your imputations, Madame. I take it your purpose in coming here is that you are seeking to have the boy acknowledged?"

"*Certainement*, Madame!" said Blanche, sensing Mavreen's confusion and now anxious to consolidate her tenuous position. "What would *you* do, Madame la Vicomtesse, if you were me? You are a mother, are you not? You can understand that I love my son and must seek what is best for him. You would not have me rear the child of an aristocrat in the filth and poverty of the dung heap that is our farm?"

Indeed, Mavreen thought wryly, one could not imagine this little princeling setting foot near a farm, let alone dirtying his soft white hands employed thereon. Yet surely he had been raised by his mother at home?

She was not given time to ponder the conundrum, for at that moment Dickon appeared with the sweetmeats she had ordered — and Gerard preceded him into the room.

It was obvious to Mavreen, as she went forward to greet Gerard, that he had no prior recollection of the woman called Blanche Merlin. Nor did the name appear to revive any memories when Mavreen explained who her visitors were.

"Mademoiselle lives at Noyer Farm," she said, watching Gerard's face closely as she mentioned the name.

With his customary good manners Gerard bowed to the woman and glanced curiously at the boy sitting quietly beside her.

"You do not know me, Monsieur le Vicomte?" Blanche asked. "Is six years so long ago that you have quite forgot when last we met?"

Only then did the faintest of memories stir in Gerard's mind. But this sour-faced, gaunt, middle-aged woman could not be the apple-cheeked buxom young kitchenmaid with whom he had taken his pleasure one summer's afternoon in the hayloft, he told himself.

But even as the thought crossed his mind he knew that it was so.

His glance went to the boy and the color rushed to his cheeks. There was no longer any puzzlement as to the reason for these strangers' visit. The boy was his child. He even looked a de Valle, reminding Gerard poignantly of the portrait of his father that had once hung in this very room. The likeness was uncanny, permitting no room for doubt.

As if on cue, the boy stood up and gave Gerard the same courtly bow he had given Mavreen.

"My name is Antoine, Sir," he said in the quiet educated voice he had copied from the nuns. "It is my great pleasure to make your acquaintance."

"And mine to make yours," Gerard replied,

going forward on the impulse to shake the child's hand. His mind held only one overriding thought — this boy was his son, the son he had lost all hope of acquiring after the death of the infant born to his late wife Faustina.

So intense was his joy in this discovery that he gave no consideration to the consequences of his behaviour in accepting paternity of the boy. He needed no proof, for apart from recognizing the boy's family likeness, he was aware of an instant feeling of kinship. Nor did he consider what effect this extraordinary turn of events must be having upon Mavreen, his wife. His briefest of peccadillos with the kitchenmaid had meant nothing to him beyond the claiming of his *droits de seigneur*, and the girl had been willing enough. He was unmarried at the time and had believed Mavreen dead. The episode had had no import for him, and but for the presence of Blanche Merlin and her son this day he would never have given the woman another thought.

"Bring the boy here to me tomorrow," he said. "I would talk with him alone and there is no time now for I am waited upon by my architect." He put his hand in his pocket and drew out a gold louis which he handed to Antoine. "Here, take this," he said. "I would like you to buy yourself some little gift. I will see you tomorrow."

The boy's eyes narrowed as they fell upon the gold. He snatched the coin as eagerly as any street urchin. He was too young to hide his greed beneath a façade of indifference, even had he been aware that good manners required of a

223

gentleman that he should appear disinterested in money even were he starving.

The woman, however, concealed her reactions more successfully. With only the smallest smile of triumph twisting the corners of her mouth, she stood up and curtsied once more to Mavreen and then to Gerard.

Only her softly muttered words betrayed her sense of victory. Looking directly into Gerard's face she said:

"I will bring your son to you tomorrow at this hour, Monsieur le Vicomte."

When the visitors had departed, Gerard turned to Mavreen in the now empty room. His face revealed the intensity of his excitement.

"There is no doubting the boy is a de Valle!" he exclaimed. "And to think I have been father of a son these past five years and known nothing of it!"

Mavreen was trying desperately not to reveal to Gerard her innermost feelings of revulsion. It was not simply that she objected to the mere idea of Gerard having lain with such a woman as Blanche Merlin, although she would have expected him to have shown more fastidious taste in such matters. Examining her conscience, she was honest enough to accept that her resentment could stem from an acute jealousy of the woman's potency. She, Mavreen, was unable to give Gerard a son. The one child she had borne him was female, and even Tamarisk did not carry his name. This boy, judging by Gerard's immediate and unqualified acceptance of him, was clearly of the greatest import to him. Until now Mavreen had had no idea just how greatly he had desired a son.

Her failure to have foreseen this secret longing of Gerard's filled her with misgivings. She had overlooked the most salient of facts — that with Gerard's death the name of de Valle would vanish forever; and even were he to leave the Château de Boulancourt to his daughter, Tamarisk, she could not perpetuate his title.

And now a farmer's daughter had produced for him a son and heir.

They discussed the subject far into the night. So thrilled and excited was Gerard, Mavreen kept silent about her own secret misgivings. She agreed that the boy was beautiful; that he definitely bore a marked likeness to the de Valles; that he had extraordinary refinement of appearance, speech, manners.

"It would be a simple matter to absorb him into our family, would it not?" Gerard said, his eyes shining. "For I am in no doubt that this is what we must do! It would be unfair to the boy himself to leave him in such humble circumstance; and naturally I would like to rear him myself. You do understand, do you not, my love? You would not object to such an undertaking?"

Mavreen paused only fractionally before shaking her head. But deep down inside her, apprehension grew. She could not give it name or reason for it was no more than an instinct which demanded that she beg Gerard to leave the boy in France with his mother, to forget his existence. She could not justify her resentment by saying to Gerard: "His smile is too contrived! Too beautiful! His manner and appearance are too angelic! Do not trust him! He may be your son, but he is also a Merlin and you know nothing of his mother's character."

Gerard would be justified in imagining she was prejudiced against the boy. Even she could not be certain as to the real reason for her fears. So she kept her counsel.

During the week that followed, both Gerard and Mavreen became more and more reinforced in their divided attitudes. Antoine was a daily visitor at the Château and was his father's shadow. They walked together around the estate, Gerard almost childlike in his eagerness to recount the de Valles' past history and stories of his own childhood in Compiègne. His son was proving even more rewarding than Gerard had anticipated. Gerard's delight was touching to observe, and Mavreen, loving him so much, would have been happy for him but for her own instinctive mistrust of the boy. This had become as heavily strengthened as was Gerard's approbation. Yet still she remained silent.

Antoine's manner toward her was impeccably correct — too correct for a child of five years, she thought. He spoke no word, took no action on youthful impulse. His self-control was quite remarkable. The only time he showed any emotion was when some small circumstance arose when he found himself wanting in matters of etiquette. Such occasions were rare, but when they occurred his face turned an angry red and his sweet smile gave way to a sullen, angry scowl.

He had a very adult way of watching to see what his father or Mavreen would do and follow their example. He was quick to imitate; intelligent enough to be well aware of his shortcomings and sharp enough never to make the same mistake twice. Had Mavreen's instinct not been so strong she might well have succumbed, as did Gerard, to the pathos of the boy's desperate anxiety to please and to prove himself worthy of his father's affection and attention.

"Is it not laudable for a child of such tender years to show such concern for my approval?" Gerard said dotingly. "I believe Antoine has become genuinely attached to me. You would not object, would you, my dearest, if we took him back to England with us when we return? The boy seems to have little attachment to his mother and positively despises his grandfather! I would not want to leave him in such company."

At last Mavreen was stung to speak her mind.

"One might feel more liking for Antoine, Gerard, were he a little more loyal to the woman who has beggared herself to give him the few advantages she felt due to him because you were his father. I have been making inquiries about the Merlins through Dickon. It is everywhere said that the old man has always had to go without in order that the boy should live in comparative luxury. Do you not agree with me that it behoves Antoine to show them some affection when they have so sacrificed themselves?"

Gerard, hearing the sharpness of Mavreen's tone, looked at her anxiously.

"I did not know there was such a degree of poverty in the family," he admitted. "But if what you say is fact, then I will take it upon myself to instruct Antoine in his duty to his mother and his grandfather. I will, of course, see that they are reimbursed financially." He frowned thoughtfully. "Do not judge the boy too harshly, my love. He is but five years of age and far too young to consider the ethics of the matter. One cannot expect a child to have knowledge of that branch of philosophy which is concerned with human character."

"It is clear that he has been brought up to consider himself above his station," Mavreen argued, "and on that account may be partially excused his derisive opinions. Nevertheless, his heart should surely dictate a natural regard for his mother which needs no philosophizing."

"It is natural for a child of such tender years to be concerned with little but his enjoyment of life," Gerard insisted. "Did I tell you that I have decided to order a gun for him? A replica of the double-barreled flintlock sporting gun dear Maman gave me when I was a boy. When he is older I shall take Antoine out in the forest, as Jules once took me, and teach him the art of hunting. It will give me the greatest pleasure."

He was so fired with enthusiasm, Mavreen had no desire to pursue her criticism. Gerard's

228

happiness was, as always, her main concern, and she had not seen him so young in heart, so physically energetic, or so uplifted since their earliest sojourn together at The Grange fifteen years ago. His severe head pains seemed to have ceased altogether, despite the fact that he was actively engaged, as was she, most hours of every day.

At night, when they had supped and wined at the auberge and retired to bed, Gerard lay with his arms about Mavreen, planning with ever increasing enthusiasm the renovations to his home. It was now his hope that he could buy back those farmsteads which were once part of the estate surrounding the Château.

"'Tis my opinion the Emperor will topple from his throne ere long!" he surmised. "And if that should happen, there may well be a Royalist revival and the return to France of her lawful King. Do you understand, my love, what this would mean? Life in France will revert to all its former glory. The *aristos* will return and the de Valles will be respected and great once again."

Mavreen was becoming accustomed to the tempering of her real opinions. But since this matter did not concern Antoine she now voiced her disagreement with Gerard's desire to set the clock back twenty years. It was one thing for those like himself, born in a privileged class, to long for reinstatement. But those starving millions who had brought about the Revolution would not want to return to the inequalities of former days, she told him. She herself, close in heart and spirit to Farmer Sale and his

229

family, understood all too well the huge chasm between the rich and the poor, the educated and the uneducated. She strongly supported the reformers who were struggling to improve the lot of the working class in England. Gerard knew of the existence of such injustices but was never closely enough involved to be moved by sympathy for the poor. When he did come face to face with such matters, he was saddened but convinced that the chasm between classes neither could nor should be breached.

"It is breeding that produces intelligence, intellect, and refinement in men," he stated, and added, smiling, "Is it not one of your English proverbs that, 'You cannot make a silk purse from a sow's ear'?"

"Yet it was a Frenchman — your famous François Voltaire was it not — who said: '*Les mortels sont égaux; ce n'est point la naissance, c'est la seule vertu qui fait la difference*'?" Mavreen quoted aptly.

Amused but unmoved by her quick riposte Gerard smiled.

"One does not always agree with such maxims," he said. "If, as Voltaire suggests, it were truly virtue and not birth which distinguished one man from another, then one would have to accept that there was no difference between your Dickon — a man of great virtue by your own estimation — and me!"

Mavreen's eyes flashed.

"But don't you see, Gerard, your simile proves my point! Had Dickon been born into *your* world, given *your* education and *your*

230

upbringing, he would indeed have been as refined and venerable a man as yourself."

To her intense annoyance Gerard refused to be drawn into a serious discussion.

"You were ever prejudiced in Dickon's favor," he said indulgently. "And were I not fully aware of your wholehearted love for me, I might even be a little jealous of the great regard you have for him. As it is, I admire your loyalty to all the Sale family."

"I do not speak from loyalty . . . " Mavreen began, but broke off as she realized that Gerard was not really anxious to have his point of view disproved. Most men of gentle birth would, she knew, hold the same opinions. Had it not been for the broad, liberal education she herself had received at the hands of dear old Mr. Glover, and her first experiences of life in a household of extreme poverty, she too might have shared the more common view that God had modeled the working man in an inferior mold.

Gerard, unaware of any real point of controversy between them, took her hand and kissed it tenderly.

"I have been awaiting the opportunity of expressing my appreciation of your attitude toward Antoine," he said softly. "Many wives — and I would not blame you had you been likewise — would have refused most adamantly to have anything to do with their husband's *coup d'hasard* nor dreamed of permitting such a child to have access to their homes. I cannot imagine how unhappy I would have been had you refused either to accept my son or allowed me to mention his name in your presence. But as always, my own dear love, you have given me complete freedom to indulge my wishes, regardless of your own feelings. Your generosity of heart has not gone unnoticed nor unrewarded, Mavreen. If it is possible, I love you now even more than I did before I knew my son existed."

As was becoming habitual now, Mavreen held her tongue. She longed to ask Gerard if he would have loved her less had she raised her rightful objections to the inclusion of his bastard within their family. She longed also to know what would be the outcome were she to ask him to choose between her and the boy. She could see all too clearly how his son tugged at his heartstrings.

Sadly, Mavreen reflected, the past was not as dead and buried as she had supposed when she married Gerard. Then, whenever he had had to make a choice between her and his family, he had rejected her, not once but many times. It was not that she mistrusted his love then or now; there could be no denying its reality. But Gerard's sense of duty and purpose were always dominant in him, and this she could not forget even whilst she understood her secondary importance to him.

Happily there was no necessity for him to make a choice between her and the boy. It seemed Blanche Merlin was prepared for Gerard to take on full responsibility for Antoine. She was willing to renounce all claims to the child — and this before she knew of the financial settlement Gerard intended to make upon her and the grandfather.

Although Mavreen could never like Blanche Merlin, she respected her readiness to give up all right to her son if it were for his benefit. It proved the undemanding selflessness of her love.

Gerard and the boy were now inseparable. Antoine was naturally intelligent and learned quickly. Young as he was, he remembered everything Gerard taught him. He was quiet, well-behaved, and in Mavreen's presence made himself as unobtrusive as possible. Gerard was determined to take Antoine back to England with them, there to have him tutored until he was old enough to be sent to Eton, where Gerard himself had been educated.

"He can include in his studies the French language, literature, and history," Gerard said enthusiastically. "And when he has completed his education, he will be well fitted to return here to Compiègne and take over the running of Boulancourt. I myself will only be able to keep an occasional eye upon the estate, but Antoine, when he is a young man, can make this his home and give it all his attention!"

But Gerard could not rest happily even when Mavreen had given her consent to such plans. He could not bear the fact that his newfound son was not his lawful heir and did not carry his name.

Saying nothing to Mavreen, he rode into Compiègne and visited a Monsieur Mougin — a much-respected local avocat. His question

233

was simple enough in the asking. Could he give Antoine the name of de Valle and make him his heir?

Monsieur Mougin regarded his visitor with interest. The avocat had moved to Compiègne from Paris only five years previously and had, therefore, no prior knowledge of the de Valle family. He had heard, naturally enough, that the Vicomte had recently arrived from England with his beautiful English wife and was busily engaged upon the restoration of his ruined home. Beyond these simple facts he knew little about his new client and nothing whatever about the Merlin family.

Gerard's opening question was, therefore, something of a shock. What had begun as a dull routine morning now looked exceptionally interesting, he thought.

Whilst it was not in the least uncommon for a man of gentle birth to beget a child by a serving girl, it was unusual for the gentleman to desire publicly to acknowledge the child; and even more unusual for a wife to tolerate her husband's bastard — especially if it were intended to put him on an equal footing with her legitimate offspring.

Monsieur Mougin took a closer look at Gerard. He judged his client to be in his mid-thirties, a handsome, aristocratic-looking man dressed in what he assumed was the latest English mode — long gray trousers over soft leather boots, a short-waisted jacket with elaborate waistcoat and neckcloth relieving the severity of his over-garments. Gerard had removed his black gloves and placed them with his walking stick and three-cornered feathered hat upon the avocat's desk.

"Well, Sir?" Gerard prompted impatiently. "Will you reply to my question? Can I make the boy my legal heir?"

"I will need to know more about the background before I can give you your answer, Monsieur le Vicomte," the avocat replied. He took a sheet of paper from a drawer and began to write upon it with a quill pen. "The simple solution would be for you to marry the boy's mother, but I assume this is not possible?"

"No, for I married six months ago," Gerard replied. "The child in question was conceived six years ago."

"And his mother? Is she married?"

Gerard shook his head.

For a moment the older man was silent. Finally he said:

"Forgive me for asking, my dear Sir, but may I inquire why it is a matter of such importance to you to make this natural child your legal heir? Now that you are married — and still in your prime, if I may be permitted to say so — is it not likely that you will have one or more sons within the legality of your marriage?"

"It is most unlikely!" Gerard replied curtly. "So let us waste no more time on speculation of that nature. I wish Antoine Merlin to be made Antoine de Valle . . . and, when I die, to inherit my estates and my title."

"Yes, well . . . !" The avocat sighed. "Then we must see what can be done. Naturally I will need a little time to look into the matter, but speaking extemporarily, there appears to be no reason why you should not recognize the child as yours. I am assuming he is not adulterate?" Seeing the puzzled expression on Gerard's face, he added, "That neither you nor the boy's mother was married to another at the time the child was conceived?"

"That is so," Gerard affirmed. "As far as I am aware, Blanche Merlin never married. As for myself, my first wife died in 1806."

"Those facts would have to be verified, of course. A mere technicality," the avocat added quickly, seeing the haughty rise of the young Vicomte's head as he assumed his word was being questioned. "A matter of legal verification only. This being accomplished," he continued, "a document could be drawn up accordingly and the boy could then bear your name and inherit your estate — if that is your wish. He could not, however, inherit the title of nobility."

"But why not, pray?" Gerard asked, disappointment quickly replacing the satisfaction that followed the avocat's previous remark. "I have no other heir, no living male relation to whom the title could pass!"

"Nevertheless, it could not pass to the boy in these circumstances. The title would, I regret, die with you, Sir."

Gerard drew a deep breath.

"There must be some way around this absurdity," he said. "I do not care what it costs, *but it must be found!*"

Monsieur Mougin took off his spectacles and

carefully polished the lenses.

"I am afraid such matters are governed by the law and not by money," he said, his voice barely concealing his causticity. "It might have been a possibility if you had been free to marry the boy's mother. But I do not imagine you are prepared to contemplate divorce from your present wife merely in order to pass on your title to your natural son?"

"Divorce?" Gerard repeated scowling. "Of course such an idea is out of the question. I love my wife very dearly!"

"Of course! Of course!" said the avocat placatingly. He was a trifle embarrassed by the vehemence in Gerard's tone. For the most part he dealt in business and property legalities, and although passions sometimes ran high in disputes between injured parties, passions of the heart were not often heard in the confines of his dull and dusty chambers.

"In any event," Gerard said, as if to conclude his point, "even if I wished for a divorce, there are no grounds for one."

"You are perhaps unaware of the law introduced in 1804 — a part of the Code Napoléon. By this law, divorce is permissible, by mutual consent, after two years of marriage. Were your wife to agree to such a step, it would be possible and legally obtainable."

"I would not consider such a thing," Gerard said without hesitation. "So that is your final word on the matter?"

"As I said before, Monsieur le Vicomte, I require a little time to consider the problem. If you could return in, say, three days from now, I will have had the opportunity to look more deeply into it."

Gerard rose, and picking up his hat, gloves, and stick, bowed formally as he said:

"I would be grateful if you would make as detailed a research as possible. I will return on Wednesday, Monsieur Mougin. Let us hope by then you will have discovered some method by which I may fully legalize my son."

He rode home in a mood of elation. His disappointment at his apparent inability to pass on his title he quickly put out of his mind. The lawyer had given no final ruling and he could still hope a way would be found. In the meantime he could not wait to impart his good news to Mavreen.

He found her in his mother's salon, supervising the laying of the carpet. Without waiting to remove his outergarments he drew her over to the window, out of earshot of the carpet layers, and quickly related his afternoon's adventures.

"So you see, my love, nearly everything can be worked out as I desire. Antoine Merlin can be made Antoine de Valle and can inherit the de Valle estate. I am so happy, I cannot adequately describe my feelings."

Mavreen looked into his shining brown eyes and tried vainly to match his enthusiasm.

"I am most happy for you, my darling," she said, "but a little worried lest this Monsieur Mougin should prove unable to find a way by which the boy can inherit your title."

Gerard shrugged off such misgivings.

"I have little doubt that he will! There are loopholes to be found. Since it is possible for the title to be passed on were I to divorce you and marry Antoine's mother, then there must of a certainty be other loopholes too."

He spoke without considering the effect of his words upon Mavreen. Until this moment the word 'divorce' had been omitted from his account of his conversation with Monsieur Mougin. There had seemed little point in relating to her that part of the avocat's solution to the problem which he had rejected out of hand.

"*Divorce?*" Mavreen repeated in a small cold voice. "Did you then discuss such a possibility, Gerard?"

"Of course not, my love," Gerard said, trying to take Mavreen's hand in his. She pulled away from him. "That is to say, the subject of divorce was discussed, but naturally I told the avocat that it was quite out of the question." He attempted a more lighthearted tone as he added with a smile, "Indeed, I believe I quite shocked the old fellow when I stressed how dearly I loved you!"

Mavreen's eyes blazed.

"You may consider it amusing, Gerard, but I do not. I can see no reason why our relationship should be a matter for your discussion with the avocat when your purpose was to take legal advice about legitimizing your child."

Gerard stared at Mavreen in surprise. He could not understand why she should be so upset — nay, even angry.

239

"*I* did not raise the topic of divorce!" he said, his tone now as cold as hers. "Monsieur Mougin raised it. He wished only to point out to me, as was his duty in the circumstances, that we could, by invoking the Code Napoléon, divorce by mutual consent; and that were we to do so, and were I subsequently to marry Blanche Merlin, Antoine would become fully legitimate. As I have already informed you, I was not prepared to discuss the matter."

"Perhaps it would have been wise for you to do so," Mavreen said, her anger suddenly abating and a deep-felt uncertainty filling her with misgivings, "for it is becoming very obvious that your son's legitimacy is of prime importance to you!"

"Important, yes!" Gerard said. "But of prime importance, no. You cannot in all seriousness believe Antoine means more to me than you do. I love you! How can you doubt me, Mavreen?"

But Mavreen had every reason, she thought, to doubt the depths of Gerard's love. Memories rose painfully from the past. At the tender age of fifteen she had trusted Gerard completely when he had taken her in love and promised to marry her. But when he had been forced finally to choose between her and his family obligations, he had not hesitated to put the de Valle family's demands upon him before his love for her.

She had forgiven him but never forgotten her horror and humiliation when he had told her he must marry a girl of wealth and good title in order to fulfill his promise to his mother to restore the family fortunes.

The logical part of Mavreen's mind accepted that Gerard must keep that vow, but her heart had never accepted his broken promises to her. Now suddenly, like a ghost from the past, the de Valle dynasty had risen to form a new barrier between her and Gerard. His newly discovered son was fast becoming the most important factor in his life. Was it only a matter of time before Gerard accepted that divorce was desirable after all in order to legitimize the boy and pass on the title that he held in such proud esteem?

Unable to bear such considerations Mavreen ran into his arms and kissed him with a fierce possessiveness.

"I love you so much," she said. "*Too much!* Forgive me if I seem unreasonable, but the very mention of the word 'divorce' frightened me unbearably."

"As indeed it came as a shock to me," Gerard confessed, hugging her closely. "Calm yourself, *mon amour.* 'Twas but lawyers' phraseology!"

Gerard never again mentioned the subject except to inform Mavreen when the avocat confirmed his pronouncement that there was no other way to legitimize the boy. He attempted unsuccessfully to conceal his disappointment.

"It is of no great consequence," he told her. "Monsieur Mougin says that as soon as Antoine attains the age of twenty-one and I myself have reached fifty, I may legally adopt the boy. That must suffice."

But that could not happen for sixteen years and was at best small comfort, Mavreen thought.

Divorce remained the only method by which he could achieve his dearest wish.

The whole affair might have preyed more continuously upon her mind had Mavreen not received news from England which put all other considerations to one side. Tamarisk was once again in trouble. A letter from Clarissa left Mavreen in no doubt that she must return home at once.

'*We are powerless to confine Tamarisk within Barre House,*' Clarissa wrote, '*for she is under the auspices of the Princess of Wales. Tamarisk has informed me that it is the Princess's intention to make her a lady-in-waiting when she is old enough, although I myself doubt such an honor would be bestowed on her and that it is no more than idle talk. Miss Gurney is convinced that Tamarisk is in some way involved with that dreadful Sapio family and I fear this could be so, as rumors are rife concerning the Princess's involvement with them. But your daughter will hear no criticism of them or of the Princess herself.*

'*I would not suggest your return to England if I did not fear for the child — more especially because of her impressionable age but also because, as you know, she is become headstrong and willful these past months and will not listen to reason.*'

"Who is this family called Sapio that Clarissa is so concerned about?" Gerard questioned

242

irritably. "What have they to do with Tamarisk?"

Mavreen frowned.

"They are Gypsy musicians employed by Princess Caroline and in whom she is said to be taking a most improper interest. We cannot allow Tamarisk to be associated with them, however indirectly, and Aunt Clarrie is quite right to advise me of the danger."

"'Tis but the exaggerated fussing of a woman too old for rational judgment," Gerard remarked when Mavreen showed him Clarissa's outpourings. "Think no more of it, my love. 'Tis but a storm in a teacup, I dare swear."

Mavreen stared at him aghast.

"How can you, her father, be so indifferent to your daughter's reputation?" she cried. "Why, Gerard, Aunt Clarrie would never have written such a worrisome letter without good cause for her concern. As for your opinion that she is unfit to assess a situation rationally, I can only say that that makes you no judge of character. She is as sane as you or I."

Gerard looked anxiously at Mavreen's flushed cheeks and flashing eyes.

"'Twould be a most inappropriate moment for us to go back to England," he muttered. "We cannot leave all these workmen without proper supervision. And there is too the documentation regarding Antoine. The preparation of the papers is underway and will require my presence."

Unable to believe her ears, Mavreen stared at him in shocked disbelief. Then she said in a cold, hard voice:

"If that is how you see your duty, then stay

here and see to matters! I shall return to England forthwith."

"You would go without me?" Gerard asked.

"You would *let* me go without you?" Mavreen countered.

He looked away from her, his eyes uneasy.

"You are being most unreasonable, my love," he said after a moment's silence. "You must see why I cannot leave now . . . "

"I see very well why you cannot leave!" Mavreen interrupted. "Moreover, I am not asking you to go with me. But do not attempt to detain me, Gerard, for I believe my first duty in this instance is to our daughter."

So saying, she left Gerard in no doubt that she felt it to be his first duty too.

But all he said was:

"I am not convinced Tamarisk is in any real danger. You must do as you wish, Mavreen. But I shall remain here."

13

"**I** HAVE not come all the way from France, leaving your Papa alone, to have you disobey me, Tamarisk!"

Mavreen's voice was sharpened by her secret misgivings. During the journey back from Compiègne, she had more or less succeeded in convincing herself that Gerard was right — that she was wrong to mistrust Tamarisk. But now that she was home and her daughter refused outright to cease her visits to Montague House, all her earlier fears were renewed.

Davinia Gurney, whom she questioned closely, could give her but the barest facts.

"Not long after thy departure to France, Madame," the girl said uneasily in her quiet voice, "Tamarisk accompanied Princess Charlotte upon one of her rare visits to her mother. I did attempt to assert my opinion that thou would wish me to go with thy daughter, but Tamarisk assured me my presence was not required by her and had not been requested by the Princess Charlotte. I did not feel it behoved me to insist in the circumstances."

"Quite!" said Mavreen, curbing her impatience. "Pray continue."

The young governess looked pale and unhappy.

"As far as I could ascertain from Tamarisk

245

on her return, Her Royal Highness, the Princess Caroline, had taken a great fancy to her and had invited her to take luncheon at Montague House on the following day."

Davinia Gurney looked at Mavreen anxiously.

"Once again I expressed a wish to accompany Tamarisk," she continued, "but she informed me that the Princess was sending her own carriage to collect her and one of her ladies to escort her; and that therefore I would be very much *de trop*! I did not feel that it would be correct for me to insist."

"I see," commented Mavreen, who understood very well what had transpired. This girl, albeit Tamarisk's senior by six years, was no match for her daughter in the matter of willpower. Tamarisk had ingeniously rid herself of her chaperone.

"Since that first occasion Tamarisk has been invited to attend the Princess more and more frequently. 'Tis my opinion, Madame, that she is flattered by Her Royal Highness's attentions — more especially as the Princess has expressed most strongly her desire to travel abroad and has told Tamarisk that if she wishes, she may accompany her as one of her ladies!"

There was little else Davinia could tell her and Mavreen realized that Miss Gurney was clearly ignorant of the less innocent pursuits of the unhappy Princess of Wales. It was from Clarissa that Mavreen was able to divine that the poor woman's behavior was become ever more eccentric. The unsavory Sapio family was firmly installed in the house the Princess had provided for them in Bayswater, and from all accounts the Princess was now as scandalously involved with the younger Sapio as she had once been with his father.

Tamarisk, however, was tight-lipped about the subject. She would admit no more than that she found the Princess amusing — her unconventional behavior a deal less tedious than the boring life she, Tamarisk, led at Barre House with no better company than the prim Davinia and music lessons with poor old Herr Mehler for entertainment.

"The Princess is most kind and affectionate toward me," she told Mavreen defiantly. "I think she has been treated quite disgracefully by the Prince Regent and in no way deserves it. If my company gives her pleasure, and I enjoy the society she keeps, why should you seek to prevent my association with her?"

"Because I have expressed a wish that you cease these visits," Mavreen replied. She was at a loss to understand what possible attraction the coarse and vulgar woman could have for her daughter. She suspected that Tamarisk's interest lay not in the Royal household but centered around some man whom she was at pains not to mention. She hoped that it was not one of the Sapios, but her tentative questioning was met with a stony reticence.

Mavreen lost patience.

"Your wishes are immaterial to me, Tamarisk!" she said finally. "My mind is made up. We are leaving at once for Finchcocks and will spend Christmas there."

"And if I refuse to accompany you?"

Mavreen's eyes blazed as she met Tamarisk's defiant gaze.

"You are in no position to refuse," she said. "Barre House will be closed and I shall instruct Aunt Clarrie that she is not to invite you to stay with her."

"Perhaps Princess Caroline will invite me to Montague House!" Tamarisk muttered darkly.

It was a threat Mavreen felt she could not ignore. She pondered the possibility of appealing to the Prince Regent. But she was loth to resort to such extreme measures for what would indubitably seem to him problems of a minor domestic nature.

As she sat down that evening at her bureau with the intention of writing to Gerard, she noticed Gideon's wedding present to her — reposing in a box in her secret drawer. No sooner had Gideon entered her thoughts than she realized that he could well prove to be the one person capable of bringing Tamarisk to her senses.

The proposed letter to Gerard remained unwritten. Acting on impulse, she composed instead a note to Gideon. Of necessity, it began with the apology now long overdue to him.

'I trust you will find it in your heart to forgive me for so readily believing Tamarisk's falsehood,' she wrote.

'Since I was unaware of her association with another man, I had no reason to disbelieve her

248

at the time although, in retrospect, I should have had more faith in you . . . '

The words flowed more easily than she had thought possible, for she truly regretted her behaviour that night. She went on to explain what had subsequently transpired with Tamarisk's affairs and her own present predicament.

'I do not wish to act too autocratically toward her lest I project her into the arms of some undesirable character — a possibility I dare not exclude,'

she wrote, hoping that Gideon was in London and would be on hand to advise her. As she dispatched the letter to be delivered at once to Harley Street, it occurred to her that Gideon might have taken serious umbrage and would now refuse his friendship. Yet somehow, deep within her, she knew she could count on his forgiveness.

She was not mistaken. Gideon sent no written reply but within the hour called in person at Barre House.

As her butler showed him into the library, where she had adjourned when told of his arrival, Mavreen's pleasure in seeing Gideon so promptly was mixed with an unaccustomed embarrassment.

"It is good of you to come, Gideon," she said awkwardly as he made his formal bow and then kissed her hand.

The face he raised was instantly familiar in its

249

expression as a sardonic smile hovered about his mouth. He said:

"Come now, Mavreen, admit that you never doubted my prompt attendance! You took it quite for granted!"

Embarrassment forgotten, Mavreen withdrew her hand which he had retained in his and said indignantly:

"I did no such thing, Gideon Morris. I did not know even if you were in London, far less that you would be prepared to overlook my past vilification of your character."

"After such fulsome apology as you wrote to me, how could I refuse?" Gideon replied. "That would have been most churlish, would it not?"

With easy familiarity he seated himself on the leather chair favored by Sir John and stretched his long legs toward the warmth of the fire. He looked remarkably elegant in a corbeau-colored double-breasted coat. He was sporting ankle-length black pantaloons — a new fashion introduced by Beau Brummel.

"Still playing the dandy!" Mavreen remarked, the regret in her tone of voice ill disguised.

Gideon looked surprised.

"You know I have no alternative, m'dear," he said in his most foppish voice. Then added more seriously, "I must continue with my rôle whether I like it or not as long as I wish to remain in Society. You know very well, Mavreen, what would happen were anyone even to suspect I was not Sir Peregrine Waite. Gideon Morris, highwayman and thief, is a wanted man, and I cannot believe you would wish to see me hung!"

Mavreen sighed, knowing that Gideon was justified in taking every precaution lest he be apprehended.

"Nonetheless, the fashion suits you," she admitted, smiling as she appraised his attire.

Gideon, in turn, remarked Mavreen's appearance. She was looking in far better health than when he had last seen her. Her skin was tanned a delicate pale gold and she had regained the delightful curves she had lost during the rigors of her journeying in Russia.

She was dressed informally in a light-green muslin peignoir which enhanced the darker green of her eyes. They were now sparkling with pleasure in finding that their former easy relationship was so simply reestablished.

William had left ready for the visitor a tray with wine which Mavreen now poured for them into two crystal goblets. As soon as she was seated opposite Gideon on the far side of the fire, he broached the main topic of Mavreen's letter.

"Tamarisk is in trouble again?" he prompted.

As briefly as possible Mavreen related her account of the past four months and voiced her concern for Tamarisk's future.

"'Twould appear she is intent upon defying me," she said at last. "It is beyond my understanding for I do not think I have been lacking in maternal affection toward her, especially in view of her conduct."

Gideon laughed.

"You would have the girl docile and repentant," he said. "But that is not her nature anymore than it is yours, Mavreen."

Mavreen sighed.

"I know not what to think, being certain only that I seem unable to discipline my own child."

"She is nearer woman than child now," Gideon remarked thoughtfully. "Would you have me speak with her, Mavreen? I am most willing to reason with her although I cannot be sure that she does not harbor a resentment against me."

"I have told Tamarisk that it is my intention to repair to Finchcocks for Christmas . . . " She broke off as an idea suddenly occurred to her. "Why, that would be the solution, Gideon! Do you come also to Finchcocks. I will arrange some entertainments to celebrate the festive season and invite a number of guests to include yourself. I am convinced that Tamarisk will agree most willingly to remove to the country if she knows you will be there."

"Then count upon me to accept your invitation," Gideon replied at once. "To tell you the truth, Mavreen, I am most heartily sick of London and its frivolities. I would greatly enjoy some country air and the possibility of a few gallops on one of those magnificent horses you keep stabled in Kingston."

Mavreen smiled, well content as she rose to pour another glass of wine for Gideon.

"You are a good friend, my friend," she said, smiling as she handed it to him.

Gideon reached out and caught her arm, forcing her to face him as he asked:

"And are you good friends with your Gerard?"

Mavreen's pause was so fractional that none other than Gideon who knew her so intimately would have noticed it. Head high, she looked directly at him and lied.

"We are always in accord," she said gaily. "It is a most rare event for us to disagree in our opinions."

Gideon let go her arm, and as she turned quickly away from him, he said in his old mocking tone:

"How singularly dull you must find such domestic bliss! And how uninspiring for your husband not to see you in one of your towering rages, for it is then you are most desirable, my dear!"

As he had anticipated, she turned upon him, her color heightened, her expression thunderous.

"Kindly keep your opinions to yourself, Gideon Morris, for I most certainly did not request them. Besides which, you can know nothing of wedded bliss since you have no experience of it."

Gideon, not the least subdued, laughed unrestrainedly.

"I will hold my tongue if that is your wish," he said. "But I will also hold to my opinions even whilst I keep them to myself."

Despite her irritation with him Mavreen realized that she was as stimulated by their verbal sparring as she was annoyed by it. No one else in the world spoke his mind so honestly, with so little regard for his impertinence or for her feelings as did Gideon. She would not tolerate from another man such liberties of speech.

"Think what you wish," she said, relaxed once more. "It is of no consequence to me and would most certainly be of no import to Gerard. We are very happily wed."

"As Hamlet would have it: 'The lady doth protest too much, methinks'," quoted Gideon wickedly.

But Mavreen had her emotions under control and merely smiled.

"This lady is also becoming weary and would retire to her couch," she said.

Gideon stood up at once. He was smiling no longer but in earnest as he said:

"I am happy that you called upon me for assistance, Mavreen. I will do what I can with Tamarisk."

When Tamarisk heard that he was one of the guests her mother intended inviting to Finchcocks, her manner toward Mavreen was transformed. Gone were the sullen scowls, the narrowed eyes, and the sulky tone of voice. She chattered ceaselessly to Mavreen as if there had been no differences between them, making suggestions for the entertainments they might have at Finchcocks, demanding a new ball gown, radiant and so much her former happy self that Mavreen too was infected with enthusiasm.

Since it was now determined that they would spend Christmas at Finchcocks, she resolved to put all regrets from her mind that she would not be with Gerard. She wrote a long letter to him, begging him to attempt to arrange his affairs in Compiègne so that he could join her in England. But she doubted the few weeks that remained before the arrival of Christmas were time enough to allow for her letter to reach him and for him to make the journey home.

She tried not to think of Gerard alone at the Château with only Antoine for company, although in her heart she was aware that he would not be unhappy if his son was with him. This paternal side to his nature was still new and disturbing to her, for she had thought to know him so well. But equally she could lay her uneasiness at the feet of the boy Antoine. She had been irritated enough with Tamarisk in her darker moods, but even these seemed preferable to the boy's everlasting self-control and watchful desire to please. In a harsher frame of mind she could condemn him, young though he was, for being calculating. Yet to do so seemed uncharitable and unreasonable.

But once installed at Finchcocks, the thought of Compiègne dwindled into the background as the house became gay and alive with its many occupants. Not only had Gideon arrived as promised, but there too were Sir John and Clarissa, the Wordsworths with their three children, the Lade family, and the Baroness Eburhard — each with their retinues of nurses and servants.

To Mavreen's delight, Madame de Staël had also accepted her invitation and brought with her to Finchcocks her eldest son, her daughter, and her handsome young lover, Albert de Rocca. Her eldest son was now twenty-three and her

255

daughter sixteen, providing ideal companionship for Tamarisk.

Large though it was, Finchcocks was therefore stretched to capacity.

During the daytime various activities were arranged by way of entertainment. There were driven shoots for the gentlemen, Punch-and-Judy and Magic Lantern shows for the younger children. The older ones performed a Nativity play and in the evenings music, cards, back-gammon, and billiards assisted the passage of time most pleasantly.

Mavreen was particularly pleased to note how avidly Madame de Staël's son shadowed Tamarisk, his admiration undisguised. Tamarisk appeared to enjoy a flirtation with the young man and to give him every encouragement. Mavreen was not to know that this was but a ploy by her daughter to show her beloved Perry that others found her pretty, charming, and worthy of their attentions even if he did not. She did not dislike her young admirer but was in no way enamored of him. Comparing him with the man she loved as greatly as ever, the boy seemed a callow youth for all his easy manners and social graces.

But the great event was the fancy-dress ball to be held on the twenty-seventh of December in honor of Tamarisk's birthday and to which a hundred friends and neighbors were invited. To Tamarisk's great delight, Princess Charlotte had been permitted by her father to accept her invitation.

'It is not yet publicly known, but I am now engaged to marry the Prince of Orange!' Charlotte wrote to Tamarisk, *'and it is my father's wish that I forget frivolity and study the duties of a wife. He has, however, relented this once, being happily pleased with me now that I have agreed to marry as he wishes . . . '*

She went on to say that she believed her future husband *'to have a warmth and openness of heart'* and that their *'tempers and minds would perfectly suit.'*

Tamarisk envied her Royal friend this seemingly happy engagement. She saw no hope of a happy marriage for herself in the foreseeable future. Perry was proving kind, forgiving, understanding, sympathetic, friendly, affectionate — but never loving. He maintained an attitude that might best be described as paternal.

But whilst his manner left no room for romance to blossom, at least Tamarisk could once again enjoy his company and draw comfort from the fact that he appeared no more romantically inclined toward her mother than he was toward herself.

Tamarisk was happy to be at Finchcocks — not only because Perry was there, but because she was relieved to be away from Montague House. Wild horses would not have dragged from her a confession that she had permitted herself to become involved in an unsavory mess of pottage; but even before her mother returned from France for the very purpose of curtailing her visits to Princess Caroline, Tamarisk herself had become reluctant to continue them.

At first she had been greatly flattered that the Princess of Wales took such an instant and uncritical liking for her company. The Princess was lavish in her compliments, laughed at Tamarisk's sallies; she applauded her looks, grace, accomplishments, and fussed over her and spoiled her as if she and not Charlotte were her daughter.

It had seemed vastly amusing for a little while. But soon the Princess began including the Sapio family in their entertainments and her lack of observance of etiquette became embarrassing to Tamarisk, who was no longer in doubt as to why the Princess favored such low décolletages. The younger Sapio was constantly leaning over his Royal hostess' shoulder and even upon occasions shocking Tamarisk by laying his hand upon her. He would sit close beside her on the sofa, shamelessly pressing his knee against the Princess's ample thigh. He seemed in no way repulsed by the fact that she had removed her stays, so permitting her gown to bulge as unbecomingly as if she were heavy with child.

Perhaps even more disturbing was the manner in which the Gypsy let his eyes rest upon Tamarisk herself. She deeply resented the familarity of those glances. It was as if he were able by some Gypsy spell to see beneath her thin muslin dress to her naked body beneath.

Tamarisk would have been relieved if the Princess had lost interest in her company. But the invitations increased by number rather than lessened and she was not sure how she might extricate herself without giving offense. Mavreen's unexpected return to England indicated clearly enough to Tamarisk the extent of her mother's mistrust; and although she had done no wrong, she realized she had been foolish in permitting the Princess's flattery to blind her to the unsavory facts of her Royal patron's behaviour. But her pride forbade such admission to Mavreen and it came as a welcome solution on all to counts when Mavreen gave her no alternative but to go with her to Finchcocks; once Tamarisk knew Perry was going too, she gave way, outwardly meek but inwardly aglow with happiness.

Perry, adopting as usual the attitude and appearance of a dandy, flirted openly with all the ladies, none of whom took him in the least seriously. The men ignored him, with the exception of William Wilberforce. Tamarisk surprised them alone together one evening in the billiard room, discussing with great seriousness Mr. Wilberforce's lifelong efforts to have the trade in slaves abolished; and as always she was puzzled by this fresh evidence of Perry's personality. Amusing though he could be when he was aping the Court fops, it was the serious, intelligent, knowledgeable Perry she loved.

On the night of the Masquerade, Finchcocks blazed with the lights of hundreds of candles. Caught up in the spirit of festivity, Mavreen had provided costumes even for the footmen.

Tamarisk had selected for herself the long, loose stola of a Roman lady. The folds of silk draped her body and were fastened by brooches along her upper arms to form sleeves. A brilliant peacock blue, the dress was startling in its simplicity and she knew it became her well.

Both Mavreen and Gideon had refused to divulge the secret of their chosen attire. During the lavish meal provided in the great banqueting hall, Tamarisk was convinced that the tall masked figure of Henry VIII was Perry in disguise. She was by now quite certain that her mother was dressed as a Roman priestess, a diadem in her hair and twisted gold wire rings and bracelets covering her hands and arms — the effect a more sophisticated version of Tamarisk's outfit.

Princess Charlotte was most charmingly attired as a fifteenth-century Yorkist Lady, her beautiful damask gown, fur-trimmed at hem and neck, providing a Royal elegance. The butterfly headdress with a floating gauze veil raised high at the back of her head flattered her features. Her fair hair was enclosed in a gold net cap.

To add piquancy to the occasion Mavreen's invitations had demanded that no one should remove their masks before the hour of midnight; that in order to preserve anonymity, guests would not be announced upon their arrival but must introduce themselves to fellow guests by the name of the character they had chosen to represent.

Tamarisk therefore found herself dancing in turn with Henry VIII, Caesar Augustus, Lord Nelson, and the Emperor Hadrian. As the moment came when masks were finally removed, her eyes searched amongst the gaily clad assembly for Perry. There seemed no sign of him although she wandered eagerly from ballroom to banqueting room, through hall and gallery, library and billiard room in search of his familiar face.

"Have you no dancing partner, Tamarisk?" Mavreen inquired as her daughter passed by her unescorted.

"I had promised the next dance to Perry," Tamarisk replied, the lie falling glibly from her lips. "But there are so many people, I fear we have become separated. Have you seen him, by chance?"

"I cannot assist you," Mavreen said, shaking her head, "for I know not in what guise he dressed. Now that we are all unmasked, we shall come upon him shortly."

Mavreen was moderately certain that Gideon was disguised as the Protector Cromwell, doubtless finding it amusing to exchange his brilliant Beau Brummel finery for the harsh, drab, colorless doublet and cassocklike coat of the puritan. She had been invited several times to dance by Oliver Cromwell, and although he spoke little she was convinced that he was Gideon mocking her with his pretense.

There was no doubt that the party was proving a great success. Young and old all seemed to be enjoying themselves; and despite the lavish supply of wine, no man had yet disgraced himself by becoming drunk and upsetting the ladies. Conscious of her role of hostess, Mavreen decided to ascend the great curved staircase and view the assembly the better from the vantage point of the picture gallery.

There were fewer candelabra on the gallery walls, so the light was consequently dimmer than below. Someone must have opened one of the long casement windows, for the candles on one section of the east side were smoking as if recently extinguished. Mavreen looked about her for a footman to bring a fresh spill with which to relight them. A movement from behind the window curtain startled her. Then a gloved hand covered her mouth and a rough uncouth voice said:

"Doant 'ee move one muscle, Lady, else I'll strike 'ee deader'n any crow!"

Even more angry than frightened, Mavreen berated herself for her thoughtlessness in not placing guards outside the house. The masquerade was the talk of the tradesfolk for miles around, for there were few who had not been asked to provide some fare for the occasion. She should have considered the likely advent of pickpockets and thieves choosing just such an evening's jollification to line their purses. There were few women present who were not adorned with expensive jewelry, and Finchcocks itself was filled with art treasures of immense value.

Unable to call for help or move from within the imprisoning viselike grip of her assailant, Mavreen's eyes searched the gallery in the hope of seeing an approaching guest. But a group of Gypsies had begun their dancing in the hall below. The strange, wild Spanish-type flamenco had drawn the attention of the revelers who now clustered around the Gypsies eager to see the spectacle. The thief had well chosen his moment to attack her, she thought.

She realized suddenly that he was inordinately silent. Moreover, he had removed his hand from her mouth and was now standing behind her, still retaining his grip upon her arms.

"Will 'ee pay a ransom if'n ah let 'ee go?" the voice demanded, the roughness of his speech convincing her of his base origins.

"What ransom do you speak of?" Mavreen asked, too proud to display her fear. When he did not at once reply she repeated her question:

"If your demands be reasonable, I will pay your ransom. What be they, Sir?"

"They be no more nor less'n I deserve," he now replied. "They be a kiss, Lady — mebbe two!"

Only now did she recognize the voice.

"Gideon!" she cried furiously, twisting herself free so that she stood facing him. "May the devil take you!"

Her anger turned swiftly to laughter as she saw that he was costumed in his own highwayman's attire.

"Why, you are incorrigible!" she cried.

He too laughed, delighted with the success of his trickery.

"You accuse me because I dared come to your masquerade as *myself*! Would you have preferred me then, to come as Sir Peregrine Waite?" he asked.

Mavreen's mouth twitched.

"I did glimpse a highwayman dancing earlier this night," she admitted, "but never thought it might be you!"

"There will be easy enough pickings tonight for a gentleman of the road when the carriages roll down the drive!" he said, grinning. "However, I'll not rob your friends — or mine! That is, not if you pay the ransom, Mavreen."

"Which I refuse most adamantly to do!" Mavreen told him flatly. "You'll not blackmail me, Gideon Morris!"

"And you'll not deny me!" Gideon replied. With no further ado he put his arms around her and kissed her long and hard, most effectively silencing the protest she was about to make.

"Confound you, Gideon!" Mavreen gasped when at last he released her. "You had no right to do that!"

"'Tis true enough," Gideon replied unrepentantly. "But I have thought of little else since the moment I espied you descending the stairs this evening looking like a Greek goddess."

"A Roman Princess!" Mavreen corrected.

Gideon laughed delightedly.

"'Tis all the same to me. Whichever, you looked so very beautiful I knew I could not let the night pass without expressing my admiration."

Despite herself, Mavreen's mouth trembled once again as she tried to withhold a smile.

"Words would have been adequate compliment," she said. "There was no need for . . . for . . . "

"Assault? Rape?" Gideon broke in, mocking

her as he reminded her of the last time she had accused him of such behavior, although with far better reason. "Come now, Mavreen, admit that you did not really object to my kiss."

"Gideon, this is enough tomfoolery!" Mavreen said with an attempt at severity. "I am now a married woman and must forego such . . . such . . ." Once again words failed her and Gideon supplied them.

"Such delights?" he said softly. "Then I am content to leave it thus, for one kiss which pleases you is better far than two which you regret!"

Mavreen let go her breath, unaware until now that she had been holding it. Eyes closed, she leaned against him in sudden weakness.

"I do not know if I hate or love you," she said. "Or perhaps the two combine and make it impossible for me to feel indifferent toward you. I do not know. But I *am* certain that it is wrong for us to remain here alone lest solitude and memory weaken our better natures. I have no heart to betray Gerard, whom I love; nor do I think that you desire to cuckold him even were I so willing."

Gently Gideon put her away from him, his very action somehow bringing them closer in spirit than ever bodily contact had united them.

"We will rejoin the gathering," he said quietly.

They were too engrossed in the emotions of the moment to notice the young girl crouching on the opposite side of the gallery.

Too far distant to hear their words, Tamarisk saw only that long, passionate kiss.

14

December – February 1814

WHILST Tamarisk strongly suspected that the couple she had seen embracing and talking so earnestly together were her mother and Perry, she could not be certain. The candlelight was very dim and many of the ladies were wearing draped dresses similar to Mavreen's. As for the tall, dark, cloaked figure, he was too indistinct in the shadows for positive identification.

She emerged from her hiding place and descended the stairs, determined to search out Perry to discover his costume. She knew that she was torturing herself yet could not put her miserable suspicions out of her mind.

They were not, alas, to be assuaged. She thought she saw Perry, attired in a highwayman's cloak, waltzing with Mistress Dorothy Wordsworth, but there were several other becloaked figures on the dance floor — a Spanish grandee, Sir Walter Raleigh, a matador — all of whom could equally well be the phantom in the gallery. Moreover, she espied two other ladies wearing diadems not dissimilar to her mother's.

Although never at a loss for partners, the most persistent of whom was Madame de Staël's son, Tamarisk was quite unable to enjoy the lighthearted spirit of the ball. Her thoughts remained jealously centered upon Perry and she looked continuously for his familiar face amongst the dancers.

It was already nearing two of the clock when Perry finally sought her out to dance with him. He seemed indefatigable as he whirled her around the great ballroom to the haunting strains of a Viennese waltz. His brown eyes were as bright as if the evening had just commenced and his whole body seemed to Tamarisk to radiate happiness.

By no means unaware of his young partner's more somber mood, Gideon drew her to a quiet recess when the dance ended and seated himself beside her.

"May I fetch you some refreshment?" he asked. "You look tired, my little Princess. Have the night's festivities proved too much for you?"

Tears trembled on Tamarisk's lids. She longed to tell Perry that the only particle of the evening's entertainment she had enjoyed was dancing with him; that there was no happiness for her that was not dependent upon his presence! She longed to ask him if it were he whom she had seen kissing her mother in the gallery; and most of all she longed to hear him deny it. But Perry had left her in no doubt that he did not wish her to be involved in his affairs and she dared not express her feelings lest she antagonize him.

"I *am* a trifle tired," she said meekly. "But it is very restful sitting here talking to you."

"Then we will remain so," Gideon said kindly. He felt sorry for the child, sensing that she still retained romantic notions regarding him and understanding very well the pangs of unrequited love. Nevertheless, however hopeless his own future might be, he was strangely happy. Though Mavreen had allowed him but one kiss, it had been sufficient to reveal to him that she had neither forgotten their shared past nor become immune to him; and although he had long since abandoned all thought of ever making her his own, it was solace to his wounded pride to discover that she still cared for him.

He and Tamarisk were still sitting together quietly talking when the first exhausted guests began making their departures. Tamarisk's tongue was loosened sufficiently by then for her to confide in him her discomfiture in the presence of the Sapio family at Montague House and her mixed feelings toward the Princess of Wales. So engrossed were they both in their discussion that they were unaware of the slow exodus of the guests. They were astonished to find themselves quite alone in the anteroom when Mavreen's voice startled them back to an awareness of their surroundings.

"The ball is over," she said quietly. "Is it your intention to remain here until dawn?"

Mavreen thought her measured tone excluded the shaft of painful jealousy she felt at the unexpected sight of Gideon and Tamarisk, obviously so intent upon one another that they had been oblivious to the party's ending. Gideon was holding one of Tamarisk's small white hands between his own, as if imprisoning a bird within them. The expression on his face seemed to Mavreen to be one of purest tenderness. Tamarisk's expression, unguarded, was unmistakably that of a girl deeply enraptured by the proximity of the man she loved.

Mavreen knew she was being irrational. She had, after all, asked Gideon specifically to talk to Tamarisk and, if possible, gain her confidence. Nevertheless, their close intimacy in this moment seemed pointedly to exclude her. She was both hurt and angry.

Her impulse was to run forward and separate them; to sit herself in her daughter's place beside Gideon and force his attention to herself. But she kept her emotions in check, reminding herself coldly and logically that Gideon Morris had once been her lover but was no more; that she was married to Gerard whom she loved devotedly. If Gideon now preferred Tamarisk's company to her own, she had no right to raise any objection nor even to care if he was attracted by her daughter's youthfulness and beauty. And Tamarisk did look beautiful at this minute and strangely mature. The glance she gave Mavreen convinced her that Tamarisk sensed her jealous envy but was disregarding it, secure in the knowledge that she held all the advantages over an older, married woman.

What kind of mother am I? Mavreen thought, to be jealous of my own daughter!

Gideon rose to his feet, his eyes quizzical as he watched the changing expressions on Mavreen's face.

"'Tis long past midnight, Cinderella," he said, stooping to assist Tamarisk from her chair. "Time you were abed! It has been a wonderful party, Mavreen — a great tribute to you as hostess. I dare swear your masquerade will be the talking point of the Season."

But when Mavreen retired to her bedchamber and lay alone in the great canopied double bed, thoughts of the success of her party did little to lift the deep depression that seemed to have settled upon her spirits.

She tried to believe it sprang from fatigue, for she was indeed exhausted. She reminded herself that despite her marriage to Gerard, yet another Christmas season had passed without him beside her to share in the festivities, and that this thought alone should suffice to explain her strange unhappiness.

Yet it was Gideon Morris, not Gerard, who haunted her subsequent dreams. Dressed as a highwayman, he was galloping toward her across the mist-shrouded Sussex Downs astride his great black stallion. She was certain that he would stop and lift her up beside him, but as he swept past her, she saw there was a woman clinging to his waist. Her golden hair streamed backward from her masked face and Mavreen knew at once that it was Tamarisk who rode with Gideon. Neither turned their heads to look at her but rode relentlessly onward, disappearing into the mist, heedless of her frantic cries to them to halt. The tears were still wet upon her cheeks when she awoke, her feeling of desolation so great she knew it was the cause and not the result of her dream.

Although, as Gideon predicted, the newspapers

did give mention to the occasion of the masquerade at Finchcocks, it was the weather that occupied everyone's attention. A fog descended upon the country so dense that even the carriage horses had to be led and people scarce dared venture upon the streets. The *Times* commented that its density and duration had never been equalled. The cold intensified and the frost was so keen that by the thirty-first of January the River Thames was frozen solid between London Bridge and the new Blackfriars Bridge.

Although it had been Mavreen's intention to remain some weeks at Finchcocks, she made the decision to return immediately to Barre House. She was delighted to find on her arrival a letter awaiting her from Gerard. Penned the week before Christmas, it stated that he and Antoine would be commencing the journey to London on the first day of the New Year. He hoped therefore to be reunited with Mavreen very soon afterward. He loved her devotedly and missed her beyond bearing.

'*Not a day nor an hour passes that I do not think of you, chérie!*' he ended his letter. '*May the time fly swiftly until I can once again hold you in my arms. Je t'aime! Je t'aime — toujours.*'

Mavreen felt a great surge of happiness. She believed her decision to return to London was the result of some sixth sense advising her that Gerard could arrive home at any moment. Now she would have time to prepare for his return and enjoy the anticipation of his arrival.

Tamarisk, on the other hand, was far from happy when the sojourn at Finchcocks was cut short. It meant that Perry would no longer be under the same roof but would return to London to his own house. Not even the surprising news that her father was bringing back to England a five-year-old son could arouse more than a passing curiosity.

She assumed, as were all their London friends to do, that Antoine de Valle was the child of Gerard's first marriage. Mavreen did not disabuse her of this notion since it counteracted any future questioning as to Antoine's origins and at the same time gave the boy himself a fairer start than if he were known to be illegitimate.

Tamarisk's lowered spirits rose, however, when Perry called unexpectedly at Barre House and offered to take her and her mother sliding with skates upon the frozen lake in St. James's Park. To her secret pleasure Mavreen declined to accompany them and Tamarisk was permitted to go alone with him, unchaperoned by the dull Miss Gurney.

Perry was in great humor. He proved to be most proficient upon skates whilst pretending, as he nearly always did in public, to be as fashionably effeminate as the other dandies they espied, many of whom waved gaily to him in passing recognition.

One day, Tamarisk thought, she would discover why it pleasured him to play the fool.

The continuation of the extreme cold of the weather in no way inconvenienced Tamarisk as it did her elders. Mavreen professed herself made listless by it, despite the huge fires burning in every room of Barre House. Sir John and Clarissa failed to make their weekly visit, writing to tell Mavreen that they were both 'in a state of stupidity,' so cold were they in the big draughty rooms in Wyfold House. They were thinking of removing to the smaller Orchid House for better comfort, they said.

When Gerard and Antoine failed to arrive by the conclusion of the month of January, there seemed little doubt that the adverse weather had caused them to postpone their journey. Sir John braved the cold to take Tamarisk to see the phenomenon of the River Thames, so solidly frozen that the many people crossing from one side to the other named the route Freezeland Street.

Tamarisk surveyed the scene open-mouthed, as she gazed excitedly at the fantastic fair that had sprung up overnight on the ice.

"Just look, Grandpapa!" she cried. "Did you ever see such a spectacle?"

"'Twas much the same in '78 — or was it '79?" Sir John replied, smiling as Tamarisk's eyes widened in wonder. "Come along, then. 'Tis too cold to stand about. We will go and warm ourselves with a hot potation, shall we?"

For a magical hour the old man and the young girl made their way from bookstall to skittle alley, past the Punch-and-Judy show and gambling booths. They bought pieces from the piemen, a freshly baked loaf from the baker, and brandy balls for Tamarisk to suck. They declined to partake of the beer, gin, and ginger beer on sale but did stop to buy sixpenny cards, produced on a printing press set up on the ice, with their names upon them and stating the year and place of printing.

As always, time passed far too swiftly, seeing how well they were enjoying all the entertainments, and Sir John had to remind Tamarisk that the coachman would be freezing to death awaiting them at the end of the bridge to drive them home.

"We will come down to the river again," he promised, "and bring your mother and Miss Gurney and your Aunt Clarrie to see the sights!"

But this promise could not be kept. Five days later, on the fifth of February, the temperature rose, a sudden thaw occurred, and the ice began to break up. There now followed a tremendous snowfall lasting for six weeks.

By some miracle of timing, Gerard managed to reach England the very day the snow began to fall. He and Antoine arrived at Barre House late one night, their cloaks so covered by snowflakes, they looked like snowmen upon the doorstep. They and their coachmen were frozen to the marrow and shivering violently. Gerard was quite incapable of speech until he had partaken of a tankard of mulled ale, which he drank gratefully before the blazing fire in the salon. The boy stood silently beside him, his face blue with cold.

As Gerard urged his son closer to the heat of the burning logs, Tamarisk viewed her young half-brother with curiosity. She could not fail but admire his ashen gold curls and was at once captivated by the sweetness of his features and expression. An only child for so long, she had oft wondered what it must be like to have other children around her. She decided that she would show affection and kindness to this shivering little French boy. As the pinched blueness of the cold gave way to a warmer rosy hue on his cheeks, she stepped forward to introduce herself.

Antoine de Valle, né Merlin, did not return Tamarisk's smile nor reply to her words of welcome. For the past four months he had been the sole recipient of his father's love and attention. Within a week of his first meeting with Gerard, he had known he must share his father's affection with the Vicomtesse, but although he was aware they had a daughter in England, Tamarisk was but a name to him. He had not anticipated the deeply affectionate welcome his father would give her upon their arrival, holding the girl in his arms, kissing her upon both cheeks, calling her '*chérie*' and 'my little sweetheart' and leaving not the slightest doubt as to his devotion to her.

Tamarisk had addressed Antoine in English, a language he could not speak. His face flushed.

"*Je ne parle que français,*" he said in his own language.

Gerard, now seated upon the sofa beside Mavreen and holding tightly to her hands,

275

smiled fondly at his two children.

"Antoine will soon learn English," he said. "He is most intelligent and I am certain will be quick to pick up the language."

He was immensely happy to be reunited with Mavreen and to see his small family gathered around him. At long last he could feel totally satisfied. He had for his wife the dearest woman in the world — as well as the most beautiful — the most charming of daughters; and now his son Antoine completed the circle.

"As soon as Antoine has recovered from the rigors of the journey, I wish him to commence his education," he said to Mavreen. "Miss Gurney can teach him until I can find a tutor for him. Then, when the weather improves, Miss Gurney will prove most useful conducting Antoine around London so that he comes to know the city in which he will be living for the next few years. You approve of my plans, my dearest?"

"Of course, if these are your wishes," Mavreen replied, caring for naught else but that Gerard was home once more, well and happy and behaving as if there had been no rift or misunderstanding between them. For his sake, she was pleased he had been successful in having the boy officially recognized as his and that he had encountered no obstacles to bringing Antoine to England with him.

"I have prepared the nursery wing for Antoine's use," she told a delighted Gerard. "And lest he should feel lonely on the third floor, I instructed Davinia to move up there as soon as you both arrived home. There are still quite a number of Tamarisk's books and toys in the schoolroom which might amuse him. I hope he will not consider himself too old for the rocking horse!"

"*Un cheval à bascule*," Gerard translated for Antoine, and laughed to see the scowl that creased his young son's face at the prospect of being given a toy horse to ride when but a few weeks since he had demanded a live pony of his own.

Mavreen too laughed and reassured Antoine that he would find other amusements better befitting his age — tin soldiers, an iron hoop, a set of puppets with a miniature stage upon which to display them, and boards for the playing of backgammon, draughts, and chess.

"Antoine is unused to playing with toys," Gerard remarked in English to Tamarisk. "The Merlins, who took care of him until recently, had little money to spare for such things. But Antoine will soon learn to enjoy childish pastimes. He has already mastered the rudiments of chess."

He looked proudly at the boy who rose at once and came to lean against Gerard's knees. Gerard released his hold upon Mavreen's hands and put his arms about the child.

"You will be happy here in England," he promised, as if the boy's face betrayed doubts about it. "You shall lack for nothing you desire."

Tamarisk, who understood enough French to comprehend her father's remark, said thoughtfully:

"Would that not be spoiling him, Papa?"

Gerard shook his head.

"Perhaps! But there are nearly five years of deprivation for which I must make amends," he said. "I do not know if your mother has already told you, but unhappily I was unaware of Antoine's existence until I arrived in Compiègne last autumn. I was at war, a long way from home when he was born, and no one sent me information about him."

By now a hot meal had been prepared for Gerard and Antoine. Both ate ravenously, but the child was almost asleep before the meal was over. Mavreen sent for Davinia to take Antoine up to bed. A fire burned cheerily in his room and warming pans had been put between the sheets. The atmosphere was homely and welcoming.

Surveying his new quarters, Antoine was not too tired to realize that life at Barre House was an improvement upon the discomforts of the semi-restored Château. He was as impressed by the obvious wealth as by the retinue of servants attending him. There was even a nurserymaid assigned to his exclusive service. And late though the hour was, the girl came hurrying up the three long flights of stairs with jugs of hot water for his washing. At the Château there were as yet no such refinements as personal servants — other than his father's valet.

"Work at the Château is progressing most satisfactorily," Gerard told Mavreen later as they too prepared for the night. "I have left a most excellent fellow in charge of building and know that I can trust him."

"Then you are in no hurry to return to Compiègne?" Mavreen asked. She was attired in her nightrobe and sat at her dressing table brushing her hair — a task Dorcas normally performed for her. Tonight Dorcas and Gerard's valet had been dismissed so that she and Gerard could enjoy their privacy.

"There is no need for me to go back before the summer," Gerard replied to Mavreen's satisfaction as he climbed between the sheets.

He lay back upon the pillows, his arms behind his head, and observed his wife's movements. The raising of her arm uplifted her firm full breasts. At once he felt the familiar stirrings of desire for her deep in his loins.

"How beautiful you are!" he exclaimed, the fatigue of his journey forgotten as his eyes lingered upon her. "You are more beautiful every time I see you."

Turning, Mavreen smiled.

"Methinks your vision is colored by your affection for me, dearest Gerard."

"'Tis far more than affection I feel for you," he replied huskily. "'Tis love, my darling. I have never loved you more deeply."

Mavreen put down her mother-of-pearl hairbrush and went to him without coquetry. As she leaned over him, her hair fell about his face. His mouth found her lips. As he kissed her, his hands reached for the ribbons of her nightgown. He felt her trembling as he freed her breasts from their confinement. Her flesh was cool in the night air, soft and delightful to his touch.

279

"Come into bed," he whispered, his need for her now fierce and urgent as he drew her in between the sheets. "Ah, my love, *mon amour*, how I have missed you!"

"And I you!" Mavreen whispered back, although there was none to hear them. Her hands sought Gerard's face and she drew his mouth downward. Hungrily, like a child, his lips closed about her breast whilst his hands traced the curve of her waist and downward toward her thighs.

Mavreen, who had thought Gerard might be too exhausted by the long days traveling to have the heart for lovemaking, was excited by the unexpected force of his passion. But he was intent upon pleasing her and withheld the consummation of his desire whilst he took his pleasure slowly and sensually, kissing each part of her body until she believed herself one conflagration of loving.

"*Je t'aime, je t'aime, je t'aime!*" he said. "You are mine, all mine! No other man shall ever take you, touch you, kiss you. You belong to me alone!"

For the fraction of a second Mavreen's thoughts went to Gideon — the highwayman who had claimed his ransom at the masquerade. She remembered his kiss — one kiss only, but enough to arouse in her desires so similar to those she now felt for Gerard that the memory itself seemed like a betrayal.

But then Gerard finally took possession of her, and as they rode united to the great peaks of completion, coherent thought disintegrated and only awareness of sensation remained. When thought returned, she opened her eyes and looked deeply at the face of the man she had married — the man she loved with all her heart.

"You were away too long!" she murmured drowsily. "Never leave me again, Gerard . . . not for one night . . . not for one day! Promise me we shall not be parted again!"

But he made no answer, gave no promise, for his eyes had closed in sleep even as she spoke.

15

February 1814

THE weather being far too inclement for the enjoyment of outdoor activities, Mavreen and Gerard decided to keep Antoine and Tamarisk gainfully employed by sitting for their portraits. They engaged for the purpose a painter by the name of John Constable. Mavreen had noticed his picture, 'Boys Fishing', hanging in the Royal Academy the previous year. She had been so impressed by it, she was convinced that the artist would one day make a great name for himself. He was more than happy to accept a fee of twelve guineas for each portrait, it being his intention, he told Mavreen, to marry his childhood sweetheart as soon as he had sufficient means to do so.

Mr. Constable was not the only man to be harboring romantic thoughts. Young Charles Eburhard paid a call upon *his* childhood sweetheart despite the terrible difficulties of travel. The streets were piled high with snow and the great white flakes fell as if the sky would never empty itself.

Tamarisk received her visitor in the morning room, her boredom so acute that even this dull, unromantic suitor was welcome.

"I am pleased to see you did not perish in America after all," she said kindly as she seated herself opposite him by the fire.

His round, boyish face reddened with pleasure as he smiled shyly back at her.

"Indeed, not, Lady Tamarisk!" he said, "although the surgeon did once despair of my life. But I was determined to come back to England." His shyness was obviously getting the better of him, but Tamarisk was feeling well disposed toward him, the more so because he had addressed her formally, thereby acknowledging that she was no longer a child.

"I am very pleased to see you — and looking so well despite your wounding," Tamarisk said. He did indeed look far more handsome than the spotty youth she recalled from memory. He had filled out a little and although by no means stalwart was more manly and quite impressive in his uniform. His blue, long-tailed coat was double-breasted, the waisted front and cuffs sporting rows of gold buttons. The turned-back cuffs and lapels were likewise gold as was the braid on his dark-blue cocked hat. His blue pantaloons fitted very tightly his long, well-shaped legs. Not least did Tamarisk admire the impressive sword he wore, with which she surmised he must already have killed many men in defense of his life. The blue of his uniform enhanced the color of his eyes, which were now gazing into hers with open adoration.

The wound to his thigh had healed and mercifully amputation had not after all been necessary, but he had been left with a slight limp which reminded Tamarisk uncomfortably of her one and only lover, Lord Byron. To her consternation she felt her cheeks burning at the sudden, unexpected memory of the poet naked as he limped away from her after her seduction. Shame engulfed her, firing her cheeks an even deeper red, and swifly she turned her head aside so that Charles might not see her blushes.

"You may call me Tamarisk, Charles," she said gently. "'Tis more friendly, do you not agree?"

Thus encouraged, the young man at once became more voluble. He had been some weeks in England on sick leave, he told Tamarisk. He was now fully recovered and had a further week's convalescence before he joined the frigate *Undaunted*. Proudly he announced that he had been promoted to sub-lieutenant.

Tamarisk offered her congratulations and wished him a safe passage to wherever he might be going.

With some difficulty and a great deal of hesitation, Charles finally managed to give expression to the real reason for his visit. It might be some time before he returned to England, he said. In the meantime he desired most earnestly to know if he might formally ask her father for her hand.

By now Tamarisk had anticipated his proposal of marriage and prepared her refusal.

"I am but sixteen years of age," she told him, "too young, I think, to know my own mind. I would greatly prefer it if we could remain the good friends we have always been, for I am not yet ready to consider matrimony."

Her wounded hero made one further attempt

to convince her that an engagement could endure as long as she wished — until she was in her twenties, if that was her desire. He wanted no more from her than to know that one day they would be married, he persisted.

Once again Tamarisk was reminded of her lost virginity as she tried not to imagine the look of shock which would shatter Charles's adoring face were he to know she was not the innocent he believed.

"It would be wrong of me to make any promises I am not certain I could keep," she replied. "But thank you for the honor you have paid me, Charles. Perhaps we may continue our correspondence and so remain in communication until we are both older and more certain of our feelings."

She softened her refusal by promising to go to the opera with him, since the weather made riding out of the question.

"If Mama will not permit me to go alone with you, then we will take Miss Gurney with us," she said, and extricated herself nimbly from the danger of prolonging their tête-à-tête by taking him to meet her young governess.

Later that evening, when Mavreen inquired if Charles had declared himself, Tamarisk nodded.

"I like him very well, Mama," she said. "But I have no wish to marry him. He is far too young."

"But very eligible," Mavreen countered, hiding her smile at Tamarisk's scorn of a youth three years her senior. "The Baroness tells me he has excellent prospects in the Navy — indeed, that his current promotion is premature. Moreover, he has private means that would ensure the utmost luxury for you and any family you might raise."

Tamarisk's mouth tightened.

"I do not love him, Mama!" she said. "And I will not marry a man I cannot love. My mind is made up upon the matter."

Wisely Mavreen did not press the point although she was far from relinquishing the idea that her daughter would do well to marry this boy. Tamarisk was still very young and in a few years hence she might change her mind about her sub-lieutenant. Mavreen was puzzled by her daughter's continued reluctance to join in any of the festivities arranged for her young female contemporaries to launch them into matrimony. But for the time being she was not unduly worried. Tamarisk had wealth, looks, a title, and a young man already dedicated to the idea of making her his bride.

She herself, in company with Gerard, braved the snow to pay a call upon her father and Aunt Clarrie. As always, Sir John was well up to date with current world affairs and was delighted to discuss at length the invasion of France by the Allied armies. He had drawn a map of the battlefronts and now used this to demonstrate the progress of the war. The Allies, he pointed out, had crossed the French boundary at the Rhine. Napoleon, in his headquarters at Châlon in the frozen plains of eastern Champagne, had managed to recruit an army of fifty thousand men whilst the Allies numbered two hundred and twenty thousand. On the twenty-ninth of January Napoleon had attacked the Prusso-Russian Army and forced Field Marshal Blücher to retreat.

But Sir John had not yet heard the very latest news from the battlefront. On the first of February Napoleon was defeated at La Rothière, his men outnumbered four to one. The Allies were marching toward Paris. Murat, whom Napoleon had made King of Naples, had deserted him and was engaged in the signing of a treaty with his enemies. There was now no hope left that Prince Eugène might cross from Italy to attack Napoleon's enemies in the rear.

The city of Paris was in an uproar. Rich ladies departed hurriedly to their country houses, their jewelry sewn into their corsets. Forty-hour prayers and the Miséréré were ordered by Cardinal Maury. Napoleon ordered Marie Louise and his little son, the King of Rome, to leave Paris. He contemplated negotiations for a peace treaty but never dispatched the request. Instead he fought six victorious battles in nine days and almost wiped out Blücher's army.

By the twenty-eighth of February the Allies had crossed the Seine and were only forty miles from Paris. The peasantry rallied to Napoleon's aid and fought side by side with his soldiers to defend the city. But Paris had a soft center. The old nobility living in Faubourg Saint-Germain were anxious to welcome the invaders.

Had the Parisians supported the defenders, the outcome of the war might have been otherwise; but instead of building redoubts, the citizens were removing their valuable furniture to the country and burying their napoleons in their gardens. Napoleon himself was busy, some one hundred and thirty miles east of Paris, cutting the enemy lines of communications. He was convinced that if Paris held firm, victory might yet be his. But dispatches informed him of the defeatism rampant in the city and he ordered his army to march there. But it was too late. On the first of April the Allies entered Paris.

Napoleon resolved to fight on. He still had a very strong army of sixty thousand men. But many of his marshals and generals were anxious that Paris should not share the same fate as Moscow. Deferring to them, he agreed to abdicate in favor of his son, the Empress to act as Regent. But the Tsar was aware that the army was still behind Napoleon and rejected the Regency, insisting Napoleon should abdicate unconditionally.

Meanwhile, Marshal Soult was confronting Wellington's troops across the River Garonne. On the tenth of April they went into battle and Soult was forced to retire to Carcassonne. On the twelfth of April Wellington entered Toulouse and received the keys of the city in the name of King Louis XVIII. By now news had arrived from Paris of Napoleon's abdication, and on the eighteenth of April Wellington signed a friendly convention with the defeated French marshal.

Two days later Napoleon departed with four hundred of his guards to the island of Elba. On the same day the Prince of Wales led the fat, gouty French King through the decorated streets of London.

It was impossible not to feel excited by these events, Tamarisk decided as she walked with Davinia and Antoine in the direction of Albemarle Street. They joined the crowds hoping to see the French King who was holding a levee in Grillon's Hotel. The Prince Regent was to invest him with the Order of the Garter. Gross and weak though Louis was, the fact that he was to be restored to the throne of France after twenty-four years lent him an aura of glamor. This was heightened by the knowledge that England had given him refuge and been instrumental in restoring his monarchy.

Gerard took great pains to instruct Antoine as to the importance of this historic day. He wished his son to be fully conversant with the events that led to the downfall of the Emperor and the return of the Bourbons.

"As a member of the French nobility," he said, "you must give your allegiance to the King. I have requested an audience with His Majesty, and it is my hope and intention to present you to him before he leaves for France!"

In the eight weeks since his arrival, Tamarisk's feelings toward her half-brother had been of growing dislike. In this she and her mother were for once in unspoken accord. They had not discussed the matter, but Tamarisk had seen from time to time the expression on her mother's face when the boy's duplicity was too obvious to be ignored. Away from his father, Antoine was proving to be self-willed, arrogant, secretive, and so spoilt that there were tantrums whenever he could not instantly acquire what he demanded.

Mavreen tried to find excuses for the child. She had met Blanche Merlin and was well aware how the besotted mother had raised the boy to consider himself a little Prince — someone with rights that superseded those of ordinary people. Gerard's adoration of his son had furthered the boy's belief that those around him existed only to serve, indulge, or amuse him. Mavreen had upon several occasions felt obliged to reprimand Antoine for his dictatorial manner with the servants, all of whom were hard put to conceal their dislike of him. They served him — but grudgingly.

Antoine was still only six years of age and young enough for correction to be effective. But if he lacked any other quality, he did not lack for intelligence, and with the shrewdness that he doubtless derived from his peasant origins, he managed perfectly to conceal from his father all his short-comings. With Gerard he was smiling, docile, obedient, respectful, and adoring. With a perception unusual in one so young, Antoine had realized that he must show a like respect for Mavreen, but when he obeyed her orders he was unsmiling and clearly resented her authority.

Gerard, unfortunately, would hear no criticism of his son. When Mavreen complained that Antoine was forever provoking Tamarisk, Gerard excused the boy on the grounds that he was an only child and unused to the give and take of family life. Given time, he said, Antoine would

290

stop teasing his elder sister. And meanwhile it would do Tamarisk no harm to realize she too was not the only goose in the gaggle.

"But, Gerard, she is ten years older than Antoine and, if nothing else, has a right to the privacy of her own bedchamber," Mavreen reflected. "On two occasions she discovered Antoine in there without her permission."

"'Tis but a boy's curiosity," Gerard replied. "I will speak with him about it."

When later he reported that he had reprimanded Antoine, Mavreen was aghast to hear from Gerard that the boy had strongly denied any offense. He maintained that Tamarisk did not like him and had invented the story to get him into trouble.

"You would doubt Tamarisk's word?" she asked Gerard.

"Why should I doubt Antoine's?" Gerard countered.

"Because he might have denied his guilt for fear of arousing your disfavor!" Mavreen replied. "It would be natural enough."

"He has no reason to fear me — and well he knows it," Gerard retorted. "I really do not feel inclined to discuss this matter further, Mavreen. Antoine has the noblest of instincts, and to infer that he lies when he has no way to prove himself innocent is, if I may say so, unjust and most unbecoming of you — and Tamarisk!"

Mavreen was deeply disturbed. She had a long talk with Davinia Gurney in whose charge Antoine was for the most part of every day. But the girl was clearly unwilling to support

Mavreen. Mavreen supposed that she feared for her dismissal by Gerard if she voiced a true opinion of his son. But this was not the case. The boy had sensed Davinia's weakness of character and played upon it. He had but to smile or to plead and she fulfilled his every whim. On Gerard's son Davinia was able to lavish all her pent-up devotion for Gerard himself. Without realizing it, she was releasing her guilty frustrations each time she indulged the child, kissed his forehead, or smoothed his bright gold curls. Her devotion to Antoine was not reciprocated, for the boy seemed incapable of feeling emotions of love, but he permitted her to fuss over him as once his own mother had done, and Gerard, noticing this, praised the young governess for the gentle sweetness of her nature. He could not understand why Mavreen and Tamarisk should so dislike his son and was glad to be able to cite Miss Gurney's good report upon the boy in answer to their criticisms.

Mavreen had no way of proving to Gerard that Antoine needed discipline rather than cosseting. Fortunately Gerard had agreed to the employment of a tutor to take on Antoine's education, and Mavreen resolved to leave the problem until such time as the tutor arrived.

Whilst Davinia, Tamarisk, and Antoine were observing the Royal activities in Albemarle Street, Mavreen and Gerard were interviewing a prospective candidate — a Mr. Alfred Mumford. The elder son of a clergyman, the young man now standing before them looked far from prepossessing. His morning coat and breeches, although attention had clearly been lavished upon them, failed to conceal their age and shabbiness. His leather boots, carefully polished had seen better days. Ignoring the fashion, he had kept his side-whiskers, possibly hoping to give an appearance of strength to a receding jawline. His pale blue eyes were downcast and it was obvious he was painfully shy.

Mavreen felt sorry for the would-be tutor. She recognized at once that he did not possess the character to deal with young Antoine. Gerard, however, seemed to have no such misgivings. It soon became apparent under his questioning that from a tutorial point of view, Mr. Mumford was more than well suited for the teaching side of the job he would have to do. He had spent part of his childhood in southern France with an aunt, the warmer climes being necessary for his somewhat delicate health as a boy. As a consequence he was almost bilingual and had an excellent knowledge of French history, literature, and art. Upon returning to England as an adult, his spinster aunt who had become greatly attached to him sponsored his further education at Cambridge where without difficulty he had obtained a science degree.

Armed with these facts and without first consulting Mavreen, Gerard promptly engaged him. Subject to his references proving satisfactory, he was to begin work at once, his annual salary to be twenty-five guineas. He would be provided with a new wardrobe of clothes, affording him suitable attire in which to escort his young charge wherever he might have need to go.

As soon as the pathetically grateful young man bowed himself out of the room as if Gerard were Royalty, Mavreen turned to her husband with a worried frown.

"I cannot agree, Gerard, that Mr. Mumford is a wise choice! I understand very well how knowledgeable he is, but I doubt strongly that he has the forcefulness of character required to control a boy like Antoine."

"I have not engaged him to form Antoine's character," Gerard said, "but to provide him with the rudiments of an education. The boy cannot go to Eton quite ignorant, else he will be disparaged by his classmates. The dunce is always a matter for ridicule, you know."

"It will come even harder for him at school if he cannot accept discipline," Mavreen rejoined. "The boy needs a firm hand."

Gerard's mood, until now complaisant, changed to one of irritation.

"What is it you have against the boy, Mavreen?" he asked coldly. "'Twould seem you can find no good in him. Can it be you resent his presence in the house because he is not *your* child?"

Mavreen's face tautened in anger.

"Although Antoine is not my child, as you say, I was more than anxious to give him my love and a happy home simply because he is *yours*, Gerard. But although you do not believe it, Antoine is by no means as innocent or charming as he chooses to appear to you. His faults are only in evidence when you are absent, so I understand your disinclination to accept what I say. Nor am I lacking in understanding of the boy. I know as well as you do the vagaries of his upbringing by Blanche Merlin; and I think it is her fault, rather than the child's, that he is spoilt, arrogant, and self-opinionated. It is not his fault that he has never been instructed in the virtues of truth, honesty, and gratitude. But if you love your son, Gerard, surely you must be the first to desire that there should be no doubt about the nobility of his character."

For a moment Gerard remained silent, his face pale, his quickened breathing alone betraying his anger. Then he spoke in a cold, hard voice:

"I think it is best if you leave Antoine's welfare entirely to me and cease to concern yourself further with him," he said. "It is obvious to me that you have no love for him. In any event he is my responsibility — not yours!"

Mavreen was bitterly hurt. Her conviction that her estimate of the boy was nearer the truth than Gerard's began to wane. She asked herself a hundred times if perchance she was being too harsh in her judgment, too premature in expecting Gerard's son to reflect his father's nature.

She longed to discuss the matter with an impartial third party but felt any criticism of Gerard's son to an outsider would be a form of disloyalty to Gerard himself. It suddenly dawned on her that she might seek advice from the one friend she could trust to be both honest and discreet — Gideon Morris. When she herself had failed to do so, he alone seemed able to understand and manage Tamarisk. It was as if he had a special insight into the mind of a child. It was possible, she thought, that he would have some helpful suggestion to make with regard to Antoine. Gerard might claim sole responsibility for his son, but as long as Antoine lived beneath her roof, the boy's behavior had an effect upon her and everyone else around him.

Of one thing she had no doubt — that if Antoine were not better directed, he would before long be the cause of a serious rift between her and Gerard.

16

May 1814

"CAN the boy really be such a little monster?" Gideon asked, his face alight with laughter. The gravity of Mavreen's expression as she came to the end of her account of Antoine's behavior gave way to a tentative smile.

"That is the very question I want you to answer," she replied.

They had met, at Mavreen's suggestion, at Somerset House, ostensibly to view the paintings in the Royal Academy. The meeting was unknown to Gerard, for the longer she withheld even the most casual of references to Gideon, the more difficult it had become to speak of him. Hating her deception, Mavreen had allowed Gerard to suppose her to be on a shopping expedition this day; and whilst her rendezvous with Gideon was totally innocent in its intent, nevertheless she felt guilty in so deceiving her husband.

Gideon, warned by Mavreen of the need for secrecy, had omitted to wear one of his more outrageously dandified costumes. He was quite simply attired in buckskin breeches and a dark brown swallow-tail coat adorned with gilt buttons.

Mavreen, however, was dressed *à la mode*.

Her military hat was the latest fashion designed to portray the patriotic feelings aroused by the news of the Allies' occupation of Paris. The low neckline of her dress was filled by a lace bayadere to protect her throat from the cold. The long, narrow scarf had been disarranged by the light spring breeze and Gideon now straightened it for her. His eyes were gentle as he looked down at her anxious face.

"All young boys are tiresome little animals," he added by way of consolation. "In truth, I doubt they ever grow quite as civilized as little girls."

"'Tis no laughing matter, Gideon," Mavreen said. "I would have no objection if it were mere mischievousness of which I speak. 'Tis the boy's underhand ways that most concern me." She paused and added almost inaudibly, "I dislike having to say this, but I verily believe him to be a liar and a thief!"

Gideon led Mavreen to a bench in the hallway and sat down beside her. He was serious now as he said quietly:

"Is that so surprising, bearing in mind his start in life? Have you forgotten that I was no better myself in childhood? Yet I would not call myself a dishonorable man now."

"But, Gideon, that was quite different!" Mavreen cried. "You were starving and you had your poor mother to support. You were forced to steal to survive. Antoine has every conceivable luxury. And his lies are merely to guard himself against Gerard's displeasure. He has no cause to fear his father for I believe

Gerard would excuse him *any* wrongdoing. I defy you to tell me you were ever *sly!*"

"At the risk of incurring your displeasure," Gideon said thoughtfully, "I must ask if unwittingly you are prejudiced against the boy? After all, you are not his mother. And, Mavreen, though you may not know it, 'twould be quite natural for you to resent your husband's bastard taking the place of the son you have not been able to give him."

He had feared Mavreen would hotly deny his suggestion. But she merely nodded her head, saying:

"I have searched my conscience many times upon just such a possibility. But it is not so, Gideon. I did not imagine it when I saw Antoine deliberately put out a foot to trip the maid on the landing. He did not know I could see him. When I raised the subject, he swore upon his oath that the maid had lied if she had said any such thing to me, and he demanded that I dismiss the poor girl. I could name a dozen such incidents. As for his thieving, I found in his bedroom three gold guineas — a deal too much money for the boy to come by honestly. He informed me that my father had made him a present of them, but when I spoke to Father he said he had given him only one florin to spend and a napoleon as a keepsake."

"And Gerard takes the boy's word in preference to yours?" Gideon asked.

"He thinks, like you, that I am prejudiced against his son," Mavreen excused Gerard quickly. "I understand his sentiments, but

299

you, Gideon, can appreciate my difficulty. The boy could well come between Gerard and me. Already he has disrupted the harmony of the household."

"You know that I will assist if it be possible, but what would you have me do?" Gideon asked.

"If you would just see the boy," Mavreen replied. "I think if you were to spend some few hours in his company, you could assess his true character without prejudice. If you believe him harmless, quite normal in his behavior and attitudes, then I will accept that I am judging him unfairly and I will attempt to be more tolerant."

"But if I endorse your suspicions?"

Mavreen bit her lip.

"Then I think I could find the courage to insist that Gerard go more thoroughly into each incident as it occurs. Sooner or later the boy will betray himself. But I do not want to go to war with Gerard over his son unless it is absolutely necessary. Will you see the boy, Gideon? We can arrange to meet casually in the park. Now that the weather is warmer, we shall resume our practice of riding there every day. Tamarisk would be more than delighted to see you. I fear she is finding life somewhat tedious at the moment; and she has no more affection for her half-brother than have I."

"Very well, then," Gideon agreed, helping Mavreen to her feet and walking with her toward the door into the street.

"Is it not strange, Gideon," Mavreen said,

"that I, who am usually so assured in my choice of actions, should find myself so uncertain in the upbringing of children while you, who have never had children of your own, seem able to understand Tamarisk far better than I — better even than Gerard?"

"Let us hope I can prove myself equally perceptive with young Master Antoine," said Gideon. "But be warned in advance, Mavreen, lest my sympathies lie with the boy. You will not care for my opinion if I find you at fault."

Far from returning his smile as he had expected, Mavreen regarded him seriously.

"I think I would welcome it," she said quietly. "It gives me no happiness to feel such antipathy toward Gerard's son; and my inability to hide my distrust is causing Gerard much distress. 'Twould be best for us all if I have but imagined the boy's faults."

"Imagination can be a powerful deceiver," Gideon replied with equal seriousness. "And although you were ever honest in your dealings, I have known you less than honest in your thinking."

"How so?" Mavreen asked, an edge of defiance in her tone.

Gideon hesitated momentarily and then said: "I have always believed that you deceived yourself as to the reality of your love for Gerard and even more so regarding his love for you. You clung to your young girl's dream of romantic love and refused to see that the young man you wanted had no such need of you. His early rejection of you touched upon that obstinate streak in your nature which cannot accept defeat. So you found excuses for him. And although he disappointed you again and again, you would not admit to yourself that he had forfeited your respect and, as a consequence, your love."

Mavreen's eyes were cold.

"You know not of what you speak!" she said angrily. "If 'twere true what you say, then why would I have married Gerard? Or been so happy in my marriage?"

Gideon met her gaze steadily.

"You have deceived yourself so long, Mavreen," he said quietly, "that you have convinced yourself the habit of caring about him, protecting him, *is* love."

"That is a ludicrous suggestion — and not worthy of you, Gideon. You take advantage of my call upon our friendship to read me a lecture upon the meaning of love within marriage, yet you know naught about the subject."

Despite the fact that her eyes were flashing dangerously, Gideon smiled nonchalantly, as if her words held no import for him.

"I have spent whole summers long at The Grange living with you as man and wife. I know very well what I am saying. We were more than lovers, Mavreen. We were friends, companions. Not only were our bodies in total harmony but our minds too. We were as one person and that is something you can never be with your Gerard."

"I will listen to no more such impertinence!" Mavreen said icily.

302

Her attempt at haughtiness only deepened Gideon's smile.

"You are quite impossible," she said, greatly discomfited. "But I shall not quarrel with you over such absurdities. It is obvious to me that you disparage Gerard only because you do not know him well enough. I shall effect a proper introduction soon so that you come to know him better. You may then appreciate his worth and understand why I love and respect him."

"'Twould appear your loyalty exceeds your honesty," was Gideon's reply.

Mavreen's sense of humor suddenly reasserted itself.

"You did ever enjoy sparring with words," she said. "But you talk nonsense and I have no more time to waste this morning, Gideon Morris. Kindly escort me to my carriage else I shall never reach my milliner before dinner."

Dinner at Barre House was a formal meal eaten in the big dinning hall at three of the clock. Footmen stood behind each chair serving the many dishes of rich food. Without haste the family partook of fine soles, nicely grilled, boiled ham and chicken, rump of roasted beef, barberry pye and cheesecakes, and then coffee to drink.

Throughout the meal Tamarisk had little to say. Antoine, beneath his father's close scrutiny, spoke only when addressed and then with the utmost deference. Davinia Gurney who, despite her lowly status as governess, was nevertheless permitted to eat with the family when they did not have guests, spoke only when questioned. Opposite her sat the new tutor, Mr. Mumford, hopelessly in awe of the Vicomte and his Lady, stuttering so severely that he was left to eat in silence.

Mavreen, seated at the far end of the table from Gerard, was bored and restless. She was half regretting her impulsive decision to involve Gideon Morris in her private affairs. His audacious comments about herself were ridiculous and impertinent. Yet they irritated like a small rose thorn in the flesh. She could not stop herself from remembering his words and was angry for allowing them recall.

But as if to dispel her misgivings, as the meal ended Gerard leaned forward and spoke to the silent Mr. Mumford.

"Antoine tells me you have insisted he remain indoors despite your assurance that he might go riding today if he completed his Latin translation this morning."

The tutor looked up nervously.

"'Tis true, S . . . Sir, I have curtailed his riding b . . . but only b . . . because he f . . . failed to f . . . finish the work he had been s . . . set."

"The boy says he did complete the work and that you must have forgotten the page at which you said he could stop."

"I am absolutely p . . . p . . . positive . . . " Mr. Mumford began but Gerard broke in:

"There has clearly been a misunderstanding, and I feel it would be wrong if Antoine were to be penalized because of it. Some exercise will do the boy good and he can continue his translation if necessary when he returns."

Seeing the unmistakable glitter of triumph in Antoine's eyes as they encountered her own, Mavreen was certain that the tutor had not made any mistake. Gideon, she trusted, would see that she was right about the boy, and the sooner the better for all concerned.

Two days later, as planned, Mavreen went riding in the park with Tamarisk, Antoine, and the head groom, who was intructing the boy in horsemanship. It was Tamarisk who first espied Gideon cantering toward them.

"Mama, 'tis Perry!" she cried, waving her riding crop in Gideon's direction. He reined in his horse and bowed to them.

"This is indeed a pleasant surprise," he said, exchanging a wicked glance with Mavreen. He stole a quick look at the boy astride his plump chestnut pony, noticing the child's handsomeness of feature and restless feet and hands. It was clear the boy resented this interruption to their progress.

Mavreen said:

"Perry, may I present Antoine de Valle who has but recently come from France to live with us. Antoine, this gentleman is Sir Peregrine Waite."

The beautiful pale face beneath the black riding hat looked up at Gideon haughtily.

"I am the *Honorable* Antoine de Valle!" he said, his French accent in no way impairing his meaning.

"Antoine!" Mavreen's voice was sharply reproving. "That is not so and even if it were . . . "

"My father told me that in England the son of a Viscount has the title of 'Honorable,'" Antoine interrupted, his treble voice barely masking his anger.

"If it be true, then try to behave like a Viscount's son!" Gideon said. "Bragging, you may not be aware, is hardly considered the attribute of a gentleman; nor is it considered polite to interrupt ladies when they are speaking!"

The boy's face turned a furious red. It was obvious he was not used to being rebuked and resented it bitterly. But he did not speak again.

Tamarisk was attempting to hide her delight. Her resentment of her father's indulgences to her half-brother had amounted almost to hatred. She sensed that her mother disliked Antoine, and now here too was Perry openly criticizing him before everyone.

"Think you not that it has become a trifle chilly?" Gideon asked Mavreen. "What say you to curtailing the afternoon's exercise and repairing to my house for some hot chocolate?"

"How agreeable that sounds!" Tamarisk cried eagerly. She was made doubly happy because of this unexpected meeting with Perry and because he seemed equally pleased to see her. And now Mama was saying "I think it an admirable scheme," as she turned her horse's head.

"I would prefer to continue with my exercise. Papa wishes me to have so much lessons as possible." Antoine's voice was quiet but emphatic.

306

"As *many* lessons as possible," Mavreen corrected automatically. "However, I am afraid your riding lesson for today is over."

The boy's eyebrows drew together in a fierce scowl. He muttered ominously:

"I do not think Papa will be pleased when he hears of this!"

Mavreen's face flushed an angry red, but otherwise she gave no sign that she had heard Antoine's obvious threat.

Riding northward across the park toward Harley Street, Gideon, Mavreen, and Tamarisk drew ahead of the boy and the groom. Tamarisk said to Gideon:

"Is Antoine not the most odious child you ever encountered, Perry? I have tried very hard to like him, but I really cannot."

Gideon smiled down at her.

"I seem to remember a spoilt little girl of the same age who was very nearly as tiresome."

Tamarisk laughed.

"I was not nearly so objectionable, was I, Mama?"

But Mavreen refused to be drawn into an open admission of her dislike for Gerard's son.

"You were very spoilt," she said, but her voice was gentle and her eyes were smiling.

The hour spent at Chiswell House passed all too swiftly for Tamarisk's liking. It was the first time since her disastrous nocturnal visit to Perry that she had entered his home. Her immediate feeling of discomfort was soon dispersed as he sought to put her at ease, joking with her in the old familiar way of a favorite uncle.

Pretending to be the dandy — for Antoine's benefit, Tamarisk supposed — he was flicking imaginary dust from the immaculately clean *objets d'art* with his lace-edged 'kerchief.

If her adored Perry's eyes wandered frequently to the quiet golden-haired boy sitting hunched in one of the big armchairs, Tamarisk did not notice, for he seemed intent upon amusing her. He called her Mama "*Madame la Vicomtesse,*" sweeping her low courtly bows as if she were Royalty, causing Mavreen to smile and Tamarisk to dissolve into delighted giggles. He aped the Prince Regent and mimicked the Prime Minister, Lord Liverpool. But Antoine stayed rigidly aloof.

"'Tis time we were on our way," Mavreen finally announced as the afternoon sky began to darken slightly with the approaching evening. "Your Papa will be worried about us if we tarry longer."

"Why, 'tis early yet," said Gideon, feeling in his waistcoat pocket for his gold repeater watch. "Well, now! 'Pon my soul," he exclaimed. "I could have sworn I had my watch about my person. Mayhap I have lost it out riding in the park."

"Oh, Perry, you have not lost your watch?" Tamarisk cried. Her very first memory of him was of his kindness to her when, in a room full of tedious adults, he had taken note of her boredom and relieved it by pressing the magic button on his gold watch, causing the repeater to strike the hour and the quarters of the current hour with pretty chimes. The gold dial had white gold inlays for the hours and minutes. Its case was beautifully engraved. "A perfect example of Thomas Tompion's craftsmanship," Perry had told her, addressing her as if she herself were grown-up and well informed enough to know the difference between a Tompion and a Breguet!

"'Tis merely mislaid," Gideon said now, and keeping his face averted from the boy, said pointedly to Mavreen:

"You, Madame la Vicomtesse, and your most beautiful daughter doubtless wish to retire to the boudoir before you leave for home. I will ring for the butler and have him show you the way."

Tamarisk was on the point of refusing this offer, but Mavreen took hold of her arm in so tight a grip and spoke so firmly that her demur died on her lips.

Puzzled, and not a little curious, she followed Mavreen from the room.

Gideon turned to his remaining quest.

"*Stand up, Monsieur the very honorable de Valle!*" His voice was no longer foppish but like a whiplash. The boy's head rose in surprise, but he remained seated.

"Up!" Gideon reached out and pulled Antoine to his feet. "Now kindly return my watch!"

Antoine stared back at him with a look of such innocence as was certain to have convinced anyone less prepared than his host.

"I do not know . . . " he began. But Gideon broke in even more sharply:

"Return my watch, boy, else I'll call the police."

The eyes narrowed. The red, curved lips

tightened ominously.

"You would not dare!" he challenged, but his voice trembled. "My Papa would not allow . . . "

"Your father is not above the law of this country," Gideon interrupted. "Now hand over my watch, boy, before I lose all patience."

When Antoine still hesitated, Gideon caught his arm and twisted it sharply behind his back. He paid no attention when Antoine cried out in pain but reached with his free hand into the boy's pockets. Within a minute he had recovered the watch.

Barely glancing at it, he pushed Antoine roughly forward so that he was doubled over a footstool. Holding him there Gideon proceeded to administer a sound thrashing with his other hand.

When finally Gideon released him, Antoine was sobbing — great angry gulps that were a mixture of pain and mortification. Gideon stared down at the wet, furious face, his eyes steely.

"'Twould seem that no one has advised you of the penalties for stealing!" he said, his icy voice strangely compelling. "You could be transported in a convict ship to the Colonies; or thrown into a filthy prison with rats and rogues for company. But that is only one point I wish to make clear to you. The other is that you seem to be proud of the fact that your father is a nobleman. But if he were to hear that you were an accomplished pick-pocket, I doubt he would wish to continue calling you his son. I, for one, would not. You not only disgrace yourself, but you disgrace the family whose name you bear."

"You are going to tell my father?" The boy's voice was shrill with fear.

"I do not know," Gideon replied truthfully. "I will consider it."

Antoine stumbled forward and fell at Gideon's feet where he knelt, hugging Gideon's legs.

"Do not tell him, I beg of you! I will pay you anything you ask. See, here is my new riding crop! Its head is silver, engraved with our family crest. Papa had it made especially for me in France and it is very valuable."

"Be quiet, boy!" Gideon's voice barely hid his scorn. "There is another lesson you had best learn — a gentleman does not buy silence from another. Now stand up and straighten your clothing. The Vicomtesse will return at any moment, and if you do not desire your thieving to be known to her, you had best hide your chagrin at being caught."

When Mavreen did reappear, she at once noticed Antoine's red-rimmed eyes. But even more quickly she intercepted the look of utter hatred the boy gave Gideon when his back was turned. There was no opportunity for private conversation, and Mavreen had to be content with the glance of reassurance Gideon gave her as he escorted her to the front door.

Only Tamarisk, ignorant of the undercurrent between her elders, chatted happily as they rode homeward. Perry had kissed her warmly on both cheeks and in return she had hugged him — the exchange of embraces so spontaneous that there had been no embarrassment between them.

Mavreen paid only cursory attention to Tamarisk's chatter. She was trying to decide whether or not to tell Gerard of their meeting with Gideon. Finally she decided to say nothing unless Tamarisk or Antoine raised the subject. She suspected that Antoine would lose no time in reporting the full details of the afternoon to his father, but to her surprise he said nothing. Tamarisk too remained silent, not wishing to betray her secret love for Perry. So the subject remained undiscussed, as if by tacit agreement.

Antoine, however, was merely biding his time.

★ ★ ★

On the seventh of May Gerard took Mavreen and Tamarisk to the theater. Antoine, too young for such entertainments, was left at home in the care of Mr. Mumford and Miss Gurney. Edmund Kean was performing for the first time as Iago in *Othello*.

During an interval they received a visit from Lisa von Eburhard. Resplendent in satin and ostrich feathers, her large bulk all but filled the limited space of their box.

"My dears!" she said conspiratorially. "Have you heard the latest gossip? Augusta Leigh gave birth to a daughter last month and some are saying that the child is not her husband's but the offspring of . . . " She broke off belatedly as she noticed Tamarisk listening avidly to her every word. Then she smiled at Mavreen with a knowing look and said pointedly, "By the way, Lord Byron is in the audience tonight with his

312

friend Thomas Moore. Would you care for an introduction?"

"I think not, thank you, Lisa," Mavreen replied, a glance at Tamarisk's face having showed her how *bouleversée* the girl was by this suggestion.

Indeed Tamarisk was deeply shocked by the Baroness's latest piece of scandal. She looked surreptitiously at the box where the poet was sitting with a group of his friends and decided that there could not be a word of truth in the gossip. Her knowledge of the young man had been limited, she thought, her cheeks flaming at the memory, but it had been very intimate. And although she had been frightened and dismayed by the act of love, she had nevertheless sensed in her lover a desire to be gentle, tender, and reassuring. She was convinced that he was neither as immoral nor as bestial as the Baroness's implications inferred.

But Lisa had already forgotten Lord Byron and was describing how, a fortnight earlier, her coachman had driven her to Dover to watch the departure of the French King for his native land.

"A most spectacular occasion," she chattered on. "His Majesty was escorted across the Channel by eight ships of the line, under the command of the Duke of Clarence. You know, my dears, we really must go to Paris soon. All my friends are arranging to pay visits. 'Twill be most exciting to return there after all these years!"

"'Twould be strange to see Paris without the Emperor Napoleon in charge of affairs," mused Gerard.

"Oh, *he* is doubtless settling down on that strange little island of Elba," the Baroness said unfeelingly. "I hear he has taken four hundred of his guards with him and is to have full sovereignty there."

"Nevertheless he does not have the company of his wife and child," Gerard remarked. "I feel it demonstrated his affection for them that he did not insist — nay, even request of them — that they should go into exile with him."

"No more they should," said Lisa with a shrug of her ample shoulders. "What would an Empress, a Princess of Hapsburg, do on a remote little island? Most improper!"

She turned to Tamarisk and with a twinkle asked:

"Have you had word from poor dear Charles? I have had no news of him except that I heard the other day Napoleon left France in the *Undaunted*. If that be true, then Charles must even now be in the environs of Elba. Doubtless we shall hear from him soon."

She stole a brief, shrewd glance at Mavreen's daughter. Tamarisk was growing up fast, she thought. Her figure was become quite womanly and Mavreen must be thinking seriously of finding a husband for her. If the girl were to marry Charles, it would be a satisfactory match. Her nephew might not be the most handsome of young men, but he was certainly one of the most eligible — and quite taken with Tamarisk, judging by his lovesick behavior on his last visit home.

The interval had now elapsed, and with a wave

314

of her beringed hand the Baroness fluttered away like a fat wood pigeon.

"One day," Gerard said thoughtfully to Mavreen, "that dear friend of yours is going to find herself in trouble. Her gossip borders on the slanderous at times!"

Could Byron have fathered Augusta Leigh's child? Mavreen wondered as the audience began to return to their seats in the stalls below. What tragedy for all concerned if he were truly in love with his own half-sister! And what weakness of character if he could not keep such scandalous emotions under control. Augusta must be weak-willed, too, to give way to temptation, however unhappy her marriage to a worthless husband.

Yet Mavreen, whilst in no way condoning, could not condemn. She knew only too well the overpowering influence a man could exert over a woman if *his* desire were strong enough; how easily he could woo her to submission if he knew and understood a woman's weaknesses. In the past, had she not found herself succumbing to Gideon even whilst she was still voicing a protest? Even the strongest of women was prey to the determined man. And Lord Byron, Mavreen thought, was handsome to a degree, wildly romantic, and, judging by his poetry, sensuous and passionate.

She turned her head and looked at Gerard's face, in profile as he leaned forward over the edge of the box, totally absorbed by the actors on stage. How dear his features! How stirring to her senses to imagine his eyes fastened upon her with that same rapt attention! Yet how disturbing

315

to remember the cold reticence with which he regarded her whenever they discussed his son! He seemed utterly blind to the boy's faults, allowing no criticism, seeing only the beauty and charm of the child's appearance and never the character beneath.

Mavreen had little doubt as to what had transpired at Chiswell House. Gideon's missing watch; his pointed suggestion that she and Tamarisk should retire, leaving him alone with Antoine; the boy's red-rimmed eyes and sullen expression on her return — all pointed to the fact that Antoine had stolen the timepiece. Innocently the unfortunate child had selected for his victim the one man who, himself once a thief, knew only too well how to detect a pickpocket. Gideon's boyhood crimes were motivated by a desperate need to support his starving mother and to rectify the injustice done to him by his father who had made no provision for them after his death. Antoine had no such excuses. Gerard had showered upon him every luxury, offered him every advantage, cossetted and indulged him. The boy lacked nothing he desired.

Horrified by her own emotions, Mavreen realized that Gerard's weakness with his son not only dismayed but sickened her. It threatened to undermine her respect for the man she so ardently loved.

Never before, since the time she had first fallen in love with him, had she had occasion to doubt that love.

17

June – August 1814

IT was perhaps fortunate that social events during the summer of 1814 involved Mavreen and Gerard in so much activity outside Barre House, that neither had a great deal of time to devote to domestic differences.

On the seventh of June, Alexander, Tsar of Russia, together with the other Allied sovereigns, visited London at the invitation of the Prince Regent. Baroness Eburhard was a personal friend of the Tsar's sister, the Grand Duchess Catherine of Oldenburg; and upon hearing that Mavreen had made the Tsar's acquaintance in Russia at the finale of the French defeat at Moscow, she took her friend to see the Grand Duchess at the Pulteny Hotel. So it was that Mavreen and Gerard were invited to meet the Tsar and attend the various celebrations given by the Regent in his honor.

The Tsar was gracious enough to remember his encounter with Mavreen in the streets of Vilna. He showed equal friendliness toward Gerard and informed him that he had some few months previously met with the French King at Gerard's birthplace, Compiègne. He had found the town delightful. But he had little good to say about King Louis who was rude, offhand, and ungrateful for the part the Russians had played

317

in his restoration. The Tsar had felt obliged to cut short his stay, since his allotted rooms in the Palace at Compiègne were as inferior as the French sovereign's manners!

Tamarisk, who could have enjoyed the festivities had she so desired, loyally joined Princess Charlotte, whose outings were being restricted by her father.

Their only outing into the beflagged and decorated streets of London consisted of a ride round the Ring in Hyde Park. Briefly they were part of a gay, sunlit pageant that included all the Kings, Emperors, and Grandees, foreign and English, displaying themselves to the delight of the crowds.

But they missed not only the gala performance of Pacitta's opera *Aristodemo* and the ballet that followed, but also the commemorative races at Ascot, the feasting, banquets, and excitements of a nation determined to celebrate victory.

On the sixteenth of June Charlotte broke off her engagement to the Prince of Orange, her main reason being, she told Tamarisk, that she feared he would force her to live abroad.

July was barely into its second week when Charlotte was summoned to see her furious father at Carlton House. She was informed that she was to be sent to Windsor with new ladies-in-waiting to live in the isolated Cranbourne Lodge in the middle of the forest. She was forbidden to see anyone except her grandmother, the Queen, once a week.

The Princess, in a state of utter despair, hired

a hackney cab and fled, panic-stricken, to her mother, the Princess of Wales.

Soon all London buzzed with the story of Charlotte's flight, the Regent's insistence upon her return, and the failure of her legal adviser, Mr. Henry Brougham, to discover any lawful means by which she could rightfully defy her father.

Tamarisk received a letter from the unhappy Princess, smuggled out of Carlton House, where she had been taken on leaving her mother. It was written on torn scraps of paper.

'You have no idea of my situation . . . ' she wrote. *'I am a complete prisoner. Not a letter or anything could get to me except by some merciful private hand . . . '*

She begged Tamarisk to try somehow to obtain the Regent's permission to visit her again, if not at Carlton House then at Cranbourne Lodge where she was to be conveyed the following Monday.

"Oh, Mama!" Tamarisk pleaded with Mavreen. "Please use your influence with the Prince so that I may be permitted to go to Charlotte! Surely *you* could make him believe that I cannot influence her against his wishes, whatever they may be; that I constitute no threat. Will you try, Mama, I beg you?"

But although the Prince of Wales received Mavreen civilly enough, he would not consider granting Tamarisk's request. Charlotte, he stated, was to be kept in isolation. She was not being sent to Cranbourne Lodge for her pleasure.

It was clear to Mavreen, as to everyone in the country, that she was to go there as a punishment for defying her father.

Tamarisk was partially diverted from her disappointment by the arrival of a lengthy, descriptive letter from Charles Eburhard. Despite her lack of any real interest in him as a suitor, Tamarisk was impressed by the adventure of his life. His own excitement communicated itself to her as she read of his sentiments when he learned that his frigate *Undaunted* had been selected to take the vanquished Emperor Napoleon to his island of exile.

'*He led the most scholarly life during the voyage,*' Charles recounted, '*studying mathematics and composing a history of Imperial victories. However, 'twould seem the poverty of his new subjects on Elba has inspired in him different ideas as to how he will pass his time on the island. He is even now planning an efficient agricultural policy for the Elbans. He has sent to Corsica for olive trees to plant. Potatoes, lettuces, cauliflowers, onions, and radishes are already in the ground.*

'*Perhaps I can better illustrate the extra-ordinary quality of our notorious "prisoner" if I tell you that not three weeks have passed since our arrival at Portoferraio and he has already sailed to the island of Pianosa, taken possession of it, and has plans for one hundred*

*families to settle there to grow wheat! He left
some of his troops on the island to build a
fort against the possible invasion of pirates
and has now returned to Elba where he has
set builders to adding a story to his house,
I Mulini. He even digs the garden himself
and, hard though it is to credit, he has tried
his hand at ploughing and has been out with
the fishermen harpooning tunny!'*

It became obvious to Tamarisk that Charles
was profoundly impressed with the deposed
French Emperor. Prisoner and former enemy
he might be, yet Charles did not attempt to
conceal his admiration. 'Old Boney', it seemed,
was by no means the ogre of nursery threats!

The remainder of this long letter professed
Charles' great regard and affection for Tamarisk.
That she did not feel able to return his regard,
caused him great distress. He pleaded with her
to take pity upon him — if in no other manner,
then at least by the writing of a letter in reply
to his.

*' 'Tis likely I shall remain here some long
while,'* he wrote. *'And letters from England
and, in particular, from your Dear Self, would
greatly ease my feeling of separation from
those I hold dear.'*

"I shall most certainly pen a letter to him,"
Tamarisk said in answer to Mavreen's question
as to her intentions. "But I have not altered my
mind in any respect regarding my affection for

321

him. Charles does not arouse in me any feeling beyond that of friendship. I shall never marry him, Mama!" She did not add that she would never be married at all unless it were to Perry.

Mavreen's mind was also centered upon Gideon but for very different reasons.

She could no longer deny to herself the fact that the presence of Gerard's son beneath their roof was seriously impairing their happiness. Although Gideon had, in some way of which she was ignorant, cured the boy of stealing, nevertheless the child seemed to dominate the household. Mavreen strongly suspected that he was so terrorizing his tutor that poor Mr. Mumford lived in fear of dismissal and allowed Antoine to dictate to him his daily program. Davinia Gurney, Mavreen had recently discovered, was employed by Antoine as if she were some servant whose purpose it was to run errands for him when no footman or valet was available.

"It is right that he should leave all menial tasks to the servants," Gerard defended his son when Mavreen drew attention to the boy's behavior. "After all, my dear, he will one day be in command of the de Valle estates and must learn how to give orders. 'Tis my opinion you yourself are far too liberal with the servants. It is their duty to serve!"

"They are people nonetheless," Mavreen argued. "That little nurserymaid is on her feet up and down the stairs from dawn till dusk. It is not right that Antoine should double her duties. Yesterday he rang for her to bring

322

him some hot water 'at boiling point,' and when she brought it, he sent her downstairs again for cold water, when it would have been perfectly simple to request warm water in the first place. He invents errands for the pleasure of seeing others at work whilst he does only what pleases him."

"Then you must employ further staff if you feel those we have are inadequate," was Gerard's final comment upon the matter.

"Gerard!" Mavreen's tone was half angry, half pleading, as she attempted to reach his understanding. "It is for Antoine's sake even more than for yours or mine that I must try to make you see him as he is. The boy is often cruel. For example, James, the second footman, has a slight cast in his eye, as you have no doubt noticed. Whenever Antoine gives him an order, he follows it up with a command to the poor man to look at him when he addresses him."

"My dear, you have most certainly lost your sense of proportion," Gerard replied. "That behavior is no more than a boy's mischievousness."

"It is not an amusing prank but a cruel one," Mavreen reiterated. "And I have told him so! But he continues the practice behind my back."

"If it is behind your back, how do you know of it?" Gerard's voice was now icy cold.

"Because I have asked James to report to me if it happened again."

Gerard regarded her, his eyes dark with anger.

323

"I will not have my son spied upon by the servants. If anyone is to report on his behavior, it is Mr. Mumford, and I have had no word of reproach for the boy from him. Once again, Mavreen, may I remind you that Antoine is not your responsibility but mine! You take too much upon yourself."

Mavreen was now most seriously concerned for Gerard who, sooner or later, would discover the truth about the child he adored so blindly. His disillusionment would be the more devastating the longer he lived in his fool's paradise. If only some third party would open Gerard's eyes to the truth!

Her thoughts went instantly to Gideon. Despite her reluctance to involve him a second time, there was no better person to handle the boy. He was never at a loss for a solution, however extreme the problem. But if she were to enlist his help, then it was necessary for her to introduce him to Gerard — something she would have preferred not to do. Yet there was no valid reason why she should keep the two men apart. Gideon was no longer her lover and had ceased to be the day she learned that Gerard was still alive. Gerard had no cause for jealousy and if Gideon were willing to give his support . . .

They had not met since that afternoon in the park, although Tamarisk had caught a glimpse of him one night at the opera and pointed him out to Mavreen. This elicited from Gerard a query as to who Sir Peregrine Waite might be. Sir John, who was with them, voiced his poor opinion of the man he termed 'Beau Brummel the Second', and Mavreen was grateful for the hot denial of Gideon's worthlessness that poured from Tamarisk's lips.

She now decided that it was high time she overcame her strange reluctance to effect an introduction. She arranged a dinner party for twenty-four guests to include Gideon.

Sir Peregrine arrived in the full regalia of a dandy. His purple trousers were gold braided down the outer seams, his coat of black velvet elaborately fastened with crystal buttons. The long, lace ruffles at his wrists were an immaculate white as were his gloves. Over these he wore gold and diamond rings. From a gold chain around his neck hung a single circle of glass which he raised constantly to one eye when he exaggeratedly quizzed a passing lady. His lace-trimmed 'kerchief was heavily perfumed.

Gerard took an instant dislike to him. In a whispered aside to Mavreen he inquired what could have possessed her to invite such a fool to a dinner party comprising so many of the intelligentsia.

"Sir Peregrine is an old friend, and as Tamarisk has already told you, he is by no means the fool he appears," Mavreen replied. "See, Gerard, how seriously he is engaged in talking with young Percy Shelley! And Mr. Disraeli seemed equally interested in his conversation before dinner was served."

Gerard looked bewildered.

"How came you to know such a strange apology for a man I cannot guess," he said. "But that you include him among your friends surprises me even more. I have no time for dandies."

Gideon was well aware of Gerard's antipathy but unconcerned by it. In a quiet moment alone with Mavreen he said:

"You will readily understand that I have no desire to be your husband's friend. We have little in common, I think, beyond our shared passion for *you*."

Whilst Mavreen was still trying to find words to express her annoyance at Gideon's remark, he disconcertingly changed the conversation.

"I have news for you, Mavreen. Young Shelley just told me he is on the point of eloping with William Godwin's daughter Mary. 'Twill cause the greatest scandal. He and Mary will need courage for such action." Suddenly he smiled. "What say you to the idea that you and I elope, Mavreen? We will go with them to the Continent — begin a new life together."

"You have imbibed too much champagne," Mavreen said curtly, "else you would not seek to embarrass me with such nonsensical talk."

"But I mean it, Mavreen," Gideon said, his eyes no longer smiling as he stared down at her. "Come with me, now, before we become too old to live our lives with passion and adventure."

"I will hearken to no such absurdity!" Mavreen said quickly. She realized that Gideon was perfectly sober and intended every word he said. She was painfully aware that the color had come into her cheeks and her hands were trembling. She took refuge in anger at his ability to embarrass her.

"Go flirt with Miss Annabella Milbanke," she said tartly. "'Tis said she has a good head upon her pretty shoulders, and you may find her more receptive to your tomfoolery than I."

"If it is matchmaking you have in mind, Mavreen, then put such thoughts from you," was Gideon's calm reply. "I shall never take a wife unless it be you, my Mavreen."

She caught sight of Gerard's eyes upon her from the far side of the room. Feeling a quite unreasonable guilt at her prolonged conversation with Gideon, she excused herself and moved away to speak with another of her guests. She wished now that she had adhered to her instinct to keep the two men apart. Gerard clearly disapproved of Sir Peregrine Waite, the dandy. Her hopes of Gideon's successful intervention were now dashed. She knew there was nothing to be done until Gerard himself woke up to the unpalatable truth about his son — a day she could not doubt must come.

A few days later Gerard and Mavreen, in company with most of the population of London, went to Green Park to watch the spectacular ascent of Mr. Windham Sadler's colorful balloon — an event planned to mark the centenary of Hanoverian rule. There was great excitement as the balloon sprung into the air when it was released. Then from the sky above them the balloonist dropped hundreds of jubilee programs which his expectant audience rushed to secure.

Tamarisk and Antoine were also upon a sightseeing tour. Under the watchful eyes of

Mr. Mumford and Miss Gurney, they had gone to admire the yellow and black Chinese Pagoda built across the canal in St. James's Park for the celebrations. They planned to continue to Hyde Park to enjoy the ornamental booths and stalls, arcades and kiosks, swings and roundabouts, set up for the great occasion.

Gerard and Mavreen preferred to watch the splendid regatta on the Serpentine. Gerard was particularly desirous of seeing the staged sea battle that was to succeed the regatta, for it represented the Battle of the Nile and was rumored to conclude with a destruction of the French fleet by fireships.

"'Twill be vastly amusing for me to observe the pageant," he said to Mavreen like an excited schoolboy, "since I was present at the real battle!"

"How long ago it seems," mused Mavreen, "since you were called Mr. George King and had forgotten my existence as well as your real name. And I, not knowing what had happened to you, believed you dead . . . "

Gerard held her gloved hand more tightly.

"Despite my loss of memory, I still remembered you in my dreams," he said tenderly.

Mavreen was silent. She too was recalling that past era of their lives and how soon after Lord Nelson's victory in Egypt, Gerard, despite his memories of her, married another girl. How cruelly Fate had parted them not once but many times!

Her face must have portrayed her somber thoughts, for a voice at her elbow said:

"Can it be possible you are not enjoying these magnificent entertainments, m'dear? Nor you, Sir?"

Mavreen swung round to see Gideon smiling down at her. He swept off his beige beaver hat and bowed in turn to her and Gerard.

"On the contrary, Sir," Gerard replied coldly, returning Gideon's bow with a stiffness that clearly indicated his displeasure at the encounter. "We are vastly entertained."

Gideon pulled out a cotton 'kerchief and holding it daintily between thumb and second finger made pretense of mopping his brow. The 'kerchief was printed with a brightly colored caricature of Napoleon.

"What think you of this?" he inquired of Mavreen in his dandy's voice. "I purchased it this very morning at a booth in Hyde Park. Is it not the most amusing 'kerchief you have seen?" He turned to Gerard and as if the subject were of the greatest import said, "Do you know, Sir, that one may also obtain such 'kerchiefs sporting a portrait of our renowned Duke of Wellington?"

Mavreen sensed the stiffening of Gerard's body beside her. She was furious with Gideon for mocking them. But before she could find adequate words to indicate her reproach, he drawled:

"But how amazingly beautiful you are looking, my dear Vicomtesse. I swear I have never seen you more becomingly begowned."

He seemed impervious to Gerard's stony silence and Mavreen guessed rightly that he was enjoying her discomfiture.

"You intend to watch the firework display, of course!" he went on in the same affected voice. "Have you seen that magnificent edifice, the Gothic Castle in Green Park? If you have not, pray allow me to escort you there. I am reliably informed the building is over a hundred feet high!"

"'Tis no building but a painting upon canvas, Sir," Gerard corrected Gideon. "And we have our own carriage close by, so we must refuse your offer to assist our way to Green Park."

"But what good fortune I should meet with you, my dear Vicomte," Gideon replied imperturbably. "For I have no carriage and perchance you will have just a tiny little corner in yours so that I may rest my legs. Why, I am so weak with exhaustion I fear I cannot stand upon them a moment longer."

Good manners prevented Gerard from declining this request; nor could Mavreen invent some quick excuse to be rid of Gideon. He therefore rode with them, his flippant chatter filling the silence so adequately that it appeared he was quite unaware he was not welcome.

Mavreen longed to demand that he cease playing the fool for Gerard's benefit. But forced to hold her tongue, she maintained an icy coolness toward Gideon until the firework display began. Then she forgot him as from the battlements of the Gothic Castle erupted an astonishing and wondrous array of roman candles, serpents, maroons, catherine wheels, firepots, and girandoles.

"Five hundred men have been engaged for a whole month preparing for this spectacular," said Gideon, as rocket after rocket shot into the sky to the excited cheers of the vast crowds.

"I have never seen the like!" Mavreen cried, forgetting in her excitement her resolve not to speak to Gideon. "Is it not marvelous?"

The air was so filled with smoke that it became impossible to see the yellow and black walls of the pagoda and the gas jets spluttering on its blue roof. The Japanese lanterns hanging on the trees were also obscured as was the Gothic Castle itself. Suddenly the smoke cleared. The castle had vanished and in its place, as if by some stroke of magic, appeared the brightly illuminated Temple of Concord — an edifice erected especially for the occasion. Its walls displayed allegorical pictures, the theme of which was the Triumph of England under the Regency.

"Our Prince is not the most modest of men," drawled Gideon. "But since the populace do not, as a rule, applaud him, one can understand his desire to applaud himself."

Mavreen laughed.

"'Tis growing late," Gerard said beside her. "We should return home, I think."

"Oh, Gerard, let us not leave yet awhile," Mavreen pleaded. "There has never been a day like it and I assure you I am not in the least tired."

"Why, 'tis early, not yet ten of the clock," said Gideon, looking at his timepiece. "Let us walk toward Buckingham House, if these vast crowds

331

permit, and see if we can espy our Royal family there."

"We should go home!" Gerard said forcefully to Mavreen. "I am concerned lest the children are not safely returned. Much harm could befall them amongst so many people."

"But Gerard, both Mr. Mumford and Miss Gurney are with them. What possible harm could befall them?"

Gerard frowned.

"You choose to forget the temper of the populace, I think," he said coldly. "Riots by mobs are become almost a daily occurrence, and with these crowds . . . "

"They are in good heart today," Mavreen broke in. She was as excited as a child by the atmosphere of jollification generated by the long day of festivities; and far too mentally stimulated to be desirous of the quiet solitude of Barre House.

"The authorities would not have ordered so many troops to stand by had they not been afraid of trouble," Gerard countered.

Mavreen's eyes flashed.

"There has not been the smallest disturbance as yet," she replied. "The Regent clearly intended the people to enjoy themselves today at his expense and that is what everyone is doing. Despite his unpopularity, I am convinced there will be no uprisings against him this day."

"You cannot be certain of it," Gerard persisted stubbornly. "It takes but the smallest incident to change the mood of a crowd from festive to dangerous. You may do as you please, Mavreen.

I intend to reassure myself that Antoine has come to no harm! I am not altogether convinced of Mr. Mumford's authority in any crisis."

Antoine! Mavreen only just succeeded in biting back an angry repetition of the boy's name. Gerard's attitude toward his son was fast becoming obsessive! If anyone were at risk, it was Tamarisk, not Antoine.

Her mind rebelled against the thought that her own wishes should be set aside for so weak an excuse. But one glance at Gerard's face convinced her his spirits were incapable of rising to the gala occasion this night, tormented as he was by fears for Antoine's well-being.

"Very well, Gerard, we will go home if you wish," she said quietly.

Gideon made no comment. It was clear he had no intention of becoming involved in a domestic dispute. But Mavreen, silently rebelling at the unnecessary curtailment of the evening, felt doubly resentful that Gideon should have witnessed Gerard's absurdity. She had wanted him to share her regard for the man she had married, not despise him for his irrational doting upon his son.

Silently, with no further demur, Mavreen allowed her two escorts to force a way across the park in the direction of their waiting carriage. The crowd seemed to have swelled to a multitude. They were jostled upon all sides by men, women, and children of all ages and ranks. Gerard, in an impatient attempt to clear a path more quickly for Mavreen, edged himself forward. There was a sudden surge of people in the direction of Buckingham House as the Royal party appeared on the lawns outside. Suddenly Gerard disappeared from view.

In vain Gideon struggled to break through the circle of people now enclosing them. But despite all his efforts he and Mavreen were carried along by the urgent momentum of the crowd.

Close by them there was a sudden flare of bright yellow light. The first shouts of warning became a thunderous roar as a great sheet of flame rose upward into the sky. The crowd about them halted and all stood staring toward the Temple of Concord. It was blazing furiously.

Several people began to applaud, believing the conflagration to be part of the night's entertainment. The cries of alarm turned to shouts of approval as the crowd pressed forward once more for a closer look at the spectacle. Gideon and Mavreen were carried with them. Mavreen clung to Gideon's arm, partly for support but mainly in order not to become separated from him. She felt a sudden thrill of excitement as the heat of the flames touched her face. The danger was slight — but it was there! And she had not experienced even the smallest adventure in her life since her return from Compiègne. She stole a quick look at Gideon's face and saw that he too was enjoying himself.

But the burning of the temple was no planned amusement and now, as they stood close beside it, it began to topple sideways. A shower of sparks was blown toward them. Quickly Gideon pulled Mavreen against him, covering her face and hair as best he could by making a shield of his body. A woman screamed. A man nearby gave a horrified gasp. A moment later the giant, burning edifice tumbled into the lake.

The danger from fire was past, but now there was a greater fear lest the crowd should panic, perhaps trampling each other to death if they attempted a mass exodus. Gideon took an even firmer hold upon Mavreen.

"Do not be frightened," he said. "Stay still. I will take care of you."

"I am not in the least frightened," said Mavreen indignantly. Her voice was muffled. She struggled to free her face which was pressed against Gideon's coat.

She heard the quick rumble of laughter in his chest.

"Then you ought to be," he replied. "We could be trampled to death by this rabble!"

"More likely we shall be lynched for calling them so," Mavreen argued, her face now free although Gideon still held her in a bear's grip as they were jostled to and fro. On the edge of laughter, Mavreen's voice trembled as she added, "Oh, dear, I fear poor Gerard will be most dreadfully alarmed for my safety."

"Your husband's alarm does not appear to have kept him waiting," said Gideon tartly when, five minutes later, they reached the street where the carriage should have been standing. "'Twould seem your Gerard has returned home without you."

He saw the flash of anger in Mavreen's eyes and said more gently:

"He could not know how long it might take us to rejoin him, Mavreen."

"That does not excuse him!" Mavreen cried, too hurt and annoyed to conceal her feelings. "How could Gerard be so . . . so . . . so ill mannered, so . . . so uncaring!"

"He would have known I would bring you safely home," Gideon vouchsafed in an attempt to console her.

"You!" Mavreen cried. "Why, for all Gerard knows, you and I may have become separated by the crowd, just as he was from us. And besides, as far as he is aware, you are no better than the stupid dandy he believes you to be."

"And therefore thinks you in no moral danger in my hands," said Gideon, "though hopefully man enough to protect you."

Mavreen's chin lifted as she glared back at Gideon with blazing eyes.

"So! Then I will give him cause to regret such assumption," she said furiously. Before Gideon realized her intention, she stood on tiptoe and kissed him fiercely on the mouth.

Had Mavreen's kiss been less passionate and less prolonged, Gideon might have found the strength to resist her. But unknown to her, he had been celibate far too long, wanting no woman but her and knowing only too well the folly of trying to imagine another was she. After her marriage to Gerard, he had attempted to drown her memory in other soft, perfumed bodies; in other delicate white arms; between other moist, warm thighs. But his hunger was for Mavreen, for her alone, and could not be assuaged.

Heedless of any passerby who might recognize them, heedless of the lights, the shouts, the sheer folly of such public exhibition, Gideon's arms encircled Mavreen's waist. Through the thin muslin gown he felt her body trembling beneath his touch.

As Gideon returned her kiss, Mavreen tried weakly to conjure up the voice of her conscience. But now memories of a past that did not include Gerard were flooding through her with fierce, angry insistence. Her desire to yield to Gideon became no less intense than his hunger for her. He covered her face with kisses, pressing her closer and closer against him.

"You are mine, my woman!" he whispered. "I love you, Mavreen. I need you. You belong to me."

Only when he drew away from her so that he could look into her eyes did she find the strength to deny not only him but herself too.

"No, Gideon, no!" she said. "I am not your woman, nor ever can be. I am Gerard's wife! I can never be yours again!"

18

1814 – 1815

GERARD, upon discovering Antoine safely tucked up in bed, regretted at once his precipitate behavior in leaving Mavreen in the care of Sir Peregrine. He was about to venture forth in search of her when he became aware of a dull throbbing in his head and realized that it was the onset of one of his migraines, brought on, he supposed, by his state of anxiety. With a sigh he sent a servant to summon Miss Gurney.

Davinia had already retired for the night. Hurriedly she pulled her daydress over her nightrobe and, conscious of the urgency of the summons, made no attempt to dress her hair in its customary prim style. At first Gerard did not notice the unusualness of her appearance as he lay back on the chaise longue, his eyes shut whilst the girl's cool hands stroked his forehead. But as the pain slowly dispersed and eventually disappeared, he looked up at her gratefully and was startled by the change in her.

"Why, Miss Gurney, how young you look, and how pretty. 'Tis your hair, I think," he murmured with genuine surprise. "It becomes you well, if I may say so. You should wear it loose more often."

He was quite unprepared for the painful blush

338

which spread across Davinia's face. Fearing that he had embarrassed her, he at once apologized for the personal aspect of his remark whereupon, to his great consternation, the girl burst into tears.

Nonplussed, he sat up and laid his hand upon her arm. She trembled violently. Quite misunderstanding the reason for it, Gerard said gently:

"How thoughtless I have been to call upon you at such a late hour. Doubtless you were already abed and now you are shivering with cold and fatigue. Please forgive me, my dear. I fear my demands upon you were most selfish!"

"It is I who needs forgiveness!" Davinia cried in a small choked voice, but before Gerard could question her, she had run from the room.

Mavreen's return put a speedy end to his bewilderment. On any other occasion he would have spoken of the strangeness of Davinia's behavior to Mavreen, but now he was concerned only in making amends for having left his wife in such inadequate care to find her own way home. Forgetting Davinia he hurried across to Mavreen and took her in his arms. Mavreen, hurt by Gerard's behavior and confused by her own, would have preferred to sleep alone that night, but Gerard was intent upon reassuring her of his devotion. He reiterated that it was his duty toward Antoine that had motivated him; that his deepest love was for Mavreen. She was not convinced but could see nothing to be gained by arguing the matter. She desperately desired to believe him and regain her trust in him. With such hopes in mind she welcomed him to her bed.

Lying in his arms later that night, she persuaded herself that her love for him was as deep and lasting as it had always been; that nothing had changed. Gerard had been a tender, thoughtful lover anxious to please her, falling asleep in her arms only when she had reassured him that he was completely forgiven for "abandoning her to the care of that popinjay!"

For the remainder of the year Mavreen took the utmost care to avoid any meeting with Gideon. She also attempted to put him completely from her thoughts.

But with the new year, a belated birthday present arrived for Tamarisk from him — a beautifully bound copy of Jane Austen's *Mansfield Park*. Tamarisk took it at once to show her mother, together with the letter he enclosed wishing her well and expressing a hope that he might call upon them.

To Tamarisk's chagrin Mavreen refused to be pinned down to issuing an invitation or to give good reason for her refusal. Tamarisk felt her mother was most unsympathetic to her wishes and selfishly unaware of her boredom.

The long days of winter dragged by but eventually brightened to spring and thence to early summer. An afternoon visit to the Princess came as a welcome relief to the uneventfulness of Tamarisk's life at Barre House.

"My life is become no less tedious than yours," she complained to Princess Charlotte as they walked together in the garden of Warwick House.

The young Princess regarded Tamarisk thoughtfully. There was considerable sympathy in her somewhat protuberant Hanoverian blue eyes.

"You are so pretty," she remarked, sighing. "I cannot think how you can be without a bevy of beaux! After all, Tamarisk, you are not limited as am I to Royal suitors!" She glanced at her young companion speculatively. "Do you ever regret that Lord Byron has married another?" she inquired.

Tamarisk shook her head, her cheeks coloring slightly at this mention of her one and only lover. She regretted she had given way to the longing to confide to a sympathetic Charlotte the details of her unfortunate liaison with the poet.

"You know that I never loved him," she replied simply. "I wish him well in his marriage to Annabella Milbanke. 'Tis rumored she is already with child."

"And he whom you did love?" Charlotte prompted. "Do you no longer see him?"

Tamarisk's color deepened. Haltingly she tried to describe her feelings for Perry. Charlotte, to her surprise, was remarkably understanding. She herself, she told Tamarisk, had experienced the strangest attractions to men much older than herself — to her uncle, the Duke of Sussex, for example.

"'Tis not unnatural that I should need someone to add excitement to my daily life, and if there are no young men, then I must

341

make do with old ones," she said, smiling.

Tamarisk sighed.

"I am convinced Perry was once my mother's lover," she confessed. "And would be still were *she* willing! But she dotes upon Papa and puts him first in all things. 'Tis on account of Papa's head pains that we so seldom entertain or go to parties. As for Papa . . . " she added bitterly " . . . he dotes upon my half-brother, and I sometimes feel I am quite superfluous in our household."

"At least you do have a mother who takes some interest in you," Charlotte spoke quietly. "Mine is somewhere on the Continent behaving, so I am informed, in an even more outrageous fashion than was her custom in England! I have promised my father I will cease all correspondence with her."

Happily, so the young Princess informed Tamarisk, her relationship with her father had somewhat improved. Moreover, she was corresponding, through a friend, with Prince Leopold of Saxe-Coburg and had invited him to visit her. Twenty-four years old, the tall, handsome young officer was, despite his youth, in charge of the Russian Cavalry. Charlotte had met him quite accidentally during the Tsar's visit to London. She had encountered Leopold on a back staircase of the Poulteny Hotel where she had called to see the Tsar's sister, the Grand Duchess of Oldenburg. She was instantly infatuated with the beautiful, dashing but impecunious young Prince, but they had occasion to meet only twice more before he was obliged to leave England to go to Vienna. Nevertheless, the romance had blossomed sufficiently to give Charlotte the courage to break her engagement to Prince William.

Unfortunately events on the Continent were making it impossible for Leopold to return to England as Charlotte had hoped. These events were so momentous that they could not be ignored.

From a letter she had received from Charles Eburhard, Tamarisk was aware that Napoleon, who had escaped from Elba in February, was now back in France with many battalions of the French Army rallied to his flag. True to his boast he reached Paris on the twentieth of March — within three weeks of arriving on French soil. The French King had fled to the Netherlands. The Allies were now massing in Belgium where the Duke of Wellington was poised to lead an attack upon the Emperor. He lacked the best of the British Army who were still in America or upon the high seas returning from thence — not to the peace they had expected when the war in the United States ended, but to renewed hostilities with France.

"However dangerous it may be, war does sound so exciting," Tamarisk remarked wistfully. "My grandfather related to me an account of the battle for the American city of Washington last August. 'Twas easy won and our troops set fire to all the city's important buildings, including the President's house where, 'twas said, they found a table set for dinner."

Charlotte nodded.

"So completely did we trounce the Americans that Philadelphia and New York were in positive terror of a further attack upon them," she said. "Papa informed me the people built fortifications all around New York and as many as fifteen thousand militia were stationed on Staten and Barn Islands, in Brooklyn, and on the farm country of Haarlem Heights."

"Had I been born a boy, I would have joined the navy rather than the army," Tamarisk mused. "Charles writes of such interesting experiences that I envy him more than I can say. Even Grandfather wishes he were young enough to have been part of the British flotilla which attacked Baltimore. Had *he* been there, we might not have lost that battle to the Americans."

"Nevertheless I am glad the war with America is over," Charlotte commented. "And I wish this tiresome war in Europe would reach a final conclusion so that Prince Leopold can visit me!" she said with a sigh. "I fear he is not proving quite so daring as I would have wished, for he doubts my father will approve our marriage and is fearful of approaching him on the subject."

Tamarisk was sympathetic.

"Charles suffers the selfsame lack of audacity," she said. "He reminds me ever of a puppy begging for a bone. If he were just to take me in his arms and kiss me without asking my permission . . . "

The two girls dissolved into merriment.

Forgetting their dissatisfaction with their feminine rôles in life, they imagined how bravely and persistently they would pursue the objects of their affections had they been men.

But the brief hours of happy companionship passed swiftly and with them Tamarisk's raised spirits. All too soon she was back within the confines of Barre House with nothing but her journal in which to confide her desperate longing for excitement — and love.

The war in France was however to provide her with a glimpse of both not two weeks after her visit to Charlotte. On Sunday, the eighteenth of June, the Duke of Wellington fought a bloody but victorious battle on the fields of Waterloo. Napoleon retreated to the Biscay coast, and on the eighth of July Louis XVIII was again restored to the throne. England was once more celebrating peace. The Prince Regent commanded a Royal performance at the King's Theater, and on this occasion Mavreen agreed to Tamarisk's request that they should attend.

It was a gala night. All London Society seemed to be gathered at the theater in their most brilliant plumage. Tamarisk wore a new gown hastily made for the occasion. The white satin of her petticoat was soft and silky against her skin, and the gold Brussels drapery and fringe of her dress sparkled in the lights as she moved. The gold on her green velvet train, like the diamonds in her white ostrich-feather headdress, enhanced the excited sparkle in her eyes as she gazed at the extravagant habiliments of the assembly. She was not surprised when the Baroness, whose box they were sharing, confided to Mavreen that the dress she herself wore had cost her a thousand guineas!

The great actor Edmund Kean seemed to excel in his performance that night. But Tamarisk's eyes were not upon London's idol. Whilst her mother and father listened entranced to Kean's impassioned voice, Tamarisk was watching the movements of the young man acting the part of page. With his long fair curls and the features of a young Greek god, he epitomized the Prince Charming of fairy tales, the Romeo of Shakespeare's great love story. As her heart quickened in delight, he seemed to her to be glancing more and more often in her direction. Upon one occasion she was certain that he smiled at her; upon another that he was actually singing to her when his part in the play demanded that he sing a ballad to the accompartment of his mandolin to entertain his lord.

She longed to know his name, but although in one of the intervals she inquired if other members of the cast were listed upon the program, the lesser actors were unnamed and she had to contain her curiosity. She wished sadly that there was one person to whom she could turn and say:

"He is very beautiful, is he not? I have never seen a young man more comely!"

But she knew her parents would disapprove of her interest in a common actor, no matter how accomplished or handsome he might be. Since her marriage, her mother scrupulously observed the conventions that governed the behavior of the titled and wealthy, with the exception of her 'friendship' toward Dickon and Rose and the rest of the Sale family. As for Papa, he made no secret of his objection to even this association with the lower classes.

"Servants are servants," he frequently commented, "and should be treated as such!" By which he meant there should be no familiarity with them.

Tamarisk sighed. With the single exception of the Sale family, her mother never defied Papa's wishes in anything and even tolerated the objectionable Antoine for his sake. It seemed her one objective was to make him happy, and to this end she often forfeited her own pleasures to live the secluded life he preferred.

Remembering the masked ball at Finchcocks and the soirées and drawing rooms her mother had held in the old days, Tamarisk reflected that their lives had been so much gayer before her parents' marriage. Her mother had had such a wonderful sense of fun and adventure. Everyday life became exciting when Mama was present. Tamarisk had admired and loved her more than anyone in the world and longed to grow up to be like her. And now, when at last it seemed as if Papa's head pains were becoming less frequent and less exhausting, he was planning to take them all to Compiègne for the remainder of the year.

There was little doubt that after her thoughtless escapades when her parents had last left her behind in London, they would not leave her alone again. Now she would be forced to live in dull retirement in the French countryside. At least in London there were rare moments, such as this evening, when she could dress herself in beautiful clothes and feel a part of the bright world of Society! She could ride every day in the park, albeit with the tiresome Antoine and dull Mr. Mumford, and hope that by some happy chance they would encounter Perry; or maybe meet some handsome young stranger with whom she could engage in flirtation. She envied Princess Charlotte who at least had her Prince Leopold to dream about, even if he had not yet come to England to claim her hand in marriage.

The play was drawing to an end and obviously Tamarisk was not the only person regretting it, for the young page was scarcely bothering to conceal his interest in her. Using her fan to conceal her face from her parents, Tamarisk permitted herself to bestow a smile upon him. If only she knew his name! It would be easy enough for him to discover hers. Her mother was a notable member of Society and a talking point in London drawing rooms. She was recognized whenever she appeared in public.

Wistfully Tamarisk mused on a Fate that had destined her to be born into a class which denied her so much entertainment. Had she been more lowly born, she might have made a brilliant career for herself upon the stage, she thought — become a second Mrs. Sarah Siddons — acclaimed not only by Royal personages but by the world. Many of those dull, tedious hours spent playing the piano-forte or embroidering her samplers might have been passed rehearsing her part in a play with — and why not? — her handsome young page taking the lead rôle opposite her!

In a daze of dreams Tamarisk returned home and wrote in her journal:

'*I am quite intrigued by a young man whose name I know not! Whose age I know not! Whose domicile I know not! I know only that he is almost as handsome as Perry and has the most beautiful of smiles. It would be vastly amusing to see him again and speak with him.*'

She wished fervently that she need not go to Compiègne. That wish was to be granted, although not even Tamarisk would have wanted it achieved at the cost — for the price of her remaining in London proved to be poor Aunt Clarrie's ill health.

By way of making his own celebration of the peace, Sir John had volunteered to take his wife, together with Tamarisk and Antoine, upon the river to ride in the paddle steamer *S.S. Marjory*. It was the first ever steam packet to ply to and from Gravesend. Only sixty-three feet long and twelve feet wide, the little boat had wooden paddles that drove her at a speed of seven knots. It was unfortunate that the July day, beginning so sunny and warm, ended with the most violent of thunderstorms. Despite every effort to protect poor Clarissa, she, like everyone else, was soaked to the skin by the time they reached home. Two days later she succumbed to the chilling and was so seriously ill that Sir John had two physicians and both night and day nurses in attendance upon her, and was in fear for her life.

When Sir John's footman called with news of Clarissa's serious condition, Mavreen was already partly packed for their impending departure to France, for Gerard was in a fever of impatience to be gone. With the advent of peace there was now no impediment to their simple crossing of the English Channel and no further likelihood of danger to threaten their safe arrival in France. He was like an eager boy waiting to go upon his holidays.

Mavreen, watching the enthusiasm glow in his face whenever he discussed their imminent journey, felt unable to broach the possibility of a curtailment. But she knew that if Aunt Clarrie were to die, she herself could not leave her father who would be inconsolable. For a week she continued to hope Clarissa would recover in time for them to depart on schedule. She spent several hours a day at Clarissa's bedside, watching the poor plump little frame shrivel to wraith-like proportions. Sir John was like a man demented. Clarissa was only semiconscious and her doctors could offer no real hope that she might survive the pneumonia that now plagued her lungs.

It became clear that there was no possible hope for her recovery before the proposed date of their departure. Gerard, now aware of the gravity of Clarissa's condition, agreed to postpone their leaving a further week. But still Clarissa clung to life as if she herself were unsure whether to cease the fight or continue to battle against her sickness.

"I cannot leave Father in this state," Mavreen was finally forced to confess to Gerard. "He is like a child clinging to me as if my faith alone convinces him Aunt Clarrie will live. You must go to Compiègne without us, my love. The children and I will follow the very instant she is better."

Gerard looked away unhappily.

"I do not wish to leave without you," he said simply. "I swore we should never be parted again and I meant that vow. I will remain in London with you."

Sensing his bitter disappointment Mavreen said quickly:

"I too have no wish for us to be parted, my love. But there is a vast amount of work you must attend to at the Château which cannot be ignored. It is duty as much as pleasure which takes you to France. And Gerard . . . " she added, seeing his hesitation, " . . . it is not as if by staying here with me you can assist in any way. You are not necessary to Father as am I. In many ways it will be easier for me to devote myself more fully to him and to Aunt Clarrie if I do not have you too to worry about!"

Gerard, his look of relief undisguised, put his arms around her and hugged her to him.

"No man has a more understanding wife," he said, kissing her. He sighed. "Poor Clarissa! I shall continue to pray for her. In the meanwhile, my darling, I will act upon your judgment and depart for Compiègne without further delay. As you say, there will be much there requiring my presence."

They discussed the possibility that Gerard might take Antoine with him. Mavreen would have been happy to have the boy gone, for she had come no nearer to liking the child and was often at pains to conceal her dislike. But somewhat to her surprise, Gerard desired that Antoine should remain with her. The boy had been pale and listless since an attack of scarlatina some weeks previously and Gerard felt a longer convalescence would give him a chance fully to recoup his strength before undertaking the long journey abroad.

Despite her own conflicting inclinations Mavreen made no further demur, reminding herself that no matter how sly and precocious the boy was, he was Gerard's son and she had long since steeled herself to put this salient fact before any other.

The child seemed to have an uncanny instinct for self-preservation. Young as he was, he knew better than openly to defy Mavreen; and if his father was present, he even appeared affectionate and eager for her approval. In fairness to Gerard, Mavreen could understand why he expected her to like his son and why he thought her unreasonable to complain of the boy's behavior. She dreaded the day, which she believed must surely come, when Gerard discovered for himself that the son he idolized had a spurious, malevolent character; one which seemed incapable of encompassing the sweet affections of a normal child. Even the outward show of devotion he gave to his father Mavreen was convinced was made to further his own interests. It was as if the natural springs of love had been curtailed by the deprivations of his childhood and by his mother's obsessive determination to bring him up as a Prince among paupers. He was now the supreme egoist.

No sooner had Gerard left for Compiègne than Antoine dropped his façade and became openly rebellious. He refused to apply himself to any of the studies the unhappy Alfred Mumford set him. He was dictatorial and insulting to the servants, ate only those foods he liked, and threw tantrums if he could not get his own way. He found ways of plaguing Tamarisk which in another small boy might have been no more than mischievous teasing of an older sister, but which Mavreen knew very well were carefully devised for the sadistic pleasure it gave him to see her distressed. When he upset an inkwell on Tamarisk's new house gown, he professed it to be an accident and Mavreen felt unable to mete out a punishment since she could not prove his carelessness was intentional. Such incidents forced Tamarisk to avoid the child whenever possible and it became her habit to accompany Mavreen on her daily visits to Aunt Clarrie.

Clarissa had now been ill for three weeks and at long last it began to look as if she might, after all, recover. The coma in which she had lain gave way to bouts of delirium alternating with spells of coherent speech. The physician informed an overjoyed Sir John that they could now hope for a slow but steady improvement.

Tamarisk, whose affection for the old woman was little less than Mavreen's, insisted upon spending time at Clarissa's bedside.

"Aunt Clarrie recognizes me now, Mama!" she told Mavreen, "and I am certain poor Grandfather would be glad of your company whilst I attend in the sickroom."

So it was that Tamarisk was quite alone one afternoon with Clarissa whilst Mavreen strolled in the garden with Sir John. The day nurse had welcomed a brief respite from her duties and left her patient in the care of her young relative.

For a while Clarissa conversed weakly but with intelligence, telling Tamarisk of the wild stormy night of her birth and the subsequent days when she had cared for Mavreen at The Grange in Sussex; of the devotion of the faithful Dickon and Rose; of Mavreen's slow recovery.

Tamarisk listened delightedly to the old woman's tales until suddenly she realized that Clarissa's conversation was no longer coherent, her sentences rambling from one event to another, her times and years and seasons lost in a confusion of memories.

" . . . so wild and unmindful of her reputation!" the old woman muttered. "Poor girl! She was mourning the death of her beloved Gerard . . . " She paused and her eyes closed for a moment. When she reopened them it was to look directly into Tamarisk's face.

"You can have no idea how frightened I was for you, Mavreen," she murmured. "Keeping company with that madcap highwayman! Even sharing his exploits! And in broad daylight too! When the pair of you held up your father's coach that afternoon, I thought I would surely die of shock!"

The frown on her forehead suddenly disappeared and she smiled — a young feminine smile of complicity.

"Mind you, my dear, I will concede your Gideon was a very handsome young man — and a gentleman for all his roguery. And not unlike Gerard to look at. But it would have broken your father's heart if he discovered you had taken a highwayman for a lover . . . and the infamous Gideon Morris with a price upon his head! You must take care, child. One day some farseeing person will penetrate his disguise and poor Sir Peregrine will find himself hanging from a gibbet . . . "

She continued to ramble, but Tamarisk was too shocked to listen. Her hands, ice cold, locked together on her lap as the import of Clarissa's words took hold of her. Aunt Clarrie, she realized, was reliving the past. Her mother had taken a highwayman for a lover and that man was Perry, alias Gideon Morris. Or was it the other way round? Instinct told her that the foppish Sir Peregrine was the fake; the highwayman the real man — the man she loved, with whom she had ridden and so much admired for his superb horsemanship! The man who talked of the countryside as if he were

355

intimate with Nature herself; the man she had always suspected was her mother's lover.

Tamarisk's heart beat furiously in her breast. Her excitement was intense as thoughts chased one another across her mind. How thrilling it must have been for her mother to ride beside Perry, holding up coaches and galloping away from danger to laugh and love the night away in his arms! Oh, how she envied her! How incomprehensible that her mother should have preferred to marry her father, the quiet, conventional Vicomte, rather than her dark, secret lover! And how simple now that she knew the truth to understand why Perry had rejected her, Tamarisk; why her mother had discouraged his visits to Barre House since her marriage.

Of one thing Tamarisk had no doubt: Mama was completely devoted to Papa. Was it possible nonetheless that she was unfaithful to him, she wondered?

The return of Clarissa's day nurse relieved Tamarisk of her vigil by the sickbed. As she descended the stairs to rejoin her mother and grandfather, she resolved to keep her newfound knowledge to herself. Instinct told her that her mother would not be at all happy to know her secret past had been revealed to her daughter. Maybe one day, Tamarisk thought, she and her mother could discuss the past openly. For now she contented herself by confiding her discovery to her journal. This she kept in the secret drawer in her bureau together with her private possessions.

For some reason she would have been hard put to explain, she had retained the letters she had received from Charles Eburhard. They were tied up with blue ribbon and hidden with her other keepsakes.

They were, after all, the only love letters Tamarisk had so far received in her young life. Although she felt no sentimental attachment to Charles, she admired and envied him. His latest letter described the excitement of the July day when he witnessed the sailing of the warship *Bellerophon* from Rochefort Harbor. Her destination was the tiny island of St. Helena in the South Atlantic to which she was carrying the defeated Emperor Napleon.

'*It must have been a bitter moment for Bonaparte,*' Charles wrote, '*when our Prince Regent refused him asylum in England, although surely 'twas unlikely we would trust that revolutionary spirit of his! Our crew were jubilant and in high spirits, but I felt a moment of pity for the man as his ship passed ours, taking him to exile on an island so remote that escape, even for him, must be impossible.*'

His letter ended, as was now becoming his habit, with a winsome paragraph expressing his hope that Tamarisk had not quite forgotten him; that she would make time in her busy life to pen him a line to reassure him of her friendship. This, he said, must suffice until his duties could be laid aside, freeing him to call

357

upon her once again to assure her in person of his undying love.

Though Tamarisk could not return his sentiments, she was nevertheless grateful to him for adding to her life one small spark of excitement and adventure. Meanwhile she had not forgotten the young actor who had caught her eye at the King's Theater.

In the same way as Charles's letters comforted her, her flirtation with the actor meant no more nor less than small recompense for Perry's disinterest. It was Perry whom she loved — whom she would always love, although she was now beginning to accept that he would never love her. If she was to have any romance in her life, she decided, it would not be with Perry nor yet with the absent Charles. It would have to be with her handsome, unknown admirer.

She took the program of the evening's entertainment, 'borrowed' from her mother, and hid it securely with her journal in her secret drawer.

19

1815 – 1816

ALTHOUGH Clarissa had fully recovered by the end of the summer, Mavreen's intention to follow Gerard to France was precluded by a letter from him announcing that he would shortly be returning home. There was a severe outbreak of smallpox in the district, he said, and he did not wish Antoine to be brought into contact with the disease. Unlike Tamarisk, the boy had not been vacinated to protect him and Gerard was unwilling to risk subjecting his son to such a fatal hazard.

Mavreen took her small family, which included Sir John and the convalescent Clarissa, to the quiet country air at Finchcocks. Gerard joined them there in the autumn, and shortly after his arrival they returned to Barre House for the Christmas celebrations.

London, however, was not in festive mood. The acute financial depression that had gripped England since the end of the war was bringing many to the edge of ruin. The *Gazette* was filled with bankruptcy notices and tradesmen's lists of bad debts. The banks closed their doors and stopped payments.

"Hardship is striking rich and poor alike," remarked Sir John, for once pessimistic. "Cotton spinners in Lancashire and on the Clyde, hardware workers in Birmingham and ironmolders at Merthyr Tydfil are all hard hit. And so too are the Spitalfields silk weavers, the Leicestershire stockingers, and the Nottinghamshire hosiers. All are hungry, angry and clamorous. Servants are being dismissed in numbers that must horrify their like lest their employers too cannot keep them in service."

His pronouncements were far from exaggerated. By early spring Beau Brummel had fled the country because of his debts; Sir William Beechey, the artist, was rumored to have been begging for a settlement of his account with the Royal household; art prices had fallen to a level previously unknown; and the playwright Sheridan was said to be dying of privation.

Few, rich or poor, were unaffected by the economic climate. Mavreen, who had heard no word from Gideon for some long time, feared that he too could be facing the devaluation of his assets. His apparent absence from London Society lent credence to this supposition.

Unknown to Mavreen, Gideon was in fact sojourning with Percy Shelley in a house in Bishopsgate on the edge of Windsor Forest. Mary Godwin, with whom the young poet had eloped to the Continent the previous year, was now on the point of birthing a child. When the baby was subsequently born in January, Shelley insisted that Gideon become the child's godfather. Gideon had loaned him a considerable sum of money to pay some of his debts and Shelley consequently looked upon the older man as one of his true friends.

But when the Shelleys invited Gideon to go with them to Geneva, he at once declined. Despite the fact that he was without interest or purpose to keep him in England, still he could not bring himself to leave the country.

Although a full eighteen months had passed since he had been in Mavreen's company, their last meeting had given him cause to worry about her. He was convinced that she was far from happily married. He knew from the gossip of mutual friends that she was a devoted and attentive wife. There were few hostesses who had not at some time or another received a refusal of an invitation from Mavreen on account of her husband's migraines. Because of Gerard's health, she had withdrawn from the hectic round of entertainments. He knew also of Clarissa's illness and had hoped in vain that he might be invited to Finchcocks when the family moved there in the autumn. Mavreen's persistent silence encouraged his suspicion that her marriage was far from perfect. If her relationship with her husband was fully rewarding, he surmised, she would have no cause to fear *his* hold upon her. If she could trust herself to be indifferent and aloof, there would be no reason to keep physical distance between them.

Nevertheless he respected her disinclination to pursue their friendship and made no effort to encounter her. It was not his wish to endanger her present happiness, however precarious he felt that to be. Common sense told him that he should do his utmost to forget her once and for all; to remove himself totally from the past and, if possible, begin a new life — maybe take a wife and beget a family before he was too old to do so. Yet still he could not take any steps that would put him beyond Mavreen's reach were she ever to need him. He saw such behavior on his part as weakness, but even this knowledge could not persuade him to sever himself irrevocably. His life in London no longer held meaning or excitement for him. Its lack of purpose depressed him beyond measure and had led to his visit to the Shelleys. Now that they were departing for the Continent he realized that he must find some other way to fill the hours of the day; and perhaps even less easily, the lonely hours of the night.

Gideon was not alone in his mood of uneasiness and depression. Mavreen and Tamarisk were finding little to occupy their time. Gerard's migraines were recurring and the doctors could advise only rest and quiet as a cure. He spent many hours in a darkened room neither sleeping nor reading nor requiring entertainment of any kind. Sympathetic though each was to his suffering, which they knew to be intense, neither Mavreen nor Tamarisk could sit silently hour by hour holding his hand and soothing his brow as did the quiet, patient Quaker girl. Their restless spirits demanded physical and mental activity, and since Gerard's condition did not allow the entertaining of friends, they were forced to turn to one another for companionship. But they had drifted apart to a degree where they seemed like strangers to each other.

Mavreen could not understand Tamarisk's

remoteness. Knowing nothing of her daughter's discovery of her past Mavreen was hurt and disappointed by Tamarisk's rejection of any intimacy between them. Yet she was convinced Tamarisk was as lonely and bored as was she.

Tamarisk was now eighteen years of age and no longer a child. Although she had vaguely suspected that her mother and Perry may once have been lovers, she had never really believed it, and she was deeply shocked to have those suspicions confirmed by Clarissa's ramblings. Reluctantly she was forced to admit to herself that her mother could hardly be blamed for loving Perry, yet she condemned her for marrying another man.

Must Mama have every man at her feet? she reflected bitterly. But for Mama, Perry might have returned her love! When she herself found a lover, she would take good care that he did not fall under Mama's spell!

In an attempt to overcome Tamarisk's reticence, Mavreen endeavored to share in her interests, now apparently much concentrated upon the stage. She accompanied Tamarisk whenever possible to the theater. Baroness Eburhard was always ready to offer them seats in her box at Drury Lane.

Tamarisk lived for these evenings. She now knew the name of the young actor, Leigh Darton, who so engrossed her thoughts. She had had no occasion to speak to him, but she was in no doubt that he looked for her as she looked for him, their eyes exchanging glances that clearly spoke their interest in one another.

She was convinced that one day, somehow, they would meet. She wondered if he would fall in love with her. She found the prospect exciting. Her heart beat swiftly each time he made an appearance upon the stage, and more so when he looked toward her. The color rushed to her cheeks whenever he smiled. From behind her fan she returned those secret looks, made the more intriguing by virtue of the necessity to conceal her emotions from her mother and the Baroness.

Whenever she could she pushed the memory of Perry to the back of her mind. When she could not she reminded herself that he had forfeited the right to her exclusive devotion. For the first time ever he had failed to present her with a Christmas gift, nor had he called to give her the Season's or birthday greetings.

Hardening her heart against Perry, she opened it wide to daydreams about her new admirer and to the possibility of sharing with him all the glamor and excitement of a life in the theater. She would be Juliet to his Romeo; Ophelia to his Hamlet; and they would have all the world's audiences at their feet!

Tamarisk longed to confide her feelings to her only close friend and confidante, Charlotte. But the Princess, who had finally become engaged to her romantic Prince Leopold, was now busily occupied in preparations for their marriage.

This Royal event took place on the second of May at Carlton House. Despite Charlotte's plea that her friends should be present, the Prince Regent refused her request and invited a large assemblage of distinguished guests of his own choosing. He was determined upon his only child's wedding being a glittering and elaborate occasion and one in which the public was to be allowed a share of entertainment.

"Doubtless he hopes to regain some popularity thereby!" the Baroness remarked shrewdly.

"We shall observe everything from the Mall," Mavreen told her daughter, seeing her disappointment when no invitation was forthcoming. "I will order the coachman to be ready for an early departure so that we may obtain a place of advantage. Do you know, Tamarisk, I can recall in detail watching with dear Aunt Clarrie for the Princess of Wales's arrival for her wedding to Charlotte's father. I was younger than you are now. How disappointed I was at first sight of the poor soul!"

But there was no disappointment for Tamarisk when the day dawned fine and sunny and she set off with her family from Barre House. Their coach found station in Pall Mall from whence they could obtain an excellent view of Prince Leopold when he drove from Clarence House. They would have equally good outlook upon the bride too when she was driven from Buckingham House to her wedding at Carlton House later that evening.

There was plenty to entertain them throughout the day. As the size of the gathering crowds increased, so too came other carriages with friends with whom they could gossip and pass the time. Gerard, free from migraine, was much of the while pointing out matters of interest to Antoine. The boy for once was displaying a normal child's happy excitement. He was genuinely admiring of the magnificent team of elegant matching gray horses being taken to Clarence House for Prince Leopold's inspection. Soon afterward, the Prince himself, in the splended uniform of a General of the British Army, passed by them on his way to pay a morning visit to Charlotte and to inspect the new traveling carriage which had been built for them.

So eager were the people to see the bridegroom that there was a near stampede when he tried to leave his curricle. But although from their position in the Mall they heard the roar of the massive crowds, they were too far away to view Leopold when he appeared on the balcony of Clarence House.

To the delight of all, a full guard of honor of the Grenadier Guards, preceded by the band of the Coldstream Guards in full dress, marched from St. James's Park into the courtyard of Carlton House. The crowds were further entertained by a troop of the Life Guards trotting down Pall Mall, followed by two Bow Street magistrates at the head of fifty police officers and constables.

Since the wedding itself was not to take place until the evening, they decided to return to Barre House on foot to partake of luncheon, leaving the carriage to secure their vantage point until their return at seven of the clock. By now the crowds were so dense that Gerard had the

366

greatest difficulty in securing a passage for his family.

"Beware of pickpockets!" he cautioned. "For they will be rife in such conditions!"

By virtue of their persistence, they obtained in due course a perfect viewing of the young Princess. She was seated beside her grandmother, the Queen. Her two senior aunts, Augusta and Elizabeth, sat opposite her as she rode down the Mall to the cheers of the multitudes.

The crowds were in no way disappointed by the bride whose gown truly befitted a fairy-tale Princess. Her dress was of transparent silk net. It covered a white and silver slip and was embroidered all over with shimmering silver lamé in a design of shells and bouquets. The sleeves and neck were trimmed with Brussels point lace and the manteau, with its long white and silver train, was fastened with a diamond ornament.

Wearing diamond rosebuds around her head, the diamond necklace and earrings given her by her father and a diamond armlet presented by Prince Leopold, Charlotte glittered even more brightly than the evening star.

"Oh, I hope she will be happy!" Tamarisk cried as the strains of the national anthem reached them faintly from Carlton House where the Princess's bridegroom now awaited her.

Sensing the wistful envy in her daughter's voice, Mavreen put an arm about her shoulders.

"Soon enough it will be your turn, my dearest," she said. "And you shall have a gown every bit as beautiful, I promise!"

Mavreen felt suddenly guilty that she had made so little effort to find Tamarisk a husband. But circumstances had seemed to conspire to curtail the regular round of activities that would have enabled the girl to establish her place in Society. Gerard's ill health made entertainment at home undesirable, and since he was unhappy if she went out without him, she had not been free to escort Tamarisk to the balls and soirées to which they were often invited.

She had not felt Tamarisk's needs to be pressing in view of her youth and her seeming disinterest in young men, but now, suddenly, she was aware that her daughter was eighteen and should have a home, a family of her own. She wondered how young Charles Eburhard's postal courtship was progressing. Tamarisk did not show her his letters and she had not demanded to see them as was her parental right. Although Charles was still very young and scarcely to be considered handsome, he had impressed Mavreen with his steady rise up the promotional ladder in the navy and by his unquestionable courage. The boy's character seemed to show stability and reliability and he would make a good husband for her willful, tempestuous, and emotional daughter. Hopefully his duties at sea would lessen now the wars were over and he would return to England where he could more ably conduct his courtship. The Baroness had long since informed her of Charles's determination to marry none other than Tamarisk.

As they made their way home, Antoine asleep

368

against Gerard's shoulder, Gerard's free hand enfolding her own, Mavreen reviewed the past three years of her own life. A few weeks ago she and Gerard had celebrated the third anniversary of their wedding. In all honesty they could not be said to have been the happiest years of her life, she reflected sadly. Yet she could find no valid reason for thinking thus. Her love for Gerard had in no way lessened, even if the substance had changed in some subtle way and had become more maternal. Doubtless Gerard's continued ill health had brought about this alteration to what had once been a predominantly passionate relationship.

Looking back to their youth Mavreen could see now that the very transience of their encounters had lent them a spurious excitement that could not continue within the permanence of married life. Yet foolishly, she now saw, she had believed without question that to live side by side with the man she loved must ensure happiness, requiring only that her love be returned for Utopia to be theirs.

Why then, she thought, had life become mundane — even dull upon occasion? She had learned to live with Gerard's first attention centered upon Antoine and steadfastly she refused to allow jealousy of his child to come between them. Antoine's presence had not enhanced the marriage. Yet how different might have been the effect of the arrival of a son had *she* been able to provide Gerard with the heir he so desperately wanted! Her barrenness made Antoine's unwelcome presence within the family necessary; and for this she could not lay blame at Gerard's door. Born to nobility, Gerard could not disregard his obligations to his heritage, and so in fairness she had always felt obliged to support him in his acceptance of his son.

As for Tamarisk, Mavreen thought, *their* daughter had little import for Gerard, and although he showed her a gentle kindness and affection he took no interest in her education and development as he did in Antoine's. He believed, as did most men, that females were not required to be scholars.

"Educating females is a waste of time and money!" he pronounced to Mavreen's astonishment and disbelief. "A man should be capable of doing his own thinking, forming his own opinion, and has no need of a wife giving voice to hers!"

Indignantly Mavreen pointed out to him that he had chosen her for his wife despite the fact that her father had seen fit to educate her as a man rather than a woman.

"That was an unfortunate whim of your father's — probably brought about because he had no son," was Gerard's infuriating reply. "I love you in spite of your intelligence, *mon amour*, and not because of it!"

With an effort Mavreen had remained calm. She tried to reason logically with him.

"Your mother was a very intelligent woman," she said quietly. "And you respected her for it, Gerard."

"Maman," replied Gerard, "was early widowed

as you know and was forced to shoulder the responsibilities of a man."

"As indeed could happen to Tamarisk," concluded Mavreen. "What then, Gerard, if she has not been taught to reason for herself?"

"I would be at hand to advise her," he argued stubbornly.

"And were you, too, to die?"

"Then she would have you to turn to."

"But Gerard, you are proving my point. Women cannot always be sure of having a man to think for them."

"But you do have a husband, my love! So permit me to decide for you what is best for our children."

So angry had Mavreen felt at this illogical and obtuse rejoinder, she had come close to losing her temper from sheer frustration. Fortunately, perhaps, Gerard had been overcome by the fire in her eyes and the bright color in her cheeks. Declaring that she never looked more ravishing than when she was angry, he put an end to the argument by taking her to bed.

A woman had much to learn about wifehood, Mavreen thought, more aware at this moment than she had ever been before of the change wrought in herself since her marriage. Self-control, never one of her strongest traits, was all too oft required of her. She laid no blame at Gerard's door for her failure always to be content in her conjugal state. She believed herself different from other women in her inability to combine her attitude of mind with the desires of her body. But that rebellious and independent mind of hers refused to accept that loving a man must necessitate agreement with his opinions: Whilst her body could and did submit, her will would not, and this division of herself was the main cause of her dissatisfaction.

Perhaps, she thought, as the carriage made its way out of the Mall and toward Barre House, Gerard was right and women were the happier for remaining ignorant.

It was Gerard who suggested they might enjoy a brief sojourn at The Grange in Sussex. The late spring weather continued so fine and sunny, he thought they might all benefit from the country air. Mavreen was overjoyed at the prospect. They had not visited the little manor house since their honeymonth, and although Dickon and Rose who were caretaking had written regularly to say all was in good order there, she longed to renew her close association with the Sale family and the home surroundings of her childhood.

Tamarisk was less enthusiastic. Departure from London would mean no hope of seeing Perry or her young actor at the theater. But she too longed to discard the trappings of London finery and to run, as would Mavreen, barefoot through the dewy grass, watch the apple blossom falling in the orchards, greet the arrival of the new calves and lambs. At The Grange she would be permitted to help Rose bake bread, her arms elbow deep in yeasty-smelling dough. And best of all she could ride freely over the meadows and Downs with no more irksome companion than one of the rosy-cheeked, red-haired Sale boys as grooms.

Davinia Gurney and the pale-faced Alfred Mumford were given a holiday. The tutor decided upon a visit to his relatives in Canterbury; the prim Miss Gurney upon a visit to her aunt, Mistress Fry, who was far from well.

"I shall supervise Antoine myself," Gerard announced. "He is so well behaved these days that I have only to state my wishes and he treats them as commands."

Mavreen, ignoring Tamarisk's gasp of dissent, nodded her agreement and hurried away to begin preparations for their departure.

For the last two weeks of the month of May all their hopes of a perfect holiday were realized. Each day the sun shone bright and warm and they basked in the eager welcome given them by Dickon and Rose and their three sturdy young sons.

They went together on Plough Monday to watch the blessing of the ploughs in the village church of St. Augustine, and afterward followed the parson and his parishioners out into the sunshine to witness the blessing of the fields. The parson, a jolly, round-faced man of middle years, had replaced the previous elderly cleric who, coming from his birthplace in Yorkshire, was talked of as a foreigner and indeed had never been able to master the Sussex dialect. The Reverend Cripps, who came from nearby Bishopstone, was happy to turn a blind eye to smugglers and was known to keep an excellent cellar which he liberally dispensed to all callers at the Vicarage.

The last occasion upon which Mavreen had entered the little church of St. Augustine, she realized, was to witness Dickon's wedding to Rose — eight years ago. Yet standing beneath the lychgate, it suddenly seemed as yesterday. How brightly the sun had shone that day too; how joyous the congregation! How typical of Gideon to appear uninvited and then monopolize her for the day — and night! With what gusto he would have enjoyed today's ceremony, his rich baritone raised above all others, a wicked smile in his eyes as he sang to the Lord to 'Protect us from the thieves of the night'.

Despite herself, Mavreen smiled at her thoughts. No moment spent in Gideon's company was ever dull. Searching her memory for the day's ending after Dickon's wedding was over, she recalled how pleasurably she and Gideon had made love. Gideon had been a dominant but tender lover. They had talked far into the night, discussing the wedding ritual. Gideon expressed his opinion that no parson nor yet the Archbishop of England nor even the King himself could make two people man and wife if they were not suited to be so.

"I believe that all true loves are predestined," he had vouchsafed; "that we cannot fight our destiny. If when we meet it face to face, we open our hearts and accept it, only then can a man and woman truly be called wed in the eyes of God."

She had not disputed his opinion. It matched

her own belief that she and Gerard were destined to meet and love one another. She had never lost that faith throughout the long years of separation. Only eight years later did she realize that Gideon had spoken from a heart filled with love for her, that he believed they were destined to meet and be wed. Yet if God fashioned one man for one woman, how then could Fate have destined her for Gerard, as she believed, and for Gideon, as he believed? Clearly no one could be so certain in opining of their own Destiny.

She would have liked to discuss this conundrum with Gerard. But he had not come to church with her, preferring to remain at home to rest in the garden where she had left him reading Sir Walter Scott's new novel *Guy Mannering*. But even were Gerard here, she thought sadly, Gideon was a subject that must not be mentioned between them. Hopefully the day would come when she could tell Gerard about her former lover. She wanted to share everything with him — even her past. Silently she vowed there would be no other secrets between them.

But within a few days, the necessity to lie to him was forced upon her. Dickon, ever as discreet as he was faithful, brought her news she could not impart to Gerard — news of the impending trial of an unnamed highwayman at Lewes Assizes.

"'Tis talked of everywhere!" Dickon said. "No one knows who he be. The prisoner has steadfastly refused to give his name since he was apprehended in the very act of robbery on Ashdown Forest. 'Twill mean pressing if he does not speak, and though many have been questioned, none know his identity." He glanced meaningfully at Mavreen. "'Tis said he is a gentleman, above ordinary man's height, dark haired, and of middle years. 'Tis also said that he shows no concern for his condition but keeps up a merry conversation with his gaolers, any one of which would willingly release him were it in their power, so well liked is their prisoner!"

There was little need for Dickon to elaborate further. Gideon's name was as good as spoken and Mavreen now used it openly.

"If Gideon Morris is to stand trial for his life, Dickon, *I must be there at the hearing!* I have money which you, Dickon, must use as you think best in his interest. Bribery may secure his escape before the trial. It has succeeded many times in the past. When is the trial to be?"

"Day after tomorrow," Dickon replied.

"Then we have no time to lose!" Mavreen cried. "Go at once, Dickon, and see what can be done for him. I myself will change my clothes and go to Lewes gaol where I will demand to see the prisoner. They will not refuse me the privilege when I say who I am."

Dickon raised a cautionary hand.

"'Twould not be proper for the Vicomtesse de Valle to befriend a thief!" he said. "Nor could you keep secret your identity. You would be instantly recognized in these parts!"

It was on the tip of Mavreen's tongue to reply that she cared not one jot for her reputation, but the next instant she knew that Dickon was right — it was not her name but Gerard's which must be protected.

"Then I will go incognito!" she declared. "'Twill not be the first time I have passed myself off in disguise — as a man if needs be!"

Still Dickon frowned.

"Such action now could be the prisoner's undoing. It is most certainly his wish to remain unnamed. If you, a friend, call to visit him, all will realize he is not unknown to *you*. You would be questioned, perhaps even imprisoned yourself for not revealing the name of a felon. Upon oath you could not deny you know him, and to withhold such knowledge might bring the wrath of the Justices upon your head. If he heard of you being in trouble, Mr. Morris would confess his name. Few men would risk pressing without good reason to conceal their identity. No, I fancy a visit to him would give him no pleasure."

It was a long speech but filled with shrewd wisdom. Knowing her so well, Dickon had obviously anticipated her first impulsive reaction to his news and thought wisely for her good as well as Gideon's.

"You are my dear friend," she said softly, putting an arm about his shoulders. "And being so, advise me then what can I do?"

"There is little, I fear," replied Dickon. "Mayhap you could attend the trial disguised if you so desire. But meanwhile I will call upon certain friends of mine, all smugglers once, who, for sufficient reward, may be willing to attempt a

377

rescue. When the trial is over, the prisoner will be conducted back to the prison. An ambush, if 'tis well planned, may succeed by virtue of the fact that 'twould be totally unexpected."

"*May* succeed!" Mavreen echoed. "But if it does not, Dickon, he might suffer pressing!" White-faced, she thought with horror how Gideon would be laid on the bare ground, naked, his arms and legs drawn with cords fastened to the several corners of the room. Body irons and stones would be laid upon his body until he could bear no more and the weight increased day by day until he died.

"There's been no pressing these last twenty years or more," Dickon broke in on her thoughts. "Most likely 'twould be a hanging from the gallows if they find him guilty!"

But the thought of Gideon hanging on some high, windy hill — on Ashdown Forest in all probability, near the scene of his crime — was little better. It haunted Mavreen's mind to such an extent that on each of the two nights before the trial she awoke screaming in her nightmare. Gerard did his best to soothe her, begging her to relate what troubled her dreams. But soaked in perspiration, shivering and feverish by turns, Mavreen could only weep silently into his shoulder and pray that her dream would not become reality.

Dickon's continued absence from the house was explained away by a false account of a horse he had heard was for sale in the neighboring county of Kent. A further lie was required from Mavreen when she declared her intention to go shopping in Lewes on the day of the trial.

"'Tis a nonsensical notion," Gerard remarked when he heard it. "On a day when the Assizes are held, there's no room even to pass safely in the streets! Besides, it has started to rain. 'Tis sheer folly!"

Tamarisk, sensing her mother's agitation and impatience to be upon her way without further question, was well aware of her motives. She too had heard rumors of the trial of the unnamed highwayman and her quick mind had leapt to the obvious conclusion. She thrilled to the thought that Perry's highwayman days were not, after all, that long past; that his affluent financial state had not precluded the quick, dangerous gains of the highway robber. But she dared not reveal her knowledge to her mother lest she forbid her to go to Perry's aid. Though unaware as yet of how she might conceivably assist him, nevertheless she was determined upon his rescue at all costs — even if it meant sacrificing her very life.

"It is my intention to spend the day at Owlett's Farm," she announced casually. And when no one questioned her intent she went out to the stables to saddle her horse, her father's pistol firmly secured in its holster about her waist.

Mavreen took the curricle, insisting upon her ability to drive herself. She knew that Gerard was irritated by her defiance of his wishes but was resigned to his ill humor. Beneath her cloak she was attired in the rough, homespun dress of a farmer's wife. Her fashionable bonnet was quickly replaced by a mobcap once she was out of sight of The Grange.

Leaving the curricle at an hostelry on the outskirts of the town she hurried on foot toward the Court House, unnoticeable amongst the crowds that had gathered to hear the trial. The press of eager spectators was so great that men and women jostled and pushed at her elbows as they fought for a good viewing point in the public gallery. Many had brought food and wine with them and all were clearly looking forward to the day's entertainment.

Although it was a long time since Mavreen had had occasion to speak the language of the common people, her knowledge of the Sussex dialect now stood her in good stead, her neighbors on either side being anxious to talk. Brief though her replies were, her voice gave no cause for suspicion. She, like Gideon himself, must remain unnamed and unremarked this day.

It seemed an eternity before the court was hushed as the legal dignitaries began to arrive. One by one the seven lawyers engaged by the Crown for the prosecution took their seats in the body of the court. The jury, consisting of twenty men, was sworn in and sat down to one side of the court. The clerk called for silence, and the two Assize judges, bewigged and impressively robed, walked to their seats on the dais above the floor. The clerk stood beneath them.

"Call in the prisoner!"

The crowd which had been quiet now rose to their feet in their anxiety to catch sight of the hero of the day's proceedings. Mavreen, who

380

was ill placed behind a tall, burly farmer, was unable to see the prisoner now being led into the dock. Around her, comments were many and detailed.

"He do be a handsomer man than my Master!"

"They've chained his hands lest he try escaping!"

"That be a laementable purty neckcloth he's awearin'!"

"See how he smiles for all they're agoin' to 'ang 'im!"

In an agony of frustration she stood on tiptoe and would have overbalanced had not a strong arm steadied her.

She turned her head and found herself looking straight into the quizzical gaze of Gideon Morris. He, too, was attired in rough laborer's clothes.

Speechless, she continued to stare at him disbelievingly.

"And what brings you here, Mavreen?" he inquired. "I'd not have thought *you* someone to find pleasure in today's events!"

"Pleasure!" Mavreen gasped, the pallor of her cheeks now changing to an angry red. "Why, I thought the prisoner was . . . "

Gideon's hand closed over her mouth. Gently he eased her to the back of the gallery. His face was unbelievably gentle as he said softly:

"Ah, now at last I am beginning to understand. *You thought I was the unfortunate wretch in the dock!*"

Mavreen nodded. Now Gideon's eyes twinkled as he teased her.

381

"And you wished to see me sent to the gallows!"

"Oh, Gideon!" Mavreen protested. "You know very well if 'twas really you, I'd not have let them hang you, much as you deserve to swing!"

"And how, pray, would you prevent it?"

"You think I would not at least attempt to save you?" she asked, her eyes flashing. "Why, even now Dickon is somewhere in the streets with men paid to effect an escape for you — I mean for the prisoner — as he goes back to . . ."

The look on Gideon's face brought her to a faltering halt. His hand gripped her arm.

"'Tis the truth you speak, Mavreen?" he asked. "For this could matter a great deal to me. That poor fellow in the dock once saved my life. I'll not reveal his name, for he is a married man and if he be convicted by name his estate will be forfeit to the Crown. I came here today in the vain hope that somehow I could assist him. But if the stout Dickon has a plan and men to put it into effect, then I doubt I could do better by myself."

"I cannot tell you of Dickon's plan for I know no detail — only that he is paying men to effect a rescue. But Gideon, how came you to hear your friend was on trial?" she inquired curiously. "Lewes is a long way from London!"

"As well I know! One of my servants informed me. Years ago he was a footpad before I took him into my service and he knew I owed this fellow my life. I had held up a coach in Barnet and one of the postilions shot me. I fell from my horse and would have been captured but for the timely intervention of my rescuer. With the same idea as myself, he had been awaiting the coach further along the highway, not knowing, of course, that I was ahead of him. When he heard shots he guessed what had transpired, and instead of galloping off to save his own skin he came forward to save mine. He took me up behind him on his horse, carried me off to his home where I remained until my wound was healed. I'd give a deal to be able to save *his* life this day!"

"Oh, Gideon!" Mavreen said weakly. "Will the day ever come when you do not surprise me? I had never thought it possible to meet you here — a free man. I was so certain 'twould be you in the dock. Dickon too was convinced. The description of the man exactly fitted you. Moreover, I'd had no word from you these past twenty months and you were not seen about London. Then, too, there is this terrible depression affecting so many men's wealth, and putting all together I had no difficulty imagining you had returned to your old ways and haunts. Sussex, after all, is one of your territories, is it not?"

"Was!" Gideon corrected. "I've not robbed a coach since I last did so with you at my side, Mavreen!"

The angry shushing from the people around them caused them to cease their talk. Moreover, the trial was now reaching its conclusion. The unhappy highwayman had been caught with his loot still upon his person. He offered no defense and his guilt was not in doubt. Despite his remaining mute as to his identity, he was convicted of felony and sentenced to be hung four days later.

One lusty farmer's wife nearby exhorted her husband to take note of the day and time of the hanging lest they should miss the prospect of a day's outing with the spectacle of the hanging by way of free entertainment. But her husband, obviously wiser than she, said:

"Adone-do with your fussing, Missus. The prisoner be a gentleman if ever I did see one, and no hangman's rope'll hang him if he do have five hundred pounds at his command."

"Is that true?" Mavreen asked Gideon as they left the Court House. Gideon shrugged.

"We'll know soon enough how well Dickon has placed his bribes — and there are few men honest enough in these hard times to refuse a sovereign or two."

"I told him to discount the cost," Mavreen said.

The rain was cascading out of the skies as Gideon steered her toward the Star Inn where they could take shelter and wait for such news as might be forthcoming. In a darkened corner where they were less likely to be observed, they drank mulled wine to warm them and ate a goodly serving of game pie to keep up their spirits. An hour or two passed swiftly enough as each told the other of the happenings in their lives since last they had met.

"Was Gerard content to let you come to my

384

trial?" Gideon asked curiously. "And in such attire?"

Mavreen laughed.

"These clothes were hidden beneath my cloak when I left home," she explained. "As for Gerard, he believes me to be shopping."

Understandably enough, the inn was packed with people who had attended the trial. The atmosphere was cheerful and noisy until a sudden outcry by the door brought about an uproar as the word spread — the prisoner had escaped!

Elbowing his way through the gossiping crowd, Gideon was able to speak at firsthand with the messenger who brought the news. Within minutes he was back at Mavreen's side, his face radiant with pleasure.

"'Tis true!" he said, drawing Mavreen to her feet and hugging her. "The fellow saw it happen with his own eyes. A band of ruffians jumped the wagon taking the prisoner back to gaol. The constables guarding our friend never so much as fired a shot — due to Dickon's bribes, I'll warrant. There were two horses waiting saddled in a gateway, one mounted, he said, by a ginger-headed fellow with a mask about the lower half of his face. The second horse was for the prisoner. They galloped off together toward the Downs and that was the last seen of them!"

Mavreen sat down on the oak settle, her legs buckling with relief.

"They'll not be caught!" she said. "For that would be Dickon himself escorting your friend, and he knows a hundred hiding places from his smuggling days. Oh, Gideon, I am so glad — almost as glad as I would have been had you been the prisoner!"

Gideon, who had remained standing, now took her hand and held it to his lips in a courtly manner quite unbefitting their appearances.

"I owe you much," he said softly. "You have paid the debt that was owing for my life, Mavreen. And I thank you too for your courage in coming to my aid today when you believed 'twas I destined for the gallows."

"I risked nothing," Mavreen said honestly.

"Your husband's displeasure and mayhap your reputation!" Gideon argued. "And now I think you should return to The Grange whilst neither is in serious jeopardy. I'll not answer for my behavior if I look much longer into those eyes of yours. I love you still, you know — perhaps more than ever I did. So bid me farewell, my lovely Mavreen."

"I shall say no more than *au revoir!*" Mavreen's voice trembled with a sudden aching sadness. "We shall meet again doubtless when I return to London."

"God willing," was Gideon's brief reply; and with one last long look at her, he turned on his heel and was gone. It was as well that he could not see Mavreen's face as he strode out into the rain. Her cheeks were wet, as through her closed eyes there ran a slow stream of unaccountable tears.

Gideon was but a hundred yards distant when a damp disheveled figure ran from the shelter of a doorway and flung itself upon him.

"Oh, Perry! Perry, you are safe! They are not going to hang you after all! I'm so happy I could die of it!"

Gideon looked down into Tamarisk's rain-drenched face with an admixture of affection, exasperation and surprise.

"Devil take me! What brings you here this day, Tamarisk?"

"I came to save you . . . I thought they . . . "

Gideon's face revealed his astonishment.

"You mean you knew that I was a highwayman with a price upon my head?"

Tamarisk nodded.

"Your mother told you?" Gideon urged.

Briefly Tamarisk related how she had discovered the truth about his past. By the time she had finished they were both soaked by the rain. Belatedly Gideon drew her back into the shelter of the doorway.

"So you too believed me guilty. Why, since I'm damned by so many, regardless of whether I be innocent or no, I may as well renew my illegal activities!"

"I do not know how you can jest about such serious matters!" Tamarisk cried. "If it had been you . . . "

"But it was not!" Gideon broke in firmly. "And even had I been the prisoner, there was naught *you* could do, Tamarisk. Would I be right in supposing your mother is not aware of your presence here in Lewes?"

Tamarisk's eyes narrowed.

"Why should I tell her?" she countered. "As to there being naught I could do . . . " She pulled the pistol from its holster and brandished it in front of Gideon.

But instead of the look of admiration she expected to see in his eyes, there was only an ill-concealed laughter.

"You would have shot the judge, the gaolers, the jury, and heaven knows how many spectators with that? Why, 'twould take you five minutes to reload!"

Scarlet-faced, Tamarisk stared at him defiantly.

" 'Twas not my intention to rescue you within the Court House," she declared. "I was waiting until you were journeying back to the prison and would then have held up the cart."

"And Dickon and his friends forestalled you," Gideon said, his face serious once again. "And most effectively too, as doubtless you already know. But I thank you all the same, my Princess, for your intent was brave if misguided. Great heavens, girl, not even your mother would have attempted such a task alone! She had sense enough to engage ruffians well suited to effect a rescue in such circumstances."

"You are both cruel and ungrateful!" Tamarisk cried, only anger holding back her tears of mortification. "And I should have known better, as you say, than to attempt to best my mother. In your eyes I can never do that, can I?" Her voice broke as she wrenched her arm from his restraining hand. "I loved you — I loved you so much I would have died to save you!" The tears fell freely now. "Now I hate you. I wish you really were hanging from a gibbet. I wish you were dead!"

She turned and ran from him, her small figure a dark shadow in the narrow street.

For a moment Gideon thought to pursue her; to ask her to forgive him if inadvertently he had belittled her gesture and allowed her to feel he was ungrateful. But common sense and a deeper wisdom held him back. He knew that it would be best for her, for Mavreen, and, less importantly, for himself if Tamarisk realized once and for all that he loved her only as a child — a daughter; that there was only one woman in the world he could love — and that was her mother, Mavreen.

20

1816

THE summer that had begun so well turned miserably wet and cold. There was little doubt that if it continued thus, the farmers were going to face a disastrous harvest. There were few entertainments to be derived from the dripping countryside and no voice was raised in dissent when Gerard suggested they should return to London. Antoine, in particular, was fractious and constantly demanding attention. He refused to play with Dickon's sons, and to Mavreen's irritation Gerard supported him in his objection to having farm boys for companions.

"You forget, my love, that he was raised on a farm, and my main purpose in bringing him to England is to educate him in the ways of the aristocracy!"

"Then he would do well to learn some manners from Rose's boys," Mavreen argued angrily. "They never answer back or grumble and complain as does Antoine, no matter how hard we all try to please him."

But as always Gerard found excuse for his son on the grounds that he was still far from fully recovered from a bout of severe toothache and allowances must be made for him.

It was therefore with relief that the family

returned to Barre House at the beginning of July. Mr. Mumford and Davinia Gurney were advised of the change of plan and the tutor was already at the house before them. Davinia, however, was not present but had posted a letter tendering her resignation. It said little more than that she felt her services were not as fully engaged as they might be and that she would be better employed assisting her aunt, Mistress Fry, who was but recently brought to bed with her tenth child.

Mavreen passed the letter to Gerard.

"There is good sense in what the girl says," she commented.

To her surprise Gerard reacted to the news as if Davinia Gurney's resignation was a major tragedy.

"We cannot possibly allow her to resign her position here!" he said. "*You* may not hold her in great regard, Mavreen, but she is of inestimable value to me when I suffer from my migraines. No one can cure me but Miss Gurney. She must return at once!"

"But Gerard, you have had no head pains these last three months! In all probability you will no longer be troubled by them now that you are fully rested and in good health again."

"I wish I had your confidence," Gerard replied. "But I do not, Mavreen, and I most earnestly desire Miss Gurney's presence in this house."

The girl's salary was not high and she was so unobtrusive that her presence made very little difference to the household, Mavreen thought.

"Very well" she conceded. "If it will make

you happy, I will call to see Mistress Fry and discuss the matter."

The situation was not, however, as simple as she had supposed. Elizabeth, whose older boys were at school and whose daughters were staying with relatives at Runcton, admitted that she was adequately staffed without Davinia's assistance; despite the size of her family. Under pressure from Mavreen she revealed the true reason for her young relative's resignation.

"The poor girl discovered her respect and admiration for thy dear husband were but part of a far deeper emotion," she told the astonished Mavreen. "In short, she feared that she was committing the grievous sin of adultery, albeit only in her thoughts. She felt it best to remove herself from thy household."

"This is unbelievable!" Mavreen cried. "She gave no sign, no indication, of how she felt, and I am certain that Gerard never once gave her cause to imagine . . ."

"That I already know from Davinia herself," Elizabeth interrupted. "There is no blame attached to anyone — least of all to thy husband." She sighed. "I suppose it is not quite so extraordinary as at first it appears. The girl is of an age when she should have someone to love and to love her; and in the absence of a young man, she has doubtless fastened her affections upon an older one who is not only handsome but gentle and kind. She and the Vicomte were often in close proximity, were they not, when she used her power to heal him? Innocent though thy husband may have been in

392

intention, his need of her was real enough and must have been transmitted to her."

"This will come as a great shock to Gerard," Mavreen said quietly. "He was distraught when I showed him Davinia's letter of resignation. I had no idea he had become so dependent upon her."

"Which would seem to confirm her correctness in what she has elected to do," replied Elizabeth sagely. "As for thy husband, you will know best whether to tell him Davinia's true reason for leaving thy house. Perhaps a small untruth saying I have greater need of Davinia and will not allow her to return would be the wiser course." She smiled. "Sometimes, however wrong in the eyes of our Church, a falsehood creates less harm than the truth. Do thou not agree, my dear? In this instance the truth can serve no purpose and will only distress thy husband."

Mavreen decided to heed such counsel and at the same time to do what she could to obviate the necessity for Davinia Gurney's presence in her home. At all costs Gerard must be kept from harassment of any kind, for it now seemed clear that worry and tension were the most likely cause of his migraines. She therefore planned a moderate way of life.

They entertained seldom and received only their closest friends, the Baroness among them. She was as ever ready with current gossip. The playwright Sheridan had died in dire poverty, she told them, but she had attended in person the magnificent funeral in Westminster Abbey provided by his friends.

"A little more financial aid whilst he lived might have benefitted him more than the generous donations for his funerall" she said wryly.

By the end of July gossip about Sheridan's death was supplanted by talk of the marriage of the King's fourth daughter, Princess Mary, to her cousin, William, Duke of Gloucester.

"Perhaps marriage is better than spinsterhood," Tamarisk commented shuddering, "but I would rather be dead than married to that fat old man with his bulging froglike eyes!"

She thought enviously of Princess Charlotte and her handsome young husband now on the point of moving into their delightful new home, Claremont, in Surrey. The Princess had written to her describing it as '*a real paradise*.' Although she had suffered a miscarriage in June, she told Tamarisk, she was in good health once more, and but for Leopold's toothache, which pained him most severely, they were enjoying married life. She had found repose and a deep fulfillment beyond her wildest hopes and wished devoutly the same good fortune for Tamarisk.

Although marriage hardly seemed a likely outcome, Tamarisk was at long last enjoying a secret romance. By the strangest chance, but one which Tamarisk believed to be the intervention of Fate, she had finally come face to face with her secret admirer. Whilst shopping in Old Bond Street for a birthday present for her father, with no one but the shortsighted Alfred Mumford to observed her, she had encountered the young actor as he purchased for himself a new cravat. Their mutual recognition was instant. He introduced himself in the most proper fashion so that the tutor was without suspicion; and when, as if it were the most natural thing in the world, he offered to escort them home since he was going in their direction, Mr. Mumford raised no objections. In such manner Leigh Darton was able to ascertain Tamarisk's address.

As they neared Barre House, he whispered too softly for Mr. Mumford's hearing:

"I would most dearly like to call upon you but greatly fear your parents would not permit such a liberty, Lady Tamarisk."

Conscious of the fervent admiration in his eyes and ardently desiring to see him again, Tamarisk whispered back:

"I would be very happy were you to take that liberty, Mr. Darton."

"Then I am indeed flattered," the young man said truthfully enough. With her heightened color, her look of grace and breeding, her trim, dainty figure and unconcealed interest in him, he had every cause to be flattered. But he understood the limits imposed by his social standing even if this young girl did not.

"I fear your parents would not open their doors to me," he said. "A penniless actor cannot expect to be received by the Vicomte and Vicomtesse de Valle!"

Tamarisk's cheeks burned a brighter red. She knew that he was justified in his remarks. Yet having met him at last, she could not allow their association to end before it had scarce begun.

Her heart beat so swiftly she feared her voice would tremble as she said hesitantly:

"Unless 'tis raining, Sir, I ride every morning in the park at eleven of the clock."

She was instantly rewarded by a radiant smile. In a low, vibrant voice, he murmured:

"Then I too shall ride in the park at eleven of the clock."

Leigh Darton's ability as an actor enabled him to bid Tamarisk and the tutor so casual a 'good day' that even Tamarisk wondered if she had imagined his whispered promise to keep their rendezvous. Mr. Mumford gave the incident no further thought and the encounter was not referred to by either of them throughout luncheon.

As Tamarisk surmised, neither Mavreen nor Gerard was in the least suspicious when she resumed her daily rides, sometimes in weather so dismal that few young ladies would have braved the elements. But Tamarisk's love for horseriding had been consistent since her earliest years and Mavreen only worried about the possibility of her daughter catching a chill.

As the summer days gave way to autumn and then to the early frosts of winter, Mavreen was content that Tamarisk seemed so much happier. The girl positively glowed with good health. Hearing her singing about the house, seeing her bright rosy cheeks and ready smile, Mavreen had no inkling of the secret romance Tamarisk was now enjoying.

Barely a day passed when Tamarisk did not meet Leigh. They were now such intimate friends as to have dispensed with formalities and called each other by their given names. Leigh, Tamarisk wrote in her journal, professed himself deeply in love. He had openly declared himself unable to eat or sleep for thinking about her. She derived intense enjoyment from his courtship and her wish to prolong it prevented Tamarisk from risking an introduction of Leigh to her parents.

They would no more approve of him than had Clarissa approved of Mr. Edward Crowhurst who, despite his bad manners, was at least well bred. Tamarisk had all but forgotten him and would have liked to be able to banish Lord Byron as easily from her memory. But of late he was all too often in her thoughts. She feared that there might be some way by which Leigh could read in her face or manner the fact that she was not a virgin; or worse, that she had carried a child. It seemed impossible that events which had wrought such changes in her body could leave her appearance unmarked.

These fears were lessened in Leigh's presence, for he seemed to find her faultless.

Since the presence of Tamarisk's groom made the exchange of kisses impossible whilst she and Leigh were riding in the park, by the end of November they were discussing the possibility of meeting at Leigh's lodging house. That this arrangement would be highly dangerous in that it was open to easy discovery, Tamarisk knew very well. But instinct told her that Leigh was becoming impatient. *She* might be content with the heady excitement of their

397

daily meetings in the park upon horseback, with the occasional touching of hands and the exchange of passionate glances, but she sensed that such romantic philanderings were not enough to satisfy her ardent young admirer. When deteriorating weather made the choice of an alternative rendezvous imperative, Leigh's lodgings seemed the only solution to both problems.

Most conveniently these lodgings were situated not far from Herr Mehler's home. On afternoons when Tamarisk was supposedly enjoying her hour-long pianoforte lessons, she would attend for only half the hour and slip away to meet Leigh. By arranging with the coachman to collect her from the mews behind Herr Mehler's house, she was able to play truant without suspicion, and they could enjoy a precious quarter of an hour alone together. Herr Mehler, believing the curtailment of her lesson to be her mother's wish, made no mention of it in his monthly reports on her progress.

Although now they could be alone and kiss to their hearts' content, this new rendezvous was not all joy and sweetness for Tamarisk. She was disconcerted, to say the least, by the lewd grins of the heavily painted landlady — a former actress whose present profession Tamarisk preferred not to think about.

"Why concern yourself with her?" Leigh protested, for once not in sympathy with Tamarisk's opinions. "Is it not enough that we are free at last to show our love for one another? Does your dislike of my landlady matter more to you than I do? Were she more respectable, she would not permit our encounters!"

Tamarisk could not continue with her objections, but she wished she could meet Leigh openly without need for secrecy and deception.

At first Leigh behaved with great propriety. But after a few weeks had passed with no more than loving kisses and embraces exchanged, he began one afternoon to talk of expressing their passions more freely.

"I love you so much it is only natural I want to make you mine — *in every way!*" he said between kisses that were becoming increasingly ardent. With new daring his hands cupped her small breasts. Gently he eased downward the fabric of her gown and began to kiss the softly swelling curves.

With closed eyes Tamarisk allowed herself to enjoy the warm thrill of his touch. This new proximity was arousing her to sensations that she recognized. The weakness of her limbs and the longings that accompanied this sweetness were more potent than the strongest wine. But she was all too well aware that such passions could lead to only one end. If Leigh were to bring their love to its rightful conclusion, she would suffer the same indignities as when Lord Byron had possessed her. She would find herself once again with child.

"No, no, Leigh!" she cried, drawing away from him. "I will not give myself to you — at least not outside of marriage!"

Leigh Darton had anticipated her objections

but was stunned by her talk of matrimony.

"Marriage!" he echoed. "But you know that can never take place between us, however much we both might wish it."

Tamarisk's face flushed a deep red.

"Then you do not love me enough to want to marry me?"

His ardor cooling rapidly, Leigh's look of surprise gave way to one of exasperation. Tamarisk must be aware that her parents would never consider such a liaison, he thought. Stepdaughter of the Vicomte de Valle, daughter of the late Lord Barre, this girl was destined to be married into the nobility. Everyone knew of the immense wealth of the Vicomtesse; so although the Vicomte would probably leave his estate to his French offspring, Tamarisk would probably still inherit a fortune from her mother. She would be doubly eligible on these counts alone, even were she not young and exceedingly pretty.

"You know very well I would marry you were I in a position to do so," he countered, his face now sullen and angry. "You mock me because I am without the right to ask for your hand."

"Indeed I do not!" Tamarisk cried, flinging herself into his arms. "I care not one jot for the fact that you have neither money nor title!"

The young man stared down at her in disbelief.

"You mean you would defy your parents? Marry me for no other advantage than to be my wife?"

"And why not?" Tamarisk rejoined, her determination growing apace. "I would vastly

400

enjoy a life revolving around the theater. It is so exciting! I have oft thought of late that I would love to be an actress. I could soon learn to be one, Leigh. You could teach me your art. I thrill to the mere thought of appearing on stage before a huge audience! And we would be together!"

She was disconcerted by the marked lack of enthusiasm in the glance he now gave her.

Did she know nothing, he wondered, of the hard work, the poverty, the squalor of life on the stage? Was she really so simpleminded as not to realize that behind the artificial diamond-studded gowns and tiaras of the Titanias, the Juliets, lay aching bodies, frightened spirits, and minds numbed by the fear of not knowing where the rent would come from if their performance failed to please? Did Tamarisk really not know that for every actor who was applauded and proclaimed, there were a thousand others who would never make the hoardings and the headlines? At the age of twenty-four he himself was little nearer becoming an Edmund Kean than Tamarisk would be of becoming the second Mrs. Sarah Siddons! His fair good looks had helped him to eke out a living of sorts. His charm had oftimes paid for his food and lodgings when some lonely widow had taken a fancy to him and shown an interest in him that was anything but motherly.

He felt suddenly sorry for Tamarisk, pitying her for that very innocence which as a rule he found so fascinating.

"You would not like my world," he muttered. "It is not as you see it from your privileged place in your theater box, believe me, Tamarisk. There is no security of employment for an actor, no place he can remain long enough to call home; he enjoys few creature comforts, and as often as not the scant rewards in no way recompense him for all the hard work undertaken."

"But I do not want security!" Tamarisk cried. "I have been secure all my life. I want adventure, excitement, something positive to do with my life. Do you not see, Leigh, that your world seems wonderful to me simply because it is so different from my own?"

Leigh Darton understood her better even than she understood herself. He realized she was blinded by illusions. But he was halfway to being genuinely in love with her, and moreover, he was very conscious of the enormous advantages to himself if such a marriage were possible. It was Tamarisk who put the idea of marriage into his mind. He himself would not have dared to presume such an eventuality possible.

As the weeks passed and the end of the year drew nearer, Leigh faced the possibility that with the closing down of the play, he might soon have to seek employment outside London. He would then be unable to continue these meetings with Tamarisk. The thought of marriage became obsessive. They talked of little else. Tamarisk suggested that he should approach her mother upon the matter, but he rejected such naïvety with ill-concealed impatience. Besides which, a better idea was forming in his mind.

"We could elope!" he said to Tamarisk. "Then no one could prevent us marrying!"

402

"Elope!" Tamarisk gasped. "You mean run away together and be secretly married?"

Leigh nodded.

"We could go to Gretna Green. In Scotland we could be married without your parents' approval or consent. Once we were man and wife they would be powerless to separate us!"

"But it would break Mama's heart," Tamarisk whispered. "She has spoken so often of the beautiful wedding I am one day to have. She promised me a gown even more beautiful than Charlotte wore and . . . "

Her Romeo had stopped listening, his nerve shattered by the careless manner in which she spoke of the young Princess. To elope with Tamarisk, he now thought, might even bring the wrath of the Regent as well as that of her parents down upon his head.

But the more reluctant Leigh became to pursue the idea of an elopement, so increasingly did Tamarisk warm to this prospect of adventure. No ordinary wedding, she thought, could be as romantic as that of two lovers forced to abandon home and family in order to be united in a foreign country! Scotland! She had never been there. Leigh would place a ring upon her finger and she would cease forever to be Tamarisk Barre. She would become Mrs. Leigh Darton, mistress of her own home, free to do as she pleased.

"You say you love me," she said finally. "Are you not then convinced that we belong together — as man and wife?"

But Leigh had begun to doubt himself. That

he wanted to bed Tamarisk was undeniable. The few intimacies she permitted left him with a growing frustration that overruled all other thought. He had never bedded a virgin, which he believed Tamarisk to be, and at night he lay awake hour upon hour imagining his possession of her.

But did he really love her? He was not sure what truly was meant by the word. How oft had he heard it spoken upon the stage! How unreal it sounded from the lips of this young aristocrat! What could she know of the violence and passion and cruelty of love as he had seen it! In his childhood he had seen drunken men beat the women they professed to love! He had seen women prostitute themselves to provide food for their starving children. He had seen his own father kill a man he thought had insulted his mother . . . and seen him hanged for it! He had seen two men fight each other with knives for the favors of a barmaid who cared not a jot for either of them — all in the name of love.

Love in real life, Leigh had long since decided, bore no relation to the love of the bards. Shakespeare alone came near the truth when in *As You Like It* Rosalind said: '*Love is merely a madness.*' He, Leigh Darton, would not be ruled by it nor allow it to set aside his ambition. In his brief twenty-four years he had fought hard to leave behind the restrictions of his lowly birth. From his father, a footman in the house of a rich mill owner, he had learned at an early age to ape the speech and manners of the gentry. Obtaining a position as a stableboy and then groom, he had

404

furthered his education until one day, at the age of fifteen, he was mistaken by a houseguest for one of the mill owner's sons. So clever was Leigh in the art of mimicry that when his 'prank' was discovered, his master had found it amusing and, upon occasions thereafter, ordered Leigh to dress in gentleman's attire and mingle with his unsuspecting guests. As the evening wore on the man would turn the conversation to the matter of breeding and thence to challenging his guests to detect which one among them was not born a gentleman. Often the stakes would be very high indeed, and invariably Leigh's employer won a considerable sum of money by this trickery.

Sometimes, when the truth was revealed, one of the more sensitive guests would be embarrassed, considering Leigh must be sorely humiliated by his unmasking. But Leigh was prepared to suffer such indignities. His master paid him well and allowed him many liberties, such as the use of the library, where he soon widened his knowledge. Before long he discovered his exceptional talent for memorizing words. He had but to look at a passage in a book and he could quote it verbatim.

"You would make a good actor, m'boy!" his master said one day, hearing Leigh recite one of Shakespeare's sonnets. He thereby lost himself a servant and started Leigh upon a new career.

Had it not been for his humble start in life Leigh might have balked at the hardships he had subsequently faced. But he was a past master in the art of deception and never allowed truth to stand in the way of his ambition. Eventually, by passing himself off as a distant relative of the Garricks, he obtained an audition with Edmund Kean. Unhesitating when he was offered a very minor position in Kean's theatrical company, he firmly hitched his wagon to this rising star. He considered himself lucky to receive a salary of three pounds a week, although he was hard put to pay for his keep and his costumes out of this meager sum.

Because he was romantic-looking, with aristocratic features framed in shining, naturally curly hair, Leigh soon attracted the attention of the ladies. Unlike Kean, who preferred the taverns to the aristocratic drawing rooms and the toadies and whores to the distinguished ladies now willing to open their bedroom doors to him, Leigh confined his attentions to the nobility. Again, unlike Kean, he avoided the habit of heavy drinking and so ensured that at all times he behaved with the utmost discretion. But although several married ladies had taken a fancy to him, they were careful not to introduce him to their daughters.

Then he had encountered Tamarisk, and for the first time in his life genuine emotion played as large a part in his pursuit of a female as did ambition. The young girl's youth and beauty, her bright, intelligent mind, her innate breeding all conspired to attract him. Moreover, he was intensely flattered by her interest in him. She showed no curiosity about his background and swore she was perfectly happy in his company. She backed such compliments with a foolhardy readiness to meet him secretly, braving her parents' wrath and its repercussions were she detected.

Now, to his astonishment, she professed herself ready and willing to elope with him! But although he himself had first suggested it, he was by no means certain that he had the courage to pursue such a wild notion.

The thought of the possible poverty which could result from such precipitate action unnerved him. He could not imagine Tamarisk without her fine clothes and jewels; without gold sovereigns in her reticule to spend if she felt inclined; without servants and a carriage; without her horse and her groom. When she accused him of so lacking in love that he could hesitate, he gave voice to those of his fears which concerned her.

Tamarisk merely smiled.

"You do not know my parents, else you would realize that they would never let me starve," she said reassuringly. "Why, Leigh, my mother gives away to charity hundreds of pounds a year — enough to support several families. I have heard Mistress Fry speak of Mama's generosity and Mama replied that she had so much money she never noticed the absence of a few hundred pounds. And 'tis the truth! Have no fear. If you cannot provide for us, Leigh, I will have sufficient for us both!"

But he could not rid himself easily of a last unnerving vision of Tamarisk penniless despite her expectations, required to contribute to his tiny income. He could not imagine her even in the relatively easy job of wardrobe mistress at the theater, pricking her tiny white hands with needles and pins in cold, draughty dressing rooms; or eating the often unsavory food provided by landladies. In fact he could not imagine her at all without a retinue of servants at her beck and call.

If her parents refused to give her a suitable dowry, *he* could not support her except in the most primitive of fashions, he tried to warn her. But Tamarisk would not listen to his muttered words of caution. Without the slightest idea of the costs of living in the style to which she was accustomed, she said brightly:

"If needs be, we can sell my jewelry, Leigh. I know 'tis worth a small fortune, for Mama said I must guard it most carefully. Such monies as it realizes should be sufficient to keep us in comfort until you are become famous like Edmund Kean!"

Leigh was too proud to put the supposition into Tamarisk's mind that he might never rise to stardom. He looked into her large trusting eyes, luminous with excitement and happy anticipation, and felt a surge of passion so forceful that it overrode his doubts. If he could have possessed her without the complications of marriage, he would not have given the elopement a second thought. But it seemed the only way he could hope to bed her, and his desire to do so was far too strong to be much longer denied.

Plans for their elopement were discussed at their next encounter and a date set for the first week of December. Leigh was now about to appear in George Colman's play *The Iron*

Chest, to be shown for the first time at Drury Lane Theater on the twenty-third of November. But Kean's portrayal of Sir Edward Mortimer was so impressive that further performances of the play inevitably followed and the date set for the elopement had to be postponed.

Tamarisk went instead to Brighton with her parents. The Prince Regent was in residence there and Princess Charlotte and her husband were visiting him. Tamarisk was invited to take tea with her friend — a pleasure she had not been able to enjoy since Charlotte's marriage. The two young girls were able to exchange confidences as of old. At first Charlotte could speak of nothing but her husband. She was obviously deeply enamored of her Leopold. She confessed herself entirely happy with their simple existence together at Claremont, despite the minor disappointment of her miscarriage.

Tamarisk noticed a quite remarkable change in the Princess. She was now quite calm and equable, no longer concerned with her own happiness but only with pleasing her husband. She and Leopold, she told Tamarisk, were constantly together in each other's company and lived in the greatest harmony. If there was any cloud over her contentment, it was caused by the occasional news which filtered back to England of her mother's outlandish behavior in Europe; and by the fact that she knew her father, the Prince Regent, was trying to find grounds for divorcing her.

But married life was quite perfect, she told Tamarisk, smiling, and Tamarisk must find a good and loving husband like her Leopold to bring her the same joy.

At last Tamarisk had someone to whom she could tell of her secret meetings with Leigh Darton. She now launched into a full account of her young lover and their plans to elope. When Charlotte showed less than a heart-felt enthusiasm for the project, she was not a little hurt.

"You know nothing of his background, his breeding!" the Princess cautioned her young companion. "He cannot be high born else he would have told you of his family. It is one thing to consider a common man for a lover, Tamarisk, but 'twould not be right for you to *marry* one!"

"But we love each other!" Tamarisk protested. "Surely *you* believe in the importance of love above all things, Charlotte?"

"No one knows better than I the happiness that comes from being a loved and loving wife," Charlotte agreed. "But you cannot disregard the question of respect. I look up to my dear Leopold in everything. 'Twould not be possible if he did not have the attributes, the refinements of a gentleman. You must know your parents would never agree to such a marriage, Tamarisk!"

"My mother is scarce in a position to criticize my choice," Tamarisk said, her eyes sullen. "*Her* mother was not of gentle birth!"

"Nevertheless, your grandfather, Sir John Danesfield . . . "

"My grandfather would not stand in the way

410

of my happiness," Tamarisk broke in. Her mood changed as she dropped to the floor and buried her face in Charlotte's lap. "Do not try to dissuade me, dearest Charlotte," she begged. "If you could but meet Leigh you would understand why I am so taken with him. Even if he be no gentleman, I swear you could not guess it for he is so courteous, so sweet and well spoken. His manners are quite beyond reproach. Besides . . . " she added, her face suddenly sad, " . . . you know full well that I can entertain no hope of marrying the only man I truly love. The excitement of my life with Leigh would offer great compensation."

The Princess forbore to offer further cautions feeling herself ill equipped to advise Tamarisk. Her secluded life had given her no experience of actors. Nevertheless her unwillingness to give the affair her blessing and approval had a marked influence upon the younger girl, and when Tamarisk next visited Leigh her enthusiasm for the planned elopement was clearly somewhat diminished. Now it was Leigh's turn to change from vacillation to determination as he saw his beautiful young prize slipping from his grasp.

"'Tis clear you do not love me, else you would come with me!" he challenged her as once she had challenged him. And with a dramatic groan equal in eloquence to the great Edmund Kean himself, he swore that he would end his life if Tamarisk were to desert him.

Tamarisk took great courage from this dissertation. Never in her eighteen years had anyone professed her worth dying for!

411

"Then I *will* go with you!" she promised and abandoned herself to the brief ecstasy of his embrace.

A new date was set for the elopement. It was now to take place on the first day of the new year, one week after Tamarisk's nineteenth birthday.

From Clarissa, Tamarisk received a Lyons flowered silk shawl which she secretly determined to include in the limited trousseau she would take with her to Scotland. Unsuspectingly Mavreen and Gerard presented her with a valuable watch in a rare enamel case made at Bilston in Staffordshire in 1761. The design of pink roses and blue harebells upon a dark blue background was delicately patterned and very pretty. Sir John gave her an armlet containing nineteen perfectly matched diamonds — one for every year of her life.

With only a tiny sigh of regret Tamarisk estimated that if these birthday gifts had to be sold, she and Leigh could live quite comfortably upon the proceeds for several years.

21

January 1817

THE new year had scarcely begun happily, Mavreen thought as she cast a worried glance at Gerard's inert figure in the darkened drawing room. His migraine had worsened steadily since luncheon; now he was in considerable pain and there was no Davinia Gurney to soothe his forehead.

"Can you not send a carriage for her?" Gerard asked despairingly. "You know very well, Mavreen, that she is the only one who can cure me!"

"I fear the Frys are not in London," Mavreen murmured, unsure if it were the truth or a downright lie. Her conscience smote her. She had never told Gerard that Davinia had nurtured a secret love for him and that this was her true reason for resigning her post.

Deceiving him had not been to Mavreen's liking, for already she believed she held too many secrets from him. Moreover, she was not altogether sure of her motives. Mistress Fry had supposed Gerard would be embarrassed by the knowledge of Davinia's feelings, but there was always the possibility that he would have been flattered and intrigued, and Mavreen had oft chided herself in the past for nurturing an unworthy resentment of Gerard's dependence

413

upon the girl. Now facing Gerard's obvious suffering, she had no option but to continue with the lie and refuse to send a servant to St. Mildred's Court to ascertain Davinia's availability.

To add to her general feeling of unease, Mavreen was further concerned for Tamarisk. The girl had retired to her bedchamber some hours ago, also complaining of a severe ache in her head. She had refused to see a physician and insisted so obdurately that sleep was all she required for her recovery, that Mavreen did not like to disturb her.

But as the evening wore on, Mavreen's worry intensified. It was the second occasion Tamarisk had been smitten with a migraine so similar to Gerard's that she could not ignore the strong possibility that the complaint was inherited. She regarded Gerard's prostrate form anxiously.

"Will you not permit me to call two of the servants to carry you to your bed?" she asked Gerard. His intense pallor and the trembling of his limbs frightened her despite her familiarity with the symptoms. The clock had long since chimed the hour of seven, and despite the huge fire burning in the grate, Gerard was shivering as if with the cold. "I have had warming pans put ready in the bed," she added. "Do you not think you would be more comfortable between the sheets than on this hard sofa?"

Unwilling to put his feet to the ground, Gerard agreed to be carried up to bed. By the time he was resting comparatively peacefully in the darkened room, the time-piece at Mavreen's waist showed eight of the clock. She decided to tiptoe along the landing to Tamarisk's bedchamber.

At first it seemed to Mavreen that her daughter was sleeping peacefully, the coverlet pulled upward over the soft mound of her body. But some sixth sense caused her to stand for a moment longer before leaving. Suddenly she realized what was wrong: there was no sound of gentle breathing, no rise and fall of the body.

For a full second fear paralyzed her. Could Tamarisk be dead? But as she hurried forward to pull back the smothering bedcovers, her fear turned to anger at the realization of her daughter's trickery. Tamarisk's migraine was but an excuse to leave the house upon some illicit nocturnal escapade. No other reason could account for the faked figure made to look so real, that had Mavreen done no more than glance through the open doorway, she would have believed Tamarisk to be sleeping.

Mavreen found the tinderbox by the candle on the bedside table and, keeping her trembling hands as steady as possible, lit the chandeliers. The room was now revealed in all its disorder. Clothes, gloves, reticules, slippers — all were scattered as if sorted and discarded in a great hurry. The top drawer of Tamarisk's bureau was open and the casket in which she kept her jewels was unlocked and empty.

Horrified, Mavreen began to wonder if some intruder had forced his way into Tamarisk's room, stolen her jewelry, and then abducted her. She was on the point of rushing downstairs

415

to tell Gerard when she remembered that he was ill — and unlike Tamarisk, genuinely so. She hesitated, her heart thudding. But again some instinct made her pause before calling the servants and alerting the night watchman. Her eyes searched the room, noted a crumpled sheet of paper lying on the thick Indian carpet. It was half concealed by the fall of the bed curtains.

She bent and picked it up, smoothing it so that she could read the writing thereon. It was the second page of a letter. The signature — that of someone called Leigh — was unknown to her. Her eyes went back to the top of the page.

' . . . *reserved first class passage for us on Sherman's Royal Mail coach, departing from the Bull and Mouth, St. Martin's-le-Grand, at half past seven of the clock. I will be waiting for you in a hackney cab at the corner of Piccadilly and Swallow Street an hour earlier. Be not a moment later. Wear your warmest attire and bring only one box, or two at the most.*

'Meanwhile my sweet wife-to-be, I am trying to possess my soul in patience. When you did not call to see me last week I feared you had changed your mind and only your dear, loving letter revived my spirits.

'I love you, my darling,
'Your devoted,

Leigh.'

Mavreen let go her breath. There was no doubt now that Tamarisk had eloped with the

416

writer of the letter. Glancing at her timepiece she realized that the mail coach would have departed London an hour previously. There was no way she could stop the elopement.

She sat down on the edge of the bed and tried to think calmly and logically. Somehow Tamarisk must be stopped. Had this proposed marriage been acceptable, there would have been no reason for Tamarisk to keep secret her mysterious suitor. If only she knew who Leigh was, she might better be able to judge the situation. There was no address on the sheet of paper she held between her hands and a quick search did not reveal the first part of the letter.

She tried to recall any of Tamarisk's interests these past months which might throw some light upon the situation. But she could think of nothing out of the commonplace — unless it were Tamarisk's growing interest in the theater; her apparent hero-worship for the impressive actor, Edmund Kean . . .

Suddenly Mavreen remembered the handsome young actor, Leigh Darton who so often played supporting rôles in Edmund Kean's plays. It had seemed of no consequence at the time, but now the frequency with which he had stared up at their box appeared highly significant. Gerard had remarked upon it and gently teased Tamarisk, telling her that her pretty face was attracting the young player's attention.

An actor! Mavreen thought. That would explain everything. Tamarisk would know Gerard would never permit such a suitor. She too would have discouraged such an association, however charming the young man.

She cut off such thoughts as wasting time. This elopement must somehow be curtailed. She assumed from the letter she held that they intended a secret wedding. The Royal Mail coach leaving London at this late hour traveled to the North. She could therefore divine their most likely destination to be Gretna Green in Scotland — a border town where weddings took place with no questions asked of bride or groom.

At least, she thought, she now had a likely trail to follow. The Royal Mail coach was run on a strict timetable. Horses were changed and mail delivered every fifteen miles or so. If she took her fastest carriage, sent a footman ahead to arrange for fresh horses, and left immediately, she could surely catch up with the fugitives. So long as they did not alight too soon — at Barnet, Welwyn, or Baldock — she could obtain news of the young couple from the various staging posts. Tamarisk would not go unremarked, however unobtrusive she tried to be. She was too pretty!

Mavreen decided to waste no further time. As she hurried to her room to change her attire, her concern for her daughter increased. Tamarisk had already had one affair leading to a pregnancy that could have had disastrous effects upon her future. Now it was to be supposed that she had permitted herself to be seduced by her secret lover and a further pregnancy might well be the reason behind these hasty marriage plans.

If only there was some way, Mavreen thought, sighing, that females could avoid getting with child as soon as they gave way to the passions of the body! What tragedies might be avoided! Not a month ago poor unhappy Harriet Shelley had committed suicide by drowning herself in the Serpentine. Made pregnant by some man other than the husband from whom she was separated, it was to be presumed that she was unable to face the consequences. Mavreen had been shocked to hear that Shelley had married his mistress, Mary Godwin, not three weeks after his wife's suicide. It seemed unfair that it must always be the female who bore the dishonor and shame of illicit love.

It took Mavreen but five minutes to change into her dove-gray carriage costume, a little longer for her maid to button her half-boots. Outside the casement a bitterly cold north wind had brought the night temperature to near freezing and Mavreen had no hesitation in selecting her ermine-lined cardinal mantle with its warm hood to protect her from the cold.

A glance into Gerard's bedchamber showed him sleeping peacefully. She decided not to wake him and perhaps aggravate the attack of migraine by revealing the necessity for her sudden departure. Instead she penned a quick note telling him of her intention to waylay Tamarisk on her northward journey and bring her home as soon as possible. She enclosed the page of Leigh's letter so that he might better understand the urgency of her mission.

The coachman had already been alerted and

the carriage awaited her as she opened the great door of Barre House and stepped out into the frosty night air. The horses were stamping their feet, steam blowing from their nostrils, their perfectly groomed coats shining in the light of the gas lamps on either side of the street.

She climbed into the carriage as the nearby church of St. James's struck the half hour. Almost immediately the night watchman called: "Half past eight o'the clock and all's well."

I wish that it were! Mavreen thought.

"To Highgate! As quickly as you can!" she ordered the coachman. "I wish to reach the Great North Road as soon as possible."

The coachman weaved a way through the evening crowds in Old Bond Street. Their route to Highgate took them across Hanover Square, up Holles Street, which ran through the estate of the Duke of Portland, and into Cavendish Square where they were forced to a brief halt by the carriages leaving Harcourt House. As she sat impatiently drumming her gloved fingers on the leather upholstery, it suddenly dawned on Mavreen that she was only a stone's throw from Gideon's house. The road cleared and the coachman urged the horses forward into a fast trot up Harley Street. But as they passed the corner of Queen Anne Street, the horses had once more to be reined in. This time it was Gideon's carriage which was blocking the road as it turned out of the mews to pull up at his house.

As Mavreen leaned out of the window she saw Gideon come through his front door and walk toward his carriage. He was dressed for evening in a full-skirted, dark blue frock coat with a high rolled collar. He was carrying his hat and cane and was pulling on long white gloves. The wind ruffled the white lace neckcloth at his throat.

She called out to him. He turned and stared at her for a moment in astonishment, then hurried over to her carriage.

"What brings you here at this hour of the night?" he asked as he raised her hand to his lips. "And alone, so it seems."

His gentle, teasing smile gave way to a look of concern as she quickly outlined her purpose and the reason for it.

"Devil take us!" he exclaimed as he pulled out his repeater watch and studied it carefully. "Why, if 'tis for Gretna Green the girl is making, you'll not catch up with her this side of the border — and at very best that means a day and a half's travel. I'll not let you go, Mavreen — not in this bitter cold weather. As like as not, there'll be snow on the hills and on the moors up North. 'Twould be far too dangerous . . . " He broke off, the smile hovering once more around his mouth. "Unless I go with you. Damme, Mavreen, the idea is beginning to appeal to me! What say you? Shall we go together?"

Mavreen shook her head.

"I am not afraid to go alone," she said. "Besides, by the look of your attire, you are already engaged for the evening."

"I was but going to Almacks," Gideon replied. "And that only because I had nothing more amusing to do with my time. Be patient for but a few minutes whilst I change my clothes, Mavreen, for I am now determined upon coming with you."

Without waiting for her to raise further objections he left to give orders to his coachman and to her own. His manner was calm and competent and suddenly she felt a great surge of relief wash over her. She knew very well the possible dangers and hardships of chasing her errant daughter from one end of England to the other. But three years of conventional domesticity had not tempered the spirit of adventure which had taken her across war-ravaged Europe to Russia. Now she was thirty-six years old — at an age when most of her contemporaries were matronly figures with few interests outside their family circle. Yet she knew herself still foolhardy enough to have contemplated a long, hazardous journey without even the faithful Dickon at her side. Now a kindly Fate had brought Gideon Morris to her assistance at precisely the moment she needed his physical and moral support.

It was Gideon who now directed their mode of travel. His barouche landau — a high, well-sprung carriage — would lessen the discomfort of the rutted roads, he told her. One of his footmen was already upon his way on horseback to advise the pikeman at Highgate Archway of their approach. He would save them precious time by paying the toll in advance of their arrival.

Gideon helped Mavreen into the landau.

"The pikeman will hear our bugle as we draw

near and throw open the gates for us. We should make fast time. I understand you have already sent your footman ahead to the inns to choose the best horses. We should find them ready harnessed and awaiting us."

It seemed to Mavreen as if luck was with her this night. The smooth stoned road ran as far as the tollgate. The highway beyond was usually ankle deep with mud churned up by the thousands of livestock driven daily along it to be slaughtered at Smithfield Market. But tonight, because of the extreme cold, the mud was frozen solid, and although their passageway was uncomfortable as they crossed the fifteen hundred acres of Finchley Common, the springs of Gideon's new barouche lessened the severity of the bumps and their wheels did not sink in the frozen mire.

Their second piece of good fortune came about in Barnet where they stopped for the first change of horses. They received news of the eloping couple. Gideon took Mavreen into the welcome warmth of the inn for a tankard of mulled ale, and whilst engaged in conversation with a fellow traveler learned of the passing of the Royal Mail coach but a little over two hours since.

With a grin the man informed Gideon that there was a handsome young couple aboard the coach heading for Scotland.

"For to get themselves wed at Gretna Green, they said," he added, seeing Gideon's interest in his idle gossip.

"Your instinct was right, Mavreen," Gideon

said. "Now that we are sure of our destination, we can plan our journey accordingly."

He obtained from the landlord a list of times and places where the Royal Mail coach would stop for the necessary changes of horses. It would not arrive at Gretna Green until nine in the morning, some thirty-three hours hence.

"Barring unforeseen accidents, we shall intercept them before then," Gideon added reassuringly to Mavreen. "Come now! Let us waste no further time here but be on our way."

They reemerged into the night air to find new horses in the traces, a postboy ready mounted to ride with them to the next halt from whence he would bring the tired mounts back — a task which would earn him three pence a mile. Mavreen's groom was already on his way to alert the next staging post; Gideon's and her own coachman were mounted on the landau ready for departure.

The new steeds were in excellent condition and took off at a goodly pace. Gideon reckoned they were covering ten miles to the hour and they reached Welwyn soon after one in the morning. By the time they drew into the yard at Baldock they had gained a little upon the mail coach. They did not stay long enough to partake of the hot meal available at the inn but purchased brandy to drink and sausages to eat in the landau whilst they continued their journey northward.

Mavreen protested herself to be incapable of sleep when Gideon suggested they should both try to rest for a while. Nevertheless when she leaned back against his shoulder and he drew her fur cloak around her, she relaxed into slumber.

Gideon looked down at her closed eyelids and his arm tightened involuntarily. The face he loved so well was no longer the smooth, unlined countenance of a young girl. There were faint lines about her wide, generous mouth. The lips parted slightly as she breathed. There were tiny grooves across the smooth skin of her forehead that might be the beginning of a frown or the first approaches of age. He did not care. He would love her no differently were she twice as old, half as young. It was not her appearance that had first attracted him but her unbreakable spirit, her indomitable character. Neither the passage of years since he had met her nor marriage had altered her. Her husband, the illustrious Gerard de Valle, had not tamed her. Nor ever would! Gideon thought as with a sigh he had perforce to wake her. Not a mile from the village of Stilton in Huntingdonshire they had come to an abrupt halt, the road being blocked by another carriage.

"'Tis a yellow bounder, Sir!" said the coachman coming to the window. "Looks as if it lost a wheel and overturned."

The two occupants came stumbling toward the barouche. They were bruised but otherwise unharmed. Merchant traders, the Stockdale brothers were taking their homemade samples of double cream cheeses from Stilton to Cambridge when the accident had occurred. Their two postboys had deserted them, unhitching the horses and leaving their hirers to their fate.

The merchants were overcome with gratitude when Gideon and Mavreen offered to take them into the village of Stilton. They pressed two large evil-smelling cheeses upon their rescuers and would not listen to a refusal.

Mavreen, now wide awake, felt the pressure of Gideon's hand upon her own and tried to suppress her laughter. Gideon offered their shivering, mud-bespattered guests a tot of brandy to revive them, and by the time they reached the inn at Stilton they were all on excellent terms with one another.

Between this village and the next staging post at Stamford, it was Gideon's turn to sleep. This time it was Mavreen who offered her shoulder as a pillow and spread her cloak across Gideon's knees.

She was surprised by her strange feeling of happiness. After all, their mission was not being undertaken for pleasure since her daughter was in trouble if not in actual danger. The rattling and bumping of the coach was already taking its toll upon her aching body and the journey was not yet a third accomplished. Yet unbelievably she was enjoying this unexpected adventure.

Her mind wandered back to the last occasion when she had been in Gideon's company after the successful rescue of his highwayman friend. She had felt elated then, as now, and it would be false to pretend otherwise. It did her no credit, she thought, that the conventional trappings of social good behavior invariably struck her as dull. Never within such confines had she been

426

fulfilled as she was at this minute.

She felt the soft warmth of Gideon's dark curls against her cheek and her heart jolted in a sudden rush of tenderness. Yet she knew him to be far stronger than she was. Now sadness overwhelmed her when a moment earlier she had been happy. She wished that she could effect a wonderful and rewarding future for Gideon; that she could hand to him as if it were a parcel of Stilton cheese, a package of happiness, of joy, of love. If only emotions could be purchased, traded, exchanged like jewels! How readily would she dispense her fortune if it could guarantee happiness for those she loved — Tamarisk, Gerard, Gideon. That she did still love Gideon she no longer questioned, believing the love she bore him now to be that of a well-tried and trusted friend. Her heart, as ever, remained steadfastly true to the man she had married.

With a sudden twinge of anxiety she realized that Gerard would soon be waking to the discovery of her absence — and Tamarisk's. On reflection she feared he would not approve of her headlong flight in pursuit of their daughter. It was perhaps as well that his migraine had made prior consultation impossible, for he would most certainly have vetoed a precipitate dash into the night. Precious time might have been lost whilst he attempted to establish the facts, made elaborate preparations for the long journey. As it was, she had acted on instinct which fortunately enough had proved to be sound. Now, when she brought Tamarisk safely home, Gerard would not be able to question the rightness of her impulsive decision.

It never occurred to Mavreen that Gerard was already awake and aware of her departure. Barre House, even at this predawn hour, was in an uproar.

Gerard had wakened after a refreshing sleep to discover his headache had completely vanished. Leaving his dressing room, he went along to Mavreen's bedchamber intending to slip quietly into the bed without disturbing her.

His wife's absence at five in the morning was so inexplicable that he at once roused the servants. From Dorcas, he learned only that his wife had ordered the carriage and left in a great hurry with the coachman and one footman; and that Tamarisk's bed was also empty and some of her clothes missing. It was some minutes before a bewildered Gerard discovered the note left for him by Mavreen on the drawing-room mantel-shelf. Reading her brief explanation Gerard dismissed the sleepy-eyed servants and returned to his bedchamber.

Antoine, awakened by the commotion, stood shivering in his nightshirt beside his father. Gerard's expression left no doubt as to his mixed feelings of anger and concern as briefly he informed his son of Tamarisk's disappearance.

The boy slipped his hand into Gerard's and said in French:

"Never mind, Papa. Even if Tamarisk has run away, you still have me, and I will never leave you!"

Gerard looked down into the boy's face, his

anger slowly dissipating. Now approaching his ninth birthday, Antoine had lost none of his delicate beauty, Gerard reflected. His son's devotion was absolute. In fact Gerard sometimes felt closer to him even than to Mavreen. Antoine never disputed his opinion, never argued his decisions, and looked up to him with an adoration that held no hint of criticism and was close to worship.

He smiled down at the boy with great tenderness.

"Tamarisk has not brought me the same happiness that you have, my son," he said. "I fear she is a wayward, undisciplined girl and has ofttimes proved a great worry to your stepmother and to me."

"What will you do now, Papa?" Antoine inquired curiously.

"There is little I can do," Gerard replied, sighing as he walked with the boy back to his dressing room. The early morning was bitterly cold and he motioned to Antoine to climb beneath the bed covers. "I fear I am helpless in this present situation. I have not been very close to Tamarisk recently and do not enjoy her confidence. Such being the case, I cannot be judge of her intentions."

Antoine gave his father a quick sideways glance.

"If 'twould assist you, Papa, I know that Tamarisk keeps a journal, and I could bring it to you . . . " He broke off, hesitating as he saw Gerard's gaze fasten upon him.

"Well, my boy? You were saying?"

429

"I fear you might be angry with me, Papa, if I continue. You might withdraw your approval of me if I confess the truth."

"Then you misjudge me!" Gerard said forcefully. "I would never be angry with you for admitting the truth. You may trust me, Antoine."

The boy let out his breath on a little sigh of relief.

"In that case I feel I should tell you that I came upon my sister's journal one day — she had left it lying about — and not realizing its private nature I did read one or two passages she had written. At first I could not believe what I read and was sure I must be mistaken in my understanding. But as I read further . . . " He broke off, burying his face in his hands as if too overcome by emotion to continue.

Gerard took him by the shoulders, firmly but not unkindly.

"I do not know if I fully understand what you are trying to tell me," he said. "But by your reluctance to continue, I must assume that you read something quite unfit for your tender age. You had best bring me that journal, Antoine. If there is some mischief afoot, then it is my duty to uncover it."

"Then you are not angry with me for speaking of it?"

As gently as his impatience would allow, Gerard disentangled himself from the boy's arms.

"You did right to tell me," he said quietly. "I know I do not have to remind you that it was

430

wrong to read another person's private letters or journal; I appreciate that in this case you did so more by accident than design." He sighed. "However, I believe Fate sometimes arranges such accidents so that good may come of evil. Now fetch me the journal. I would fain discover what has brought my daughter to shame this house by nocturnal elopement more befitting a housemaid than a girl of gentle birth."

It took but a few minutes for Antoine to bring to his father Tamarisk's journal from its hiding place in the secret drawer in her bureau. Espying through her key-hole one dull afternoon when he had nothing better to amuse him, he had watched her place it there and had read it at his leisure whilst she was at her pianoforte lesson. That was over a month ago, but he had never, until now, found good reason to offer it to his father without his motives being suspect.

Despite his tender age Antoine understood very well the implications of Tamarisk's revelations. The references to his stepmother's past would, he was convinced, loosen the close bond between her and his father — that mysterious, hateful bond which he knew excluded him. It kept him an outsider on the edge of a circle of love he could not penetrate. When they exchanged glances, that special look in their eyes, or touched one another, or kissed, the boy was convinced that his father's love for him was of secondary importance. When they retired at night to their bedchamber, he had offtimes crept along the passage and pressed his ear to the keyhole, heard their soft laughter, their cries

431

of pleasure and delight, and had known very well what they were about.

He did not blame his father. He had little doubt that it was his stepmother who seduced his father, just as Eve in the Bible tempted Adam. Now, at long last, he saw that he could prove to Gerard how unworthy was the woman he had married and how much happier they would be without her. As for Tamarisk, she had condemned herself.

Antoine's self-confidence waned, however, when he saw the effect the journal had upon his father. Gerard's face became a white mask of fury as his eyes scanned page after page, returning always to the day Tamarisk discovered the real identity of Sir Peregrine Waite and his long association with Mavreen as her lover.

When he could sufficiently control himself, Gerard sent the shivering uneasy boy back to his own room. Once again he scanned the lines of his daughter's journal.

' . . . yet 'tis not so hard for me to credit, knowing how full of daring and courage is Perry, or should I call him Gideon Morris now?' Tamarisk had written in her careful script. 'I can understand why Mama loved him, loving him so well myself. What exciting times they must have enjoyed together! Yet 'tis hard to believe my own Mama once rode beside a highwayman and even assisted in his holdups!

'The more I think on it, the more strange it seems that Mama should have chosen to

432

marry so good and quiet and seemly a man as Papa. I am not even certain anymore if he is my real father — yet I think he must be since Mama did not encounter Perry until after the smugglers had captured poor Papa. But nothing is certain. Aunt Clarrie rambled so, that it is difficult to put events in order. I cannot even be sure that Perry is no longer Mama's lover, though I believe her to be in all respects faithful in her marriage. But that Perry still loves her I am no longer in doubt . . .'

Gerard's knuckles were white as his hands tightened even more strongly about the leather-bound book. His mind ached with the thoughts running torturously through it. His temples throbbed. He wanted desperately to dismiss Tamarisk's revelations as the distorted ramblings of an adolescent girl, but reason would not allow of it. By accepting these facts, all the many small puzzlements were explained: Mavreen's strange tolerance of the nincompoop Sir Peregrine; those long years when he, Gerard, had been abroad and she had appeared content to live alone; her long absence from The Grange that day last summer when the nameless highwayman was on trial; those two tiny silver pistols in their holsters that Waite had given her for a wedding present . . .

Gerard's jealous imaginings of his wife in the arms of her lover made further inaction intolerable. He jumped to his feet, rang the bell for his valet and dressed in a fever of

433

impatience. His self-torture would have been even more agonized had he known of his wife's reputation as the Barre Diamond. But he had been away from England these past nine years, and although Mavreen had attempted to confess her unfortunate past, he had not wished to hear of it.

The matter of his daughter's elopement and her safety were now of secondary importance. Uppermost in his mind was the desire to establish once and for all whether or not the dastardly highwayman was still Mavreen's lover. If it were so, then honor alone demanded he throw down the gauntlet without delay. He himself would welcome a duel and the chance to kill the man! And were he, Gerard, to be killed, then Mavreen must bear her husband's death upon her conscience forevermore.

Since Mavreen had taken the carriage, Gerard ordered the gig to be brought to the door. It was near seven of the clock when he drove himself down Piccadilly and turned into Old Bond Street. Outside the White Horse Cellar stood the Royal Mail coach about to depart for Windsor. He passed by without a glance at the crowds milling about it, urging his horse to a faster trot as he rounded Hanover Square. Crossing Oxford Street he turned up Holles Street. His impatience mounted as he neared Cavendish Square. Across the heads of the worshippers gathering outside the Convent of the Holy Child Jesus in preparation for morning Mass, he could see the beginning of Harley Street where he knew his quarry to live.

Now suddenly he realized that he could not remember the number of Sir Peregrine's residence. Undecided, he looked at the row of newly built terraced houses. He was obliged to obtain the information from a baker's delivery boy trundling his barrow over the cobbles in the frosty morning mist.

He was looking forward to the duel which he believed must be the outcome of this visit. Sir Peregrine, he decided as he hitched his horse's reins to an iron railing and rapped on the front door with his whip handle, would have to give some very convincing explanations as to why he continued to force his attentions upon their household! Moreover, there was another score he needed to settle: the man had taken advantage of his privileged position as 'uncle' to foster Tamarisk's affections, eventually driving her into the arms of the nefarious Lord Byron. Gerard now felt a new wave of antipathy toward Mavreen. Let her defend the poet as best she might; it shocked him to consider his innocent daughter's association with such a man.

Such was Gerard's mounting indignation that when the manservant who opened the door informed him Sir Peregrine was not at home, he refused to believe a confrontation was being denied him.

"I insist upon seeing your master!" he said, moving to enter the doorway. But the servant stood firm.

"I do assure you he is not here, Sir — nor even in London. He left late last night for the North. I think he may be on his way to Scotland."

435

He took a step backward at the sight of Gerard's face, distorted as it had become with suspicion and anger.

"You'll answer for it if you lie!" Gerard cried. "So you had best speak the truth. When did your master leave? At what time? Who with? Was there a lady with him?"

The terrified man made no pretense of loyalty to his employer. Afraid lest Gerard should strike him with the whip he carried, he stammered out his replies. His master had been on the point of departing for Almacks, he told Gerard, when a lady had drawn up in her carriage. He thought he recognized the lady as the Vicomtesse de Valle but he could not be certain. There had been a hurried consultation which he had not overheard, but his master had hurried indoors to change his clothes, having first alerted his coachman to bring round the new barouche landau. One of the footmen was ordered to ride with them. The stableboy told him during breakfast in the servants' hall that he understood their master was going with the lady to Scotland in search of a missing person. Beyond this he knew nothing, not if his very life depended upon it, he assured Gerard.

The news he had imparted was far more informative than Gerard could have anticipated when he demanded it. As he turned away from the house and remounted his gig, he wondered for one fleeting moment if Mavreen rather than Tamarisk was eloping to Gretna Green with her lover. But as he turned the horse's head and retraced his route down Harley Street, he knew that this was folly. Mavreen was already married to him, Gerard, whether she liked it or not!

Besides, Tamarisk too was missing from Barre House; he had in his possession part of *her* lover's letter and her journal to verify her intention to elope.

The anger which until now had sustained him was fast draining away. He was suddenly aware of the intense cold and urged his horse to a quicker pace. Before long, he thought, he would begin a new attack of the migraine — and small wonder with such terrible discoveries upon his mind! But not even calmer reflection could bring him comfort. When Mavreen had found Tamarisk gone, he told himself bitterly, she had not turned to her husband for help but had ridden posthaste to her lover! Doubtless she welcomed the excuse to be with him, alone somewhere upon the highway to the North where they could stop at will to indulge their passions. There were inns aplenty where they could hire a bedchamber with no questions asked; no one to cast looks of suspicion their way.

The thought of Mavreen, his wife, his beloved, lying naked in the embrace of another man filled him with such abhorrence that the bile rose in his throat. A hundred different memories of her came to his mind, colored his thoughts, and aroused in him a desire for her that in her absence was stronger than he had yet felt in her presence since their marriage. If he were to find her waiting for him upon his return to Barre House, he would take her and rape her without mercy. Her very resistance would only incite him to further ravishing. He could well imagine how she would fight him, her slim, beautiful body, as strong and youthful as a girl's, twisting in his grasp as he took his pleasure.

His own ardor cooled suddenly as he remembered Mavreen's responsiveness. How eager she was — had always been — for his loving! How ready to fulfill his demands upon her, to prolong the preludes so that they might miss no moment of passionate pleasure in a release achieved too soon. He had delighted in her sensuousness, her natural enjoyment of what many women of breeding looked upon merely as a wifely duty to be performed. He had marveled at the uncomplicated, almost innocent way she expressed her love for him, giving herself freely, without modesty or shame.

But that same generosity took on a different meaning now that he knew she had given herself to another man . . . other men, perhaps . . . as freely. Her responsiveness became a shocking immorality seen in such context. And he had trusted her! Allowed her an independence of thought and action far in excess that normally considered reasonable in marriage. He had even permitted her to return home to England from Compiègne without him. He never once suspected, when she gave him as an excuse that she must leave forthwith to rescue her daughter from the clutches of the unhappy Princess Caroline, that her real motive might be to meet her lover. That was four years ago, yet he could remember, now that he searched his memory, how Mavreen had indeed consulted her lover, professing that Tamarisk took advice from 'her adored Uncle Perry' and that the man was a good influence upon her.

How easily he had been tricked! Cuckolded! How naïve and foolish he must seem in her eyes; how ridiculous in his own! As ridiculous as the miserable old night watchman who normally patrolled the streets around Barre House whom Gerard now discovered imprisoned in his own wooden shelter. Some drunken young bloods had turned it to the wall, making his escape impossible. The poor old fool was hollering and beating upon the sides of the hut with his cudgel and shaking his rattle.

Gerard released the old man. Aware that the poor fellow received but eight pence a night for his work, he compensated the victim by giving him a guinea piece.

But as Gerard walked into his house, cries of gratitude ringing in his ears, he knew that nothing in the world could compensate *him* for the humiliation he was convinced his wife had inflicted upon him.

22

January 1817

AT the same time as Gerard was returning home, Tamarisk and Leigh were halted for a change of horses in the market town of Grantham. It was half past eight of the clock and the temperature was only just above freezing.

Tamarisk's spirits were nearly as low. They had now been on the road for thirteen hours and had had five changes of horses. The most recent, at the village of Stamford, had added immeasurably to her general feeling of malaise.

She was rudely awakened from the light doze into which she had fallen by the blaring of the horn announcing their arrival at The Angel in Grantham. The ostler was shouting: "Horses on!" and she heard the now familiar hustle and bustle of the coaching yard. There were stableboys, postboys, and horses everywhere; the jingle of the harnesses ringing out in unison with the clatter of horses' hooves as coaches, carriages, and bounders jostled their way in and out of the yard beneath the old gatehouse.

Maidservants, laden with food and drink for the passengers who did not wish to leave their seats for the warm fires of the inn, picked their way through the turmoil with their burdens. Indoors there was always food waiting — breakfast, dinner, or supper — and newspapers on the tables for travelers to read. Sometimes the weary passengers were pestered by peddlers trying to sell anything from black lead pencils to a tame squirrel, saw blades, pocketbooks, nuts, slippers.

Despite her fatigue Tamarisk was fascinated by the antiquity of this medieval travelers' inn. Leigh took her into the King's Room above the old gatehouse where in 1483 King Richard III had written his fateful letter to the Lord Chancellor proclaiming the treachery of his cousin, the Duke of Buckingham.

"Oh, Leigh!" she cried, pointing to the three great stone oriel windows. "Would they not make magnificent background scenery when your Edmund Kean is enacting Richard III?"

But Leigh was hungry and eager for a jug of mulled ale and had no heart for exploring their surroundings.

Had Leigh shown greater enthusiasm Tamarisk would have found such halts exciting. She was filled with interest and pleasure in this adventure, for she had never traveled before except it be in the quiet confines of her mother's private vehicles. On the few long journeys she had undertaken, she had not been permitted to leave the carriage and food and drink were brought to her. But now, suddenly, she was desperately in need of sleep, besides which Leigh's disinterest was discouraging.

Leigh too was tired and had little to say to comfort her since they had not yet reached the end of the first half of their journey. He further succeeded in upsetting her by showing himself quite unsympathetic with her shocked reaction to the sight of a dead man hanging from a gibbet on the outskirts of the town.

The body, swinging in the wind in its grizzly iron frame, was partly decomposed; but worse, it had been mutilated.

At her cry of protest Leigh merely shrugged indifferently.

"'Tis not unusual," he commented matter-of-factly. "There are always superstitious people who believe that certain parts of a hanged man will assist the potency of their remedies and potions — hair and teeth especially."

"But that is witchcraft!" Tamarisk cried. "'Tis against the law now to practice such evil."

"Nevertheless 'tis done," Leigh argued. And with the mistaken idea of lightening her fear he quoted dramatically some lines from Thomas Ingoldsby's *The Hand of Glory*:

"Now mount who list, and close by the
  wrist
Sever me quickly the Dead Man's fist!
Now climb who dare, where he swings in
  the air,
And pluck me five locks of the Dead Man's
  hair!"

He was nonplussed and not a little irritated when Tamarisk burst into tears. He could make no sense of her gasped protest:

"But that could be Perry hanging there!"

As the coach proceeded northward, passing

through Newark on the River Trent and then Ollerton, his malaise increased. It became more and more obvious that his future wife was totally unused to hardship of any kind; that her life had been sheltered not only from poverty but from even the most minor discomforts that went with it. She had already vouchsafed that at the first opportunity they must furnish themselves with their own carriage and coachman so that they could return on the homeward journey at their leisure and not at the breakneck speed required by His Majesty's mail coaches. Only fatigue had prevented Leigh from telling her there and then that it was unlikely they would ever be able to afford such luxuries.

By midday they had survived the dangers of Sherwood Forest and were near the halfway stage of the journey as they crossed the bridge over the Chesterfield Canal in Worksop. Staring out of the window Tamarisk cried out in delight as she saw one of the big canal barges, trailing its huge 'butty' barge behind, passing beneath them. Both boats were all of seventy-foot long and filled with Baltic timber from the docks at Hull. They were traveling slowly westward along the canal to Chesterfield where the timber would be used to heat the great iron furnaces. Tamarisk was enchanted by the huge carthorse whose strength surprisingly was more than sufficient to pull both boats. With each breath steam blew from its nostrils as it plodded along the path. Behind it the tiny chimney peeping through the roof of the leading barge puffed little clouds of smoke as the crew cooked their food.

But her pleasure was short-lived. It was time for yet another change of horses and by now Tamarisk was so tired she did not have the will to leave the coach. Her head drooped against Leigh's shoulder. Food was brought to them but she could not partake of it. The halt, as always, was a very short one and within three minutes she was once more being bounced over the increasingly bad road as the coach sped northward. Nevertheless she slept fitfully. When next she woke darkness had fallen and they had crossed the River Don, changed horses yet again at Doncaster, and were arriving at Pontefract.

Leigh regarded Tamarisk's white dusty face and sleeptousled hair with misgivings. Her unkempt appearance made her look far younger than her nineteen years. He felt wretchedly responsible, his protective love for her mingling with a large measure of exasperation. He tried to interest her in the race run yearly at Doncaster. A little over a hundred years previously, he told her, a certain Colonel St. Leger had instituted this race for the best horses in England. But Tamarisk desired only to know how many more miles and hours they must travel.

"We shall descend into a valley shortly," he told her as she tried to restore the lost circulation in her fingers and toes. "Then when we have crossed the River Calder, we climb upward and traverse the Roman Ridge to Wetherby. We should reach there by six of the clock. Then we must cross the Yorkshire moors."

He took care not to add the information he

444

had received from a passenger on the southward-bound coach that snow was already lying inches deep further north between Penrith and Carlisle. The journey across the bleak moorland was dangerous enough without the added hazard of becoming snowbound!

He would have been even more disconcerted had he known that by now Mavreen and Gideon had gained upon them and were less than two hours behind, changing horses at Doncaster.

Gideon too had been advised of the snow threat in the North; but he knew better than to suggest to Mavreen that they halt for the night as some coach travelers had elected to do.

Laughing, he produced a large copper warming pan he had purchased at a greatly inflated price from the innkeeper's wife. It was filled with hot coals.

"'Twill serve to keep us from freezing before ever we reach the Yorkshire moors," he told Mavreen.

"You are the most resourceful man I know," Mavreen said, unbuttoning her half-boots and warming her stockinged feet upon the pan. She was grateful to him on her own behalf but even more for his thought for the coachman and footman who, perforce, sat atop the barouche exposed to the elements. Gideon had purchased for each of them a warm sheepskin and an additional woollen muffler to tie about their heads. He had already given the coachman a welcome rest, taking over the reins himself for the long stretch of road from Worksop.

By stopping no longer than the necessary time

to change the horses and by obtaining always the very best of beasts, they were gaining slowly upon the eloping couple. They were in no doubt that Tamarisk and Leigh were still riding with the Royal Mail coach, for at each staging post there was someone who had noticed them amongst the crowds of travelers.

"Men will always notice Tamarisk, just as they have always noticed you," Gideon said. "Mother and daughter share that indefinable beauty which never goes unremarked!"

"You think her like me in looks?" Mavreen asked curiously.

"In looks and in temperament!" Gideon replied without hesitation.

He glanced at Mavreen's pensive face and gave a sudden loud laugh.

"Why, I do believe you are jealous!" he teased.

Mavreen attempted a smile.

"Tamarisk is a deal younger than I and has that advantage over me," she said. "And I am beginning to *feel* old, Gideon!"

This time Gideon's laughter was loud enough to reach the ears of the coachman.

"Old? *You?*" he exclaimed. "God's teeth, woman, how can you so say when you undertook this journey upon impulse and were prepared to suffer its rigors and dangers quite alone? It was not as if you could have expected to meet with me. In fact it is indeed a stroke of good fortune that I was not already gone to Almack's when you approached my house; or indeed had not gone with Lord Byron upon

446

his travels to Milan. Did I tell you he invited me to go with him although I know the fellow but slightly? His friend Hobhouse, with whom I am better acquainted, suggested last autumn that a sojourn abroad would be good for me."

Mavreen looked at Gideon curiously.

"I am surprised that you declined the adventure," she commented, "for such it would be, I do not doubt."

For a long moment Gideon did not reply. When he did his voice was so low she had to bend forward to catch his words.

"I could not bring myself to leave England," he murmured. "Not whilst *you* live and breathe beneath an English sky!"

Tears filled Mavreen's eyes.

"It both pleasures and pains me to hear you speak so!" she said. "Oh, Gideon, my dear friend, I realize that it brings you nothing but unhappiness to care so much for me. Yet selfishly I am made strangely happy by the knowledge that you love me still. It is a paradox I cannot explain. If I had never encountered Gerard . . . "

"Yes, I know," Gideon interrupted, his voice harsh with suppressed emotion. "Let us not talk of what might have been, Mavreen, lest my thoughts cease to be limited to those of a good friend. There now! We must be nearing Pontefract. We are stopping at the top of the hill that leads down to the town."

He leaned out of the window the better to supervise the footman as he climbed down with the skidpan ready to tie to a rear wheel so that

447

the barouche should not outpace the horses. This precaution was only required if a hill was very steep, but Gideon had complete faith in his most excellent coachman and did not question his decision upon such matters.

By the time they left Pontefract, the fresh horses snorting and eager to be on the move, the first great flakes of snow began to fall in intermittent flurries. The sky was pitch black, no stars showing. Gideon noted with a frown the deterioration of the weather. It had stopped snowing, however, by the time they reached Boroughbridge. As they crossed the river into the town, a bright moon was reflected in the dark waters of the Ure. The temperature seemed to have dropped again and frost formed slowly on the carriage windows as they climbed the hill up to the Roman road leading to Brough.

It was now nearly three of the clock as the coachman urged the new horses higher and higher onto the moors. Here, despite the dark moonlit sky, snow whitened the ground and muffled the sound of the horses' hooves. It became deeper as they neared the fifteen-hundred-foot summit and inevitably their pace slowed. Seeing Mavreen's anxious glance at her timepiece, Gideon said reassuringly:

"The mail coach will have suffered the same conditions. We are above the snow line now but presently we will be going downward again into Brough. We cannot be far behind the runaways."

Mavreen shivered. Despite fresh coals in the warming pan the temperature inside the coach was below freezing. Outside she could see the endless expanse of bleak, treeless moorland, the rocks showing darkly through their snowy blanket.

As they reached the summit the coach drew to a halt so that chains could be fixed to the wheels before their descent. Gideon alighted and took out a bottle of brandy to put fresh life into the coachman and footman. Their eyebrows and side-whiskers were frosted white, their noses scarlet with the cold, made even more bitter by the wind blowing from the North. No one doubted that there was more snow on the way and they were thankful to reach Brough before the sky filled with the dark, heavily burdened clouds.

Although she had now been traveling for thirty hours and her whole body ached with fatigue, Mavreen was in good heart, for the innkeeper at Brough told them the mail coach had stopped there not three quarters of an hour since.

"We are gaining on it," she told Gideon as they set off once more with fresh horses for the comparatively short stretch of road to Appleby. "So long as we meet no mishap we shall overtake it before long."

She drifted into a fitful sleep, her head against Gideon's shoulder. He, however, was too anxious to give way to sleep. The sky was laden with snow, and before ever they reached the small village of Appleby the great flakes were falling softly but steadily, obscuring the outline of the road and requiring from their coachman the utmost attention. Even the streams and rivers

449

that ran through the rocky crevices seemed to be silenced by the threatening skies. But for the dull thud of the horses' hooves, the jingle of harness, and the occasional crack of the coachman's whip, no sound could be heard. The silence was ominous.

They reached Penrith to discover they had gained a further twenty minutes upon the Royal Mail coach.

"'Tis a deal more cumbersome than my barouche," Gideon told Mavreen, grinning. "I do not envy their coachman or their horses!"

He decided this would be an excellent opportunity to prolong their stop for a quick breakfast.

"They'll not reach Gretna Green before us, I promise you. The snow is lying a foot deep in places!" he said reassuringly.

Mavreen did not believe herself hungry, yet when the meal was put before them she discovered she had a vast appetite. With no difficulty she and Gideon consumed thick Cumberland gammon steaks nicely browned on the griddle, followed by freshly baked bread and a delicious goats' milk cheese made by the innkeeper's wife. Washed down with tankards of ale, the repast put fresh energy and heart into the weary travelers.

"It was as well we did eat," remarked Gideon when an hour later, the coach came to an abrupt halt. Looking out of the window he could see the huge snowdrift into which the horses had blundered despite the efforts of the coachman to turn them aside in time. The men dug a passageway behind the wheels, but the walls of powdery snow collapsed as soon as the horses began to back out. It was decided to unharness them and lead them forward until they were clear of the drift. They were then brought round to the rear of the barouche and a makeshift harness of ropes arranged so that they could pull the coach out backward. With Gideon at their heads and the two men adding their strength to the back wheels, the barouche was slowly retrieved from the drift.

The wetness of the lower half of their clothes added to the cold and discomfort of the travelers. Although by the time the horses had been put back in their traces it was nearing six of the clock, there was no sign of an approaching dawn. The darkness was so complete that they caught no glimpse either of the mountains of the Lake Country to their left or of Penrith Beacon to their right. But before long they were in the narrow valley running along the side of the River Petteril and there was some small measure of protection from the biting wind.

"I am reminded of the cold of Russia," Mavreen said to Gideon. "And remembering it I am almost warm again."

The welcome sight of the town of Carlisle, bathed in the pale gold light of a fitful dawn, seemed like a glimpse of heaven to all of them. The stonework of the castle turrets showed darkly against an amber sky. The coachman blew several loud blasts upon his horn, and as if from nowhere the street began to fill with people.

Despite the early hour the staging post was a hive of activity for the mail coach had departed no more than ten minutes earlier. From the postboy they learned that it too had met with mishap on the previous lap of the journey, one of the horses losing a shoe and slowing their progress.

They were now but ten miles from Gretna Green. Making all haste, the barouche bounded along the road out of the town, crossing the bridge over the River Eden and passing the ruins of Hadrian's Wall at a spanking pace. The snow still lay upon the ground, covering the flat marshy plain, but no more fell from the leaden sky. To their left the estuary of the Solway Firth came into sight, glinting in the fitful shafts of pale sunshine.

Gideon reached for Mavreen's hand and smiled down at her.

"There it is — the border!" he said, pointing ahead. "And unless I am much mistaken, there's the Royal Mail coach not half a league ahead of us! I wonder whether our quarry will alight at the Toll Gate and have the pikeman marry them!"

Such in fact was Leigh's intent, but Tamarisk would not agree to it. First, she said, she required a room at one of the inns where she could wash, curl her hair, change her clothes.

"I shall at least endeavor to look like a bride on my wedding day," she said reproachfully, "since I do not expect to have another!"

Leigh, who cared little by now how unruly

was Tamarisk's appearance, was impatient for the pleasures of the rights the wedding would bestow upon him. Tamarisk had kept him at arm's length far too long, and he had not suffered the indescribable discomforts of the two-day journey to Scotland in order to be longer deprived of his possession of her.

Now that the wedding was about to become a reality and the benefits were almost within his grasp, his doubts as to the advisability of marrying Tamarisk were forgotten in the sheer intensity of his desire. For thirty-five hours he had sat beside her in the coach, her warm body pressed against his own, her sweet-smelling hair and the soft skin of her cheek within kissing distance of his lips. Sometimes when the coach lurched, she had been flung against him so that their legs and arms became entangled as if in the very act of love. She spoke now of washing and changing her clothes, yet it was the warm smell of her body that excited him as much as her physical proximity.

But Tamarisk was not to be persuaded into a hurried ceremony at the Toll Gate. With the resilience of youth, she was already beginning to recover from the ardors of the journey and was as bright and gay as a Christmas robin. He resigned himself to indulging her whim and consoled himself when they reached the staging post by commanding a double-bedded room for the pair of them. He knew better than to suggest to Tamarisk that he be allowed to enter it before their wedding. He therefore made his way to the fireside and ordered a comforting glass of brandy whilst she effected her toilette alone in the bridal chamber.

It was here that Gideon and Mavreen came upon him seated on a wooden bench, his legs stretched out to the blazing log fire. On oak settles around the walls sat several farmers, tankards of beer in their great work-roughened hands, their fustian jackets and smock frocks making each man indistinguishable from his neighbor. They raised their eyes only briefly at the entry of the newcomers and proceeded to stare at one another in a deep silence none seemed to find uncomfortable. Leigh, however, studied the latest arrivals with interest. He was convinced that he had seen the strikingly handsome female before. Unquestionably she was of noble birth, as was the gentleman who escorted her. Leigh was not altogether surprised when the lady approached as if she knew him. But he still had no inkling of her true identity as she addressed him.

"May I inquire, Sir, if your name be Darton? Mister Leigh Darton?"

Only then, too late, did he realize why her face seemed so familiar — it was an older replica of Tamarisk's. He rose and with a shock discovered himself standing face to face with the Vicomtesse de Valle with no way of avoiding her maternal outrage.

The color rushed to his cheeks as he bowed in confusion.

Mavreen's voice was ice cold but quietly authoritative as she said briefly:

454

"My daughter, Lady Tamarisk, Mr. Darton, *where is she?*"

Leigh hesitated, wondering if there were not some way he could extricate himself from this unfortunate encounter. But now Gideon took a step toward him and caught his arm in a grip that left no doubt as to his intention to prevent Leigh's escape.

Miserably Leigh nodded his head upward toward the ceiling.

Mavreen's look of contempt was more withering than any words she might have spoken. With a nod to Gideon and ignoring Leigh she turned and made her way toward the stairs.

Gideon looked at the tired, disheveled young man visibly drooping in front of him. A glint of amused sympathy came into his eyes but was quickly gone again as he ordered Leigh to be seated.

The innkeeper came hurrying over, took Gideon's order, and at his command sent a maidservant upstairs with a jug of wine for the two ladies.

Only when the cognac Gideon had ordered was served to him did he speak to Leigh. His voice was matter-of-fact but incisive, brooking no falsehoods.

"I take it you and Lady Tamarisk are not yet wed?"

The would-be bridegroom shook his head.

"But this was your mutual intent?" Gideon persisted.

Leigh nodded. There seemed no point in

trying to prevaricate.

"At least your intentions were honorable in this degree!" Gideon said wryly. "But in other respects, Sir, I think not. You are an actor by profession, are you not? And earn, doubtless, a very moderate salary for your pains. Do you then have private means that you presume to marry a young woman of noble birth? If I am mistaken in you and you are of gentle birth, be so good as to correct me!"

Leigh's silence was sufficient answer.

"Then how, pray, did you intend to support Lady Tamarisk?" Gideon's voice sharpened. "Could it be that you presumed *she* would support *you*? Because if that was your presumption, Sir, I regret to inform you that Lady Tamarisk is quite as penniless as you are. Nor, were she to go against her parents' wishes and marry you, would they offer either of you financial assistance."

"Nevertheless Tamarisk is not entirely penniless," Leigh said sullenly, hating to be thought the fool Gideon was making him out to be, and stung by pride to indiscretion. "Her jewelry is her own and . . . "

"And you love her so dearly that you would sell her only valuable possessions to feed and clothe you both?" Now Gideon's dark eyes were black with anger. "You take advantage, Sir, in a manner which demeans the very nature of love."

Leigh's face was scarlet, his fists clenched as he cried:

"But I do love her. And Tamarisk loves me.

456

You will see, she will not lightly give up the idea of marriage to me. She . . . "

Once again Gideon interrupted.

"You are not going to give her an option. You, Mr. Darton, are going to inform her that you have thought better of your madcap scheme; that although you still entertain the fondest of feelings for her, your love for her will not permit you to belittle her status to your own degree."

"And if I refuse?" Leigh asked with sudden courage.

"I do not think you will be so stupid!" Gideon said quietly. He called for the landlord and ordered him to bring quill, ink, and paper. When these were brought to him, he wrote briefly on the paper and without haste sanded it.

"This, I think, might persuade you to act upon my suggestion," he said, handing to the younger man his note of hand. "You will see that I have instructed my bank, Gurney's, to furnish you with two thousand guineas. If you are agreed, I will put my seal upon it."

"You mean you would bribe me to jilt Tamarisk?"

"Certainly!" Gideon said calmly, unmoved by the implied insult. "I have no hesitation in doing so since I consider it to be in her own interest! Nor do I think you will hesitate in accepting my bribe."

Leigh would dearly have loved to tear the paper in half and throw the pieces in that dark, determined face. But the number of noughts which followed the first figure was irresistible.

With two thousand guineas he might even set up his own touring company; take the lead parts that always fell so maddeningly to Edmund Kean; establish himself in the way he had always dreamed of but never dared believe could happen. He thought of Tamarisk and was shocked to discover that the enormity of his desire for her had paled into insignificance against the future possibilities that lay within his grasp.

Tamarisk was very young, he told himself as excitement mounted in him. She would soon recover from her broken heart — if indeed it did break! She would find some man far more worthy than himself to make her a good husband.

It was with no more than the faintest glimmer of regret that he handed the paper back to Gideon and watched him heat the wax and put his seal upon it.

Within minutes of Leigh's departure from the inn — Gideon having arranged that his own coachman drive the young man to Carlisle where he could pick up the southbound mail coach — Mavreen came down the stairs looking tired and worried.

"I trust you have made more headway with Mr. Darton than I have with Tamarisk!" she said dolefully. "I fear I cannot make her see reason. She insists that my purpose is to curtail her freedom — the freedom she says I enjoyed when I was her age. Furthermore, she seems to feel that her mistakes are the result of my desire to keep *you* for myself."

Seeing the look of bewilderment on Gideon's face she added:

"Tamarisk knows we were once lovers and suspects that we remain so and that is why you will not love *her*! Mr. Darton was, I surmise, but a substitute for you — her real love."

"But she cannot seriously believe I would take a child of her age to wife!" Gideon exclaimed. "Nor have I ever given her the slightest cause to think I could love her other than as an uncle loves a favorite niece. Besides which she knows that I love you."

Mavreen sighed deeply.

"Tamarisk is no longer a child, Gideon. At her age I was long since wed and had a child of my own."

Gideon frowned.

"Be that as it may, to me she remains your daughter, Mavreen, and a mighty troublesome one at that! I will go and speak with her. Perhaps I can talk reason into that pretty little head of hers."

At first Tamarisk was unwilling to believe Gideon when he told her that Leigh was departing on the southbound mail coach without her; far less would she believe that her bridegroom had been willing to give her up for money. All but incoherent with shock, fatigue, and tears, she tried in vain to wring a denial from Gideon. But his gentleness and tenderness as he took her on his knee as if she were still a little girl convinced her of the fact of Leigh's perfidy.

"You must not feel bitter, my sweeting,"

Gideon said, wiping away her tears. "After all, your young man put a very high price upon your pretty head. Why, he has come near to bankrupting me! I had the devil's own task to persuade him to give you up. Between you and me, I thought to buy your freedom for a fraction of the sum he wanted, troublesome little baggage that you are!" His eyes were twinkling as he gently teased her.

"'Tis nothing to laugh about, Perry!" she protested between sobs. "'Tis . . . 'tis humiliating!"

"I expect it seems so at the moment," he agreed, "but you must not judge him too harshly, my Princess. You have never known poverty so you cannot judge what it means to a poor man when he sees the chance to put money in his pocket. 'Tis a cruel world without it, I can assure you!"

She suddenly remembered her journal and the truths it contained about Perry's past. He had had to steal, to rob, in order to get rich! Her bitterness toward Leigh was assuaged by such thoughts, although the pain of his desertion was in no way lessened.

"Come now," said Gideon, sensing her mood correctly. "Admit that you do not really love this fellow! For I believe 'twas merely the excitement and romance of the elopement which took your fancy!"

Tamarisk was momentarily silenced by this barb of truth. During the journey to the North she had already begun to appreciate that marriage to a struggling young actor might not turn out to be so exciting as she had foolishly supposed. As for loving Leigh — he had never come first in her affections.

"I will admit that I never loved him as I love you," she said in a small unhappy voice.

Gideon removed her gently from his lap and held her hands as she stood forlornly before him.

"That too is but romantic nonsense," he said quietly but firmly. "And 'tis best put out of your mind, Tamarisk, with other such ridiculous and dangerous thoughts as concern your Mama and me. I understand you have learned some of the facts relating to a period of our lives when your Mama believed your Papa could never marry her. And do not turn your head away!" he insisted. "For I want you to hear the truth from my lips so that there can be no further misunderstandings. I loved your mother very dearly and would have married her had she been willing. But she wanted only your Papa. Her subsequent marriage to him in no way lessened my feelings for her, but I have not as yet in my life laid a hand upon another man's wife, nor intend to. So never again condemn your mother of wrongdoing. She loves you, Tamarisk, and your mistrust must hurt her deeply. Moreover, she has just risked life and limb to rescue you from your folly. That I came with her to help and protect her was the merest stroke of Fate. Therefore she has earned your respect rather than your criticism and I would like you better were you to show some sign of appreciation."

"If it pleases you, I will try," Tamarisk said.

461

"But only because you ask it of me, Perry! I will do anything in the world for you."

"Then promise you will discard the notion that I would make you a good husband!" Gideon said, smiling. "For I might be an indulgent and affectionate uncle to you, Tamarisk, but I would be a harsh despot to the woman I married! Now dry your eyes and tidy your hair so that we may go downstairs and reassure your anxious Mama!"

Sighing, Tamarisk did as he bade her, but she was all too well aware that even now Perry's first thought was not for her but for her Mama. As for Leigh Darton, already he had begun to seem of small importance. Even the memory of his handsome young face flushed with ardent desire for her paled into insignificance now that she was gazing into Perry's eyes. Compared with Perry, he assumed the guise of a gauche boy; and by his failure to stand by her had proved himself as weak and ineffectual as Perry was strong and determined. In twenty years he would never make the man that Perry was.

As she ran a comb through her disordered hair, she stole a sideways glance at Gideon. He was staring out of the window, his eyes no longer smiling but thoughtful — and sad.

One day I will make him happy! she vowed silently. He will realize how pointless it is to continue loving Mama — and then . . . then he would turn to her — to the one who truly loved him, Tamarisk thought.

When Gideon looked round at her, he was

surprised to see a faint smile upon her lips and that a soft rosy color had returned to her cheeks. He would have been less happy had he realized the true reason for her abrupt change of mood.

23

H AD Mavreen returned home at once Gerard might have been persuaded to listen to reason. But it was a full four days before, weary and utterly exhausted, she and Tamarisk stepped into the great hall of Barre House.

She looked about her in astonishment. There were boxes everywhere, all neatly strapped and labeled as if for a journey. She bent down and read one of the labels: *Compiégne, France.* She drew a deep breath and released it on a long, tired sigh.

"It would seem as if your father has had news from France requiring his return there at once," she said to Tamarisk. "I trust it is nothing serious that necessitates his presence so promptly."

Tamarisk made no reply. Half asleep, she clung to the bannister of the great staircase, longing for nothing more than the warmth and comfort of her bed. If she had awareness at all of any emotion, it was a feeling of relief — relief to be home; relief to be rescued at the eleventh hour from marriage to a man who, it was now obvious, had never loved her.

Mavreen, no less exhausted, slowly climbed the stairs in search of Gerard. She guessed that he must be in the wing where their bedchamber was situated, else the commotion caused by their arrival would have brought him to the hall to welcome them. Her steps quickened as she neared their room, her anticipation mounting as she thought of his pleasure at the news of Tamarisk's safe return. She was happy to think that no matter how pressing the requirement for his departure to France, he had awaited her homecoming before leaving for Compiègne.

She opened the bedroom door. Gerard was standing at the window with his back to her, looking down into the street below. He turned and stared at her, the look in his eyes so strange and unsmiling that she paused a second or two before running to him. But before she could reach him with her outstretched arms he moved sideways and walked past her without speaking. She swung round, a frown of bewilderment creasing her forehead, a feeling of apprehension engulfing her.

"Gerard, my love, what is it? Have you had bad news? For pity's sake, tell me what has happened? Has there been disaster of some kind at the Château? Has it to do with Antoine?"

Her familiar habit of running many questions together momentarily touched him. But almost at once his face hardened again.

"There has been no disaster at the Château!" he said in a cold, hard voice "Nevertheless I am leaving this morning for Compiègne and I shall be taking Antoine with me."

"I do not understand. If nothing is amiss, then why are you leaving?" she asked nonplussed.

465

"You must have good reason, Gerard. What is this about, pray?"

"I have every reason for wishing to leave this house!" Gerard replied stonily. "You may think me a simpleton, Mavreen, but I assure you I am not the blind fool you suppose me to be. However, since you demand I spell out my reasons for going, I will do so!" Now his voice grated with pent-up jealousy and anger as he said, "*I know that you have a lover.* I know that you have spent the past six days in his company. That, I think, is sufficient explanation of my intent to remove myself from this house and from you."

For one long moment Mavreen stared at him in total astonishment. Then anger brought the color flaring into her cheeks. Her eyes blazed brilliantly as she flung back her head defiantly.

"How dare you make such accusations!" she cried. "And by what right do you condemn me without even hearing what *I* may have to say!"

But as suddenly as it had overcome her, her anger faded. The tension left her body and she fell back into an armchair. Her voice, when next she spoke, was that of a mother addressing a small boy as she said softly:

"Let me at once reassure you, Gerard. I do not know who has put such foolish thoughts into your mind, but I give you my word — I am entirely innocent. I do not have a lover nor have had since the day I learned you were still alive. I swear it upon my oath."

The look of relief she expected to see come into his face was not forthcoming. Instead he continued to regard her with an expression of jealous hatred.

"Before you perjure yourself further, Mavreen," he said scornfully, "perhaps I should explain that I have proof that Peregrine Waite was your lover. I know the man is a deceiver and a highway robber as well as a thief of other men's wives! I even know his true name, Gideon Morris!"

Scarce able to credit her ears, Mavreen stared at Gerard, white-faced. From whence he had obtained such information she could not imagine. But that did not matter. All that concerned her now was to rectify Gerard's mistaken belief in her infidelity.

"I do not *have* to defend myself against your accusations," she said quietly. "Nevertheless it is best that you should know all of the truth since you have misconstrued those few facts already in your possession. Gideon Morris *was* once my lover. I do not deny it. But that was many years ago — before I came to Russia to find you. As you well know, Gerard, I believed you dead, and yes, he was my lover then."

She looked at him with gentle patience.

"Once I tried to tell you about those years with Gideon, but you begged me not to talk of them. You said they had no importance for you. Yet now you choose to revive the past. It all happened a long while ago, my darling, and I can only repeat that I have been completely faithful to you since our marriage."

Although the tone of Mavreen's voice and the honesty of her gaze raised a momentary doubt in Gerard's mind, he had had six days alone in which to build up his suspicions to the point where he was convinced of his wife's guilt. He had imagined this confrontation a dozen times and been certain Mavreen would admit her culpability. He had not once imagined she would deny it nor attempt to lie her way through it. So sure was he that she and Waite were still lovers that he could not now readjust his judgment of her. It was therefore an admission of her guilt he now demanded rather than an assertion of her innocence.

"Tell me one thing," he said, his hands clenched, his temples throbbing. "Did you go to your lover when you left this house the other night? I want a 'yes' or a 'no,' Mavreen!"

"Yes! No! Gerard, I cannot give you a true 'yes' or 'no' lest you misconstrue my meaning. 'Tis true I went to Scotland with Gideon in his coach; but for no other purpose than in pursuit of Tamarisk. But I did not go to Gideon's house with any such intent that night I left you here ill in bed. I had no thought then of asking Gideon's assistance. I came upon him quite by accident outside his house in Harley Street. Upon hearing my mission he at once offered to accompany me and I accepted his offer, since my journey was likely to be long and dangerous. It was but by the merest chance I saw him — and *not* by design."

Angrily Gerard swept away the hand she had placed upon his arm in an appeal for understanding. Her references to Gideon by his true name had only served to increase his uneasiness.

468

"You expect me to believe in such a fairy tale?" he cried, his voice knife-edged with sarcasm. "Then indeed you take me for a fool, Mavreen. Such a meeting by coincidence is not to be credited. It is obvious to me that you met this man by design."

Now, without warning, anger rose like bile in Mavreen's throat.

"If I take you for a fool it is because you are one, Gerard, but not for the reasons you have stated! If you cannot accept my word after all the years you have known me, if you can have so little affection for me that you can think only of your foolish male ego and not of me or your daughter, then the sooner you leave us both the better. I have no wish to live under the same roof with a husband who mistrusts me; who cares nothing for the arduous journey I have made nor, more importantly, for his daughter's safety. Do you be on your way, Gerard, and do not expect that Tamarisk or I will follow you to Compiègne. If you go, you go alone."

Gerard paused, staring at her great flashing eyes made larger than ever by the white frame of her face.

It angered him to discover himself suddenly desirous of her, his body betraying his mind by its awareness of her beauty as her breasts rose and fell with her swift breathing and she moistened her full red lips with the tip of her tongue.

Inconsequently, at the moment when he believed his marriage was at an end, he found his thoughts returning to the first time he had possessed that beautiful voluptuous body. His desire for her now was no less than it was then. He was but a boy of seventeen when first they lay naked in one another's arms. What heady delight he had found in that sweet virginal innocence, combined as it was with a total lack of girlish modesty! Like some healthy young creature from the farmlands where she had been reared, Mavreen had savored as hungrily as he the union of their bodies.

He closed his eyes, remembering the tiny, slim waist; the smooth satin skin of her shoulders, legs, arms; the delicate curves of her hips and the taut wonder of her breasts, the rose-pink nipples hard and erect beneath his lips. He was aware now of the hardening of his own body as the memory of his seduction and her surrender heightened his desire. He both hated and loved her for this power she had to stir in him the deepest, most lustful of instincts. He was tempted to push her backward onto the bed, rip her clothes from her, and wipe forever from her eyes the angry scorn. But he would not give her the satisfaction of knowing his need. He must keep in his mind the thought of that most secret part of her wantonly exposed for another man's pleasure.

Sickened by his thoughts, his desire cooled and he looked away, his eyes stricken with unhappiness. Then without a word he turned on his heel, and permitting himself no backward glance he strode from the room.

Mavreen jumped to her feet and took a step forward. His name, trembling on her lips, remained unspoken, dying there with the tiny broken fragments of her trust in him.

He cannot mean this! He cannot! she thought, as she fell exhausted upon the coverlet.

She lay in silence, waiting expectantly for his footfall. She was certain he would return to take her in his arms, hold her to him and beg forgiveness for doubting her. Some minutes later there was a knock upon the door. But it was her maid with a tray of hot chocolate. Mavreen was too proud to inquire if the Vicomte were still in the house although her heart ached with the desire to do so. Presently she heard another footfall. Raising her head, a radiant smile upon her face as she opened her arms to welcome Gerard back, she waited breathlessly for the door to open.

This time the slim white-robed figure standing in the doorway was that of her daughter Tamarisk. Tears were streaming down her face as she ran to the bedside and threw herself upon Mavreen.

"Oh, Mama, Mama!" she cried. "Papa has gone! He has left us never to return. And it is all my fault! *Oh, I wish I were dead!*"

Mavreen's disappointment mingling with anxiety and fatigue were too much for her.

Unable to stop her own tears, she cradled her child to her, rocking her gently to and fro.

"Hush! Hush, my pet!" she whispered. "Of course it is not your fault Papa has gone. How could it be?"

Between sobs Tamarisk confessed that lying open on her bed was her journal, all the pages

471

telling of her discovery of Perry's past torn out and missing.

Horrified, Mavreen could find nothing to say.

Now she understood Gerard's reactions. They were not based on idle rumor or suspicion but on the written word of their own daughter. How he had come upon Tamarisk's journal or demeaned himself to read it was incomprehensible to her until Tamarisk said tearfully:

"I have no doubt it was that despicable Antoine who discovered my journal!" She brushed angrily at her tear-streaked face. "He was forever spying upon me, Mama, and must have seen where I hid it. I hate him! I wish he had never been born!"

Mavreen was uncomfortably aware that Tamarisk's suspicions matched her own. So unsavory an action as to steal and read a person's most private writings was all too easily attributable to the child she knew Antoine to be; and to pass on such information to his father was in keeping with the underhand and malicious streak in the unhappy boy. Nevertheless she felt compelled to remind Tamarisk that there was no proof of Antoine's complicity.

"Moreover," she added quietly, "to know how it happened cannot alter the fact that your father now knows the truth about Perry. But whatever he may suspect to the contrary, I have been faithful to him since the day I discovered him to be alive, so there is nothing with which he can reproach me. I would myself have told him about my past, but he would not permit me to

472

talk of those years. That he has heard of them through your journal is perhaps unfortunate but allows no blame for his departure to be laid at your door. He will doubtless come to his senses in due course. But I do regret that Perry's true identity is known, for it could be dangerous, nay, fatal, for him if ever the fact was revealed."

Tamarisk's tears ceased abruptly as she stared at her mother.

"But surely Papa would never betray such a confidence!" she exclaimed.

Mavreen bit her lip.

"No, I do not think he would, Tamarisk. But he loves me so much I fear his reason is a little disordered by his jealousy. He might challenge Perry to a duel and one or other be killed as a result. It is perhaps as well, after all, that your Papa has gone to France. When he has had time to reconsider in a calmer frame of mind, I am sure he will realize and deeply regret that he falsely accused me of infidelity. But I must warn Perry meanwhile. If your guess is correct and Antoine too has read your journal, then the reputation of Sir Peregrine Waite is at risk."

Tamarisk dissolved once more into tears.

"I wish I had never eloped with Leigh. I wish I had never even met him!" she cried. "I have hurt everyone I love most in the world!"

Despite the gravity of the occasion Mavreen smiled.

"No, my love, you have not! No one has been hurt as yet except perhaps your Papa, and he has hurt himself by his failure to trust in my love for him."

"But you, Mama," Tamarisk sobbed. "You are all alone!"

"That is far from the case since you are here with me," Mavreen replied gently. "Now let us stop feeling guilty or sorry for ourselves and be grateful that we are safely home. Papa will be back before long, you will see. Everything will be happily resolved."

So certain was Mavreen that Gerard would soon come to his senses that she at once wrote a letter to Gideon telling him what had transpired and begging him not to call or make any kind of contact with her.

To Sir John and all her friends Mavreen explained away Gerard's sudden absence by saying that the affairs of his estate in France necessitated his presence there.

But Society had more interesting gossip to hand than the separation of the de Valles. On the twenty-eighth of January an attempt was made upon the Prince Regent's life as he drove to Westminster for the opening of Parliament. Speculation as to the culprit was rife, but the Regent was so generally unpopular and the crowds so hostile that the man who dared to fire the air gun was not revealed.

"'Tis not to be wondered at if the people are in revolt!" remarked Sir John one evening at dinner. "This country is in need of reforms and I have put my name to Hunt's petition demanding them. Some of his followers were gathered at the Golden Hotel in Charing Cross on the day of the shooting, and they say it could be one of these who was the would-be assassin."

Mavreen sighed.

"The Baroness was at a dinner party given by the Regent two weeks ago at the Pavilion in Brighton. She told me Prinny had ordered the serving of one hundred and sixteen dishes. With so many of his subjects on the point of starvation, such extravagances by the head of the Realm are unwise to say the least."

Tamarisk tried unsuccessfully to hide a smile as she said:

"I overheard my maid telling Dorcas that the Regent's stomach is now so vast it hangs to his knees when uncorseted!"

Her grandfather patted her arm warningly.

"Best not repeat servants' gossip," he said. "The Regent is so frightened for his life, everyone is suspected of treason. And what is more, Parliament too must think he is in danger, since they have seen fit to enroll special constables to guard him."

Clarissa, now restored to health though not quite so plump in figure, looked at her husband questioningly.

"Is it true the blanketeers marching from Manchester upon London have been halted by the military?"

"Blanketeers!" Tamarisk echoed. "Who, then, are they, Grandpapa?"

"Desperate men who were seeking to lodge a protest about their unemployment," Sir John explained. "They have been so named because each man carried a blanket to keep him warm whilst he marched."

"The ringleaders have been imprisoned in the

Tower," Mavreen said quietly. "They have been charged with high treason!"

"I do not know what the world is coming to," said Sir John with a sigh, "what with rebellions, assassination attempts, and now the suspension of habeas corpus! 'Tis my opinion there is no reason good enough, not even the security of the Regent, to justify a man's detention in custody without good cause stated for it."

He lowered his voice so that no attentive servant might overhear him.

"Sir William Cobbett has fled the country. They were seeking to arrest him, you know, on a matter of high treason. I heard he is on his way to America."

"'Twill not prevent him continuing with his political register, I'll warrant!" said Mavreen.

But political events, interesting although they were, could not keep Mavreen's mind for long away from Gerard. There were many occasions when her desire for a reconciliation was so intense that she was on the verge of writing to him. But on the point of putting quill to paper she realized that there was nothing new she could say to him. She had professed her innocence, and until he felt able to believe her, humbling herself by further reiteration of her faithfulness to him could achieve nothing worthwhile.

The greater the number of weeks and then months which passed without word or sign of him, the greater became Mavreen's longing to forget her pride and go to him. She was convinced that once they were together again he

476

would cease to doubt her. But always she found excuse not to go. The severity of the winter had continued into the spring, and in May the snow was still falling. With the approach of summer, however, the sun at last shone again, and upon the impulse of the moment she decided to take Tamarisk to The Grange. The Sussex countryside had never yet failed to restore her spirits, she told herself. Moreover, Tamarisk too was in need of cheering.

Although her daughter now talked openly to her mother of the secret meetings with Leigh Darton, she admitted that she had never really loved him.

"I would not have forgiven him any wrongdoing, as you forgive Papa!" Tamarisk said, sighing. "Nor would I have remained faithful to him had he doubted me as Papa doubts you. If I were you, Mama, I would as soon be hung for a sheep as for a lamb and I would take a lover again!"

"Then you do not know what true love is about," Mavreen replied, thoughtfully. "What is important in love, Tamarisk, is that which lies in your heart and your head and not the temptations of your body!"

To add to Tamarisk's depression, even the erstwhile dependable Charles Eburhard had ceased to write adoring letters to her. She supposed that he had found himself a beautiful girl abroad to occupy his heart.

Tamarisk's one great consolation was her pleasure in riding. As the summer weather continued with one golden sunny day following another, she spent many hours upon her horse, going most frequently to Firle Beacon where there was usually a faint breeze to cool the hot breathlessness of the afternoon air.

On one such afternoon Tamarisk rode in the direction of Falmer across the Downs and was about to turn her horse's head for home when she glimpsed a curricle overturned on the roadside, its driver standing forlornly by its side.

At the same moment the man must have espied her, for he withdrew a white 'kerchief from his pocket and waved it vigorously. Although Tamarisk doubted there was much she could do by way of assistance, nevertheless she urged her horse toward him.

The unfortunate driver turned out to be a fashionably attired young man who hastened to explain that he was on his way back to Lewes from the Brighton races when his curricle had hit a loose boulder and overturned. The traces had broken and his horse had bolted.

Tamarisk stared at the hapless victim curiously. His face seemed remarkably familiar. Then her cheeks flamed as suddenly recognition dawned.

"Are you not Mr. Edward Crowhurst?" she inquired.

The man stared up at the beautiful young woman in an admixture of admiration and astonishment.

"By my troth!" he exclaimed, a glint of amusement in his voice. "If 'tis not my Angel of Mercy come from Richmond to succor me once again!"

Tamarisk's blush deepened. But his mocking tone angered rather than embarrassed her.

"'Twould be a just desert were I to leave you in your predicament!" she said tartly.

He grinned disarmingly.

"And you would be justified in so doing, Lady Tamarisk!" His face became serious. "I owe you an apology which, alas, I was not permitted by your aunt to make at the time of our last encounter. I fear too much wine got the better of my tongue — a poor excuse indeed! But I do sincerely regret my behavior that day. Can you find it in your heart to forgive me?"

"I had quite forgot it," Tamarisk said truthfully. "In the meanwhile, since I can espy your horse upon that hilltop, I will endeavor to catch him for you."

Without waiting for his further comment she spurred her mount to a canter. He watched her ride away scarce able to credit that the trusting young girl who had so intrigued him — was it really five years ago — had become such a self-assured and gorgeous a creature. He was more than anxious to take advantage of this strange coincidence which had brought them together for a second time.

But even as he watched her, his excitement turned to consternation as he saw her horse swerve violently. For a moment it looked as if the rider would keep her seat, but the animal, clearly frightened, lunged forward and, to his horror, the girl was flung to the ground.

So good a horsewoman was Tamarisk that

Mavreen never feared for her safety. She was therefore deeply shocked when a carriage rolled up the driveway and a strange gentleman carried her daughter into the house.

Tamarisk was deathly pale. She attempted a smile.

"It is all right, Mama. I have had a riding accident. This is Mr. Crowhurst who has been kind enough to bring me home."

There was no sign of injury as they laid her upon the bed, but wincing with pain Tamarisk admitted she had hurt her back.

"I have alerted the physician in Lewes," said Edward Crowhurst, his forehead creased with anxiety. "He will be here directly."

But when the physician arrived betimes in his gig, he was unable to estimate the seriousness of Tamarisk's injury.

"We can but wait and see," he informed Mavreen as kindly as he could. "At least there are no bones broken and no internal injury that I can find."

When the physician had departed Edward Crowhurst explained to Mavreen how the accident had occurred.

"I fear I am entirely to blame," he said remorsefully. "I was traveling far too fast and had I not overturned my gig, your daughter would not have had to come to my rescue. Thank heaven I was able to stop a passing carriage and bring her home."

He was staying with his uncle in Lewes, he explained, and would be honored if he might be allowed to call on the morrow to inquire after the invalid who he hoped would suffer no long-term ill effects.

But there was to be no speedy recovery for Tamarisk. For the whole of the month of August she was unable to use her legs without pain. The physician ordered complete immobility but permitted her to be carried downstairs by Dickon where she could lie on her back on a day-bed by the open French windows.

True to his word Mr. Crowhurst called daily. At first Tamarisk refused to receive him. It was Mavreen who persuaded her to do so.

"He seems such a charming, likable young man," she said to her daughter. "And so concerned about you! Not only would it be a kindness to see him, but his company would relieve the tedium of the days which must seem very long to you!"

Tamarisk finally relented. As far as she was aware, Aunt Clarrie had never told her mother of her first meeting with Edward Crowhurst, and Tamarisk had no wish now to relate the incident. It would have meant revealing his references to Mavreen as the Barre Diamond and the repercussion upon herself which could only cause embarrassment to them both.

As for Edward Crowhurst, he was fulsome in his apologies. He begged Tamarisk to forgive him for his behavior which he could only excuse on the grounds that he had had too jolly a time at the tavern with his friends. His reasoning so impaired, he had quite misjudged both her and the Vicomtesse de Valle, he vouchsafed, and had never forgiven himself for so doing.

"Your statement cuts no ice with me, Sir!" Tamarisk had replied curtly, "for you know very well that you had quite forgot my existence until we met a second time!"

It was an accusation he hotly and truthfully denied. But although Edward Crowhurst proved to be far nicer than Tamarisk remembered from their first encounter, and she admired his good looks, she was disinclined to respond to the flirtation he so obviously desired.

"I cannot understand you, Tamarisk!" Mavreen said when her daughter requested that the young man should be asked to cease his visits.

Tamarisk could not explain that it was not that she disliked Edward Crowhurst but that time spent in his company was meaningless. It was Perry she longed to see! Perry whose company she needed! He and only he could have cheered the long, dull days; lifted her spirits and removed the ache in her heart.

Once Mavreen had no further cause to worry about Tamarisk's ultimate recovery her thoughts turned again to Gerard. She realized that she now had good excuse to write to him. Without too great a loss of pride, she could tell him about Tamarisk's fall and subsequent recovery and end her letter with a request that he return home soon since they would both dearly love to see him.

She wrote and dispatched the letter at once before she could yet again change her mind.

From then on her heart leaped with joyful expectation whenever she heard the sound of a carriage drawing up to the house, believing it must be Gerard come in person in reply to her letter. But their only visitor was Charles Eburhard, tanned a golden brown by the Mediterranean sun, taller, broader, and very much more self-assured than when last they had seen him.

He was not dressed in naval uniform but was handsomely attired as befitted a country gentleman. He kissed Mavreen's hand, and smiling warmly asked if he could pay his respects to her daughter. It was his intention, he told Mavreen matter-of-factly, to ask Tamarisk to marry him.

As amused as she was surprised by this unexpected and transformed young man, Mavreen told him about Tamarisk's riding accident and informed him where he might find her.

Mavreen was glad to see him although she was far from certain Tamarisk would feel equal pleasure.

Tamarisk's first reaction at the sight of Charles was one of such amazement that she quite forgot her manners.

"But where are your freckles?" she inquired as he bent to kiss her hand.

"Hidden beneath my sunburn, doubtless," he replied, sounding quite unperturbed by the personal tone of her remark. "And where, pray, are the roses in your cheeks? Or did they fall off when you fell from your horse, Lady Tamarisk?"

"You make fun of me!" she replied, tossing her head and frowning. She was suddenly conscious of her crumpled muslin gown and disheveled hair and was angry with Charles for appearing unannounced. She was also made uneasy by the change in him which she could not immediately define. His features were no more handsome than they had ever been, but he had acquired a look of distinction.

"You look older!" she blurted out.

"As indeed I am!" replied the young man, seating himself on a chair beside her chaise longue. "And as you are too, Lady Tamarisk," he added, smiling, "though damme if you do not look as if you belong still in the schoolroom!"

Made even more self-conscious by this remark, Tamarisk scowled as she said:

"There is no need to address me by my title, Charles. I do not think any the better of you for playing the sophisticate!"

If her sharp tone and her reprimand upset him, he gave no sign of it. Instead he repossessed himself of her hand and imprisoned it in his.

"I am delighted to find you so well-spirited, Tamarisk," he said. "I was unaware, of course, that you had suffered an accident until your mother so informed me."

Tamarisk halted, trying without success to withdraw her hand.

"I cannot see why my health should be of interest to you, Charles!" she said coldly. "After all, you have not concerned yourself with my well-being for . . . for a long time!"

"Ah! You refer to the lack of letters from me of late!" Charles said, sounding quite pleased with her reproof. "But you reproach me unfairly, Tamarisk. I have been at sea and only this last week reached England. I waited not one day longer than was necessary before calling to give you my news in person."

Tamarisk was momentarily silenced. This was no longer the shy, tongue-tied admirer who had bidden her a sad farewell at their last encounter. This was a new Charles — a grown-up, self-possessed, and doubtless self-opinionated young man showing very little deference to her.

"Your news is of little importance to me, Charles!" she said airily. "Now if you have no objection, I would like to rest."

She lay back against her cushions in tacit dismissal, but the visitor made no move to go.

"I fear I must object!" he said, his voice no longer teasing but determined. "You see, I came to Sussex today because I wish to talk to you on a matter of importance, Tamarisk. In truth I came to tell you that I love you very much and want you to be my wife!"

Tamarisk sat up abruptly. She was angry with herself because his sudden declaration had made her blush.

"Then you will have to go on wanting!" she said pertly. "I have told you a dozen times that I will never marry you!"

Charles seemed quite unperturbed. Smiling, he said:

"Not a dozen times, Tamarisk. Only five!"

"My answer is still 'no'!" she replied firmly.

Charles's smile faded.

"This time I will not take 'no' for an answer!" he said quietly. "I really mean that I want you to be my wife. I love you very much, Tamarisk. I have always loved you, and although I have met many girls these past few years, none can equal you in my regard. I do not expect you to love me at once, but given a little time I believe you might come to care for me. I can offer you a good life. I am to be promoted to lieutenant and have been told that my career prospects in the Navy are excellent. You will want for nothing, Tamarisk, and I will devote myself to ensuring your happiness!"

It was a long speech, and the serious manner in which Charles delivered it affected Tamarisk quite markedly. She found herself looking at her suitor with new eyes. Although he lacked the good looks of Leigh Darton or Edward Crowhurst, Charles was not without appeal. His years at sea had given him a manly breadth of shoulder which unaccountably recalled Perry to her mind.

Without warning, tears welled into Tamarisk's eyes as she thought of the hopelessness of her adoration for Perry. How near she had come to ruining her life with her foolhardy dash into the arms of Lord Byron and equally reckless elopement with Leigh! If Charles knew of her past he would very quickly rescind his offer of marriage! In fact no worthy young man, if he knew the truth about her, would want to make her his wife.

Before Tamarisk could brush away her tears Charles had pulled out a lace-edged 'kerchief and was performing the task for her, his face a mask of consternation.

"Forgive me, I beg you!" he cried. "I had no

intention of distressing you. I had hoped . . . I wanted . . . " He broke off in a confusion so complete that Tamarisk felt immediately sorry for him.

" 'Tis not your fault, Charles. I . . . I am still a little weak after my fall, and really, I do assure you, I am greatly complimented by your offer. But I cannot marry you. I am truly sorry!"

A year ago such a rejection would have silenced him. But now he said gently:

"I have to return to my ship at Plymouth almost immediately. But I have been promised long leave for Christmas. If you will allow me, I would like to call up on you again then, Tamarisk. You see, I did really mean what I said when I told you I am very much in love with you. And I see that I shall have to go on asking you to marry me until finally you do relent and say 'yes.' "

"I could not say 'yes' even if I so desired!" Tamarisk said enigmatically and would not enlighten him further. But she gave way to his insistence that he call upon her on his next leave.

To her mother Tamarisk made no mention of Charles's proposal nor of her refusal to marry him. It lay heavily upon her conscience that she had not given Charles the real reason for her rejection of him, namely, that in her secret heart she clung to the hope that one day, by some miracle, Perry would discover that he loved her and wanted her for *his* wife.

24

September – December 1817

MAVREEN did not press Tamarisk to confide in her. She was determined that however suitable a husband young Charles Eburhard might make, she would not attempt to persuade her daughter into a union with a man she did not love. Judging by the depressed state of Tamarisk's spirit, she could only assume that Charles's proposal had brought her no joy.

Not only was Tamarisk depressed, but Mavreen too was finding herself increasingly downhearted. She refused to believe that Gerard intended their separation to be permanent, yet it was already nearing the end of September and his silence remained absolute.

She decided to return to Barre House in an attempt to cheer Tamarisk and assuage her own loneliness with a life filled with social frivolities. It was on her return from one such occasion — a musical soirée at the house of her old friend the Baroness — that the miracle happened. Gerard arrived home. Mavreen was on the point of retiring for the night when she heard a commotion downstairs. She halted Dorcas who was assisting her to disrobe.

"'Tis far too late for callers, Dorcas!" she said to the maid. "Go see what the noise is all about!"

But long before her maid could return Mavreen recognized the sound of Gerard's voice. He was in the hall below, issuing instructions to one of the footmen.

Unaware of her semi-*déshabille*, of the white, naked skin of her shoulders revealed when Dorcas had unfastened her dress Mavreen gathered up her full skirts and, her heart thudding wildly, ran down the stairs.

Gerard, with Antoine standing quietly at his side, looked upward at the sound of her glad cry of welcome. For a moment he wondered if it were Tamarisk flying toward him in so youthful and undignified a manner. But as Mavreen flung herself into his arms, he was instantly reminded not of his daughter but of the glowing, vital girl who had first stirred his desires so long ago; and he knew himself as vulnerable now as then to her sensual beauty.

Oblivious of the servants, of his young son's cold, disapproving stare, of anything but the intense hunger in his loins, his arms enfolded Mavreen and his mouth came down upon hers in a long, hard kiss.

He was the first to break free. But Mavreen, bright-eyed, clung to his arm, laughing and talking both at once.

"Oh, Gerard! I am so happy, so very, *very* happy to see you!" she cried breathlessly. "You received my letter? No, do not answer me! Nothing matters but that you are home. I have missed you so much . . . "

She broke off, urging him in a low voice to follow her back up the staircase. Gerard hesitated. But his aching need for the sweet solace of his wife's beautiful body outweighed all other considerations. As he took a step forward he looked back over his shoulder at his son. There was an expression of angry resentment on the boy's pale face which his father failed to interpret.

"Go to bed, Antoine!" he said. "You look very tired. Dorcas, see he has everything he needs. We have eaten upon the journey, but a hot drink . . . "

Impatiently Mavreen pulled at Gerard's arm. Wordless, he permitted her to lead him up the stairs and along the landing into their bedchamber. As the door closed behind them he paused:

"Mavreen, lest there be any misunderstanding . . . " he began, his voice low-pitched and as serious as his expression. But Mavreen interrupted him with an embrace so loving, his cooling blood flamed once more to a fever of desire.

"Do not let us talk about the misunderstanding which separated us. All that matters now is that we are together," she said softly as she began to unfasten the gilt buttons of his coat. This done, her fingers moved swiftly and easily to the smaller pearl buttons of his shirt. Her eyes smiled up at him as she added, "I have missed you so. Help me, Gerard! Help me to disrobe myself!"

His hesitation was fractional as his eyes devoured the face and figure of the one woman in the world who never failed to arouse him. She

490

had never seemed more desirable than at this minute when she had abandoned all pretense and was openly declaring her urgent need of him. Her eyes were like two great pools of fire and her cheeks were flushed like a young girl's as her body moved sinuously beneath his hands.

It amazed him that the passing of the years had wrought so little change in her. If change there had been, it was to enhance her voluptuousness. Her breasts were fuller but firm and vibrant beneath the pressure of his lips. Her golden skin, untouched by wrinkles, was fragrant with the scent of her womanliness. Unmarred by perfumes, the half-forgotten smell of her hot, eager body pervaded his nostrils and his desire flamed to unbearable torment.

"You are too beautiful!" he cried in a strange hard voice. "No man could resist such temptation!"

Smiling happily Mavreen drew him toward the great bed.

"I do not want you to resist me!" she whispered as he fell upon the coverlet, dragging her down with him. "I love you, Gerard. I want you! I need you!"

Her voice was muffled by his desperate kisses. It was as if he were taking her for the first time. His desire was too great a force to be controlled or withheld. She felt his nails gripping into the soft flesh of her buttocks and gloried in the pain as he drove into her. This was no halfhearted lover but a man long deprived of the joys of a woman's body. His demands upon her were no less than hers upon him and it seemed to Mavreen that never before had they reached such pinnacles of mutual pleasure. Even when her body's needs were perfectly and totally satisfied, her delight in him was not lessened. She kissed and caressed him until his very immobility brought her to rest beside him.

"Talk to me, my love!" she whispered, fearing he might have fallen asleep. "I want to hear your voice. Tell me how much you have missed me! Tell me how much you love me. Tell me . . . "

Slowly, deliberately, he moved aside from her embrace.

"I think it better we do not converse tonight," he said quietly. "I will leave you now, Mavreen. We can discuss the future tomorrow."

Stunned as much by his words as by the cold, impersonal tone of his voice, Mavreen sat up and stared at him in disbelief.

"Leave me? *Now?*" she echoed. "But what is this, Gerard? What is wrong? I do not understand!"

Avoiding her eyes, Gerard too sat up. As if discomforted by the sight of his nakedness, he pulled the bed cover up to his waist. Awkwardly he said:

"I fear you have misjudged my mood, Mavreen."

Now, at last, Mavreen suspected that it had not, after all, been Gerard's intention to effect a reunion.

Her hand went to her mouth. Her cheeks colored a deep pink. Silently she prayed that

492

her suspicion was fallacious; that somehow she was mistaken in reaching such a conclusion.

"You did receive my letter, did you not?" she asked, her voice sharp with anxiety. "It *was* your reason for coming home?"

"I received no letter," Gerard replied. "I came home because, though you are obviously forgetful of it, Antoine is due to commence at Eton this term."

Mavreen drew a deep breath, pressing her hand against her mouth lest the cry of dismay within her escaped.

"*Then you did not come back . . . to me?*"

His silence answered her question.

Slowly, as if sleepwalking, Mavreen stepped down from the bed and went to the wardrobe. She took out a robe and thrust her arms into the sleeves, drawing the white velvet folds close about her body. She was shivering uncontrollably as she walked to the window and sat down upon the chaise longue.

"Then I have made a very grave mistake!" she said, her voice flat and expressionless. "My welcome was intended for my husband, for the man I loved, for the man I believed loved me."

She turned and stared at the silent figure in the bed.

"If it was not your intention to renew our life together, Gerard," she continued slowly and deliberately, "pray will you inform me by what right you participated just now in our physical reunion?"

The bitterness in her voice did not escape

him. He was made acutely uncomfortable by the implications of her question.

"You are still my wife," he said. "And I am a man!"

Now Mavreen was on her feet, her eyes blazing, her body taut with the tension of controlled anger.

"Do you think I would have permitted you so much as to touch my hand had I known that you were merely claiming your marital rights? Shame upon you, Gerard! I would feel less humiliated if I were a whore and paid for my services. But perhaps that was your intent — to make me feel so?"

The scorn in her voice silenced the denial that rose to Gerard's lips.

"But no! I am not being quite fair to you," Mavreen went on as she paced up and down the room. "Now that I recall the details of your homecoming, I see that it was I who seduced *you*! And of course *I* have no rights, do *I*, Gerard? Not as a woman, nor as your wife, nor even as a human being. You have condemned me in your mind as an adulteress and nothing I can say or do will convince you of the falsity of such accusation."

She paused beside the bed and stared down at him, body taut with the tension of controlled anger.

"I pity you, Gerard. Your misplaced jealousy is destroying not only you but our marriage; and tonight you have forefeited all right to my love." She turned away, her face bitter, her spirit crushed with desolation. "I was married once

494

before to a jealous man and *you* . . . yes, *you*, Gerard, pitied me then for my misfortune."

Now for the first time Gerard spoke.

"James Pettigrew had good cause to mistrust you," he said harshly. "And since you were unfaithful to one husband, I would be stupid to believe you could not as easily be unfaithful to me. It suits you to deny it, but I have no doubt you betrayed me just as you once betrayed him."

Mavreen took a step toward him, her hand raised as if to strike him. But her arm fell to her side. The color drained from her face.

"No woman ever loved a man more truly, faithfully, and absolutely than I loved you!" she said quietly. "Nor faced greater dangers to prove it. Until this day I have never regretted that I gave my love and my life into your keeping, Gerard, although there were many times in the past when you failed me. I wish I could say that I no longer love you, but I cannot be sure if that is true. What I know to be true is that I shall never forgive you for this night."

She turned away lest he should see the tears gathering in stinging pools beneath her lids.

"You spoke just now of leaving me," she said. "I suggest you do so, Gerard. Deliver your son to school, if that is your intent, and return to Compiègne for all the concern it is to me. I myself shall lead my own life as I please. I consider our marriage at an end."

Gerard regarded her rigid back uneasily.

"You mean you wish for a divorce?" he asked.

"'Tis not I who wish it!" Mavreen said sharply. "Do you think I have forgotten that a divorce would suit your purpose very well? That were you rid of me you could marry the wretched Blanche Merlin and legitimize your beloved Antoine? If this is your desire, be honest enough to say so."

"I said no such thing," Gerard replied.

"It is for you to act as you think best, Gerard. I do not care what you do!" Mavreen said.

"And that is part of the trouble!" Gerard burst out. "You were ever far too independent for a woman. A man should have control of his wife's actions, but you . . . you profess to love me yet you defer neither to my opinions nor to my superiority as your husband."

"Deference must be earned and not claimed as a right! That is the privilege only of Kings," Mavreen flared back. "Is there one single subject who would pay honest homage to the Regent were he not obliged so to do? But if 'tis lip service you require of me, Gerard, then you should have told me so. But 'twas always an *honest* opinion you asked of me. And now, in my *honest* opinion, I will inform you that I would rather have died on the Russian battlefields than see my love for you so debased."

"'Tis not I but you who have debased it!" he said, his voice cold once more as he thought of her in her lover's arms — a thought made even more intolerable now that he was so newly risen from her warm embrace. He realized that he had given way to temptation and that he should have resisted the driving forces of his body. But he believed Mavreen to be responsible for what had transpired, urging him to her bedchamber so eagerly that she had allowed him no time to think beyond the passionate need of the moment.

"'Twould be best for both of us if this night were forgotten," he said, mustering what little dignity he could as hurriedly he pulled on his breeches. "As for the future, it was my intention in any event to return to Compiègne where there is much still to be done. A continuance of our separation will give us both time for further reflection. I shall return at Christmas to fetch Antoine from school and we can reach a decision regarding our marriage then."

Mavreen made no answer. Her mortification was total. She was still finding it difficult to believe that Gerard had just possessed her with a cold, indifferent heart, and that the long months of separation had not brought him to his senses. Bitterly she reflected that he had not one shred of evidence on which to base his accusation of infidelity and he must be aware of it. Was it really possible, she asked herself, that any intelligent, grown man could be so blinded by jealousy that he could jump to such horrifying conclusions about a woman who had loved him unceasingly for twenty-four years? Could she herself continue to love such a man?

But when next day she stood silent and unobserved, watching from the landing above as Gerard and Antoine preceded the footmen carrying their boxes out to the waiting carriage, her eyes filled with tears of helpless misery.

Do not go! Do not leave me, Gerard! she thought. But the words were never uttered, and she knew from his implacable expression that even had she called to him he would not have relented.

Although Tamarisk knew nothing of this fresh contention between her parents, she was unhappily aware that the rift between them had intensified rather than abated. Her mother's white, unhappy face mirrored her own depression.

Tamarisk had been giving her future a great deal of consideration and had reached the conclusion that she must resign herself to a life of spinsterhood. She admitted to herself that her mother and Perry had been right to prevent her marriage to Leigh. She had never really loved him but had been carried away by the desire to do so because he brought a little color and adventure into her otherwise eventless life. But wanting to love was not sufficient reason for marriage to a man in no way suited to her and who, as it transpired, did not love her either. Leigh would never have been capable of arousing in her that deep devotion of the spirit she felt for Perry. Only *he* understood her character, her moods, her needs — sometimes even better than she understood them herself. And since he had made it painfully clear to her that his heart lay elsewhere, it was time she accepted that life did not intend to bless her with that most wonderful of all gifts — the love of the man she wanted.

Her spirits were brought even lower by the tragic and untimely death of her one true friend since childhood, Princess Charlotte. On the sixth of November Charlotte gave birth to a stillborn son and shortly afterward, to the amazement and confusion of her doctors, suddenly died. The country went into mourning. Tamarisk was no less inconsolable than Charlotte's grief-stricken husband and father.

Only shortly before Charlotte had been brought to bed Tamarisk had received one of her weekly letters stating how perfectly content she was. Tamarisk was deeply shocked to think that she would never again hear from Charlotte and that she was now bereft of her only confidante. Albeit circumstances had made their meetings few, their friendship had been nonetheless deep and thrived through their correspondence.

"How could fate be so cruel, Mama!" she wept in Mavreen's arms. "Charlotte was so happy with her Prince! She told me herself that she had discovered paradise in her marriage. They were so devoted!"

With no other comfort to offer Tamarisk, Mavreen decided to reopen Finchcocks for Christmas. Sir John and Clarissa were anxious to go to the country with them, and although the festivities would be severely curtailed by the state of mourning, Mavreen planned a small dinner party in an attempt to lift their spirits. She was not unmindful of the fact that young Charles Eburhard was due on leave. Hoping that his presence might cheer Tamarisk, she included him and his aunt, the Baroness, in her list of houseguests.

She also invited Gideon Morris. She made this decision coldly and deliberately on the afternoon Alfred Mumford called upon her at Barre House. The tutor had been living at the Château de Boulancourt since Gerard had removed Antoine to Compiègne in January. Although the boy was now at boarding school, Gerard obviously considered it worthwhile to retain the tutor for his son's holidays. Mr. Mumford's visit to London came, therefore, as a complete surprise. Mavreen had not expected to see him since Gerard had said he himself would collect Antoine from school for his Christmas vacation.

Her heart sinking in disappointment, Mavreen had her visitor shown into the library.

There, stammering even more acutely than was his wont, the anxious little man explained that he had been sent to England by the Vicomte to perform this task for him.

"He asked me to advise you that he is too busy to make the journey himself," he faltered. "He desired me to give you this letter."

Gerard's missive was brief and to the point. He was no nearer reaching a decision as to the advisability of trying to patch up their marriage, he wrote. He required further time for reflection and hoped that when Antoine was due back to school in January, he would be more certain of his sentiments regarding the renewal of their life together. In the meanwhile he hoped that his continued absence from Barre House was not causing Mavreen any social embarrassment.

"Social embarrassment!" Mavreen said furiously to Gideon, to whose house she drove immediately upon Mr. Mumford's departure. "As if I cared one jot what Society has to say about Gerard and me. Can he have no idea what heartbreak he is causing me?"

In an attempt to lighten her obvious distress Gideon said:

"'Twould seem to me 'tis your pride more than your heart which is suffering, Mavreen!" He glanced unobtrusively at her face. She was very pale and had lost a great deal of weight. Anxiously he wondered if worry were making her ill. "Come now, Mavreen, 'tis not like you to give in," he attempted to rally her. "If you have no desire to go to France in pursuit of Gerard — and I would have none in your place — then show the world you can be happy without him. I will gladly accept your invitation to Finchcocks, and we will eat, drink, and be merry this Christmastide!"

Mavreen tried to act upon Gideon's advice — to forget Gerard and enjoy herself. Despite a strange and unaccustomed lack of energy she went about the business of bringing to Finchcocks a positive whirl of festivities. She arranged a party for all the children of the estate workers and a display of fireworks for the whole village. She personally supervised the packing of baskets of food to take to the old and poor of the neighborhood.

Within the house every room blazed with lighted candles; food was piled high upon the tables; lavish presents were wrapped in secrecy and then unwrapped on Christmas morning. Not the least exciting of the gifts exchanged was Gideon's present to Tamarisk — a velocipede.

"I will demonstrate how to ride this machine!" Gideon announced, grinning boyishly as he led the household out to the drive where he proceeded to straddle this new invention. He put his hands upon the steering handle and pushed with a backward motion of his feet. The mechanical contraption wobbled perilously, the wheels revolved, and it shot down the driveway like a bolting horse. The applause of the watching audience ceased only when Gideon turned too fast to make the return journey and went head-over-heels into a flowerbed.

"At least I have succeeded in making you smile again!" he said to Mavreen as she ran to his assistance, "though I fear your father thinks me a clown," he added ruefully as they walked toward the house where Sir John stood frowning disapprovingly.

Affectionately Mavreen linked her arm in Gideon's.

"Never mind Father," she said softly. "I think you are wonderful, Gideon, to give Tamarisk so unusual a present. I have little doubt she will soon learn to balance upon it."

She smiled up at him with affection. But the sudden quick pressure of his hand on hers reminded her that Gideon was susceptible and that she must guard against words or behavior which might encourage him to believe she felt more than friendship for him.

But even as she so cautioned herself, a contrary thought crossed her mind. Why should she *not* allow Gideon to become her lover again? Gerard, convinced of her unfaithfulness, chose to deny her his company and his love. His rejection of her was cold and deliberate. But if *he* did not want her, there were other men who did; and Gideon, of all men, deserved some reward for his loyalty.

She glanced upward at his familiar profile. He was no longer a young man, she reflected with some surprise. Time was beginning to etch its marks upon his face — as indeed upon her own.

We are growing old! she thought in sudden panic.

Behind them, in the driveway, she could hear Tamarisk's youthful high-toned voice as she called to her grandfather to assist her onto the velocipede now retrieved from the flowerbed. Young although Tamarisk was, Mavreen thought, even her daughter was no longer a child. Doubtless she would marry soon and she, Mavreen, would become a grandmother! Her youth was already gone and life itself was passing her by!

"Gideon!" she said, her voice and eyes uneasy. "I have wasted a whole year of my life despairing over my marriage and I am mortally tired of being glum and dispirited. I have made up my mind to enjoy myself without regret this Christmastide. Do you approve of this intention?"

He looked down at her anxious face with great tenderness.

"I approve of anything that will bring the sparkle back into your eyes and the smile to your lips!" he said simply. "To see you happy is to be happy myself!"

And I will make you happier still she vowed silently as they went indoors.

That evening Mavreen took great pains with her dressing. She chose an apple-green and white-flowered silk gown gathered high under the bust. It was trimmed around the hem and the low, boat-shaped neckline with tiny bunches of lilies of the valley. She had a matching Lyons silk shawl to drape around her shoulders against the cold and white kid gloves on which the same green motifs were embroidered.

Dorcas spent more time than usual arranging her mistress's hair in curls and ringlets into which she scattered fresh lilies of the valley brought in from the heated greenhouses.

"You look beautiful, Milady!" she said with an admiring sigh as she selected a necklet of pale green peridot stones to fasten around Mavreen's neck.

"Do you not think my emeralds . . . ?" Mavreen began hesitantly, for it had crossed her mind that peridots were symbols of everlasting faithfulness.

"Indeed no, Milady!" Dorcas said firmly. "The emeralds are too bright a green. These are quite perfect!"

I am allowing my sensibilities to weaken toward Gerard! Mavreen thought. There was little virtue in remaining 'everlastingly faithful' to a man who believed her otherwise. Determinedly she turned to her reflection in the cheval mirror beside the dressing table.

"You do not think the ensemble too youthful for me?" she asked anxiously, for the dress was new and when ordering it to be made, she had pondered the question of its being more suitable for Tamarisk than for herself.

"Never, Milady!" Dorcas said with such conviction that Mavreen forgot her misgivings. Green was a color which always became her, she thought, for it brought out the green in her eyes; and tonight they looked larger than ever in her pale face.

"A little rouge on my cheeks, I think," she said. "I fear without it I look quite ill!"

She did not add, lest Dorcas worry, that she had not been feeling well of late. Hidden by the faint artificial coloring, however, there remained no sign of her fatigue and she descended the stairway looking radiant.

She drank freely of the many wines served with the evening meal. Her glance went more and more often to Gideon who was playing the dandy — to her father's disgust and the Baroness's delight. Secretly Mavreen allowed her mind to revive memories from the past whilst indulging in no more than the mildest of flirtations with Gideon. She planned how later that night they would turn the clock back and relive those intimate hours when time had no meaning and Gideon had breathed fire into her veins; made her feel a young girl again.

Whenever the thought of Gerard disturbed these reveries she reminded herself that her husband had only himself to blame if she were unfaithful to him. Since he was forcing her to pay the price he considered befitting her supposed 'immorality', and could not be convinced of her innocence, then she might as well pay the same price for her guilt. Such humiliations as she might inflict upon him were no greater than those he had already inflicted upon her.

Mavreen's gaze fell upon young Charles. He was staring at Tamarisk with an expression of such love that it came near to devotion. Her daughter seemed unmoved by the boy's attentions, although she was smiling in friendly enough fashion. Mavreen felt a swift stab of pain. Twenty-two years ago Gerard had looked upon her with this same undisguised devotion that young men were apt to bestow upon their first loves.

"There are a thousand ways to love . . . " he had said, "and we shall invent another thousand!" Yet when trust, tolerance and understanding were demanded of him — or at very least forgiveness — his love was found wanting.

Her resolve hardened.

At midnight the great house fell silent. The servants extinguished the last of the candles and were dismissed to their beds. In Mavreen's bedchamber Dorcas gave a final brush to her mistress's hair, curtsied, and left her sitting at her dressing table in her white lawn nightgown and matching peignoir.

For a while Mavreen sat staring at her

reflection. A little of her earlier excitement was dimmed by sheer fatigue. She felt exhausted, but her determination was as keen as ever. As soon as she was certain that the household slept, she took up her candle and left her room.

Gideon was sleeping in the guest chamber in the east turret. Unhurriedly Mavreen climbed the spiral staircase. Without first knocking she opened the door and entered his room. It was in darkness. The curtains around the four-poster bed were drawn. The sound of her entry and the light of her candle did not disturb the sleeping man.

She tiptoed across to the bed and extinguished the flame. Now in complete darkness, she untied the pale gold ribbons which fastened her peignoir and let it slip to the floor. One foot became entangled in the gold ribbon threaded through the hem of her nightgown. Impatiently she freed herself and removed the gown. Naked and shivering, she pulled back the curtain and slid into the bed beside Gideon's recumbent form.

"'Tis I, Mavreen!" she whispered.

Beside her, he woke from a deep sleep with a bemused start.

"In heaven's name, Mavreen, what do you here?" He sat up and reached his hand toward his tinderbox. But she caught his arm.

"There is no need for light, Gideon. Naught is amiss," she said, and added softly, "I came because I was in need of company — your company!"

Her perfume was all around him in the darkness. He could feel the sweet warmth of

her body as she nestled easily into the curve of
his own. It was as if the years since he had last
made love to her had never existed. They might
even now be at The Grange, newly returned
from some highway adventure, Mavreen curling
her body against his for warmth as they laughed
together about the night's exploits.

"Mavreen!" He spoke but the one word before
his mouth closed over hers. All the pent-up force
of his longing for her was expressed in that long
hungry kiss.

Mavreen's eyes closed as she tried to bring
a shutter down in her mind. She would not
think of Gerard. Not now! Not tonight! She
was determined upon giving herself to Gideon
without reserve or regret. He had helped her to
forget Gerard once before. Now he must do so
again.

Gideon's lips covered her face, throat,
shoulders with kisses. Eagerly his hands reached
out for her body, searching, remembering.

It seemed that he had waited an eternity for
this moment, but such was his joy he would
not allow his impatience to hurry him as he
rediscovered her.

"I love you. I . . . love . . . you!" he said
slowly between kisses. "Oh, Mavreen! I always
believed that one day you would need me again;
turn to me for the love I have to give you. I
could never have married another whilst such a
hope existed. And now . . . now . . . "

He broke off, his voice husky with the deep
intensity of his feeling.

"I will make you happy!" he whispered,

smoothing the hair from her forehead. "I know that I can, my love, *my only love*. We will be married as soon as possible. You must obtain a divorce from Gerard as quickly as you can. We will admit to adultery if that will hasten the matter . . . "

He broke off, sensing rather than feeling the stiffening of her body. He was suddenly aghast.

"Mavreen!" he said urgently. "You have not said one word. For the love of God, tell me what this is about. I am not wrong, am I, in supposing that you have made up your mind to part from Gerard? That it is your intention to end your marriage?"

This time Mavreen did not try to prevent Gideon as he reached for the tinderbox and lit the bedside candle. The flame flickered as he held it aloft. She turned away from the look of feverish anxiety on his face. Slowly he set the candle down upon the table. Then he took her face in his hands, turning her head so that she was forced to meet his eyes.

"*You must answer me, Mavreen!* 'Tis unlike you to be a coward! I want the truth!"

His taunt had the desired effect. She bit her lips in an attempt to stop them trembling, but nevertheless her voice quavered as she said:

"I am so sorry! I never thought . . . I never meant . . . Gideon, I still love Gerard. I wanted only . . . "

His hands dropped from her face. His arms fell to his sides.

"I see! Then I must apologize for having

assumed otherwise!" He got up, pulled on his nightrobe, and walked away from the bedside. Standing by the window, his back toward her, he said quietly:

"I will give you the benefit of any doubt and assume that you have forgotten the view I once expressed to you, Mavreen, on the subject of morality!" His voice was toneless, as if he were discussing the weather. Yet she understood very well how difficult he was finding it to conceal his bitterness. "I told you that I would never sleep with another man's wife. Nor will I, Mavreen — least of all with you! I want no half measures from you! No second best. And though I long for your body as I have never longed for any other woman's, I will never take you without you offer your heart too."

Mavreen lay back on the pillows, her eyes filling with tears. They spilled over and ran quietly down her cheeks.

"When last we were lovers, Gideon, you were prepared to take me knowing I loved another."

He turned and looked at her, his face white.

"It was but the ghost of Gerard de Valle who stood between us then," he said. "I believed him dead, as did you, though you would not admit it. My intention then was to banish that ghost — to make you love *me*, the living man, and forget the dead."

He looked at her for a long moment in silence. Then he said quietly:

"I do not doubt Gerard will return to you, Mavreen, and make you happy again, though 'tis true I have no reason to foretell that outcome.

So until the matter is decided, *I will not lie with you*. When next I do it will be because the ghost of Gerard is banished forever!"

The sight of her white tearful face upon his pillow was nearly his undoing. But with iron self-control, he walked toward her and held out her robes which he had gathered up from the floor.

"Come now, I will escort you back to your room," he said gently. "Let us both forget this interlude and remain the good friends we have always been. And dry those tears, Mavreen. Why, since you rate yourself the equal of any man, you cannot indulge in female weeping, you know!"

Mavreen wanted more than anything in the world to fling herself into his arms and hug him; tell him that she was weeping not just for herself but for him too. She realized how deeply she had hurt him by her thoughtless, selfish need to be loved and wanted. Yet he had already forgiven her unreservedly and still offered his friendship.

"I do not deserve you!" she said huskily, taking the 'kerchief he offered her and wiping the tears from her cheeks.

He made no reply but merely smiled his old sardonic smile. Irrelevantly she thought that Gideon was the only man in the world she knew who could look mocking and loving at the same time.

"I do love you, Gideon!" she cried impulsively.

"I know!" he replied quietly. "But not quite enough!"

He took her arm and led her gently but firmly toward the door.

25

1817 – 1819

THE general festivities of the household that Christmastide made it easier for Mavreen and Gideon to resume a customary friendliness without any residue of embarrassment from her incautious behavior of the night before. In the cold light of a new day she deeply regretted the impulse that had sent her flying to Gideon's arms for comfort. Her thoughtless action had hurt Gideon and even had he been less wise and less loving and taken her on her terms, deep down she had no desire to be unfaithful to Gerard. She still loved her husband, despite the injurious way he had been treating her. Moreover, she had not entirely lost hope of a reconciliation.

But when Gerard returned to Barre House in order to bring Antoine back to school after the Christmas holiday, there was little real change in his attitude toward her. But on this occasion, he informed her, he would remain in England since he had decided that he must in fairness give her the benefit of the doubt as to her fidelity.

"So your verdict upon me is not 'innocent' but 'guilt unproven'!" she commented bitterly. "Obviously it does not occur to you, Gerard, that *I* might not wish to share a life with you whilst you hold such opinion of me."

For one moment he appeared disconcerted. Then the mask of indifference closed over his face.

"That is for you to decide!" was his brief reply.

Had Mavreen been in better health she might well have pursued the discussion. But although she had no fever, she felt alternately sick and dizzy and so lacking in energy that the smallest task required an effort of will. She therefore avoided a direct confrontation with Gerard. Even he noticed her pallor. Impersonal though his attitude was toward her, within days of their resuming their life together he suggested that she should send for her physician.

"You surprise me by your concern for my health!" she said bitterly. "I am not ill, I assure you, and need no doctor."

Gerard had removed himself to his own bedchamber on his return home. By doing so he made it clear to her that their marriage was to proceed without intimacies; that there would be no attempt by him to claim his marital rights. Although he formally kissed her hand in public and paid her every courtesy, he never embraced her when they were alone and their conversation at all times was equally impersonal. Nor did he interfere with her day-to-day decisions.

On this occasion, however, he overruled her objections and insisted that Dr. Willis come at once to examine her. Too tired to argue, Mavreen acquiesced.

Only Dorcas was present in the room during the physician's examination of Mavreen and heard his diagnosis. With a beaming smile he said cheerfully to his patient:

"I think my congratulations are in order, my dear Vicomtesse. You are suffering no worse 'disease' than the early stages of pregnancy . . . three to four months, I would judge."

Open-mouthed, Mavreen stared back at him.

"You must be mistaken, Sir!" she said. "'Tis not possible . . . that is to say, I am far too old to conceive a child. No, Sir, you must be mistaken!"

The physician patted her hand.

"My dear Vicomtesse, correct me if I am wrong, but I believe you are only approaching forty? It is not uncommon for ladies of your age to find themselves with child!"

"But they are women with many children!" Mavreen cried, "whereas I have had no child since Tamarisk was born. Mistress Sale who attended her birth told me that I would be unlikely ever again to conceive."

Dr. Willis gave a patronizing smile.

"Midwives are not physicians, if I may say so, Vicomtesse. And yours was certainly mistaken. I have given you the most thorough examination and I have no reason to doubt my diagnosis. On the contrary you are remarkably well preserved for a woman of your age. In truth you have the physique of a young girl!"

Mavreen drew a deep breath of incredulity.

"You are certain you are not mistaken, Sir? 'Tis not that I doubt your ability, but you will appreciate that 'tis indeed hard for me to believe I am carrying a child after all this time!"

Mollified the doctor smiled.

"I think I can guarantee that you will be presenting the Vicomte with a son or daughter by July of this year. I will leave you now to give him the glad tidings. Meanwhile, here is a list of potions which should ease the nausea and improve your appetite."

"Shall I call the Vicomte to you, Milady?" Dorcas asked when she returned from showing the doctor to the door.

But Mavreen shook her head.

"I need time first to consider!" she said ambiguously.

The maid looked at the ashen countenance of her employer with sympathy. She knew very well of the rift between her mistress and the master of the house and how deeply it had upset the poor Vicomtesse.

"'Tis good news you have to impart!" she said. "After so long, it will come as a happy surprise to the Vicomte, will it not, Milady?"

Mavreen nodded.

"Yes, if it be true!" she said doubtfully. "But still I cannot quite believe it!"

"I mind my Mam telling me women do become more fertile when they near the end of their childbearing days than ever they were in their prime!" Dorcas said wisely. "Many's the baby born when its Mam thought she'd not be needing the cradle out again!"

Dorcas's homely remark and obvious pleasure did more to convince Mavreen than any word of Dr. Willis. She accepted the fact that she was carrying Gerard's child and her heart suddenly thrilled at the prospect. Gerard, who had so longed for a legitimate son and heir, could now hope for a male child. Her thoughts winged back to their last union nearly four months ago. Despite the bitter memory of the aftermath, she remembered as if it had been only last night, how totally she had surrendered herself; how passionately Gerard had loved her and how great had been her need for him. It was not surprising that from such tumultuous desires the miracle had occurred and her barrenness been overcome.

Lying back upon her pillows Mavreen smiled in sudden deep contentment. This baby was like a gift from God — sent to reunite them.

"Tell the Vicomte I wish to see him, Dorcas!" she said, and laughing softly with excitement, added, "Ask him to come as quickly as he can!"

Her heart beat like a young girl's when at last she heard his footfall. Gerard knocked and entered. He closed the door behind him and stood with his back to it, without expression as he regarded her across the room.

She held out a hand toward him. Her eyes were shinning brilliantly.

"I have news to impart!" she said. "Will you come nearer to me, Gerard, that I may tell you the tidings?"

He hesitated as if undesirous of carrying out her bidding. But though tight-lipped, he walked to the foot of the bed.

"Gerard, they are glad tidings! I pray they will make you as happy as I am at this minute. Dr.

Willis says I am with child!"

For one small fraction of time joy lit up Gerard's face. He took a step toward Mavreen before he halted, his body becoming rigid. His eyes narrowed and the look upon his face brought a cry to Mavreen's lips. He was taut with anger.

"You dare to call these good tidings?" he asked, his voice as cold as cutting as a rapier. "How gullible a fool do you suppose me that you foist another man's child upon me and expect me to rejoice!"

Had she not been lying upon her bed Mavreen would have hit out at him. Her pain and disappointment were equalled only by her fury at his injustice.

"You insult me — beyond forgiveness!" she cried. Desperately she fought down her rising hysteria, aware that the longed-for reconciliation with Gerard could never be effected in anger. Mustering the last vestiges of self-control she said quietly, "You know me well, Gerard, yet not well enough, it seems, to give me credit for honesty. If 'twere another man's child I carried, I would confess it to you as readily as I would confess even the possibility if it existed."

"You deny such possibility then?" Gerard asked, his eyes disbelieving.

"It should not be necessary for you to ask me that!" Mavreen cried. "Nor should I answer you. Yet I will do so. This child I carry cannot be another man's since I have lain with none other but you, Gerard, since our marriage. For you to accept one truth, you must accept both."

517

She looked at his cold, implacable face and realized that far from bringing them to a happy reunion, this child was proving but another and worse barrier between them. The pain in her heart became intolerable and she turned her face aside.

"Go away, Gerard!" she whispered. "For I can no longer bear to look upon you!"

Something of her pitiful distress stirred Gerard's heart. For the first time he wondered seriously if he had cruelly misjudged her and if she was, as indeed she sounded, innocent. But about his person he still carried one page of Tamarisk's journal — a page now tattered and dog-eared from his constant perusal of it whenever doubt assailed him. Upon it the girl had written:

'*I ponder whether they are still lovers. I think they must be so for Perry openly declared to me his love for Mama, and were it not returned he would of a certainly have found another to love. 'Twould not be the first time Mama has cuckolded a husband for she herself admitted to me that I was conceived out of wedlock . . .* '

Mavreen's own daughter had pointed the finger of truth at her, Gerard thought, his heart hardening again. None knew better than he how easily Mavreen fell prey to her bodily passions.

If only he could be certain! he thought as he left the room, his heart heavy. The past year had been far from happy, its only compensations

518

his home in France and his son Antoine. The renovation of the Château was nearing completion and it never failed to please him to see it restored to order and beauty. With a King once more upon the throne of France, deference was given to the nobility again, and through Monsieur Mougin, Gerard had been successful in reacquiring a great part of his former estate. The number of his employees had risen vastly. Even those who did not respect the aristocracy respected the affluence of the Vicomte de Valle and were forced to agree that he was good and just in all his dealings.

Antoine was Gerard's pride and joy. When they rode out together side by side, he, like Antoine, could not fail to notice the admiring glances of the estate workers and inhabitants of Compiègne. If any talked privately of the boy's humble start in life, none failed to doff their hats to Gerard's son, so beautiful in countenance and always so perfectly mannered. It did not enter Gerard's mind that one of the reasons he received only smiles and obedience from Antoine was that he denied him nothing, indulged his every whim, and praised most lavishly even his smallest achievement.

There was but one cause for concern about Antoine, Gerard thought, and that was the boy's heartfelt dislike of Eton and of his classmates. But bitterly though the boy railed against the harsh discipline, his 'unsympathetic' masters, and the unfriendliness of the boys, in this one instance Gerard was adamant. He refused to take his son away from the school he hated. Antoine must continue with his classical education in England, he told him, pointing out that he had now mastered the language so that only the smallest trace of an accent remained and was making far better progress with his studies than ever he had achieved under Mr. Mumford's tuition.

It was to this ten-year-old son he had turned for comfort and company when his relationship with Mavreen first met with disaster. And now that he was newly tormented with doubts he had believed to be subdued if not subjugated, it was of Antoine he thought constantly — a son unquestionably flesh of his flesh and no meretricious by-blow of Sir Peregrine Waite's. Gerard was convinced that once the baby was born, he would know if it were not his child from one glance at its features. He told himself that if he awaited the birth, he would be better placed to make the decision whether or not to divorce Mavreen and remove himself forever to his own country. On this assumption he was prepared to let the matter rest for the time being.

As the weeks passed he remained quietly courteous, maintaining the outward appearance of an affectionate husband whenever they were in company, but effectively putting a barrier between them in private which excluded even the smallest intimacy. And Mavreen encouraged none. To his daughter he was affectionate, as he had always been, and said nothing to disillusion her mistaken belief that the coming child had brought her parents together again.

Mavreen's health seemed to improve with

every month of her pregnancy. Her indifference to Gerard's cold, impersonal manner, however, was very much contrived. The hurt he had inflicted was a gnawing pain within her. But at the same time she was aided by the placidity of a woman approaching motherhood, and her joy in the thought of the coming child was in no way lessened by the bitterness she felt toward its father. She was unconcerned as to whether the baby would be boy or girl since she believed Gerard had no intention of acknowledging it. Tamarisk seemed delighted and was sweet and attentive as Mavreen's burden increased.

At times Mavreen was hard put not to confess her unhappiness to Tamarisk, and in particular when one day her daughter hugged her in a rare demonstration of affection.

"Dearest Mama!" Tamarisk exclaimed. "I am so very, very happy to see you and Papa so settled and content again. It pleases me to see you reunited, for I know you love him very much and were most miserable when he went to France without you!"

When Tamarisk was absent the need for pretense was gone. Preferring solitude to Gerard's silent company, Mavreen often pleaded ill health and spent more and more time alone in her bedchamber. Otherwise she took only occasional outings to spend the afternoon quietly in the company of her father and Clarissa.

Word of her condition had now got about and congratulations from their many friends arrived daily at the house. Mavreen was kept occupied in replying to these letters whilst Gerard went riding or to his club to play cards, to the opera, the theater, or to the races. Sometimes their paths did not cross for several days.

Preparations were made for Mavreen's confinement — an event which seemed to worry her physician on account of her age but which left Mavreen unconcerned. Nevertheless Gerard insisted that there should be a second doctor instantly available at the birth in case of complications. Secretly he was not unmindful of the death of the young Princess Charlotte after childbirth, and his concern for his wife outweighed his feelings of antipathy toward the child she carried.

On the tenth of July Mavreen was brought to bed. At first there seemed no cause for concern, but by the following morning Dr. Willis informed Gerard that there were serious complications.

Shocked beyond his customary reticence Gerard said impulsively:

"If there comes a choice between whose life must be saved, I care naught for the child. Please give first consideration to my wife!"

The doctor nodded, unwilling to admit at this juncture that he had very considerable fears that he could save neither. He had no wish to suffer the same disgrace as had overtaken Sir Richard Croft for his supposed mishandling of the Princess's confinement, resulting in a stillborn child as well as in her death. The unhappy man had shot himself some months ago, and however unnecessary his suicide, the physician could imagine the state of mind leading up to it.

Mavreen's labor continued throughout the day. Barely conscious, so great was her fatigue and pain, she clung to life by sheer determination. Deep within her, she was determined to provide Gerard with a son, an alternative to Antoine, a de Valle worthy of the name, upon whom Gerard could depend to perpetuate honorably his family line. It had never ceased to worry her that all his present hopes and dreams lay in Antoine. At the age of ten the boy was become even more devious and cunning than when Gerard had first lifted him out of the farmyard where he was born. Neither time nor a good home and schooling had changed the child's amoral nature. He had inherited nothing but his delicate beauty from the de Valles. In moments of honest reflection Mavreen could liken him only to a small satanic being concealed within the bodily appearance of an angel. Gerard's blind trust in the boy only increased her fear of the evil she sensed in his son.

Her suffering ended at midnight when on the verge of total exhaustion she gave birth to the son she craved. As Dorcas laid the infant in her arms, she stared down into the tiny crumpled face. Desperately she searched for some likeness to Gerard. But there was none. She could see only herself. Weakly she closed her eyes and surrendered the baby to the attendant midwife.

Dorcas, with tears of relief in her eyes, ran to tell the glad tidings to the Vicomte. But by the time Gerard came to the room Mavreen was already asleep. Reassured by the two doctors that there was no cause for alarm, he looked at the child for the first time. As Mavreen had done not a few minutes earlier, he studied the minute pink face for some resemblance to himself. Like Mavreen, he could see none.

"Oh, Sir!" said the midwife. "Is he not the most beautiful babe you ever saw? And the very image of his mother!"

He made no answer; showed no sign of the joy expected of him. Having obtained Dr. Willis's repeated assurance as to Mavreen's well-being, he left the room.

Strange fellow! Not like the usual emotional Frenchy! thought Dr. Willis with some surprise. With a sigh the doctor set aside his meditations on the strange behavior of his fellowmen and instructed that a few drops of camphor julep be administered to Mavreen when she woke, to stimulate her heart. She must be encouraged to eat, he said, suggesting such invalid diet as gruel, chicken broth, barley water. He was to be summoned at once if there were any sign of deterioration in her condition or that of the infant.

Despite his fears, despite Mavreen's age, despite her long and difficult labor, his patient surprised him by making a rapid recovery. He had not taken into account either her natural good health or her strength of will.

More than any other factor, it was the child who gave Mavreen the incentive she needed to overcome the weakness following her confinement. Whether Gerard believed it or not, she knew the baby to be his; and when she nursed the child at her breast, it was recompense for Gerard's cool indifference. The baby had not brought about the reconciliation she had hoped for, but neither had his arrival brought about a final separation. She guessed correctly that Gerard himself was far from certain about the baby's paternity. She was informed by Dorcas that he visited the nursery daily and spent long minutes staring intently at the child.

"Such devotion!" said the baby's nurse, mistakenly, to anyone who would listen to her.

In fact Gerard alternated between a violent antipathy to the fragment of humanity staring back at him from milky blue eyes and a deep tenderness which he fought hard to subdue. It was his first encounter with a tiny child, for he had not been present during Tamarisk's early years nor yet encountered his son Antoine in babyhood. But the perfection of the minute fingers and toes, each nail so perfectly formed, of the dark, fawnlike fringes of his eyelashes lying on soft pink cheeks, roused in him a protective love such as he had never felt before.

As the days passed the crumpled look of the newly born infant gave way to a satin-smooth, pink and gold complexion unmistakably like Mavreen's. There could be no doubting the child's mother, Gerard thought wryly. If only he could be convinced he was the child's father! He stayed staring silently at the infant until the pain of his uncertainty became too great to bear.

If Gerard was secretly fascinated by the baby, Tamarisk, Sir John, and Clarissa were openly adoring. Sir John, who had not been in the best of health of late, was overjoyed at the birth of his first grandson. His happiness was complete when Mavreen announced that she wished to call the boy John, after him.

Clarissa, who was equally enchanted, never having had children of her own, arrived each day to visit mother and child, bearing some tiny garment she had herself fashioned or a bauble for the nursery.

"You must be the happiest woman in the world!" she said to Mavreen, her pink face beaming, "as well as the most beautiful. You know, my dear, it becomes you to be thinner in the face — although you must try to eat more. I am far from convinced you should be feeding the baby yourself. Would it not be better for you to engage a wet nurse as is customary?"

"No, my dearest Aunt Clarrie!" Mavreen said, smiling. "It gives me great joy to feed little John myself, and so long as he thrives I will continue to follow nature's way, as I did with Tamarisk."

"Such a long time ago that seems," Clarissa mused. "And poor Gerard was on the high seas and knew nothing of his daughter's birth." She gave a deep sigh of contentment. "Now, my dear, you are happily married with your dear children around you. Who could have imagined it all those years ago?"

Mavreen did not have the heart to disillusion her. Moreover, Gerard of his own accord was behaving in public as any other proud and happy husband. It was as if they had a verbal agreement to hide the truth from everyone but each other.

Not even Tamarisk guessed his true emotions.

Gerard was secretly concerned about the health of his father-in-law, for whom he had a great affection. Old Sir John was now in his seventy-sixth year and becoming increasingly frail.

"Cannot expect to live forever!" he remarked to Gerard one evening as they lingered over their port and cigars. "Although I am a year older I have outlived our poor Queen, God rest her soul. And who would have thought that poor demented husband of hers would outlive her?"

He insisted upon paying his last respects when the Queen was buried on the second of December; and Gerard went with him. They returned together to Barre House, and still doggedly determined not to give way to his growing weakness, Sir John accompanied Gerard on his daily visit to the baby. He looked at his namesake with a sigh of satisfaction and turned with a wry smile to his son-in-law:

"Clarrie says girls always resemble their fathers and boys their mothers," he commented. "She swears Mavreen takes after me, and this boy's the spitting image of me daughter, so happen he'll also favor me, eh? You're a fortunate fellow, Gerard," he went on, "to have such a fine, healthy son."

Perhaps! Gerard thought, as dutifully he nodded. But was the body really *his* son? His doubts remained unresolved.

★ ★ ★

527

Winter had turned to spring and spring to early summer when with a sinking heart Mavreen realized that Gerard was intending to return to Compiègne without their affairs settled. It was tacitly understood that Mavreen would not accompany him, the baby, now nearing his first birthday, providing the excuse for her to remain in England.

To add to her depression, her father had suddenly aged in the most alarming way. Although he never complained Clarissa told Mavreen she was certain he was often in pain. He remained more and more frequently in his bed and had begun to take opium. He told Mavreen that this was to help him to sleep, but she, like Clarissa, believed it was to relieve the pain he obviously suffered.

The physicians could find nothing wrong with him.

"It is old age, no more!" said one. "After all, Sir John is seventy-six!"

If Sir John had been distraught when he believed Clarissa to be on her deathbed, she was no less so now that he was ill. Mavreen tried to comfort her by reminding her that her father had once said he would die a happy man if he could hold a grandson in his arms, and this he had done.

"I would not want to live if . . . if your father died!" Clarissa wept.

But the black Angel of Death was not kind enough to take her too when he came to claim Sir John. Clarissa's anguish brought more grief to Mavreen than did the loss of her dearly loved father. Even Gerard, busy with preparations for his sojourn in Compiègne, was moved by the old lady's distress.

"She cannot remain alone in Wyfold House!" he said to Mavreen. "As soon as the funeral is over she must come here to live with us. Wyfold House can be let until we decide what should be done with it. Maybe you will wish one day to give it to John. Your father would have liked him to have it, I daresay."

She had not heard him speak so warmheartedly in a long while. Touched, she thanked him for his thoughtfulness and waited for him to continue in like vein. But Gerard's moment of compassion was past. Although he remained thoughful and kindly until Clarissa and her possessions were brought to Barre House after the funeral, he left as he had planned to do the following week, with no more than a formal kiss of Mavreen's hand by way of farewell.

The month of June came in before Clarissa showed any sign of recovery. Mavreen's hopes were raised when the old lady agreed that the bracing sea air of Brighton would be a nice change.

But by the end of their month's sojourn Clarissa became oddly restless. She seemed unable to settle to anything with enjoyment, and even her interest in her chubby little grandson was diminished. Finally she confessed to Mavreen that she longed to return to London — not to Barre House or Wyfold, but to Orchid House in Richmond.

"I know you will think me a sentimental old

fool!" she said tearfully to Mavreen. "But Orchid House was our home and your father and I were always happy there. I feel I could better reconcile myself in such surroundings to my loss."

"Then you shall go back there, if that is what you really wish!" Mavreen said, hugging the little old woman. "Although I shall miss you, dearest Aunt Clarrie!"

"You see, dear," Clarissa continued, wiping her eyes, "I became accustomed in those years before your dear father was free to marry me, to his being away for quite long periods of time. I always knew he would be back, and if I were to live there now, I believe it would comfort me — the feeling I would have that at any time, any day, he would just walk in."

Mavreen was uncertain of the wisdom of leaving Clarissa to such a solitary existence but, at the same time, it was obvious that Clarissa found her greatest solace in her memories of the past. It was in total contrast to her own experience, she thought, shunning the idea of another summer at The Grange without Gerard. Barre House too abounded in memories of him and brought her daily reminders of his absence.

Clarissa packed her few belongings and with Tamarisk for company returned to Orchid House.

Mavreen now had only the baby for comfort, and there was little companionship to be had from so young a child, greatly although she loved him.

John still bore no resemblance whatever to

his father. Each day he became more like herself. When Mavreen took the little boy to visit her, Clarissa remarked constantly of his resemblance to Mavreen when first her dear John had discovered his eight-year-old daughter.

"How fascinated he was by you, my dear!" she reminisced. "And small wonder when you remember those two great ugly girls of his. All golden hair and mischievous green eyes, he used to describe you, and as sturdy as any boy. Little John has your intelligence too, dear — and your impatience!"

Mavreen laughed, for it was all too true that the child had great determination if his mind was set, and his nurse declared she had never known such a pickle.

"Let us hope he uses his intelligence more wisely than have I!" she said wryly. But Clarissa, knowing nothing of the rift between Mavreen and Gerard, insisted that Mavreen had long ago outgrown her youthful follies. By which she intended Gideon, Mavreen thought, remembering sadly that she had not encountered him since he was at Finchcocks over a year ago; neither had he written to congratulate her on the birth of her son, which he must surely have heard about even had he failed to see the announcement in the *Times*.

In an attempt to revive her spirits she arranged several small dinner parties to which she invited the more intellectual and intelligent of her friends. Among her guests was Sir William Wilberforce, whom she had known since childhood. A charming and distinguished

Quaker, he was with dogged persistence still working for world abolition of the trade in slaves. In early June he had given yet another impassioned speech in Parliament, drawing the attention of the Members to the fact that, despite their promises, France and America had still not abolished this inhuman practice.

Listening to the small, sharp-featured, elderly man speaking so eloquently at her dinner table, Mavreen felt that it was high time she involved herself in some of the many reforms the country so badly needed. Not forgetting her late father's backing of Henry Hunt's petition to Parliament, she decided to join the new party called the Radical Reformers.

Mavreen called upon Henry Hunt, a man little older than herself, who spoke fervently to her of the terrible conditions existing in the north of the country. Too little was being done to find work for the unemployed, to pay a living wage to those in work, and to improve the appalling conditions in which they worked, he told her.

He had had some success in arousing sympathy, in spite of the rigid government opposition headed by the Regent. Meetings were taking place all over the country; and in Birmingham Sir Charles Wolsely had been nominated to represent the Reformers in the House of Commons.

"I myself am addressing a meeting in St. Peter's Field in Manchester on the seventeenth of August," he said. "There will be many female reformers in attendance. Your presence, my dear Vicomtesse, would be a great inspiration to them. Although I should warn you," he added seriously, "that you would be putting your reputation and possibly your person at great risk. The government is unlikely to remain inactive, to say the least."

This challenge to her courage more than anything else prompted Mavreen to travel to Manchester so that she might be present at the meeting. Taking only Dickon with her — for she knew he would never forgive her for going on some dangerous escapade without him — Mavreen set out for St. Peter's Field in good spirits. It did not suit her, she remarked to Dickon, to lead a quiet domestic life without adventure to break the daily routine.

Nevertheless her mood became more serious when, as they neared the meeting place, she first became aware of the crowds. They were of such vast proportions that she estimated they must number at least sixty thousand men, women, and children. As Hunt had predicted, there were two bands of female reformers gathering under white silk banners.

Mavreen knew that Dickon was as interested as herself in the plight of the working man. As was natural for a man from farming stock, he had been bitterly opposed to the injustices of the Corn Laws. She was now more than thankful to have his sturdy frame beside her as they were jostled by the angry, murmuring crowds milling about them.

"'Tis as well I'm alongside of you, surelye!" Dickon agreed as nervously he eyed the yeomen standing at the ready with drawn swords.

He knew better than to suggest to Mavreen that she leave the meeting before any trouble arose. But he regretted he had not tried to persuade her when, within minutes of Hunt's opening words, the commanding officer ordered his men to advance upon the dais. Hunt was promptly arrested and the soldiers were ordered to aim at the destruction of the banners.

There then arose a terrible scene of confusion. Somehow Dickon managed to drag Mavreen aside as the horses surged forward and men, women, and children were trampled underfoot. Screams rent the air — screams of such agonized suffering Mavreen knew she would never be able to forget them.

Eleven innocent people died that day and several hundreds were injured. With others who had not fled the scene of the massacre, Mavreen and Dickon attempted to help the dying and wounded.

"Dear God!" she whispered to Dickon as she nursed a child with a crushed leg. "This is worse even than Borodina. There at least the wounded were grown men!"

"If this be the work of a Tory Government, I'll have naught more to do wi' it!" Dickon said as he used his own jacket to pillow the head of a dying woman.

They worked tirelessly into the evening, helping the wounded from the battlefield, relaying them in their own coach to their homes, although little enough could be done to ease their injuries. Where it was most needed Mavreen left money for food and doctors' bills.

But such help was, she well knew, but a drop in a vast ocean of misery. She was aware that she could achieve more at higher levels and returned quickly to London.

It was with mixed feelings she discovered Gerard had arrived home in her absence.

26

August – December 1819

AT first she felt only happiness in the fact of his physical presence within their home. But although Tamarisk had explained to him the purpose of Mavreen's visit to Manchester, it soon became obvious to Mavreen that once again Gerard was questioning her fidelity; that somewhere in the tortured imaginings of his mind he suspected Gideon might have accompanied her.

Across the dinner table on the night of her return Gerard said coldly:

"Do you not think your proper place was at home, supervising the care of your son?"

The servants had been dismissed. Tamarisk had excused herself and departed from the room, so they were alone. There was no need, therefore, for Mavreen to temper her bitterness as she replied:

"And do you not think *your* proper place was here, in London, supervising your wife?"

He regarded her furiously — the more angry because he had been exceedingly lonely in Compiègne and found himself daily more anxious to return to his home in England, perhaps to find the infant John was now grown like him, thereby making possible a reconciliation with Mavreen.

Her visit to Manchester, unexpected as it was, had merely served to revive all his earlier jealousies. As for the child, now over a year old, he looked even more like his mother and came no nearer to resembling him.

Bitterly Mavreen was forced to accept that Gerard's return was no herald for a betterment of their relationship. She turned her mind away from him and filled her time with the self-imposed task of arousing sympathy for the plight of those unfortunates, the residue of the battlefield now publically referred to as 'Peterloo'.

But there was little enough she could achieve. The Corporation of London addressed the Regent censuring the authorities for the massacre and received a stern rebuke for prejudging the facts. It soon became clear to Mavreen that the Radicals, whose strength lay mainly in the manufacturing areas, were to be suppressed at all costs. Six new Acts were introduced by the government which successfully brought about this suppression. The Acts outlawed 'seditious' meetings; imposed a stamp duty upon newspapers which prohibited them publishing facts which might influence readers to sympathize with the Radical causes; and gave the courts power to punish offenders by transportation, banishment, imprisonment, or fines.

Henry Hunt, meanwhile, refused bail and with great courage opted to become a martyr to his cause by remaining in prison. There was no man of humble origins who did not adore him, and Mavreen herself held him in the highest regard.

She determined to obtain an audience with the Regent and somehow gain, if not his sympathy, at least a less rigid opposition to the reformers. But three months of persistent attempts to see him resulted in failure, for whether by accident or design, the deteriorating health of the King provided the Regent with a good excuse not to receive her.

"'Twould be more fitting if the Regent concerned himself with those who died at Peterloo and their cause rather than with a poor old man of eighty-two whose life is drawing to a natural conclusion!" Mavreen said bitterly to Gerard. The sight of her own healthy babe would not allow her to forget the child who had died screaming in her arms beneath the hot sun shining down upon St. Peter's Field.

Gerard, though not unsympathetic once the rumors of the massacre were confirmed, refused to involve himself personally.

"Perry would have found some way to help!" Tamarisk commented privately to Mavreen. "But I fear Papa is too aloof from the common man!"

But although Mavreen privately agreed with her daughter's remark, she felt obliged to rebuke her for criticizing her father. It did not prevent either of them from wondering what had become of Sir Peregrine Waite.

As if in answer to their pondering, Gideon suddenly and surprisingly wrote Mavreen a long letter. He offered belated congratulations upon the birth of her son and went on to tell her that he had just received intelligence from abroad that his three-year-old godson, Percy Shelley's child, had died in Rome. He had therefore decided to go to Leghorn in the north of Italy, where the grief-stricken Shelleys had friends. It was his intention, he said, to remain with them for a while at the Villa Valsovano.

' 'Tis but nine months since their little daughter Clara died!' Gideon's letter continued. 'Poor Shelley! His life seems full of tragedy and I hope that somehow I can cheer him with my presence.

'I read the announcement of your father's death with sadness for I well know how greatly he was loved and respected. I wish to offer my most sincere though belated condolences to you, Lady Danesfield, and Tamarisk.

'It now remains for me to wish you and your family farewell. I shall take with me abroad the happiest memories of our long friendship which, now I am leaving England, must come to an end . . . '

Unable to read further Mavreen put down the letter. There were tears in her eyes. Silently she handed it to Tamarisk who read aloud:

'I cannot say when or even if I shall return to England. It is my intention to travel far and wide now that Europe is at peace.

'Please give my fondest regards to Tamarisk and my farewells, for I doubt I shall have occasion to voice them in person before I leave . . . '

It seemed obvious that he was intending to put the past behind him and go in search of a new life — a new love, perhaps, Mavreen thought. Doubtless the birth of little John had given him reason to suppose Gerard and herself to be totally reconciled. He had assumed she had no further need of his friendship nor was likely ever to require his love.

If he but knew how greatly I need a good friend to cheer me! she thought unhappily. But it was best he never knew of it lest it encouraged him to waste even further years of his life in the vain hope that one day she might leave Gerard and marry him.

She longed to take the carriage straight to Gideon's house; to see him once more before he left the country. But she dared not trust herself to remain calm and unmoved. Moreover, Gerard would fail to understand her innocent desire to bid an old friend adieu.

Tamarisk was meanwhile staring at her mother from a white, stricken face.

"Mama!" she cried, her voice trembling. "Does this mean we shall not see Perry again?"

Mavreen looked into her daughter's unhappy eyes. Ignorant of Tamarisk's continuing devotion to Gideon, she underestimated the shock his letter afforded her. Wrongly she supposed Tamarisk to be suffering no more than a child's distress at the pending loss of a favorite uncle.

"'Tis doubtless all for the best!" she said. "You know as well as I do that your Papa resents . . . dislikes . . . " she stumbled over the words. "Your Papa cannot overlook the fact that Perry and I were once . . . involved! It will be easier for us all when Gideon . . . Perry . . . has left the country . . . " Her voice trailed away.

Tamarisk remained silent. She knew very well what her mother implied. Her thoughts were racing. She drew a deep breath and in a deceptively casual tone of voice said:

"Perhaps you are right, Mama! But whilst I quite see that Papa would object if you were to pay a last call upon Perry to wish him a *bon voyage*, I scarcely think he could object if I were to do so. And I *would* like to say goodbye to him, if for no other reason than to let him know we wish him well and that we will miss him. After all he has done for me, I feel I owe him this last courtesy, do you not think so, Mama?"

Surprised but pleased with the suggestion, Mavreen agreed. She was suddenly struck with an idea which Tamarisk's proposed visit to Gideon would make possible.

She went to her desk and from a locked drawer withdrew a small parcel. It was wrapped and tied with ribbon so that Tamarisk was unaware of the contents as her mother handed it to her with instructions to give it to Perry. In any event her thoughts were concentrated elsewhere. Now that her mother had consented to her seeing Perry again, she could hope that she might somehow find a way to prevent him leaving England forever. The mere thought instantly revived all her old feelings of passionate adoration which had lain dormant since he had absented himself from their lives after that Christmas vacation at Finchcocks.

It was inconceivable that she might never see him again, she reflected. Yet her mother, who had professed to love him as her dearest friend, seemed almost unconcerned. Mama was too deeply involved now with Papa and baby John, Tamarisk thought; and as the notion crossed her mind, she guessed that Perry had felt this too — that this was why he was leaving England. At long last *he had realized that Mama would never return his love!*

Her heart thudded painfully. It had only ever been Mama who had stood between her and Perry, she thought. His heart had not been in his own keeping. But now he was free — free to offer his love to whomsoever he pleased . . .

Tamarisk glanced at her mother's face, lost in thought as she stared at the parcel Tamarisk was holding. Mavreen was considering the effect this one small parcel would have upon Gideon when he opened it, for it contained the tiny silver bracelet with the miniature guns and holsters he had presented to her as a memento of their shared past. He would know that by its return to him she too had accepted that their long friendship was at an end; that she was releasing him from a love that had endured ten years. Unaware of Tamarisk's reactions she spoke aloud her thoughts:

"'Tis time Gideon found a wife and settled down," she said. "He would make an excellent husband and father; and he is no longer young. He needs a woman to take care of him."

"Shall I tell him that you said so?" Tamarisk asked quietly.

With a start Mavreen became aware once more of her daughter. She gave a wan smile.

"Gideon was always his own master," she said, "and I doubt he would listen to my advice. Moreover, 'tis not my place to give it, Tamarisk."

"Very well, Mama. Then I will go this afternoon."

"Take Dorcas with you," Mavreen said. "You are too old now, Tamarisk, to ignore the conventions, and Perry's is, after all, a bachelor establishment!"

As the phaeton took Tamarisk along the familiar route to Harley Street, she prayed fervently to her guardian angel that Perry would be at home. She realized that if he were preparing for a long journey abroad he would have many arrangements to make. Her heart beat furiously in a confusion of nervous dread and intense excitement as they drew up at his house. Dorcas pulled the bell rope.

Tamarisk's prayers were answered. Gideon himself came to the front door to greet her. He conducted her to his morning room and dismissed Dorcas to the servants' hall.

"Well, my little Princess!" he said as he settled her beside the blazing fire. "This is an

543

unexpected pleasure! I had not thought to see you again!"

Tamarisk stared up into his dark, teasing yet kindly eyes and her heart lurched. She swallowed nervously and sat primly in her chair, her hands clutching the parcel her mother had given her.

"I came to say goodbye," she said. "And to give you this from Mama."

Gideon took the parcel from her trembling hands, his own far from steady as he untied the ribbon. He had but to glimpse the box beneath the wrapping paper to guess its contents. His face paled.

"Did your Mama send any . . . any message with this?" he asked harshly.

"Not exactly!" Tamarisk faltered. "That is to say . . . Oh, Perry, let us not pretend at such a time as this. We know you are leaving us — perhaps forever!" Her voice broke. "Mama says it is all for the best but how can it be? I do not want you to go! I cannot bear it!"

Gideon's face was inscrutable. He would not allow this young girl to see how her reference to Mavreen's indifference affected him. He had made up his mind to leave England some long time ago when Mavreen's and Gerard's child was born. He decided he must go far away where he could not be tempted to seek out her face at every dinner party he attended; at the theater; the opera; to watch for her carriage; to listen eagerly for her name to be mentioned by mutual friends. There could be no heart's ease for him in England whilst at any time, on any day, he could hope to encounter her.

But although he had deliberately planned this physical separation, it was not his intention to end their friendship forevermore. But Mavreen had chosen to do so by returning his token of their past links. He could only assume that she and Gerard had resolved all their differences and were now as happily married as Mavreen had always desired.

He felt no bitterness toward her and nothing but affection for the young girl seated so miserably before him. Tamarisk was as dear to him as if she were his own child and he loved her with a great tenderness which had nothing to do with the fact that she was Mavreen's daughter, although he would have loved her for this alone.

"'Tis more than likely I shall be back in a year or two's time," he said to comfort her. But she shook her head.

"Not if you marry and live abroad!" she said.

"What put such an unlikely idea into your pretty head?" Gideon replied. "Believe me, Princess, 'tis very far from my intent!"

Tamarisk looked at him from eyes brimming with tears.

"Mama says you should find a wife to take care of you!" she blurted out. "And I think she is right!" She drew a deep trembling breath. "Oh, Perry!" she gasped, "will you not marry me and take me with you? I would make you a good wife. I am twenty-one years old now and no longer a child. And I love you. I have always . . . "

"Hush, Tamarisk!" Gideon broke in gently. "You may be twenty-one years old, but you are still too young to realize what you are suggesting. *Why, I am an old man!* Nearly twice your age! A pretty young girl like you cannot tie herself for life to a man old enough to be her father!"

Tamarisk jumped to her feet, her eyes blazing.

"Mama's first husband was far, far older than you. And they were happy — Mama has often told me so. And that despite Mama being enamored of someone else and begetting a child by him. Oh, Perry, do you not love me even a little bit?"

Gently Gideon put his arms around her and stroked her soft golden hair as it nestled into his shoulder.

How like Mavreen's hair! he thought, with an ache in his heart.

"Of course I love you," he said. "'Tis because I do care so deeply about your happiness and your future that I cannot accept your very flattering offer. Do you not see, my Princess, that if I cared less for you and more for myself, I would whisk you off to a foreign land, disregarding your need for a young handsome lover, and keep you quite selfishly for my own pleasure?"

She raised a tear-streaked face to his.

"I do not expect you to love me!" she cried. "I know you love Mama and probably always will. I only want to be allowed to live with you, near you, to take care of you and love you the way you deserve."

Touched but realizing the need to be firm, Gideon said:

"I could not live with my conscience were I to behave in the fashion you suggest!" He disengaged her arms and led her gently toward the door. "To take everything and give nothing . . . no, Tamarisk, you must know me better than to believe me capable of such egoism." He lifted her cloak and put it around her shoulders.

"Believe me, you will know I am right, Tamarisk, when finally you meet the young man destined to be your husband. Do you remember how misguided you were when you eloped with that unfortunate young actor? Well, now you are once again permitting your emotions to mislead you. 'Tis pity you feel for me — and affection, mayhap — but nothing more! When real love comes to you, you will know I speak the truth!"

"When . . . are . . . you . . . leaving?" Tamarisk asked brokenly.

"I shall be sailing with the tide on tomorrow's packet from Dover. I shall be in Ostend before the day is out and from thence I shall make my way across land to Italy."

Anxious to put an end to this distressing scene, he opened the door and called for Dorcas. Tamarisk had no choice but to give him one last despairing embrace before he led her out to the waiting carriage.

Upon her arrival home she went straight to her own room. There she flung herself upon the bed and broke into a storm of weeping.

But this outburst was short-lived. Before long she sat up, dashed the tears from her eyes, and stared out at the darkening sky. Soon it would be night — Perry's last night in England! Tomorrow he would be gone forever from her life, leaving her behind to an empty, pointless existence. She would be quite alone!

Whilst her parents had been estranged, she reflected, her mother had needed her for companionship. But now her father was home and they were reunited, they had each other and her lovely baby brother on whom to lavish their attentions. Her presence in the household was superfluous. They did not need her. But Perry did. He too was alone in the world. *And only his altruism stood between them.*

Her breathing quickened as her memory recalled his words.

"*Of course I love you,*" he had said. "*If I cared less for you and more for myself, I would whisk you off to a foreign land . . . and keep you quite selfishly for my own pleasure . . .*"

Tamarisk clasped her hands together so tightly that her knuckles whitened. Did she have the courage, she asked herself, to act upon her instincts and force a decision upon Perry he would never otherwise make? She was well aware that a further appeal to take her away with him would result in yet another denial of his need of her. But all might be very different if she were to follow him to Dover, arrange a passage for herself aboard the same packet, and then, when they were out to sea, announce her presence. Then it would be too late for him to tell her to return home! He would realize at last how deeply in earnest she was in her desire to give her life to him. He would see how little she cared about the discrepancy in their ages, how wholeheartedly she loved him, and how mistaken he was in his unselfish rejection of her love.

Her excitement mounted to fever pitch. She remembered how bravely her mother had traveled across the world to be with the man she loved! Tamarisk had only to travel to Dover! She would take her little maid Elsie with her. Elsie adored her, and although she was silly and frightened even of her own shadow, she would prefer to go to hell itself with Tamarisk rather than be left behind.

And Mama! Tamarisk thought with a sudden sobering of her spirits. Mama would prevent her going were she to know of her intent. Her mother had never understood how deeply she loved Perry. She had ridiculed Tamarisk's love, calling it 'a child's adoration', 'hero worship', and 'the fantasy of an adolescent girl'.

Tamarisk's mouth curled and her eyes narrowed. It was easy enough to understand why Mama had never sympathized or appreciated the real quality of the love her daughter had for Perry. He had once been *her* lover, and even though her mother had ceased the liaison after her marriage, she had still kept Perry as her adoring slave, albeit in the guise of a friend. Doubtless she could not have borne to see her lover turn his attentions to her young, pretty daughter.

Resentment vied with a grudging admiration

549

and seethed within her. For as long as she could remember, Tamarisk had wanted to be like her mother — as beautiful, as fearless, as unconventional, as undaunted. Now she could be all these and cease to be a pale shadow of her mother's brilliance. All she needed to prove herself her mother's equal, were courage and determination.

As Tamarisk went to her bureau to find quill, ink, and paper, she was not unmindful of the last occasion she had run away from home. That elopement was indisputably misguided, she admitted freely. But it would never have happened if she had not believed Perry was still her mother's lover and therefore beyond her reach.

Tamarisk's letter to her mother was very brief:

'*I am going to join Perry!*' it said. '*By the time you read this we will be crossing the Channel together. Mayhap this will convince you that I love him. Yesterday he told me that he loved me, and I hope we can soon be married. Now that I know I can spend the rest of my life beside him, my future happiness is assured, so please do not worry about me.*

'*I hope you and Papa will find it in your hearts to rejoice for me. I will write to you once we are settled.*

'*From your affectionate daughter,*
Tamarisk.'

Tamarisk left the house soon after breakfast saying that she intended to pay a morning call upon Clarissa. Only when she had not returned for luncheon by three of the clock, did Mavreen learn that Tamarisk had not taken any of the carriages but had hired a hackney cab; furthermore, that many of her clothes and her maid Elsie were also missing.

Tamarisk's letter was brought to the door by a messenger at precisely the dinner hour. Reading its contents Mavreen understood very well why Tamarisk had chosen to have it delivered in such a fashion. She had not wished her mother to learn of her whereabouts until she was beyond recall. She would now be out to sea, and there was no way in which Mavreen could prevent *this* elopement. As for Gideon, it seemed as if he had finally succumbed to the girl's adoration.

'*He told me that he loved me . . .* ' The words stood out as if they were written in capital letters. Tamarisk had not written '*I think he loves me.*' Mavreen was shocked and strangely frightened for her daughter.

Weakly she walked into the morning room and sank into an armchair, the letter still clasped between her trembling hands. She tried to tell herself that she must feel joy and not distress now that Tamarisk had found the happiness so far denied her. She told herself that Gideon would make the girl a wonderful husband, kindly, generous, sensitive; he would never reproach Tamarisk for her past mistakes — all of which were well known to him. She told herself that it was not unnatural that Gideon should love Tamarisk, for her daughter had grown into a very beautiful young woman.

He had acted quite honorably, first making clear his intention to end his long friendship with her before declaring himself to Tamarisk. And Tamarisk was like her, not only in looks but in nature, this very day proving herself as doggedly determined as her mother to follow the man she loved whatever the consequences.

But despite all such reasoning, Mavreen felt no happiness — only a profound, unaccountable sense of loss and pain.

27

1819 – 1820

WHILST Mavreen dreaded the moment when she must inform Gerard that their daughter had eloped with Gideon, he was equally apprehensive at the prospect of imparting to her the disturbing news he had received regarding Antoine. His reaction upon hearing of Tamarisk's departure to a foreign land with the one man in the world he most hated was tempered by his far greater concern for his son.

"Tamarisk is mistaken if she imagines I will ever accept that man as her husband or receive him in my house!" he said coldly. "Her judgment of men has ever been misguided, so I am not entirely surprised by this new folly. Nevertheless I did not imagine she could sink to quite such depths of stupidity." He glanced at Mavreen searchingly. "I take it you knew nothing of this before-hand?"

"Do you think I would have encouraged it?" Mavreen cried. Her voice became bitter. "Surely *you* do not think I would want my daughter to steal one of my most ardent admirers from beneath my nose!"

Gerard flushed an angry red.

"Tamarisk may well have been influenced by your mistaken estimate of that renegade," he said pointedly, his remark nearer the truth than he imagined. "However, 'tis done now and I do not wish to hear anymore on the subject. Nor do I wish that man's name mentioned again in this house." He drew a deep breath. "Now I have something of far more importance I wish to discuss with you, Mavreen."

She looked up at Gerard's face, surprised into open-mouthed silence by his statement. What *could* be more important than their daughter's happiness?

"It concerns Antoine!" Gerard said, choosing his words with care. "I shall be leaving for Buckinghamshire first thing in the morning to collect him from his school."

"*Take Antoine away from Eton?*" Mavreen gasped in astonishment. "But I thought he was beginning to enjoy school life — to make friends and . . . "

"I have been asked by the headmaster to remove him!" Gerard broke in, his voice strangled by the depths of his emotion. "There has been the most terrible miscarriage of justice. Antoine has been held responsible for the theft of a large sum of money from one of the older boys. Of course such a thing is inconceivable, and I have no doubt that Antoine can prove his innocence and will do so to my complete satisfaction when I question him. But the headmaster is adamant in his letter to me that he believes Antoine to be the culprit; and if the man is so lacking in intelligence and judgment as to believe a de Valle capable of so base a crime as theft from a schoolmate, then I do not consider him fit to have the care of my son. I shall not hesitate therefore to remove Antoine from the school as he suggests."

Mavreen continued to stare at Gerard, her mind in a turmoil. Uppermost in her thoughts was the terrible distress Gerard must now be suffering. Even if he truly believed his son innocent, the blow to his pride in having Antoine under suspicion must be enormous. She herself believed it quite likely that the boy was guilty. It was inconceivable that the headmaster of a school such as Eton would condemn a boy without proof; even less likely if that boy was the son of the Vicomte de Valle. In no time at all it would become common knowledge that the boy had been expelled and for what reason, and such gossip would be libelous if the truth were not beyond question.

"You say nothing!" Gerard remarked. His voice was bitter as he added, "Which does not surprise me. You have never liked Antoine, have you? From the beginning you found fault with the boy. No doubt you are willing to believe the worst about him now."

"It is not fair to accuse me of prejudice!" Mavreen cried. "Antoine is your son, Gerard, and I was ready to love him for that reason alone when first you brought him home. But . . . "

"Exactly!" Gerard interrupted. "But his mother was lowly born and you resented the boy for not being your own flesh and blood. Well, I shall not bring him back to *this* household. I anticipated your condemnation and yesterday I called upon Princess Camille. She has professed herself not only willing but anxious to receive Antoine into her household!"

"*Princess Camille Faloise?*" Mavreen asked incredulously. "But Gerard, you must have taken leave of your senses! You must know her reputation!"

Aghast, she watched the expression on Gerard's face change from one of irritation to determination.

"Unlike you and your good friend the Baroness, I do not listen to idle gossip!" he said coldly.

Forgetting everything but her need to prevent this further disaster, Mavreen caught hold of Gerard's arm. Keeping her voice as calm and conciliatory as possible she said forcefully:

"'Tis not idle gossip, Gerard. The Princess makes no secret of her penchant for very young boys. Wherever she goes she takes her current favorite with her and openly dotes upon him. She is not only extremely ugly in appearance but she is perverted by nature. She is the very last person fitted to be guardian of your son."

Gerard broke free of Mavreen's restraining hand. He looked at her coldly.

"I had not thought you well enough acquainted with the Princess to be able to speak with such authority on her character. As it happens, I myself am very well acquainted with her. She was in residence in Compiègne throughout last summer and I visited her with Antoine upon many occasions. Ugly she may be, but no one could have been kinder to Antoine or more interested in his welfare. He received a great deal more by way of maternal affection from her than ever he has received from you; and he was as much in rapport with her as she was with him."

"Antoine is a very beautiful child to look upon!" Mavreen said carefully but meaningfully. "Naturally the Princess was attracted to him; and if she continually indulged him, small wonder that he returned her affection. But Gerard, do you not see that the boy's looks alone are enough to put him in jeopardy even were he not already weak of character and therefore prone to corruption . . . "

The look of fury on Gerard's face silenced her. Dismayed Mavreen realized that in her desperate effort to prevent Gerard from pursuing his ill-chosen course of action, she had used the very words most likely to make him discount her advice.

"I do not think your opinion of great value!" Gerard said, his voice edged with sarcasm. "After all, my dear, you can hardly claim your maternal instincts to be infallible when you consider the misfortunes which have befallen your daughter. In any event Antoine is not your son but mine, and I shall decide his future as I think fit. My mind is made up. He shall go to live with Princess Camille and continue his education with his tutor, Mr. Mumford. I have the utmost confidence in both of them. As for Tamarisk and . . . and that man, I consider we are most fortunate that they have left this country since they will never be welcome under my roof!"

557

"You would cast out your own daughter?" Mavreen cried, aghast. "You, who professed to love her?"

"I consider by her actions she has forfeited my regard. When first I came to know her, I was happy and proud to be the father of such a charming daughter. But she has become quite different these past few years and is as willful and wanton as once she was innocent and unspoilt!"

"'Tis time you learned the meaning of the word 'love,' Gerard!" Mavreen replied bitterly. "I am sure I have no need to remind you that it was your favorite author, Shakespeare, who said: *'Love is not love which alters when it alteration finds.'*"

"I have no wish to discuss Tamarisk further!" Gerard said coldly. "I have more important matters to occupy me!"

Gerard would have been able to dismiss his daughter so lightly had he realized that Tamarisk was still in England. Her plan to meet with Gideon aboard the packet was thwarted by the most minor of mishaps to the stagecoach in which she and her maid were traveling to Dover. When finally they arrived at the port, it was to discover the packet had departed fifteen minutes earlier.

When she recovered from the first shock of dismay on receiving this intelligence, Tamarisk took stock of her situation. Her chin lifted in stubborn determination.

"Whatever else I do, I will *not* return home!" she told the tearful Elsie who stood sniffling amongst their boxes.

"But Milady, we have no money!" Elsie wailed. "We must go back else we shall starve!"

"Nonsense, girl!" Tamarisk said sharply, although she she was unhappily aware of their financial predicament. She had brought only a few pounds with her to pay for their passages over the English Channel, assuming that Perry would thereafter make himself responsible for them. She hoped he would quickly adjust to the idea that she was going with him to Italy and had forced herself firmly not to question his compliance. She was reassured by the thought that he had admitted loving her — the only barrier between them being his misguided concern regarding their differing ages. By her actions now she would prove she was no helpless child but as resourceful as her mother.

Doggedly Tamarisk turned her attention to her present predicament.

"Stop sniveling, Elsie!" she commanded. "I know exactly where Sir Peregrine is going in Italy, even to the name of the villa where he intends to sojourn with friends. We shall join him there!"

She had no way at the moment of knowing how this could be accomplished since she had insufficient money for so long a journey.

It seemed, however, as if Fate had now chosen to favor her. At the inn where she and Elsie were debating their unhappy situation was a wealthy Italian family with a large brood of troublesome children. The wailing and gesticulations of the portly, bejeweled Signora soon brought their misfortunes to the notice of everyone at the inn. The English nurse who was to care for the children on the schooner taking them to Italy had not kept the rendezvous as arranged. The schooner was leaving for Genoa on the next tide and there was no time to arrange for a dependable substitute for the nurse.

"*Che cosa devo fare? Che cosa farebbe se fosse al mio posto?*" the woman moaned to anyone prepared to listen to her.

Tamarisk grinned.

"I know exactly what the Signora can do," she whispered to Elsie as she rose to her feet. "She can engage me as governess to her children in return for our free passage to Genoa!"

"Oh, Milady!" Elsie gasped. "'Twould not be right for you in your position to act as a governess!"

She looked so shocked that Tamarisk had difficulty in restraining her laughter.

"You are not to tell the good woman that I have a title," she said, "for by her appearance I doubt very much that she has one herself and she might not presume to offer me the post."

If Signora Galvanti had doubts as to the advisability of engaging someone who was most certainly of gentle birth to act as her servant, her husband had none. Signor Galvanti had already noticed the exceptional beauty of the solitary young woman and was more than willing to agree to Tamarisk's proposition.

"There now, Elsie! I told you it would be all right!" Tamarisk said when finally they boarded the schooner. She had to shout to be heard above the noise of the five unruly children sharing their cabin. "Genoa is no distance from Leghorn. We may even reach the Villa Valsovano before Sir Peregrine!"

Elsie eyed their five charges with misgivings. To begin with, she thought, they were foreigners and she could not understand a word they were saying. As for their parents, Elsie had only been in service with titled people and she deeply resented the thought that her young mistress, a Lady in her own right, was forced to take employment with merchants. Signor and Signora Galvanti might be rich but they were certainly not gentry.

Tamarisk merely smiled at Elsie's snobbery.

"You must try to look on all this simply as an adventure!" she advised. "We must make the best of it, Elsie. Are you not even a little excited to be on a schooner sailing to foreign places you have only read about in books?"

But Elsie did not read books; the motion of the sailing ship made her feel sick; she was nervous of the leers and winks of the crew and terrified of the enormous waves they encountered when a storm blew up in the Bay of Biscay.

Tamarisk, who discovered herself to be an excellent sailor, was exhilarated by the sights and smells of the ocean. Unfortunately both her employers were seasick and rarely emerged from their cabin; and with Elsie terrified of her own shadow, it fell to Tamarisk to attempt to control the Galvanti children. The enormity of this task left her little time to enjoy the voyage.

By nightfall she was too exhausted to lie awake pondering the finality of the step she had taken or to question whether Perry would after all receive her with open arms.

By the end of the first week at sea the weather became calmer as they sailed in a southwesterly direction following the coast of Spain. Tamarisk's task became easier as the three young Galvanti boys made friends with the sailors who good-humoredly kept an eye on them and taught them how to tie knots and cast fishing lines.

The two little girls were content to sit on deck in the sunshine playing with dolls the sailors made for them from ropes. Elsie gained a modicum of courage and was kept busy washing the children's clothes and trying to keep their cabin in some kind of order. She gave up any attempt to keep her young mistress looking like the aristocrat she was. Tamarisk had dispensed with frills and petticoats, with ribbons and curling tongs for her hair. She now moved freely in a simple cambric dress and permitted her hair to blow in the freshening wind as they turned eastward toward Gibraltar.

On the sixteenth of December they docked at Gibraltar. The schooner, carrying wool to Genoa, needed fresh water and provisions before completing the next leg of the journey eastward, through the Mediterranean, past the Balearic Islands and then northeastward toward Genoa.

They were still at sea on Christmas Day, Tamarisk's twenty-second birthday. Signor Galvanti made one of his rare appearances from his cabin, patted his windtanned, untidy children on their heads, drank too much rum with the captain, and retired below once more. The ship's cook, advised by Elsie of Tamarisk's birthday, baked a cake which she and the Galvanti children demolished without difficulty. The children, under Elsie's guidance, had secretly made little birthday gifts, and Elsie herself gave Tamarisk an embroidered 'kerchief; Signora Galvanti, a pretty glass bead necklace.

It was by far the most impoverished birthday celebration Tamarisk had ever known, yet she was never happier, she informed Elsie at the end of the day.

"And very soon now we shall arrive at Genoa," she added, her face radiant with anticipation.

Five days later Tamarisk stood on deck watching the approaching coastline with glowing cheeks and eager eyes. It had taken them just under a month to reach Italy and she was certain that they could not be far behind Perry, who would have traveled across France and over the Apennines by carriage in far more leisurely fashion. She had agreed with Signor Galvanti to remain with the family in their house in Genoa for ten days after their arrival in order to give them time to employ another governess. Although she had no wish to delay in Genoa, she explained to Elsie, they needed the money from her promised wages to pay for their journey to Leghorn.

From conversations with the burly but amiable ship's captain Tamarisk knew what to expect when they docked: a busy seaport exporting wine, olive oil, coral, paper, macaroni, and marble. The town itself he had described most vividly — a labyrinth of narrow lanes most of which were accessible only to those on foot or to pack mules carrying goods to and from the docks; but also boasting a number of palaces and some tall, handsome houses built of marble and belonging to the wealthier members of Genoese society.

It was to one of these houses that Signor Galvanti took his entourage in a fleet of sedan chairs. It required two handcarts to transport their baggage to his home. Although in no way comparable in size or luxuriousness to Barre House, it was large and comfortable, and there were servants in plenty to see to the menial tasks. With the assistance of Elsie and a young Italian maid, it did not take Tamarisk long to settle the Galvanti children into their beds on the evening of their homecoming. Later she herself was able to luxuriate in a tin bath of hot water and, laughing, permitted Elsie to wash and curl her sun-bleached hair. Elsie completed the task and regarded her young mistress with pleasure.

"You look a deal more like yourself, Milady!" she said as she helped Tamarisk into one of her prettiest muslin gowns which the Italian maid had expertly ironed for her — a suitable choice, Elsie considered, for the Galvantis had invited Tamarisk to dine with them. Only the golden tan of Tamarisk's skin caused by the sea winds gave Elsie reason to bemoan the loss of her proper ladylike pallor.

"You be almost as dark-skinned as these here

Eyetalians!" Elsie cried. But Tamarisk laughed.

"I think it becomes me," she said. "It makes my eyes a deeper green and my hair is bleached to a prettier color."

Tamarisk was not alone in believing that the sea journey had enhanced her appearance. Throughout the meal Signor Galvanti's eyes were focused upon her; and Tamarisk was uncomfortably aware of his wife's mounting jealousy as his attentions to her became increasingly lascivious.

Tamarisk's good spirits began to evaporate. The gross, balding merchant with his heavy paunch and loose-hanging jowls revolted her as much as did the smell of garlic on his breath when he leaned toward her. He drank far too heavily of the wines served with the meal and, almost as heavily after it, of a dark-colored liqueur. His remarks became more and more personal and were delivered in his halting English with a leering smile which could only be called ribald. His wife, who spoke no English, understood his mood very well, and to Tamarisk's relief she found herself peremptorily dismissed as soon as coffee had been served.

Elsie was awaiting her in her bedchamber. She looked near to tears. As she began to undress Tamarisk, Elsie confessed that she had had a terrible time with the Genoese servants.

"Oh, Milady!" she moaned. "I could not understand one word of what they was saying, but the men was that awful with their familiar looks and their hands was everywhere! As for the girls — they all hated me because of the men being interested, me being foreign-looking to them, I daresay!"

Tamarisk laughed.

"I have not fared much better," she said, relating her own experience with Signor Galvanti. "Never mind, Elsie! We will not be here long, and at least we do not now have to share a cabin with the children and can sleep in peace!"

Sleep, however, was to elude Tamarisk. Not an hour after she had retired, there was a knock upon the door of her bedchamber. Imagining it must be Elsie, she lit her candle, rose from her bed, and ran shivering to unlock the door.

To her dismay Signor Galvanti stood on the threshold.

Before she could open her mouth to protest he placed a pudgy hand over her lips and by the sheer weight of his body pushed her backward into the room. Despite his bulk he succeeded in kicking the door shut behind him; then twisting with a litheness surprising in so fat a man, he released his hold upon her and turned the key in the lock.

Tamarisk ran to the bed and grabbing at her nightrobe, pulled it around her body. But the man had already seen through the diaphanous silk of her nightgown to the enticing, youthful shapeliness of breasts, legs, hips. His face, flushed by alcohol, suffused a darker red.

Drunk though he was, the elderly merchant was well aware of the seriousness of the offense he might have to commit. He had every intention of seducing this aristocratic young girl, but if she would not submit, he was ready to use force.

He was shrewd enough to assess Tamarisk's vulnerability. Not only was she penniless, but she was unprotected. He knew her parents would never have permitted a young girl like her to travel unchaperoned except by her maid. He guessed, therefore, that she must have undertaken this journey either against her family's wishes or without their knowledge. She had told him she was going to join the man she was to marry, but he knew better than to imagine that her parents would permit such a state of affairs. He supposed that the man she hoped to wed was unsuitable in one respect or another.

Tamarisk, he concluded, had no family or friends to complain to of his conduct. As for the authorities — he was a much-respected citizen of Genoa with wealth and an excellent reputation, so they would disregard any complaint she might seek to lodge against him.

With such self-assurances and with the confidence of the intoxicated, he stumbled toward the girl and pushed her backward onto the bed before she realized his intent.

Tamarisk had time to scream only twice before her attacker rammed his sweat-stained cravat into her open mouth. Desperately she clawed at the great hot hand clutching at her breast. Even in her terror her mind seemed to sum up coldly and logically the hopelessness of her situation. The man's servants would not come to her aid. His wife, who might seek to intervene if she had heard Tamarisk's screams, would be unable to open the locked door of the bedchamber. As for Elsie asleep in the attic at the top of the house, even if she heard her mistress's cries, it was unlikely that she would have courage enough to run out of the house and seek help. Tamarisk herself did not know if there were watchmen or constabulary in this foreign town. Mustering all her strength she tried to push the man away from her. But he caught her wrists and with his knee attempted to force her legs apart. Sickened with fear and disgust she raised her leg hoping to kick him away; but the folds of her nightgown were impeding her as well as him.

He released one of her arms and ripped her nightgown with vicious strength from shoulder to hem. She struck out with the hand she had freed and felt her nails sinking into his cheek. She heard him gasp in sudden pain; but her resistance seemed only to inflame the lust that was driving him to a maddened determination to have his way with her.

In the flickering light of her bedside candle Tamarisk saw the glazing of his eyes and the thickening of his features. She turned her head away in horror. The sound of his hoarse panting came close to her ear. She felt his thick, moist lips against her flesh and her whole body arched in revulsion.

She twisted her head, hoping somehow to dislodge the choking lump of cloth in her mouth. But now the man was astride her, his white, fat, hairy legs and monstrous great thighs topped by the coarse bunched folds of his nightshirt. Sweat poured from his face, neck, and armpits, adding to the evil smell of his brandy and garlic-laden breath. Her legs and arms flailed in growing terror and panic as the weight of his gross body crushed the air from her lungs.

For one crazed moment of hope she ceased to fight. She lay still, staring up at him in appeal for pity, mercy. But he was not looking at her face. His eyes were devouring her now naked body, the skin whiter than any woman's he had known, deliciously slender and delicate in comparison with the fat, olive-skinned flesh of his middle-aged spouse. He was convinced that the girl beneath him was a virgin and the thought incited his desire to even greater heights. Whilst he savored the delights to come, he was momentarily off guard. He grunted with pain as Tamarisk's hand caught him a stinging blow across the face, temporarily blinding him. But his weight was sufficient to prevent her escape from beneath him, and as the pain subsided he was once more filled with animal lust. Wordlessly he pulled her arms apart so that both small breasts reached tantalizing upward toward his panting mouth. His knees imprisoned her legs, and with a muffled cry he plunged down deep into her body.

The scream could not force its way from Tamarisk's throat past the gag in her mouth. It seemed to travel downward into the lower part of her abdomen and join with the great searing pain as her tormentor rode wildly to his climax. It echoed in her skull until her whole body was rent by her agony and unvoiced protest. Coherent thought ceased whilst terror and pain prevailed. It returned only when he suddenly rolled off her and lay gasping beside her.

With what little vestige of strength she still possessed, Tamarisk struck out with her fist and was unaware of this lesser pain as her knuckles connected with the jaw of her attacker. She saw the shocked surprise in his eyes turn to a furious anger. Then he hit her. Mercifully blackness engulfed her and she knew nothing of the succession of blows raining down upon her head.

It was Tamarisk's stillness which brought the man to his senses. Terrified lest he had killed her, he felt for her pulse. His relief at finding her still alive was short-lived. Only now as his blood cooled did he appreciate the enormity of his folly. Sobered at last by fear, he stared down at his victim thinking that he had set about this night's work believing it would be a simple matter to seduce her; that he had never intended to rape her; that what transpired was her fault for fighting him when she should have realized that too much wine had befuddled his judgement.

Nevertheless, blaming Tamarisk for her own downfall in no way protected him from the consequences of his actions. Already there were innumerable bruises showing on her white flesh that left no doubt as to the fact that she had been assailed. Even if he paid his servants enough money to keep their mouths shut, he could not hope to avert his wife's jealous retribution. It would be better, he thought, if the unhappy girl ran away! But it was obvious it might be days

570

before she could run anywhere.

Nervously he tried to marshal his panicking thoughts. He realized that he must get rid of Tamarisk — and as soon as possible. At once his mind turned to his personal valet Guiseppe — the one man whom he had always been able to trust. Guiseppe frequently procured women for him and secreted them in and out of the house without his wife's knowledge. Guiseppe would do anything if the financial rewards were great enough. He could carry the unconscious girl downstairs, bundle her into the handcart, and dispose of her somewhere where she would be unlikely to find her way back. Not that she would wish to return after what had happened.

He opened the door and called to his servant who was lurking in the shadows, a grin upon his ugly face.

"Do not kill her, Guiseppe!" he warned the man as he explained the mission he was to undertake. "The risk is too great!"

"No need for it, Master!" the man replied. "If I leave her up in the hills in this weather and in that attire! . . . " He broke off, shrugging his shoulders meaningfully.

As the servant carried Tamarisk out onto the landing, Elsie sat crouched in the darkness at the top of the stairs above them. She had heard Tamarisk's screams but lacked the courage to go to her aid. For an hour she had sat sobbing quietly, deeply ashamed of her fearfulness but yet unable to overcome it. She was convinced that her young mistress was dead as she watched Tamarisk's lifeless form being carried down

571

the marble staircase into the dark hall below. But although her fear of the two men was overpowering, she was even more afraid of remaining in this evil house alone. Keeping to the shadows, silent as a cat, she followed at a distance, guided by the soft golden glow of the lamp Guiseppe had attached to the side of the handcart in which Tamarisk's covered body lay.

The terraced alleyways petered out into stony tracks as they climbed upward. Before long they were passing through the darkened groves of orange and pomegranate trees, and finally into the uninhabited hills. Here, in the shelter of a single dead olive tree, Guiseppe unloaded his burden. He stood for several minutes staring at the crumpled figure of the young girl from whom he had removed the covering. Horrified, Elsie wondered if the man intended her poor mistress even further harm; but mercifully Guiseppe flung the cover into the handcart and began hurriedly to descend the hill.

Not until the man was well out of sight did Elsie emerge from her place of concealment behind an outcrop of rocks. Crying, she ran to the spot where the body lay. Although Tamarisk's eyes were closed, she was moaning softly and Elsie broke into a fresh storm of weeping in relief at discovering her young mistress alive. Urgently she patted Tamarisk's bruised cheeks in a vain attempt to revive her. Removing her own rough-spun wrap, she covered the cold, naked body of the girl. She was instantly aware of the icy bitterness of the

January wind against her own warm flesh.

"Oh, mercy be, mercy be!" she wailed. "We shall die of the cold — the both of us. Our Father which art in heaven, save us! Have pity upon us!"

On the point of hysteria she began to pray a feverish jumble of prayers, hymns, and psalms.

So it was the gypsy found them, guided away from the snares he had laid nearby for rabbits by the faint echo of Elsie's frantic appeals to God.

28

January – March 1820

TAMARISK opened her eyes. She was in a dim cavelike interior. Occasional shafts of sunlight were moving in disorientated patterns on the dark ceiling of cloth above her head. Slowly she became aware of the metallic jingle of pots, kettles, and saucepans which her searching eyes discovered hanging in rows around the walls. The floor beneath her seemed alternately to sway and bump, making her aware of the pain engulfing her body.

As full consciousness returned she realized that she was in a covered wagon which, through the slit in the felt overhang which served as a doorway, she could see was being pulled by a large carthorse.

Her head throbbed unbearably and she closed her eyes. When next she opened them it was to see a strange, dark-eyed girl looking down at her in kindly concern. As the girl bent forward two gold earrings dangled down across the dark skin of her face. Her clothes were ragged but in no way concealed the strong, voluptuous curves of her body. Her walnut-brown arms were hung with silver and gold bracelets; a pendant of silver coins hung from her neck. Her body exuded a pungent odor — strange but not altogether unpleasant.

She is a gypsy! Tamarisk thought, her mind totally bemused.

Seeing the astonishment in Tamarisk's eyes, the girl's red lips parted in a smile, revealing the whitest teeth Tamarisk had ever seen. The girl was friendlily disposed, she thought as she attempted to raise herself so that she could make some kind of greeting. But the ache in her limbs was of such intensity that she fell back with a little cry.

At once the girl moved forward, holding a small tankard to Tamarisk's lips. The liquid was ice cold and tasted of herbs. The gypsy girl pointed to her forehead, indicating by her gestures that it would help disperse the pain Tamarisk was suffering. She moved to the side of the wagon and returned with a jar containing oil which she proceeded to smooth with the utmost gentleness into Tamarisk's bruised skin. Tamarisk thought she could detect the smell of honey and marjoram. The effect was instantly soothing.

Tamarisk's gypsy benefactor had not yet finished her ministrations. One concoction she forced upon Tamarisk was a Romany recipe to procure abortion.

When first Tamarisk was carried into the camp by the young man who rescued her, the old woman of the tribe, Miarka, was called at once to give her counsel. Elsie, who was shivering violently in her thin nightgown, was close to hysterics with fright and shock and unable to give an account of their misfortunes in her own language, far less in a foreign tongue.

575

Dispatching her to one of the wagons in the care of a gypsy girl, the old woman turned her attention to Tamarisk. It did not take her long to realize that the injuries the young foreigner had suffered were the result of a vicious rape.

She had at once set about boiling a concoction of aloes, cloves, ginger, nutmeg, goose grass, borage, sage, rue, and mint. To this the old woman added white wine and filtered the whole through her apron. By mid-morning, when Tamarisk first regained consciousness, the resultant decoction was ready for the girl Zorka to administer to her patient.

It was some days before Tamarisk recovered sufficiently from the shock and injuries of her ordeal in Genoa to discover that she could communicate with the Romanies in French. Poor Elsie, who spoke no foreign language, was forced to make do with miming and gesticulations which invariably reduced the gypsy children to gales of laughter. But despite Elsie's initial horror at finding herself at the mercy of 'vagabonds', as she termed them to Tamarisk, she was quickly recognizing their virtues which were far in excess of the mere fact of rescuing them from the 'villainous Eyetalians'.

Zorka, Tamarisk soon discovered, was her own age but had been married at fourteen and was already the mother of four children. Her husband, Torina, like the other men in the Yonesti tribe, was a tinsmith by trade. The motley band of nomad gypsies traveled from town to town, stopping to repair pots and pans wherever they could; and when they could not,

576

singing and dancing to earn their livelihood.

They were now upon their way to Lavagna, a small town on the coast, from whence they intended to go to La Spezia, a city near the Apennine mountains where they never failed to find work. Their route would take them on to Viareggio, past the seaport Leghorn before they turned inland to Florence, Zorka said.

"Leghorn!" Tamarisk repeated, her face breaking into a smile for the first time since her dreadful experience at the hands of Signor Galvanti. "Then Elsie and I may travel there with you . . . in safety!"

Her recovery was greatly assisted by her relief and happiness at finding herself by great good fortune actually upon her way to her chosen destination.

"Before long we shall be in Sir Peregrine's safekeeping!" she told Elsie comfortingly. The girl had not adapted to her new surroundings easily. But she was at last beginning to make the best of the limited facilities and had herself swept and dusted the wagon and wrought some semblance of order within it.

Soon Tamarisk was well enough to leave the wagon, although the bruises covering her torn body had not yet disappeared. The extraordinary metamorphosis of her life with the Romanies did help, however, to keep at bay the full shock of her recent experience. The gypsies' philosophy helped to mitigate the full extent of the horror she had suffered, for they believed in the value of lessons learned by experience and saw no purpose in worrying over the irredeemable.

They were kindly, sympathetic, and attentive to Tamarisk's physical welfare but encouraged her to look forward and not back. Unwilling to relive her fear and revulsion, she tried to push it from her memory. Fortunately there was much to occupy her mind.

When the tribe halted on the outskirts of La Spezia and camped on the wooded hills at the foot of the towering peaks of the Apennines, Zorka and Torina encouraged Tamarisk to go into town with them. They had provided her and Elsie with clothes — brightly colored peasant skirts over several layers of petticoats, topped by low-cut blouses. Heavy triangular shawls kept at bay the bitter January winds. Tamarisk was not uncomfortable in this coarse clothing; but she found the ill-fitting, roughly sewn boots caused blistering to her feet, accustomed as she was to wearing only the most delicate calfskin shoes tailored to fit her.

She accompanied the young couple into the town where very soon Torina was given work at one of the big houses repairing the copper and iron kitchenware. After several hours he emerged into the courtyard where Zorka and Tamarisk were sheltering in the stables. His white teeth showed in a wide grin as he held out a handful of coins which he immediately shared between them. Zorka told Tamarisk she might spend her money as she wished.

To the gypsies' astonishment Tamarisk purchased neither food, clothing, nor trinkets but returned smiling to the camp carrying quill, ink, and paper.

"It is a new year, Elsie," she explained, "and I wish to keep a journal once again. Then I will remember every detail of this adventure to relate to Sir Peregrine! And later I shall be able to record my new life with him."

It was the seventh of January. Before an admiring group of gypsy children who were all, like their parents, illiterate, Tamarisk began writing in her journal.

'We are remaining here at La Spezia for a further two days,' she wrote in her neat script, 'for there is much work for the Yonestis. Tonight we ate of a delicious fish stew — a welcome change from rabbit which we have eaten every day since leaving Genoa. Zorka told me her brother Michel obtained the fish from the market. I think he stole it, but I have discovered in conversation with Zorka that the gypsies do not look upon theft as a crime. "The fruits of the earth belong to all men," is their philosophy.'

Her entry for the following day referred only to Miarka. Wife of the chief of the tribe, the old woman was looked to by all for advice and counsel. She was recognized as having 'the sight', and at Tamarisk's request she told her fortune. That night Tamarisk covered several pages of her diary.

'Miarka said I have many long journeys to make before I marry!' she wrote. 'But in this she must surely be mistaken, for it is

579

but a further fifty miles to Leghorn. The gypsies call the town 'Livorno'. That my husband will be rich but not handsome was yet another prediction. I suppose Perry might not appear handsome to her, yet he has always been spoken of as such. Miarka promised me many sons and daughters and excellent health, but followed this good news with warnings of a death of someone near to me before many moons have passed.

'I do not think I believe in her fortune-telling for all Zorka swears she is never mistaken. Miarka is so old now, mayhap she can no longer see so clearly into the future! Elsie was too frightened to have her fortune told. Poor Elsie! She is forever wishing she were safe at home in England. But then so might I be wishing if I did not have the prospect of seeing my beloved Perry so soon!'

On the ninth of January she wrote:

'If ordinary people were to know the Romanies as I am beginning to know them, they would not fear them or criticize their morals. I have discovered that if a gypsy woman bares her breasts, it is not considered immodest. It is not done to incite the men but to feed their babies which they do without shame before us all. They look upon their bosoms no differently than if they were limbs such as arms or legs. They are most moral in their insistence upon fidelity in marriage and *the punishments for transgression are often severe. Prostitution and offenses against the laws of nature are forbidden under threat of banishment from the tribe.*

'*The Romanies are quite charmingly loving to all the children of the tribe. As for Elsie and me — although we are "gaujos", as they call non-gypsies, they share their meager fare with us despite the fact that we have nothing to give in return. I have no need of a chaperon in this company, for no man would lay a hand upon me — truly a great blessing! I can move among these people without fear, and at night, were it not for my evil memories, I could sleep in peace.*'

For the tenth of January her entry read:

'*Today we crossed the River Macra and came to Carara. How I wish Mama were here to see, as I did, the great marble quarry where Michelangelo chose the blocks for his masterpieces!*'

A day later Tamarisk wrote of the bitter cold of the Mistral — a northwest wind which blew suddenly down upon them in violent gusts from the Alps.

'*The sea to our right is no longer blue but gray with white-crested waves,*' she wrote. '*So rough is it I am thankful we are not aboard the schooner.*'

581

Her spirits remained high nonetheless, for they were but a day's journey from Livorno. On the twelfth of January they came to the outskirts of the town.

Fearing that her unexpected appearance in the guise of a gypsy might cause considerable embarrassment not only to Perry but to his friends the Shelleys, Tamarisk decided to send a preparatory note to him via Elsie, explaining her predicament and asking him to come to collect her in a carriage, bringing with him suitable clothing. She suggested he might take her to an inn where she could bathe and wash her hair and regain some measure of respectability before he introduced her to his friends.

Elsie made herself as neat and tidy as possible whilst Tamarisk penned her note to Perry. Torina offered to escort Elsie to the gateway of the Villa Valsovano.

Knowing they would be gone for at least two hours, Tamarisk had plenty of time to see to her own appearance. Until now, when on the point of seeing Perry again she was forced to consider her looks, she had preferred to disregard all facets of her femininity. Thinking about her body recalled the hateful memories of its violation. But now her anxiety that Perry should still consider her pretty, despite her ragged clothes, was greater than any other emotion. Like all the gypsies, Zorka would not wash in water from the streams but instead cleaned herself with the folded leaves of the jujube tree. Tamarisk did likewise and discovered that this practice kept her delicate skin from becoming chapped by the constant exposure to the cold and winds.

But the oily content of the leaves, beneficial in one respect, had stained her skin almost as dark as that of the gypsies. Moreover, it had a distinctive odor to which she and Elsie had become accustomed but to which she feared Perry would object. To the horror of the whole tribe she now washed herself thoroughly in one of the streams.

Despite her efforts, when she studied her reflection in the mirror, she had little doubt that Perry would be hard put to recognize her. Except that her hair was fairer than ever, she looked little different from any of the gypsy girls.

But when Elsie and Torina returned at dusk, there was no Perry riding beside them. Close to tears, Elsie wailed:

"Oh, Milady, Sir Peregrine's gone to a place called Napoli, hundreds of miles south of here, and likely as not he won't never be coming back!"

Tamarisk put a restraining hand on Elsie's shaking shoulders. She tried to hide her own bitter disappointment as she broke in on the maid's hysterical outburst:

"Now, Elsie, tell me quietly exactly what transpired. You took my note to the Villa Valsovano as I instructed, did you not? And you saw Mister and Mistress Shelley?"

"No, Milady, that I did not!" Elsie moaned. "Them's gone too, to live in a place called Pisa! And the owners of the Villa has gone to Rome to a funeral and won't be back for a month or more. There weren't no one there but a housekeeper and her English was that bad I barely didn't understand her. I think as how she said Sir Peregrine went off in a boat." She began to cry.

Torina, standing quietly in the background, stepped forward and said in his halting French:

"House empty. Only servants. No good you stay there. Your man he gone to Napoli!"

Tamarisk's heart sank. There was no alternative but to follow Perry to Naples. But how could she accomplish this without money? She could seek financial help from English people living in Italy, perhaps in Leghorn itself. But what respectable family would consider lending her money! Looking as she did, she would never be able to convince a stranger that she was Lady Tamarisk Barre.

As if sensing her despair, Torina said:

"We go Florence soon. Then Sienna, Rome, and springtime we reach Napoli. Then Tamara find man and marry!"

Close to tears Tamarisk said sadly:

"Thank you, Torina, for the suggestion, but I cannot wait that long!"

If Perry had sailed from Leghorn to Naples, he would almost certainly have arrived by now, and for all she knew, he might not remain there until the spring. Suddenly a faint chord of memory stirred in her mind. Torina had mentioned Florence! In Florence there lived some distant relations of the de Valles.

Desperately she searched her memory. Fragments of her mother's conversation returned to her. Papa's mother, the former Vicomtesse de Valle, was an Italian by birth. Her sister had married one of the great Florentine noblemen, il Conte dell'Alba.[1] Although it was unlikely these relatives were still living, their children would be of similar age to that of her own parents; they must be aware of their French cousins even if they had never met them.

"Stop sniveling, Elsie!" she said firmly but not unkindly. "I have just remembered that I have cousins in Florence. They will provide us with everything we need and we shall be able to make our way to Naples speedily and in comfort!"

For the ensuing week they followed the wide fertile valley bordering the River Arno and made good progress eastward toward Florence. It was now mid-January and the weather worsened. As they approached the ancient walled city, they could see that snow had fallen on the upper slopes of the Chianti Mountains. The Yonesti camped, as always, outside the town at the foot of the hills.

Torina, who seemed to possess the most remarkable memory when it suited his purpose, informed Tamarisk that he knew where to find the Villa dell'Alba. It had always 'a good sign', he told her, by which he meant the message left by passing gypsies for those to follow — in this

---

[1] The dell'Alba family, at a later period in history, feature in the novel *A Voice in the Dark* as central characters.

case a circle with a dot in the center indicating that the dell'Albas were generous and friendlily disposed.

Once again Tamarisk and Elsie did what they could to make themselves look a little more respectable. Bidding a final farewell to the tribe, they made their way to the dell'Alba estate, Torina escorting them.

As they walked up the long, straight drive leading to the magnificent balconied mansion, Torina proved a further fount of information. An old woman had recently died at the house, he informed them, noting a new sign. But it was not the mistress of the house. There was also a marriage pending.

Elsie looked bemused.

"Whatever for do you gypsies want to leave messages about such things!" she exclaimed.

Torina grinned.

"It is good for Miarka to know if she wish to come to house to tell fortunes! If she right in some things, she is believed in all and will get much money!"

In front of the house lay a round, green lawn in the center of which stood a fountain. Water splashed into a huge basin, cascading down the flanks of a bronze horse. Elsie looked hopeful.

"'Tis a fine house!" she said, relieved to be nearing at last the civilized world which she knew and understood.

But as Tamarisk bade Torina goodbye, there was an ache in her heart at this final parting from the Romanies.

"I will leave money for you all by the front

586

gates!" she promised, for they were all agreed that it would be better if she were not to arrive at the house of her relatives in the company of a gypsy nor to begin her introduction to her cousins by begging money from them! "I shall never forget you all. And if I am still in Naples when you arrive there, Torina, search for me and I will help you in any way I can!"

Torina nodded.

"And if you meet trouble here, Tamara, then return to our camp!" he cautioned her. "We will not leave Firenze for three more days."

Before Tamarisk or Elsie could speak again, he melted into the shadows of the cypress trees flanking the drive.

It was several minutes before the liveried servant who opened the great polished wood front doors would permit them to cross the threshold. He seemed intent upon diverting them round the side of the house toward the kitchen quarters. But something in the proud lift of Tamarisk's pale gold head and the imperious tone of her voice caused him to hesitate. Pulling Elsie after her, Tamarisk took this opportunity to step past the footman into the great hall.

Elsie stared in awe at the two magnificent curved staircases leading up to the gallery above. Down one of these staircases, dressed completely in black, came a middle-aged woman. Tamarisk had little doubt that this imperious-looking lady must be the Contessa dell'Alba. Walking boldly forward she extended her hand.

"I am Tamarisk!" she said in perfect French. "My father is the Vicomte de Valle and your

587

cousin, I believe, Madame?"

The Contessa was far from anxious to receive any visitors, let alone this extraordinary-looking English girl and her maid whom she regarded with considerable misgivings. But at last Tamarisk managed to convince her beyond doubt that she was a bona fide member of the de Valle family.

A strict conventionalist herself, the Contessa was deeply shocked to hear how Tamarisk had taken refuge with the gypsies and lived as one of them these past two weeks. Although Tamarisk did not recount in detail the horror of her night at the Galvantis' house, the Contessa guessed that the merchant had made unwelcome advances to the girl. She could not understand how her cousins in England could have permitted their daughter to travel to a foreign country alone with no more than a young maid to accompany her.

Upon hearing of Tamarisk's wish to proceed at once to Naples to join the man she was to marry, the Contessa's suspicions deepened.

"I am convinced the girl is eloping!" she said later to her husband, Leonardo dell'Alba. "As if I did not have enough to worry me without this responsibility descending upon my shoulders! *E molto umiliante!*"

She had reason to be vexed. Two days earlier the elderly Contessa, Leonardo's mother and sister to Marguerite de Valle, had suddenly died. Her own daughter, Maria, was on the point of marriage to a wealthy young Florentine and all the wedding arrangements had had to

588

be canceled, involving her in a great deal of work and worry. Moreover, the funeral of her mother-in-law had yet to take place.

Hurriedly she dispatched Tamarisk to one of the guest chambers and Elsie to the servants' wing so that they might immediately divest themselves of their clothing. Tamarisk suspected correctly that the Contessa would give orders for their garments to be burned forthwith.

"When your maid is more suitably attired, I will send her to you with a gown and other necessities!" she told Tamarisk sharply. "Fortunately your height and size resemble that of my daughter Maria. Later, when you have bathed and changed, we will discuss your wish to go to Naples!"

Although Tamarisk had taken an acute dislike to her father's relative, she was grateful for the luxury of the beautiful bedroom and bathroom allotted her. For the first time in weeks she was able to enjoy a hot bath with real soap, lavender-scented, to wash her body. A smiling Italian maid ran in and out with copper jugs of hot water and then with freshly laundered towels. She insisted upon washing Tamarisk's hair for her and was combing out the tangles when Elsie came hurrying into the room. She too looked pink, scrubbed, and shining, and wore a neat new uniform.

"Oh, Milady, is it not wonderful to be in a real house again?" she said, taking the comb from the Italian girl's hand, "and have respectable clothes to wear? The Contessa has sent you ever such a pretty dress, and you have a fine

treat to come because I saw the dinner menu!"
Her eyes shone as she paused momentarily for
breath and then continued, "You'll be starting
with oysters and then soup and then there's a
whole heap of foreign foods I never heared about
before, but I think one of the dishes is venison.
And then there'll be fish, joints, sweetmeats, and
all manner of wines to drink!"

Tamarisk smiled.

"It does sound wonderful," she agreed. "But
do not imagine we shall be settling down here,
Elsie. I want to leave for Naples tomorrow!"

The sumptuous repast was eaten in the great
dining hall in funereal silence — out of respect
for the dead, the Contessa informed Tamarisk
crisply when she attempted to speak. The six
dell'Alba children, including the disappointed
young bride-to-be, Maria, whose dress Tamarisk
was wearing, kept their heads bowed as was
obviously expected of them. Occasionally one
stole a curious glance at their English visitor.

It seemed a very long time, Tamarisk thought,
since she had last dined in elegant surroundings
such as these. Gold candelabra graced the long
table. Fruit and flowers formed a magnificent
centerpiece. The footmen were kept busy serving
the numerous dishes — thirty at least, Tamarisk
calculated — to the large family. It might have
borne an even greater resemblance to one of
Mama's dinner parties at Barre House but for
the lack of interesting conversation.

As soon as the long, silent meal was over, they
were dismissed to their rooms. Tamarisk, who
was by now in a fever of impatience to make

the necessary arrangements for her journey to Naples, hoped to be permitted to remain with the Conte and his stiff-backed wife in the salon. But the Contessa ordered her to bed with only the barest civility.

With no option but to obey, Tamarisk retired to her room where Elsie awaited her.

"I do declare the gypsies made us more welcome than do my relatives!" she commented wryly.

But Elsie was not listening. Her face had resumed its familiar expression of anxiety and dismay as she cried:

"Oh, Milady, I don't know as how I am to tell you this, but tell you I must. I know as how you always taught me it was wrong to gossip but . . . well, I could not resist just a word or two with that there English nurse upstairs who takes care of the youngest children. I did so want to speak my own language again with someone as would understand me . . . "

"Elsie, do not ramble!" Tamarisk broke in sharply, sensing trouble. "What have you learned that is not going to please me?"

Elsie looked on the point of tears.

"They are not going to let you go to Naples!" she burst out. "That there Contessa and her husband, I mean. Nurse told me she had heard them talking before dinner and said as how they believed it was their duty to send you straight home to your parents. The Conte dell'Alba is going to arrange passage for us to England tomorrow, and if there is a boat sailing soon, we are to be taken to the coast at once and put in the care of the ship's captain. We are not never going to get to Naples now!"

Tamarisk's face turned a deathly white beneath her tan. She grasped Elsie's arm and made her repeat word for word what she had heard. When she could no longer retain any doubts as to the dell'Albas's intentions, she drew a deep breath of resolution.

"Then we shall go to Naples without their help!" she said. "For I will not return to England until I have seen Perry again!"

29

January – April 1820

QUIETLY, but with icy determination, Tamarisk made preparations for their departure from the Villa dell'Alba.

"Here, take this, Elsie!" she said. She pulled a rug from the bed and put it around the girl's shoulders. She put another around her own. "And do not look so frightened!" she added, smiling in spite of her acute concern that their plan to reach Naples was now in jeopardy.

"Oh, Milady!" Elsie moaned softly. "I am not nearly so feared for myself as I am for you. Have you forgotten what happened to us the last time we traveled by our twoselves?"

Tamarisk's young face hardened.

"No, I have not forgotten!" she said. "And that is why we are going to rejoin the Yonesti. So long as we can find our way back to their camp, we have nothing to fear. 'Tis but two miles distant from here and we shall pass unnoticed if we skirt the edge of the town."

But they were not to make their escape so easily. The Contessa and her husband seemed in no hurry to retire for the night; and since the doors of the salon where they sat talking had been left open, there was no chance of descending the stairway without detection.

Time crawled by whilst Tamarisk waited

impatiently for the house to fall silent. It was well after midnight before she felt it safe to venture onto the landing.

Every stair seemed to creak as they crept cautiously down to the darkened hall. Elsie clung nervously to Tamarisk's skirt.

"What'll they do to us if'n they catch us?" she whispered fearfully.

"We're not going to be caught, you silly girl!" Tamarisk whispered back. "I'm now going to open the bolts on the front doors. Don't move, Elsie!"

Despite the squeaking of the heavy iron bolts as they slid backward, there was no movement from the rooms above. Grabbing Elsie's hand, Tamarisk eased open the great doors and stepped out into a bright moonlit night.

As Tamarisk forecast, they were able to retrace their steps to the camp without mishap. Their gypsy friends received them back with a childlike acceptance of the Fates. Miarka, Zorka told them, had prophesied their return. Indeed, the old woman had also declared that they would bring wealth with them; and this too was proved true when Elsie produced from beneath her rug two silver-backed brushes and a silver bowl concealed by her before they left Tamarisk's bedchamber.

Tamarisk stared at her aghast.

"But Elsie, that was stealing!" she cried. "How could you do such a wicked thing?"

For once Elsie did not look woebegone.

"The gypsies say as how taking what others

do not need is no harm done to the losers!"
she said, "and we be in their tribe now,
beant we?"

The obvious delight of their hosts at receiving
such a valuable trio of gifts did little to salve
Tamarisk's conscience; but it did prevent
her from insisting upon their return to the
dell'Albas.

"I suppose our sea passage home would have
cost them a great deal more than these are
worth!" she said to Elsie, talking herself into a
kind of rough justice which must suffice for the
present. As soon as she could, she determined to
send a note of hand to her relatives, reimbursing
them the value of the articles they had stolen.

The chief of the Yonesti thought it best
in the circumstances to move on at once.
If they lingered in Florence, the dell'Albas
might send search parties to look for Tamarisk,
knowing that the Romanies had once before
befriended her.

Tamarisk was now resigned to the fact that
she could not hope to reach Naples before the
end of February. As best she could, she tried to
quell her impatience and to enjoy the discovery
of new towns and villages. She loved especially
the beautiful little walled town of Sienna set
three thousand feet up on the summit of three
hills, to the south of Florence.

Whilst Torina and his friends went about
their work, she explored the marble cathedral
and the many beautiful churches and palaces.
The fine, orange-red ocherous earth covered her
clothes and tinged her hair, but she let it linger

there before finally cleaning it with jujube leaves. She wanted always to remember Sienna. There, sitting quietly in one of the churches, she had prayed to the Virgin Mary that she would not find she was with child as a result of the attack upon her; and later that day she discovered her prayer had been answered. She would never know if this merciful event happened because she had not conceived; if it was the result of Zorka's many herbal potions; or in answer to her prayer. She hoped that she would now be able to forget her ordeal, or at least to relegate it to the past.

She resumed her diary, noting briefly anything she felt might be of interest to Perry should he request an account of the journey she had undertaken to be with him.

'*Twenty-fifth January. We left Sienna. Weather cold!*'

'*Twenty-sixth January. Camped near the River Ombrone. The Chief is worried lest we are caught in snowstorms in the hills.*'

'*Twenty-seventh January. Snowing hard. We are sheltering in some caves. Mara, one of the gypsy women, is in labor.*'

'*Twenty-eighth January. Last night Mara gave birth to a little girl. Miarka delivered her and she suffered hardly at all. They are naming the babe Tamara as a compliment to me.*'

'Twenty-ninth January. Mara and the baby are doing very well. Mara is not the least bit shy breastfeeding in front of us all. Elsie is quite shocked, but I think it is beautiful. It is still snowing hard and the horses are hungry.'

'Thirtieth January. We crossed the hills early this morning and are now encamped on the outskirts of Nuovo. The snow is only patchy here.'

'Thirty-first January. The men have found work in Nuovo. Early tomorrow we shall leave here.'

'Second February. It is becoming much warmer. We have camped not far from the most beautiful lake I have ever seen. It is called Lago di Bolensa. But the Romanies dislike water and would not go with Elsie and me to the lake's edge.'

'Sixth February. We have reached Vetrella where the men have once again found work. Michel found three chickens wandering in the road and promptly wrung their necks. Stolen or not, they were quite delicious after so many rabbit and herbal stews.'

'Ninth February. We are camped outside Bracciano. The countryside is flat and not so pretty as the hills we came through to reach here. Mara allowed me to hold her baby. The infant looks just like her.'

'*Eleventh February. We are on the northern outskirts of Rome. Zorka says we shall circle the city, and Kako, the Chief, has forbidden Elsie and me to go within the walls lest we are attacked or become lost. I would have liked to see St. Peter's Square, the Sistine chapel, the Colosseum, and the Fountain of Trevi, but perhaps I shall be able to do this some time in the future with Perry.*'

'*Eighteenth February. We left the southern outskirts of Rome this morning and will be traveling until the twentieth when we stop at Latina.*'

Now that they were so close to Naples, Tamarisk began to grow increasingly impatient. She resented the leisurely halts at Latina, Terracina, and Gaeta, and the lack of haste that was so characteristic of the gypsies. To add to her restlessness, the rainy season was approaching.

Ten miles south of Gaeta they were halted in a heavy rainstorm by floods along the banks of the River Liri. For five days it continued to rain, and had it not been for the shelter they found in the ruins of an ancient Roman villa, they would have been as sodden and dripping as the wagons.

On the third of March the floods subsided sufficiently for them to make the river crossing. By the sixth they were on the outskirts of Naples. Tamarisk was beside herself with excitement, not untinged with apprehension.

She had made up her mind to go directly to the British Consul rather than risk a repetition of the dell'Albas' attitude. She reasoned that the Consul would be unlikely to dispatch her to England without first consulting Perry. She convinced herself that when Perry heard but a fraction of what she had undergone to be with him, he would no longer doubt the magnitude and enduring quality of her love. Despite Miarka's reading of her palm and her prophecy that Tamarisk would not marry before she had made another long sea journey, she would not allow herself to dwell on the possibility that Perry might, in spite of all, reject her.

Elsie had never quite lost her superstitious fear of the gypsies, but when the moment came for them to make their last farewells, even she was sad. Zorka gave each of them a coral bracelet as a parting gift. Tamarisk promised that as soon as she could, she would bring Perry to their camp outside Naples with presents for them all.

She changed into the only dress she had — the evening gown the dell'Albas had lent her and which she had carefully preserved for this occasion. Concealed by her thick shawl, her dress was unnoticed by the kindly farmer who offered her and Elsie a ride into the town in his cart. He left them at the Piazza del Municipio facing the harbor. There Tamarisk was able to hire a sedan chair.

"If we are to present ourselves at the Consulate," she said to Elsie, "we must at least try to give ourselves an air of respectability!

Let us hope we have the means to pay for this small luxury!"

They had between them only one coin of doubtful value which Miarka had pressed into Tamarisk's hand as they were leaving. The bearers of the sedan chair seemed well satisfied, however, with the gold Austrian ducat, although it took them a long time to conduct the English Milady to her destination. They were grinning broadly enough for Elsie to comment shrewdly that they had certainly been overpaid. She glanced anxiously at her young mistress.

Tamarisk's appearance was unconventional, to say the least. Apart from the unsuitability of her evening gown, she carried no parasol, reticule, or gloves, and was without cloak or bonnet. She was, moreover, without papers or passport with which to identify herself.

Nevertheless, with a haughty, dogged persistence, Tamarisk at last managed to obtain an audience with the Consul, Sir Henry Lushington. A man of forty-five with four children of his own and one daughter not much younger than Tamarisk, the Baronet was astonished and deeply concerned by her story.

Insofar as she dared, Tamarisk kept to the facts — her only untruth being the inference that the reason why Perry had not awaited her at Dover was due to a lovers' tiff the day previously.

Sir Henry regarded the young girl with astonishment.

"That being the case, Lady Tamarisk, surely upon finding yourself alone and without money, it would have been sensible for you to send a messenger to your parents requesting the necessary funds to enable you to follow your ... er ... fiancé?"

"I realize that now!" Tamarisk said with apparent meekness. "But I thought then of nothing but the distress my poor fiancé must be suffering. It was very stupid of me, I know, but when the opportunity presented itself so fortuitously for me to travel direct to Genoa ... well, I acted upon the impulse of the moment ... as young women in love are wont to do!" she added demurely.

I don't know what young people are coming to these days! thought Sir Henry, but refrained from speaking his mind aloud. He said instead:

"Well, my dear young lady, you are indeed fortunate to be alive! That merchant! And living with the Romanies! Good gracious me!"

"Now you understand why I have to find the whereabouts of Sir Peregrine without delay!" Tamarisk repeated, anxious to get to the vital point now that she had established her identity to the Consul's satisfaction. "Have you seen or heard of him, Sir?"

Sir Henry shook his head.

"I have not had the pleasure of meeting the gentleman!" he replied frowning. "Which is strange, to say the least, since I know all the English people living here in Naples!" He paused, looking into Tamarisk's wide-apart eyes now clouded with disappointment. "'Tis possible your fiancé may have good reason not to make his presence known in Naples," he said slowly. "Perhaps I should enlighten you as to the political situation now prevailing, Lady Tamarisk. But first I will take you to my wife. Lady Lushington will, I know, make you most welcome and doubtless there are many prerequisites you will wish to borrow until such time as you can go upon a shopping expedition," he added with another furtive glance at the girl's strange habiliments.

"And you will do what you can to help me to find Sir Peregrine?" Tamarisk persisted. Only when he had given this assurance was she willing to accompany Sir Henry to meet his wife.

Lady Lushington was barely able to conceal her disapproval of the young woman her husband brought to her. It went beyond distaste for Tamarisk's darkly tanned skin, roughened hands, and uncoiffed hair. Upon hearing the extraordinary account of her travels, she suspected at once, as had the Contessa dell'Alba, that Tamarisk's parents had not approved this journey from England; that doubtless they did not approve the marriage and that Tamarisk's impetuous dash to the English coast was, in effect, a planned elopement which had miscarried.

After Tamarisk had bathed and changed into borrowed clothes, her hostess tried to elicit from the girl the lineage of Sir Peregrine Waite. But Tamarisk dared not supply any information other than to say that he was a lifelong friend of her mother's and frequently in attendance at Court. Lady Lushington's curiosity was aroused. She was not greatly reassured to learn that Sir

Peregrine was a close friend of the poet Percy Shelley. He, despite his subsequent marriage to Mary Godwin, had put himself outside the circle of social respectability when he left his first wife to live with her.

But her husband had worse fears than for Sir Peregrine's respectability or social status. He was concerned for the man's life.

As he had promised Tamarisk, Sir Henry made her *au fait* with the current political situation in Italy insofar as it might have a bearing on her future husband's whereabouts. Ferdinand, the Bourbon King who now sat upon the throne of the two Sicilies, he told her, did so uneasily. The Italian people had been too long oppressed and, as in France during the Revolution and currently in England, were in revolt against their domestic oppressors. Furthermore, King Ferdinand was weak and afraid of revolution. He had felt it necessary to court the support of the Austrians who, since the defeat of Napoleon, were virtually in control of Italy. The people therefore had as a further reason for unrest their resentment of this foreign domination.

Secret societies were growing in number, Sir Henry told her gravely. They were formed with the object of liberating the people. Chief of these societies was the *Carbonari*. The members were sworn to secrecy on enrollment in a manner not dissimilar to that of the Freemasons. Like other such societies, it was badly organized and achieving little that was effective. Recently a number of English aristocrats had involved themselves as leaders and supporters of the *Turba* — the name given to the mob of workmen who, for the most part, formed the societies' members.

"Lord Byron, for one, is involved with the revolutionaries in Romagna," he explained to the attentive Tamarisk. "There have been uprisings there and in Lombardy and Piedmont and, quite recently, here in Naples too, though it came to nothing. I believe it to be within the realms of possibility that Sir Peregrine has become likewise involved. An Englishman was here two months ago in search of a friend of the Shelleys who had joined the Neapolitan *Carbonari*. Perhaps Sir Peregrine was on the same mission?"

Or was he that Englishman! thought Tamarisk, her heart racing as she posed the question to Sir Henry. But he shook his head.

"He was not of that name, I am certain," he replied. "Nor did the gentleman I speak of have a title."

Tamarisk's cheeks were now burning with excitement.

"Was it by chance a Mr. Gideon Morris?" she asked breathlessly.

Sir Henry and his wife looked at their young guest in astonishment.

"Why, yes, I think it could have been!" said the Consul. "A tall, dark-haired man? A little younger than I, perhaps . . . ?"

"A handsome man!" interposed his wife. "With a charming smile!"

"I am certain it was he!" said Tamarisk as feverishly she searched her mind for a plausible

604

reason why Perry should have used an alias. "Sir Peregrine is an author," she invented glibly. "And it is not unusual for him to adopt his pseudonym, Gideon Morris, when he wishes to travel incognito."

"Then I will institute inquiries at once," said Sir Henry, satisfied by Tamarisk's explanation. "But I feel it my duty to advise you, my dear, that it may be extremely difficult to trace this gentleman. The recent revolt by the *Carbonari* was ruthlessly put down; many were killed and the survivors fled back to the mountains. I heard they intended to seek refuge in Potenza."

He saw the whitening of Tamarisk's cheeks and quickly added:

"You must not worry until there is known cause! Meanwhile, you are more than welcome to remain here with us. My wife will take care of you, and if there is anything at all you need, you have but to ask!"

The Lushingtons proved to be kindness itself. But as day succeeded day with still no news of Perry, Tamarisk's spirits sank ever lower. Sir Henry established very speedily that he had signed the passport of a Mr. Gideon Morris on the tenth of January. But it was now the twelfth of March. If Perry had been involved in the *Carbonari* uprising — and Tamarisk could well believe that such an adventure was much to his liking — then either he had not survived or, a less painful possibility, he had removed himself far from Naples.

In either event Tamarisk was unable to go in search of him herself as her heart dictated.

Sir Henry had made it a condition that he would only enlist the help of his informers if she gave her word to remain quietly with his wife and young daughter. He had appointed himself Tamarisk's guardian and, despite her pleas, would not permit her to visit the Romany camp. Not unsympathetic to her wish to repay the Yonesti for their many kindnesses, he did, however, dispatch a servant with a generous monetary gift from his own pocket as a reward for their care of the young English girl.

Unbeknownst to Tamarisk, Lady Lushington discovered the truth as to her ordeal at the hands of the merchant, Signor Galvanti. Elsie had made friends with Lady Lushington's English maid and indiscreetly disclosed the truth. Lady Lushington considered whether or not it was her quasi-maternal duty to raise the subject with Tamarisk, but her husband dissuaded her.

"You cannot undo the harm the poor child suffered at the hands of that rogue!" he said sagely. "And since Tamarisk herself has made no mention of it, then one must assume she is trying to wipe the memory from her mind. I will, however, send word to the Consul in Piedmont so that he can take warning of the man's perfidy! What a terrible experience for a young girl!"

His admiration for Tamarisk's courage increased although his disapproval of her dangerous escapade was in no way lessened. It distressed him personally the day he learned the bad news that he must pass on to her. He considered that she had suffered quite enough already.

As he feared, Tamarisk looked to be on the point of fainting when he gathered the strength to inform her that her future husband, Gideon Morris, was dead.

She stared at him disbelievingly.

"I do not believe it! I do not believe it!" she gasped as he led her to a chair. "Tell me it is not true, Sir Henry; that there is some mistake!" She looked at him in helpless appeal.

"I fear there is little doubt as to the veracity of this intelligence," he said regretfully. "My informant has proved himself in the past to be most reliable. However, lest there be any cause for doubt, he gave me this . . ."

He held out a gold repeater watch. Tamarisk made no move to take it from him but stared at it, her face white and stricken, her eyes wide with horror.

"It was taken from the dead man," Sir Henry continued gently but remorselessly, for there seemed little point in allowing the girl to hope when none existed. "Perhaps you can identify it?"

As Tamarisk continued to stare speechlessly at Perry's cherished timepiece, Sir Henry had his answer.

Tamarisk's thoughts had winged back to the past: to her childhood when she had sat upon Perry's lap whilst he held the gold watch to her ear so that she might listen to the chimes; to her girlhood when she and Perry had ridden together in the parkland surrounding Finchcocks and he had looked at this same watch face and, smiling at her, said: "Time to go home, Princess!"

607

She recalled that wonderful masquerade ball when he had sat holding her hand until late into the night and had withdrawn his timepiece from his pocket saying with regret: "'Tis long past midnight, Cinderella. Time you were abed!" Now she could never hope to see that lovely smile again; nor hear his deep, affectionate voice; nor feel the miraculous, safe warmth of his arms around her shoulders.

Oh, Perry! Perry! Perry! she thought. I cannot bear it!

Her sense of loss was beyond tears. Stunned to a cold, bitter numbness, she allowed Lady Lushington to lead her away to her bedchamber so that, alone in her room, she could come to terms with her grief.

For several days she neither ate nor spoke. Elsie came to sit beside her and informed her that the Lushingtons were sending them both back to England. Tamarisk was indifferent to the news.

"What matters it now?" she said bitterly. "I care not what becomes of me!"

"To think we came all this way for naught!" Elsie wept in sympathy, remembering with horror the fears and rigors of their journey. "That old gypsy, Miarka, was right after all! She said as how you would not get wed until after another sea voyage!"

"I will never wed now — *never!*" Tamarisk said quietly and turned her white, thin face back into the softness of her pillow.

A week later, on the twenty-sixth of March, the Lushingtons escorted Tamarisk and Elsie to the harbor and handed them over to the care of their friends, Lord and Lady Greensmythe. The middle-aged couple were sailing back to England in His Majesty's frigate *Voyager*.

As the frigate glided slowly out of the beautiful sunlit Bay of Naples, Tamarisk stared back at the magnificent mount of Vesuvius, a dark silhouette against the blue Italian sky. Now, suddenly, she discovered she could cry. Quietly the tears welled from her eyes and cascaded down her cheeks from which the golden tan had almost faded.

Elsie came to stand behind her.

"Never mind, Milady dear!" she attempted to console her young mistress. "We will be home soon and this'll seem like some fantastical dream!"

A dream that can never come true now! Tamarisk thought. As for home, she dared not think about her reception or even if her parents would permit her to live with them again.

Tamarisk knew nothing of the letter Lady Lushington had given to Lady Greensmythe to hand in person to her mother.

'*Whatever your daughter may have done to cause you worry or offense, my dear Vicomtesse,*' she had written, '*I feel it incumbent upon me to tell you that she has endured more than most women do in a lifetime, and with great courage and fortitude. If punishment of any kind was deserved, then she has already suffered it.*

'*Despite what has transpired in Tamarisk's*

young life, I consider her to be a charming, sweet, brave girl whom I myself would be proud to call my daughter. She will always be a welcome guest in our house . . . '

The writer penned those words in the hope that they would ensure Tamarisk's welcome. She was unaware that by the time it reached Barre House the Vicomtesse de Valle would be at death's door and that it was doubtful if she would live to see her daughter again.

30

1820 – 1821

LORD and Lady Greensmythe insisted upon accompanying Tamarisk to her home in London although they themselves were bound for their country estate in Derbyshire. Lady Greensmythe had been gentle and kindly in her care of her young charge throughout the month's journey across the seas to England. Now, sensing Tamarisk's apprehension at the approaching confrontation with her parents, she volunteered to be the first to announce her arrival at Barre House. She still had about her person the letter from Lady Lushington for Tamarisk's mother.

But the Vicomtesse, the butler informed Lady Greensmythe when she requested an interview, was unable to receive visitors; indeed, no visitors were welcome in this house. Only the day before, old Lady Danesfield had died, the Vicomtesse was not expected to survive the night, and even her baby son was dangerously ill.

"Is there no one here to receive me?" Lady Greensmythe asked with a sinking heart as she listened to this sorry tale of misfortune.

"The Vicomte de Valle is at home, Milady, but he will not leave the sickroom," was the butler's reply.

Lady Greensmythe returned to the carriage.

As gently as she could, she broke the news to Tamarisk but without stating that her mother was dying.

"Doubtless your stepfather will be pleased to have your support at such a time!" she said, glad at least for this possibility.

Tamarisk hurriedly gathered her gloves, parasol, and reticule whilst the coachman took her boxes from the roof of the carriage.

"We shall stay overnight at the Pulteny Hotel," Lady Greensmythe added, "and you are to send word to me, my dear, if there is anything I can do to be of assistance."

The mood of despair which had engulfed Tamarisk since learning of Perry's death was quickly replaced by her anxiety for her family and an impatient desire to see them all again. The news of the death of poor Aunt Clarrie did not distress her unduly, for the old lady had lost her will to live when her beloved husband died. But Tamarisk was deeply affected to learn that her mother was dangerously ill; and the chubby, healthy little baby John too!

With only the briefest of farewells and thanks to her kindly traveling companions, she hurried into the house.

The bright April sunshine filtered only fitfully through the heavily draped windows. The great house was hushed and filled with gloom and smells of camphor and other medications. The few servants busy about their domestic tasks spoke only in whispers and moved on tiptoe to dull the sound of their footfalls.

Fear striking deep into her heart, Tamarisk

threw down her gloves, removed her pelisse, and ran up the stairs.

Her mother's bedchamber seemed at first to be filled with people. As her eyes took in the scene, Tamarisk noted with dismay that there were two doctors in attendance and a white-aproned nurse. Dorcas stood quietly by the window. Her father sat beside the bed, his eyes never leaving the face of the unconscious figure lying there. That face, framed by a mass of white pillows, was covered with a dark red rash. For a moment Tamarisk did not recognize her mother. But then another figure seated by the far side of the bed leaned forward and said in a deep, fierce voice:

"I dunnamany times I told 'ee, Mavreen, I doant intend nohow to sit here and watch 'ee die. I justabout had enough of waiting for 'ee to adone this nonsensical nonsense, surelye! Taint no use thinking as how I'll let 'ee die no more than what I would in that there Russia. You're agoing ter get well and get shut of this here sickness!"

"Dickon!" Tamarisk whispered, the sight of him shocking her into full realization of the seriousness of her mother's condition. Faithful old servant though he was, Dickon would not be in this bedchamber unless her mother was dying.

At the sound of Tamarisk's voice, Gerard turned his head. He gazed at his daughter with eyes that seemed deeply sunk in their sockets. Wearily he rose to his feet and came forward to greet her, the faintest of smiles showing about

613

the lines of his mouth.

"Why, my dear child, what a happy surprise!" he murmured.

Tamarisk would have flung her arms about him and hugged that gaunt figure, but Gerard held her at bay. Taking her by the hand, he drew her out onto the landing.

"The physicians think it unwise for one to approach another too closely in this house," he said in a quiet, exhausted voice. "We have typhus here, I am afraid to say. Your Aunt Clarrie died last night. Her heart failed beneath the strain of the fever and she lacked the will to live. Your little brother is very ill and your mother . . . "

His voice broke and tears filled his eyes.

"Typhus!" Tamarisk echoed. "But Papa . . . "

"I know!" he broke in. "I will explain everything to you, but first let us go to the morning room, for I have quite a long story to tell you."

When she was seated beside him on the sofa, Gerard related to his daughter the horror of the past few weeks.

"It is really I who am to blame for everything!" he said unhappily. "Your mother and I were not reconciled even after you had left to marry the man who . . . " He faltered but picked up his story again. "Your mother was lonely and renewed her friendship with Mistress Fry. She, as you know, has spent many years of her life campaigning for better conditions for female prisoners. Your mother became interested in this charity, and when Mistress Fry described

614

to her the terrible conditions in which those wretches were imprisoned within the rotting hulks of the old men-of-war, she determined to go there to verify these stories for herself. It was her intention to try to enlist the sympathies of our more influential friends if she found Mistress Fry's account to be accurate."

He looked at Tamarisk with unseeing eyes as he repeated a few of the horrors Mavreen had related to him upon her return from the prison hulks.

"Your mother's sympathy for those miserable, starving women was deeply aroused," he said. "But that was not all! There was an infant in that horrifying place — a child of our John's age, and starving. He was as skeletal as our son was rounded with good health and your mother found the comparison unbearable. She brought the child home since it was an orphan, its mother having died of the fever some three weeks earlier."

His eyes blazed suddenly with anger.

"The ship's captain should not have permitted it!" he said. "But he was glad to be rid of the miserable little orphan, and your mother paid him well in her ignorance of the dangers of such action."

Tamarisk listened in growing dismay as her father continued. Two days after the child had been put with little John in the nursery, it produced all the symptoms of typhus. Such was its state of emaciation, it died just over a week later despite the care Mavreen and Aunt Clarrie lavished upon it. Although it had been bathed and given clean clothing immediately upon its arrival in the house, nevertheless the typhus disease was passed on. On the eighth of April Mavreen, Clarissa, and the baby all developed the telltale symptoms.

Somehow Tamarisk found the strength to ask the question:

"Will Mama die?"

Her father covered his face with his hands and groaned. "I do not know, Tamarisk. This is the fourteenth day and the time when the crisis is reached. I sent for Dickon because your mother called out his name so many times in her delirium. I think she is living in the past!" Gerard seemed to have forgotten that he was talking to his young daughter as he added painfully, "It is as if she has no will to live. Dickon has sensed this too and is doing his best, poor fellow! There seems nothing I can do, for she cannot — or will not — recognize me!"

Aware of the pain he must be suffering, Tamarisk took her father's hand and pressed it to her cheek.

"Do not abandon hope, Papa!" she said softly. "You must know as well as I do that Mama never gives up easily. She will not submit to death without a fight!"

"You do not realize that this fight is not like those others in her past. Then, she risked everything, dared anything in that brave, tenacious way of hers, because she was convinced I loved her." Near to despair, Gerard cried, "Now she is certain that I do not love her, and it is my fault entirely that she doubts me.

But I do love her — with all my heart!" His voice broke as it trailed into silence.

Tamarisk waited until he had composed himself. Then she said gently:

"Have you told Mama how you feel?"

"I have tried, many times! But she is quite unconscious and does not hear me. I cannot bear it if she dies without first forgiving me!"

"Forgiving you, Papa?"

Gerard looked at his daughter with eyes that clearly revealed his agony of mind.

"I belittled her love for me — our love for each other!" he cried. "I failed to trust her, believe in her. I even accused her — God forgive me — of bearing a child that was not mine!"

Now at last Tamarisk understood the reason for his bitter torment. As if she were suddenly become the parent and her father the child, she said firmly:

"You were wrong to doubt her, Papa. I know her to be innocent! Perry — Sir Peregrine himself told me the truth about their relationship. He loved Mama and would have married her had she been willing. *But Mama loved only you*! As for baby John, he is your child, Papa, and my brother."

"I know that now!" Gerard moaned, wringing his hands. "In the first week of her delirium your mother often talked — rambling, unconnected sentences, but sufficiently coherent for me to understand her meaning. Does it not strike you as strange, Tamarisk, that my doubts were both evoked and destroyed by a woman's delirious words?"

617

A servant came running into the room — protocol abandoned in the urgency of the message to be delivered.

"You are to come at once to the sick chamber, Sir!" the maid gasped. "The Vicomtesse's condition has changed and the doctor said for to fetch you as quick as ever I could!"

In an agony of fear, father and daughter hurried up the stairs. Dorcas, now kneeling at the foot of the bed, was weeping noisily. One of the physicians stood with his hand on Mavreen's forehead. But on Dickon's freckled face there was a broad grin. His hand about Mavreen's wrist, he said:

"She be mending!" He looked from Gerard to Tamarisk with a beaming smile. "Her's getting tedious cold!"

"Cold?" Tamarisk echoed. "But . . . "

"The man is quite correct!" interrupted the physician. "When the crisis comes, the temperature of the body falls very rapidly. Within a few hours we can expect our patient to regain intelligence!"

Ignorant as he was of the early childhood of the Vicomtesse, he was by no means happy to have this servant, Dickon, behaving in a manner more befitting a relative of the family. He had only permitted Dickon's presence in the sickroom because the Vicomte had insisted most adamantly that Dickon alone might be able to revive life in the dying woman. The doctor neither understood nor approved this request but resigned himself to the belief that all foreigners were capable of strange behavior

618

and that Gerard, a Frenchman, behaved more oddly than most.

By the following morning Mavreen was conscious. Although too weak for conversation, she smiled first at Gerard and then at Tamarisk, whose presence seemed not to surprise her. Within days her strength began to return, her recovery made certain by Gerard's untiring devotion.

All was now well between them, and to prove his faith in Mavreen, he himself brought the baby to her room so that she could rest assured that the child too was recovering from the illness that had ended poor Clarissa's life.

"Our son is out of danger!" he said, this final acknowledgment of the little boy being all that Mavreen needed to ensure her slow but certain recovery.

At first Tamarisk withheld the news of Perry's death, fearing that her mother was not strong enough to suffer even the most minor of upsets. But as Mavreen's strength began to return, so did her natural curiosity as to the events in her daughter's life. When finally she learned of Gideon's untimely death, her heart grieved sorely for this loss of her dearest friend. She grieved too for Tamarisk. Unbeknownst to her daughter, she had perused Lady Lushington's long, informative letter and therefore knew the story of Tamarisk's unfortunate adventures in Italy.

Tamarisk's sad, pale countenance distressed Mavreen deeply. She longed to comfort her, but Tamarisk's manner precluded all discussion about Gideon or her suffering at the hands of the evil Italian, Galvanti. From Dorcas, Mavreen learned that Tamarisk was making her bedchamber into a shrine to Gideon's memory. His silhouette was displayed on a table and fresh flowers were put before it every day. Beside it were his gold repeater watch and all the presents he had ever given her in her childhood. She declined any suggestion made by Mavreen or Gerard that she should accept invitations from their various friends to entertainments and excursions that were being arranged for the young people. Although it seemed as if she had resigned herself to her loss, she was clearly unable to overcome her grief.

As the days passed and Tamarisk spent long hours at her mother's bedside, they began to develop an intimacy that had never previously existed in their relationship. They discovered themselves conversing as two close friends rather than as mother and daughter.

On one such afternoon they were alone whilst Gerard paid his fortnightly visit to Antoine at the house of Princess Camille. The room was suddenly filled with the sound of a horn as a coach bowled down Piccadilly on the start of its journey with the mails to Bath. Tamarisk's heart lurched painfully as the sound transported her back to the night she had first discovered her love for Perry. How alert her senses had been that night to the sights, smells, and noises all around her! How vividly she recalled the sound of the coach horn as they crossed Oxford Street!

Her eyes filled with unexpected tears. Seeing them, Mavreen reached out and took Tamarisk's hand in hers.

"Try not to be sad, my darling!" she said softly.

"Oh, Mama, I loved him so very much!" Tamarisk said brokenly. "When I heard Perry was dead, there seemed no point in my continuing to live. When I returned home to find you so ill and poor Papa in such distress, I realized that Perry was not the only person in the world I cared about. But much as I do love you and Papa and little John, life seems so meaningless without Perry."

Mavreen was silent for a moment whilst she pondered her reply. She too had loved Gideon but not with Tamarisk's youthful obsession. He had been her friend but was always Tamarisk's idol.

"He would not wish you to grieve for him!" she said quietly. "He always wanted you to be happy, Tamarisk, and would wish it now!"

"Yet he never asked me to marry him!" Tamarisk replied. Seeing her mother's look of surprise, she added with a bitter smile, "I wanted you to believe he had asked me to marry him, but he never did. I followed him to Italy because I hoped he would discover that I was a grown woman, and since you were beyond his reach, that he would accept me in your place." She smiled wanly. "That was presumptuous, was it not, Mama? I could never be your equal however much I tried to emulate you!"

Now Mavreen could speak without hesitation.

"I am grateful for your compliment, my darling, but you are mistaken in your reasoning. You are far more like me than perhaps you realize — as foolhardy in your impulsiveness, as violent in your loving, as daring in your pursuit of love. We both feel, do we not, that death is the only negative we can bring ourselves to accept? And even that is not easy for us to accept without a fight. I, for one, do not blame you for going to Italy to discover whether the man you loved returned your affection. I admire your courage, for I believe very strongly in that old proverb: 'Nothing venture, nothing win.' I regret only that you suffered as you did."

Tamarisk bit her lip.

"I doubt I shall ever recover now from that horrifying experience," she said quietly. "I cannot bear the thought of any man's proximity. I think I would have overcome such abhorrence if . . . if I was in Perry's arms. I trusted him — and he was always so gentle with me!" She sighed. "Mayhap I have learned one good lesson from so much evil — that the sufferings of the body are nothing in comparison with the sufferings of the mind!"

Mavreen nodded her agreement, for Gerard had recently made the same comment when speaking of the dreadful agony of mind he had suffered believing her about to die before he could beg her forgiveness. Their joy in one another was now absolute. If on very rare occasions she was saddened by thoughts of Gideon's untimely death, she would not allow them to linger in her mind but gave all her strength and energy to regaining her health and restoring her marriage. Their reconciliation had brought them closer than ever before.

There was to be no such happy reconciliation between Royal husband and wife. When news reached the Princess of Wales of the death of her father-in-law, King George III of England, she at once made plans to return from Italy. When she arrived at Dover, she was greeted by thousands of cheering subjects, but her husband, the new King of England, was conspicuous by his absence. He had already stated that he had no intention of crowning her Queen. Such was his unpopularity, however, that he was obliged to postpone his own crowning until the summer of the following year.

By then Mavreen was more than fully recovered. Her newfound happiness with Gerard brought peace and contentment that were all the tonic she needed for perfect restoration of her health. At Christmas they had celebrated their daughter's twenty-third birthday and had received a surprise visit from young Charles Eburhard. He was still unmarried and determined to remain so, he told Mavreen and Gerard, until such time as Tamarisk accepted his proposal.

But Tamarisk had rejected him yet again, and although she appeared to enjoy his company she was clearly no closer than she had ever been to considering the faithful Charles as a possible husband.

In July baby John celebrated his third birthday. He, like Mavreen, had fully recovered his health and strength and now possessed the energy of a child far older in years. He had also developed an unusually strong determination to have his own way. Gerard, his pride tinged with amusement, called him *'mon petit Empereur!'* But Mavreen was not too pleased with this title, however apt its meaning, for news had just arrived in England of the death of Napoleon in May. Alone, a prisoner on the remote island of St. Helena, he had suffered a long time from a painful recurring illness to which he had finally succumbed.

"It saddens me to think of that once so powerful man brought to such an end!" she said. And suddenly smiling at Gerard, she added, "You may call our young tyrant after the Duke of Wellington instead, or after Lord Nelson, if you prefer!"

The Baroness, still vigorous and as busily engaged as ever in her round of social activities despite her seventy-five years, and as ready with the latest gossip, spoke knowingly of the circumstances in which France's former Emperor had died. His incarceration had led to hepatitis the year previously, she related, but although painfully thin and depressed, he had continued to dictate his memoirs.

"He wished to leave an accurate record of his life for posterity," she said. "It will make interesting reading, I dare swear!"

Sadly Napoleon's last dictation was a letter to his wife, Marie Louise, telling her that his heart and his love were hers only. He had requested that his heart be sent to her after his death but she, so it was rumored, had refused it.

"Which is just as well!" remarked the unsympathetic Baroness, "since she most certainly did not deserve it!" And she turned the conversation to her plans to be present at Prinny's coronation on the nineteenth of the month.

"Queen Caroline is as determined to be present as Prinny is to keep her away!" chuckled the Baroness.

Not a week later she was back at Barre House relating how the Queen had arrived at Westminster Abbey but had been refused admittance. As she left, the excited mob had shouted and hissed at her.

"I felt deeply sorry for her!" the Baroness concluded, "for I hear that this incident has finally broken her spirit and that she is now seriously ill!"

Although this gossip proved to be true, the Queen did make one final appearance at Drury Lane to applaud Edmund Kean in the part of Richard III; but a week later, on the seventh of August, she died in great pain. To the King's consternation, she had asked that her body be transported to Brunswick for burial.

"He fears that there may be demonstrations by the people on the route the funeral cortège would take to Harwich," said the Baroness shrewdly.

Tamarisk looked distressed.

"Doubtless the King is rejoicing at his wife's death!" she remarked bitterly. "Did you hear, Baroness, that when Napoleon died and the

King was told of the death of 'his greatest enemy,' he replied: 'Is she, by God!' Even if this be untrue, no one can deny he loathed his wife. But whatever the rights and wrongs of her conduct, she was ever kindly to me and I shall send flowers as a mark of respect."

The government ordered that the cortège should not, as planned, go through the City but go directly from Hammersmith to Chelmsford. Gerard saw no reason, therefore, why he should not pay his usual fortnightly visit to Antoine at Princess Camille's house in Warwick Lane.

Since his reconciliation with Mavreen, they had talked frankly about the boy. Despite her secret misgivings, Mavreen had offered to have Antoine home. But Gerard decided to leave his son with the Princess, not merely because he seemed exceptionally contented there, but because Gerard now felt he had been unfair to expect Mavreen to welcome the child some other woman had borne him. He regretted that he had lacked the sensitivity to anticipate her feelings. It was a matter of some concern to Mavreen that Gerard was still unable to see anything but good in his son, so making it impossible for her to explain that it was the child himself she objected to rather than the circumstances of his birth.

Gerard's mood was one of perfect happiness as he drove off in the gig to visit his son. The August sun shone down upon him with agreeable warmth as he turned his horse's head. His day was well planned, he thought, for after luncheon he, Mavreen, and Tamarisk had arranged to take John to see the swans and ducks on the Serpentine River in Hyde Park. The little boy adored his 'Papa' and made no secret of the fact that Gerard was his favorite visitor to the nursery.

The child still bore no resemblance to him or to his family; but now Gerard found himself delighting in the little boy's striking resemblance to his beloved Mavreen. The baby blue of John's eyes had changed to the selfsame hazel-green as Mavreen's and always shone with the same lovely smile of welcome. His long curls were corn gold and he glowed with good health. His nurses adored him despite his mischievous nature and they proudly informed his father that he was quite fearless.

Gerard, therefore, was without a care in the world as he guided his spirited horse along the thoroughfare toward Warwick Square. There seemed suddenly to be an unusual number of people about, increasing as he neared Ludgate Hill. Here he met with a congestion of carriages and carts which halted by vast congregating crowds. From a nearby coachman Gerard learned that despite Government's orders that the Queen's funeral cortège should not be driven through the city, a mob of demonstrators had put obstacles across the road and forced the procession to go toward Temple Bar. Even now as Gerard watched, the cortège crossed Ludgate Hill on its way to the Essex Road.

Suddenly a shout rose from amongst the milling crowds. Two men, locked in a private quarrel, staggered into the road in front of

627

Gerard's horse. The startled animal whinnied and then rose on its hind legs. Terrified by the close confines of the carriages and people surrounding it, the frightened gray attempted to bolt. Desperately Gerard gripped the reins. But now the horse's hooves slipped on the cobbles. Before Gerard could jump clear, the horse in its helpless confusion fell sideways, overturning the gig.

It was but a matter of minutes before two men secured the animal's head and a dozen more lifted the gig upright. But the man beneath lay motionless. The excited onlookers fell silent as the coachman to whom Gerard had spoken earlier bent down to listen for a heartbeat.

Hushed now, the crowd watched and waited. Some saw the lips of the injured man move and the whisper grew to a murmur of relief as word passed around: "He lives!"

But even as they began excitedly to discuss the possible extent of Gerard's injuries, the coachman stood up, removed his liveried jacket and respectfully covered Gerard's lifeless face.

A woman screamed. She was promptly hushed lest her noise brought about another accident. A gentleman, Sir Robert Wilson, stepped down from his carriage and himself helped the coachman to lift Gerard's body into his own vehicle. He had no need to search Gerard's pockets for identification, for he had recognized him instantly as the Vicomte de Valle.

"To Barre House as soon as you can extricate

628

us from this mêlée!" Sir Robert instructed his driver.

But it was more than half an hour before the crowds which had gathered to see the passing of the Queen's coffin dispersed sufficiently for them to take Gerard's body home.

31

February – May 1822

"'TIS six months since your Papa died!" the Baroness said to Tamarisk. "If your mother continues to grieve in this manner she will be seriously ill!"

The old lady and the young girl were alone together in the morning room.

"I know!" Tamarisk agreed unhappily. "But nothing seems to stir her. All day long she sits by the window in her bedchamber staring down into the garden. But she sees nothing. Her thoughts are elsewhere — in the past. Neither Dorcas nor I can make her eat more than enough to keep her alive. She neither reads nor talks unless the conversation is about Papa. She receives no one — not even her close friends."

The Baroness nodded, her wrinkled little face creased with lines of concern. She patted Tamarisk's hand sympathetically.

"It must be hard upon you, child!" she said. "At your age you should be enjoying life — going to parties and balls and finding yourself a husband. How old are you, dear? Twenty-four?" Her faded blue eyes twinkled. "You should be married, my girl, lest you miss your chance and find yourself on the shelf!"

Not that the Baroness believed such a thing possible. In the first place she knew that her

630

nephew, young Charles, was determined to take Tamarisk for his wife even if he had to wait another ten years. The rascal had told her so! But in the second place, even if Charles was not handsome enough for the girl's taste, she had grown into a very lovely young woman and would not lack for suitors once she came out of mourning for her poor Papa.

The events of Tamarisk's young life had given her an unusual wistful beauty. She seemed to combine a girlish innocence with the subdued passions of a unfulfilled woman. Looking at her, the old Baroness was reminded of Mavreen at the same age. She sighed. No wonder young Charles was so taken by the girl! But she had not come to Barre House today out of concern for Tamarisk's future but for Mavreen's.

"I have tried everything that I can think of to bring Mama to take some interest in life!" Tamarisk was saying despairingly. "But it is to no avail!"

When the first shock of Gerard's sudden death was over, Tamarisk hoped that little John would afford some comfort to her mother. But, strangely, Mavreen had turned against the little boy.

"I do not wish to see him!" she said in a dull, lifeless voice when Tamarisk first brought the child to her. "He does not look in the least like his father!" she added, tears filling her eyes. "Gerard wanted him to be a de Valle, not a Danesfield!"

"But Mama, Papa loved John!" Tamarisk

cried. "He took the greatest pride in him and . . . "

"Take him back to his nurse!" Mavreen interrupted. "The child does not need me! And I do not wish to be disturbed by his chatter."

The shock of Gerard's sudden death, coming after her near-fatal illness, had proved too much for Mavreen. For a month she had lain in a darkened room whilst the doctors feared for her sanity.

Before succumbing to the full severity of her grief, Mavreen had ordered that her husband's body be taken to France and laid to rest in the graveyard where his mother and father were buried.

"He loved Compiègne. It was always his spiritual home!" she announced when she made this decision. "I shall go with him!" But she was too ill to travel with the coffin, and it had fallen to Tamarisk, with Dickon to help and comfort her, to lay her father to rest. On her return home she had tried to raise Mavreen from her abyss of grief by reminding her constantly of the last words her father had spoken before he died and which Sir Robert had faithfully recounted:

"Mavreen . . . surveille-toi Antoine!"

But although this dying request to Mavreen to watch over his elder son did move her to pay one call upon the Princess Camille, it was only to learn that the French woman had departed the country at the end of August, taking Antoine with her on a prolonged sojourn to foreign lands. She had dismissed her servants. The elderly caretakers Mavreen and Tamarisk questioned said that they did not expect the Princess to return for at least a year — perhaps longer! She had left no forwarding address.

"Then there is nothing more I can do!" Mavreen said, and returning to Barre House began her self-imposed vigil by her window.

Various of her friends called to offer their condolences, in particular Mistress Elizabeth Fry who tried to offer the comfort of religion. But her mother seemed beyond comfort, Tamarisk now told the Baroness. She confessed her secret fear that her mother might even be willing her own death in order to be near her father again in another world.

The kindly old lady nodded her head thoughtfully.

"I believe there may be a remedy," she said slowly. "Just now you spoke of something your Mama said about the child John . . . that he had no need of her?"

Tamarisk sighed.

"And I fear 'tis true! John's nurses care for him most excellently. And I see him every afternoon. He progresses very well and is most advanced for a child not yet four."

"*So there is no one who needs your mother, eh?*" commented the Baroness pointedly. "John does not. You are grown up now and do not. But . . . " her walnutlike face screwed up in a grotesque wink, " . . . but you, Tamarisk are not going to feel at all well on the morrow. The doctors will prescribe a change of air, but you cannot bring yourself to contemplate a holiday alone. You are not well enough. Do you follow

633

my meaning?" she asked. "You, my dear girl, are about to become so weak and helpless that you are greatly in need of mothering."

"I doubt Mama will listen to the doctor's suggestion," Tamarisk said.

"But she will listen to me because I shall insist upon it," said the Baroness. "'Tis one of the few advantages of old age that politeness demands your Mama does not dismiss me if I enter her room unannounced. I shall tell her this very afternoon that I am most concerned about you. I shall tell her that it is her duty to stop thinking about the dead and turn her attentions to the living lest she be responsible for your *imminent decline!*"

Tamarisk smiled wanly.

"It would do no harm to try," she said doubtfully, "although I am loth to add myself to her worries!"

"But that is exactly what is required!" cried the old lady, rising stiffly to her feet. "Now go and find some chalk to rub on those rosy cheeks of yours. You look far too well to play the part I have designated for you!"

It took a further two weeks and the month of March was nearly at an end before the Baroness's ruse succeeded and Mavreen agreed to accompany Tamarisk to The Grange to take the benefit of the country air. Together with the nurse and John but with no other servants, the family drove down to Sussex to a loving welcome from Dickon and Rose.

Reluctantly Mavreen had agreed that they should dispense with the wearing of mourning attire when they left London. She did so only because the Baroness had persuaded her that these dark, depressing clothes were in part responsible for Tamarisk's melancholy.

Despite Mavreen's conviction that she would never again find joy in living things, she discovered herself stirred by the familiar sights and sounds and scents of the Sussex countryside. Spring was in its full glory, the hedgerows a delicate green. Primroses, cowslips, and dog violets were growing in great profusion along the roads and lanes. In the garden of The Grange, daffodils and azaleas, bluebells and polyanthus, foxgloves and jasmine, forget-me-nots and borage were flowering in haphazard abandon. The leaves of the great oak tree beyond the rose garden were still enfolded in yellow-green buds. But the swallows had not yet arrived to vie with the blue tits, robins, nuthatches, and goldfinches fighting for places to build their nests.

Like Mavreen in her early childhood, her little son John now shadowed Dickon as he discovered this budding new world of nature, his chubby legs struggling to keep up with the grown man as Dickon went about his tasks — chopping wood for the cooking stoves, supervising the stableboys in their care of the horses, throwing corn to the chickens. Best of all, the child loved to collect the big brown speckled eggs from the nesting boxes.

Every evening Dickon related the day's adventures to Mavreen.

"You justabout should've seen your little lad

635

this arternoon! That there old skinny-looking cockerel did chase arter him and the poor leetle Master John shruck till he could shruck no longer!" he recounted the story, grinning. "I done fixed a leetle bow and arrer for 'en and tolt him he best shoot that unaccountable bad old bird next time he runs arter him!"

But although Mavreen listened dutifully, it was without real interest. She sat each afternoon in the garden, looking about her, listening with that same remote disinterest. When the child came running to her, she nodded, ran a hand absentmindedly over his tousled curls, but did not turn her head when he ran off in another direction in pursuit of a butterfly or a bird or because he had caught sight of Dickon, Tamarisk, or Rose on his horizon.

But one day, a month after her return to The Grange, Mavreen was seated with Tamarisk in the garden. She looked up as the sturdy little boy came hurrying toward them. On his rosy face was a look of bewilderment.

"Mama! Mama!" he stammered in his haste to form the words. "There is a strange animal sitting in the tree!"

Mavreen made no effort to follow the line of his small pointing finger.

"Mama!" He tugged at his mother's arm impatiently.

Tamarisk looked up from her embroidery. Not ten feet away, on a low branch of the great oak tree, she caught sight of the little rust-red animal which had attracted the child's attention.

"Why, that is a squirrel, John!" she informed him. "Is it not pretty?"

The boy stared for a moment and then raised the little bow Dickon had made for him. He was about to attempt the task of inserting an arrow as Dickon had taught him, when his arm fell suddenly to his side.

"No! I will not kill it!" he announced. His rapt little face glowed with pleasure as the tiny animal sat up upon its haunches and began to wash its face with two miniature hands. "Look! Mama! Look!" he cried in delight.

To Tamarisk's astonishment Mavreen's arms suddenly reached out and drew the child to her in a rare gesture of affection. She bent her head so that her cheek lay softly against his, and said tremulously:

"In France a squirrel is called an *écureuil*, John. Your father would not kill one either! He used to call me . . . "

She broke off as tears suddenly poured down her face. Small sobs burst from her throat. The child, perplexed, eased himself from her arms and ran away across the lawn.

Tamarisk knelt beside Mavreen and held her mother in her arms as now, at long last, she found relief in tears.

"Oh, Mama, do not cry, I beg you!" Tamarisk pleaded, near to tears herself as she witnessed for the first time in her life her brave, courageous mother succumb totally to grief.

The child had run to Dickon in his distress and now Dickon came hurrying across the lawn. He stared down at Mavreen, his face thoughtful, his eyes full of wisdom as he said softly to Tamarisk:

"She'll get better now! 'Tis best thing for her to cry!" He put his arm around Mavreen and, with Tamarisk assisting, led her slowly toward the house. "And doant 'ee start wailing, young lady," he added with a grin at Tamarisk. "One's enuff, surelye!"

Dickon's prognosis was proved correct. Mavreen began almost at once to regain her interest in life. Not two days after her collapse, Tamarisk discovered her in the parlor playing the piano. She had not touched the instrument since the day of Gerard's death when she had sat at the Broadwood in the music room at Barre House writing the score for the little French song 'Vert-Vert,' which Gerard so loved to hear her sing. As her mother's voice sang softly now in accompaniment to her playing, Tamarisk remembered the horror of the moment when Sir Robert had come into the music room and told them that Papa had met with a fatal accident.

"It cannot be so!" Mavreen had cried. "I have just started writing 'Vert-Vert' for him. No, you are mistaken, Sir. I promised to sing this for Gerard as soon as he comes back!" Her mind, distorted by shock, refused to accept that the husband she loved so dearly was really dead.

Now, at last, Mavreen was able to put the nightmare behind her and begin to live in the present once more. She began to ride again and she and Tamarisk spent many hours on horseback, Mavreen delighting in visiting with her daughter places they both loved — the Downs; Firle Beacon; the fields around her first home, the Sales' farmstead. She was deeply concerned to discover the worsened conditions that prevailed there. Dickon's younger brother, Henry, explained as best he could the trough of depression into which the country's agriculture had descended. Common pastures had been enclosed by the landed gentry, denying the farmers valuable grazing. In addition they had withdrawn the strips of land on parish fields which many husbandmen used not only for grazing but as a source of fuel and manure.

As the farmers became poorer, they could no longer afford to fence and drain their fields and were forced to sell some or all of them to richer neighbors. Nor could they poach for food since the old poaching grounds were now enclosed. To be caught doing so meant transportation; and a single blow delivered to an apprehender invoked a penalty of death by hanging.

Men — good honest men and friends of the Sales — had been killed by spring guns whilst poaching for their starving families; some had been caught in mantraps. At least one fifth of the villagers and farmers were receiving some form of parochial relief.

"Last year's harvest," Henry informed Mavreen, "was a lamentable waste of a year's work, for there was no profit to it, the price of corn being what it is."

Mavreen sent urgent letters to London to inquire if anything could be done. Her old friend, Mr. Wilberforce, wrote back to tell her that Mr. Brougham had asked Parliament to take action to relieve the distress. There were changes in the Cabinet, he said, and duties were to be lowered on wheat, salt, and leather.

With every sign of her old energy and spirit, Mavreen sat talking with Tamarisk late into the evening about the need for reforms and how pleased she was to think that they might soon become a reality.

"The Whigs won the day last summer with their support for the poor unfortunate Queen Caroline!" she remarked. "So now the Tories have been forced to consider reforms lest they lose the opportunity to continue in government. We may see great changes soon, Tamarisk. They cannot come soon enough! They are needed everywhere — and not least by those who were seeking them at Peterloo. Never again should there occur such horrors as I saw that day with Dickon."

Not only was Mavreen's interest in politics renewed but so was her interest in her son and in Tamarisk's future.

"It is time we found a husband for you, my darling!" she said. "It shocks me to realize how selfish I have been this past year. I have given no thought whatever to my children's happiness, so lost was I in my own misfortunes!"

"I am by no means as unhappy as I was, Mama!" Tamarisk replied, gently: "You are most excellent company now that you are well again; and I love it here at The Grange!"

Mavreen looked at her beautiful young daughter anxiously.

"You are not still grieving for Gideon — Perry?" she inquired.

"I shall never forget Perry!" Tamarisk admitted openly. "And I shall always love him." She looked away from Mavreen, her eyes betraying the confusion of her thoughts. "After my experience at the hands of Signor Galvanti," she said hesitantly, "I feared all men. I hoped and believed Perry would be able to overcome my fears. He was always so understanding of my problems. But now he is dead . . ."

Her voice broke off in mid-sentence, her words leaving Mavreen strangely uneasy. Until now she had not realized how deeply Tamarisk was scarred by her misadventure in Genoa.

"Perry would not want you to grieve for him. You must look to the future. There are others you could love — if not in the same way as you loved poor Perry."

"Even if such a man existed, I could not bear to lie with him!" Tamarisk murmured.

"You must not be afraid," Mavreen said softly. "If you are lying in the arms of the man you love, you will think of no other."

Yet even as she voiced this innermost conviction, she recalled that this was not always so. There had been many times when, lying in Gerard's arms, she had thought of Gideon. She had loved Gerard with every fiber of her being. Yet when she had learned of Gideon's death, she had felt as if some secret part of herself had died too. Was it possible, she asked herself, to love two men, not equally but differently? But the answer mattered not, she thought, for both

Gerard and Gideon were dead and she must learn to live with her happier memories of them. It was not her future but Tamarisk's that was important now. When the summer was over, and they returned to Barre House, she would start entertaining again.

Now, at last, Mavreen was able to face the fact of Gerard's death. She knew that the total occupation of her mind was the only way to keep grief and loneliness at bay. Deliberately she renewed her former interest in books and music; brought herself up to date with the world's events. Her health improved and she was even heard to laugh again — to Dickon's and Tamarisk's delight.

Tamarisk had no fear in leaving her mother alone upon occasions. She struck up a friendship with Dickon's sisters, Patty and Anna, and, like Mavreen before her, made plans for a bigger and better school for the village children. She paid frequent visits to the Sales.

It was now the month of May and as the weather was so pleasantly warm after the long winter, she chose to be outdoors as often as possible. For the past five days, Charles Eburhard had been a house guest and Tamarisk was aware that it pleased her mother to see the two young people enjoying each other's companionship.

It was on one such afternoon, while Tamarisk and Charles were paying a visit to Owlett's farm, that Dickon entered the room where Mavreen sat alone contentedly reading Sir Walter Scott's new novel *Ivanhoe*. She had not heard the arrival of a carriage in the driveway and was surprised when Dickon announced that she had a visitor who desired to remain nameless.

There was a strange look on Dickon's face which puzzled Mavreen more than the identity of the caller whom she supposed might be the parson.

"I explained as how you'd been tedious ill and was not receiving," Dickon said, "but the gentleman said as how he would not likely stay long unless you wanted and it was important you receive him, seeing as how he had come a tedious long way."

"Very well!" Mavreen agreed, putting down her book reluctantly. It was a perfect spring evening, the air soft and sweet, the dew falling gently amongst the young leaves and on the newly scythed grass. The birds were busy about their evensong and her mood was relaxed and contented. "Show the gentleman in, Dickon. And bring the decanters and goblets too, will you? If he has come far he may be in need of refreshment."

Still Dickon made no move to go. His voice hesitant, he said:

"He's come from a good long ways away — from Italy!"

Mavreen looked up in surprise. Was her visitor then someone from Tamarisk's past? Lord Greensmythe? Il Conte dell'Alba? Sir Henry Lushington? Perhaps even Mr. Percy Shelley with word of poor Gideon's unfortunate fate.

"Show the visitor in, Dickon!" she said again.

She was suddenly stirred by an irrational certainty that it was indeed none other than Mr. Shelley who was calling upon her and that she was about to receive news of Gideon. Her heart beat in a combination of curiosity and apprehension. She was by no means sure if she was strong enough to hear tales, if they were unpleasant, of the death of the man who was once her closest friend. Gideon had seemed to haunt her memory of late — a fact which had not surprised her, for no one had been closer to loving, as she did, Sussex in springtime. Like Dickon, he knew where every kind of bird nested; where to find the cuckoo when it called; what animal rustled in the undergrowth; how to tread the woods so silently that even the deer and the badgers could not hear his coming. He could tickle trout, track any animal. He knew as well as Dickon where to go to watch the hares at their mad March gamboling; where to poach pheasant or rabbit; where to look for the cruel gin traps which he always destroyed, believing that there were many kinder ways for a man to kill if he was hungry. He knew where to find every species of herb and how best to use each one for curing sickness. And as for horses — not even Dickon could judge them so well.

But that was all past, she thought as Dickon returned, holding open the door for her visitor. The visitor, leaning heavily upon an ebony stick, came forward from the hallway. Now suddenly she understood why Dickon had regarded her so anxiously, spoken so hesitantly. He had known her caller's identity would be a shock to her.

"Gideon!" Her lips shaped his name.

Her shock was twofold. Not only had Gideon appeared from the dead, but he looked so ill and frail — Gideon, whom she had last seen upright, broad of shoulder, abounding with good health and well-being! As he came toward her, he limped heavily. His shoulders were bent at an awkward angle as he used his stick for support. His face was pale, lined, drawn with fatigue.

As Gideon led her to the sofa, he too was suffering from shock. Mavreen's loss of weight frightened him. The great hazel-green eyes seemed to have grown larger in her thin, pale face. Her hands were like frail white birds as he sat himself awkwardly beside her and took them in his own.

"Oh, Gideon!" she murmured, half laughing, half crying. "You cannot know how pleased I am to see you!"

"Or I you!" Relieved to see the color coming back to her cheeks, he smiled down at her as he added, "I have only just learned from Dickon that you believed me dead! Otherwise I would have written first to advise you of my visit! As you can see, I am no ghost!"

"But you look so ill!" Mavreen protested.

Gideon tapped his leg lightly.

"I am suffering from the aftereffects of a serious leg wound," he explained. "It happened a long time ago and I believed myself quite recovered. But last year, whilst in Switzerland, I slipped on some mountain rocks, reopened the wound, and contracted a poisoning of the blood which laid me lower even than the wounding

645

itself. But I am better now; the leg is healing and I'll not need this confounded crutch much longer! And you, Mavreen, you are recovering your health too, Dickon tells me."

"Yes, 'tis true, I am much better. Every day I grow stronger. But before we talk of my misfortunes this past year, I must know how it is you are alive! Your death in Italy was reported not as a rumor but as a fact! We heard from the British Consul in Naples that . . . that your body had been found and identified by your gold repeater watch. 'Twas known to the Consul that you were involved with the *Carbonari* in the regions of Naples."

"Perhaps it would be best for me to recount my adventures in Italy from the time of my arrival there," Gideon said. "That is, if it would interest you to hear of them."

Mavreen smiled, the color now fully restored to her cheeks.

"You know that I am agog with curiosity!" she said. "Do not keep me longer in suspense."

"Then I will satisfy that eager curiosity of yours," Gideon replied, his voice gently teasing as he added, "for I have not forgot how impatient is your nature!"

When he had gone to Leghorn two years ago, he related, it was with the intention of cheering his friend Shelley after the death of the child who was his own godson. But he arrived only to discover that the Shelleys had been comforted by the birth of another son.

"They were preparing to move to Pisa," Gideon continued his story, "and all was well

646

with them both except for the fact that one of their closest friends, a young Italian aristocrat, was long overdue from a mission to Naples. A member of the *Carbonari*, the fellow's life was known to be very much at risk. Having nothing better to do, and rather enjoying the prospect of some adventure, I offered to go to Naples and search for him."

"At risk to your own life!" Mavreen exclaimed.

Gideon smiled in mock reproach.

"Nay, Mavreen, none knows so well as you what excitement is to be had by putting one's life in danger!" he exclaimed. "So to Naples I went. I did not find Shelley's friend, but if you know anything at all about the conditions of the working classes in Italy, you will understand how I became interested in their cause. I joined one of the many secret societies and became a member of the *Carbonari*. I took part in one of the unsuccessful uprisings in Naples. We were without adequate arms and far from well organized. In a very short while we were chased into hiding in the hills outside Potenza."

He looked at Mavreen anxiously.

"I am not tiring you?" he asked solicitously.

She shook her head.

"On the contrary, I cannot wait for you to tell me the end of your story!"

"There is a deal more to relate," Gideon said. "For although our revolt was most effectively put down, I could not bring myself to abandon my comrades and return to Pisa. It was obvious to me that we badly needed money for arms if ever I could hope to reorganize the survivors.

But I had been wounded in the leg and could not travel north myself to seek financial aid. I sent a man, Pietro, in my name. He was to have called upon Shelley to ask if he could raise funds for arms. I gave Pietro my only possession — my gold repeater watch — so that Shelley would know the request for money came from me. I heard later that Pietro was killed soon after he left our camp, but I did not know what had become of my watch."

Mavreen stole a quick glance at Gideon.

"Then you do not know that Tamarisk has it in her possession? That it was given to her by the British Consul, Sir Henry Lushington?"

"Tamarisk?" Gideon repeated, astonished. "But how so? I do not understand!"

As briefly as she could, Mavreen recounted Tamarisk's adventures from the time she too had left England. Only when finally she came to the end of her tale did Gideon speak. His eyes were dark with distress as he said:

"I had no inkling of all this! What can I say, Mavreen, to convince you that I gave the girl no encouragement, no reason whatever to suppose that I loved her other than as a child; far less reason to suppose that I would marry her! And to think that she endured so much . . . "

Mavreen quickly covered Gideon's hand with her own.

"You must not blame yourself," she said. "I suspect that she hoped to force your hand by following you to Dover."

Gideon smiled.

"I have always maintained the girl was as

648

determined as her mother!" he said. "I loved her for her resemblance to you and perhaps she read more into those feelings I did have for her than I ever intended. Mavreen . . . " he hesitated, searching her face for signs of fatigue before he went on, "I have more to tell you. I too have a daughter. Does it surprise you? Those months when I was living rough with the *Carbonari* in Potenza, I was cared for by a Neapolitan girl whose husband had been killed in the fighting. She was very good to me. I think she loved me in her simple way, and I became fond of her. In November — nearly two years ago now — she bore me a child. It was a little girl whom we called Lucia because she was born at break of day, that being the meaning of the name. By March of the following year — last year — I had had no word from the Shelleys and the *Carbonari* were disbanding following a series of further defeats. My leg was mended and I decided to take little Lucia with her mother to the Shelleys in Pisa. I could not leave them alone in the hills unprotected and without the means of survival. Unfortunately, whilst the child survived the journey northward, her mother died of milk fever. I had no alternative but to put my daughter into the care of Mary Shelley, who most kindly offered to act as foster mother."

"Oh, Gideon!" Mavreen broke in. "I do not know if you wish me to be pleased or sorry; but for my part, I am delighted to hear that you are a father! You were always so good with Tamarisk!"

"But not much good with a four-month-old infant!" Gideon replied, laughing. "So I decided to take a prolonged sojourn to Europe. As you know, my last visit when hastening after you to Russia left me no time to see any of the sights. I went to Vienna, to Munich, to Switzerland — where I came near to dying — and finally to Paris. It was there, by the most extraordinary piece of good fortune, I found myself at the gaming tables seated next to a delightful old French gentleman by the name of the Marquis de Guéridon!"

"The Marquis!" Mavreen exclaimed. "He was a great friend of Gerard's father and . . . "

"When he discovered that I knew you and Gerard, he told me all the family history," Gideon interrupted. His eyes suddenly serious, he added, "He also told me of Gerard's death. I decided to come straight back to England instead of returning to Italy as was my intention. Mavreen, I cannot express how deeply sorry I was to hear about Gerard! Fate could not be more cruel than to take your husband from you when you had waited so long to be together!"

To her surprise Mavreen discovered that she could talk to Gideon of Gerard's death without difficulty, without tears.

"You were wont to tell me that I did not truly love Gerard," she said, "but it was as if life itself was blotted out the day I learned of his death. We were so perfectly happy together that year before he died."

Gideon stood up and limped away from her to the window. He stared out into the gathering twilight and said thoughtfully:

"I had no right ever to set myself up in judgment of your feelings! I think it was only jealousy that made me voice an opinion I was not qualified to give. Love is not something which can be quantified, evaluated, compared. It is, after all, an emotion felt by human beings, and who can say if any two people ever feel exactly the same about anything. I believe now that you did love Gerard; that a part of you will always love him. No woman ever proved more steadfast and enduring than you in your affection for him. I am happy for you both that your days together before he died were so idyllic. But if he loved you, which I do not doubt, he would not wish you to grieve indefinitely for him."

He turned and came back across the room, seated himself beside her, and took one of her hands, holding it tightly between his own.

"What Gerard must have loved most about you, Mavreen — as indeed do I — is your magnificent zest for life. To imprison that vitality behind self-imposed barriers would be to destroy your very self. You are still a young woman, a very, very beautiful woman, and I, for one, will not stand by and see that life wasted. You must not retire from life's merry-go-round."

Mavreen stared back at Gideon, her eyes confused.

"I am forty-two years old!" she said. "I have a little son to whom I must devote my remaining years, and Tamarisk too to care for — at least until she marries."

To her surprise Gideon threw back his head and laughed.

"Forgive my amusement, Mavreen!" he said, his eyes still sparkling. "Especially since your maternal sentiments are admirable, to say the least. But you cannot really believe one young child will fulfill your every need. When you are fully restored to health, you will require a companion who can satisfy you intellectually as well as physically. If you think otherwise, then I must claim to know you better even than you know yourself! You will still need to love and be loved when you are twice your present age."

"That I will not!" Mavreen argued, frowning. "Love brings nothing but pain in its wake. I want no more loving in my life!"

There was no smile now on Gideon's face as very gently he released her hand and put his arms around her. Slowly his face came down to hers, nearer and nearer until she could see her own reflection in the dark pools of his eyes. Then his lips touched hers in a long kiss of such loving tenderness, it seemed to Mavreen as if her heart was melting.

"Gideon! Gideon!" she murmured, her arms reaching to his head where silver now threaded the dark brown curls. "It has been so long . . . I have been so lonely . . . and I am terribly confused. Suppose that I cannot love again?"

Now he was smiling again as he interrupted her in a firm, vibrant voice:

"I was ever one to enjoy the taking of a risk, Mavreen, and in this instance I feel the odds are very much in my favor." He smiled his gentle teasing smile. "Come now, admit that you always did love me — just a little?"

Suddenly she too was smiling.

"A little, yes! But Gideon . . . !"

"No 'buts,' Mavreen. Do you remember, many years ago, when I pointed out to you the dangers that might threaten were you to join me in my highway escapades? You laughed and said: 'I care not one jot for what *might* be, Gideon. If I did, I would have no excitement in my life. I beg you, Gideon, to allow me to accompany you . . . and devil take the consequences! I swear I shall not blame you if I live to regret it.' Do you remember, Mavreen?"

She nodded, surprised that he had recalled that conversation so accurately.

"Then trust me with the future — your future and mine!" he said. He laced his fingers through hers, joining them by this simple gesture. "Know you this couplet, my Mavreen?" He smiled as he quoted: *"A mighty pain to love it is, and 'tis a pain that pain to miss!"*

Now she was laughing and crying at once. As he rocked her in his arms, his cheek warm and rough against her forehead, she felt for the first time since Gerard's death as if she had an anchor again. Gideon, she thought, had the oddest understanding of her. Mayhap he really did know her better than she knew herself! If he had tried today to persuade her with passion, with that same violence he had used the first time he had declared his love for her, she might as easily have revolted against his physical dominance as once she had succumbed to it.

But he had led her gently, with tenderness and humor, to an understanding of herself and her dormant need for warmth, love, life itself. She had not, after all, died with Gerard, although she had many times wished it. Gideon made her feel that there was a future; convinced her that neither time, distance, nor the passing of years had lessened his love for her.

It was twelve long years since Gideon had first declared himself, insisting that she was as much a child of nature as he and that they belonged together. "'Tis only with me you can be your true self — wild, headstrong, passionate, without restraint," he had said then. And now she knew it to be true. Without fear of disloyalty to Gerard's memory she admitted the truth to herself — that she had had to control that side of her nature which never pleased her husband and which was the cause of his mistrust of her.

She smiled at Gideon, her heart at ease.

"I too can quote from the past," she said. "Do you remember promising me that you would cease to play the dandy when I agreed to marry you?"

Gideon laughed.

"I do . . . and I will! But it might not be easy, Mavreen. I cannot ever reveal that I am Gideon Morris, a man with a price upon his head. You would have to marry Sir Peregrine Waite, and whilst marriage might well reform that tiresome dandy, I fear you could take little pride in bearing his name."

Mavreen smiled.

"It seems a small price to pay for your safety,"

she said softly. "And to me, you will always be Gideon Morris."

"Then 'tis agreed!" Gideon said contentedly. "In any event I had determined to build a new life for myself because of my daughter. I would not wish her to grow up believing her father to be a fop." He looked at Mavreen anxiously. "I had thought to leave her with the Shelleys until she was old enough to be sent to a convent. I met Lord Byron in Italy who told me he was well pleased with the Convent of San Giovanni Battista in Bagnacavallo where he has placed his four-year-old daughter by Claire Clairmont. It was my intention to return to Italy and reside there. But . . . "

"But I need you here in England!" Mavreen broke in, smiling. "And 'twould seem you need a mother for your daughter, Gideon, and I need a father for my son."

"Then 'tis agreed we shall marry!" Gideon cried.

Mavreen's eyes darkened with sudden distress.

"In our concern for our future, we have forgotten Tamarisk!" she cried. "I had begun to believe our marriage was possible, Gideon, *but it cannot be*. I cannot deal Tamarisk a further blow! 'Twill be shock enough to find you still alive. Oh, she is well enough! The natural resilience of youth has restored her to full health long since. But I fear time has not helped her to forget you. On the contrary, she has enshrined your memory."

She looked at him anxiously.

"News of your death, coming as it did

after her ordeal at the hands of that vile Genoese, must have put a terrible strain upon her mind. Fortunately she was living with kindly people; and mayhap the severity of my illness which confronted her on her return to England helped to divert her thoughts from her own unhappiness. In any event it brought us close again. There was a time when I think she hated me because of the way you loved me; but once she knew you were beyond her reach — or mine — that resentment vanished. We are now the best of friends and I cannot bear to hurt her again."

Gideon's eyes were thoughtful.

"What would you have me do, Mavreen? To remain a memory cannot be the solution, more especially if, over the passage of time, Tamarisk has persuaded herself that the affection she had for me was the one true love of her life. Yet if I 'return' from the dead and *do not love her*, that too will hurt her even if I keep silent as to my love for you. And time is not on our side, Mavreen. We are neither of us young. The years left to us are infinitely precious. I need you *now*. I want to make you my wife *now* — not at some distant date in the future."

"I know! I understand!" Mavreen cried, taking his hand and holding it against her cheek. "But I am loth to shatter Tamarisk's dreams." She glanced anxiously at the clock upon the mantelshelf. "She will be back very soon now. Charles Eburhard has taken her to visit the Sales at Owlett's Farm. You remember the young lieutenant, Gideon? He is on leave and, as happens every time he is back from his ship, he called to ask Tamarisk to marry him."

Seeing the look of hope on Gideon's face, she shook her head.

"She has told me she will never accept him, that she could never love him, or any man, as she loved you. She believes you were the only one who could have overcome her fear of the proximity of men — the fear resulting from her raping in Italy."

For a few moments Gideon said nothing. Then he stood up, drawing Mavreen to her feet, his eyes indicating his resolve.

"'Tis best we tell Tamarisk the truth," he said quietly. "No happiness was ever derived from deceit. Moreover, I do not believe I could hide from her my love for you even if I wished. You must trust me, Mavreen. I am certain 'twill be better for her to face up to life. Mayhap it will hurt her very deeply. But somehow a kindly way must be found to disillusion her. 'Tis not the loss of my love for her that will be hard to bear; she must know full well it was never hers. No, 'tis the loss of *her* love for *me* which she will find hardest to relinquish, for this is the substance of her dreams. Tamarisk must finally face reality, as must we all if our lives are to have any lasting worth."

"So we must now be cruel in order to be kind!" Mavreen said sadly. "'Twill not be easy to break her heart a second time."

"'Right wrongs no man'!" Gideon quoted. "Come, my dearest, let us go to meet her.

Together we will find the courage to do what must be done."

He picked up his ebony walking stick and leaning heavily upon it, he led her slowly through the French windows into the garden.

32

May 1822

OUTSIDE the house, the soft spring air was filled with the evensong of the birds. A faint breeze stirred and rustled in the leaves of the trees, and a light dew lay upon the grass like a faint covering of frost.

As Tamarisk came through the garden gate from the field, Charles looked anxiously at her thin slippers.

"You will catch cold!" he said solicitously.

Tamarisk laughed.

"Fiddlesticks!" she cried. "Let us take off our shoes, Charles. I like nothing better than to run barefoot!"

Without waiting for his reply she bent to remove her shoes and then, holding on to his arm for support, rolled down her stockings.

Charles sighed, even as his heartbeat quickened at the sight of Tamarisk's slim white ankles. He wished despairingly that she would not treat him always as if he were a brother, albeit a beloved one. But she would only accept his company on such a level.

"You are my dearest friend," she said, "and we have the greatest amusement together. Do not spoil it, Charles, with talk of love."

She seemed to have no idea how much it hurt to realize that she considered his unwavering devotion to her must spoil her pleasure. During the past five days, they had ridden out together, walked, talked about everything under the sun. She had even permitted him to hold her hand. But although she freely admitted that she was fond of him, that they were excellent company for one another and agreed on most matters they discussed, she was adamant in her denial that these were perfect grounds for marriage.

"Love is all that matters in marriage!" she declared. "And I do not love you in the way you want, Charles. It would not be fair to you if I were to pretend otherwise. I wish I *could* love you!"

She voiced this wish with such regret that he did not doubt it was true.

"So there is someone else?" he had asked inevitably.

"Not any longer!" she replied, her eyes filling with tears. "But there was someone once whom I loved with all my heart. He is dead and I shall never see him again. But I cannot stop loving him. Can we not remain friends, Charles? There is no one whose company I enjoy more than yours. I am happy to be with you. Will that not suffice?"

With such small compensation he was trying to be content. But it was not easy for him. He had loved Tamarisk faithfully for nine years. He was now twenty-seven years old and had traveled to most countries in the world yet never found another girl he could love as he did Tamarisk. Not even her confession about her past — made no doubt to discourage

660

him — had lessened that love. If anything, it had added another dimension, arousing as it had a desire to protect her from further misfortune. He bitterly condemned the unnamed man who had taken advantage of her youth and innocence and left her with child. As for the despicable Italian merchant, Charles had every intention when next he visited Italy of seeking him out and killing him. And he understood now why Tamarisk avoided any close contact with him. Each day he tried with gentle persistence to encourage her to overcome this fear. Now, of her own accord, she kissed his cheek before they all retired to bed at night.

He watched her with an ache of longing as she danced away from him barefoot across the lawn, her eyes bright with laughter as she challenged him to catch her. With sudden determination he removed his boots and stockings and ran after her, his long strides swiftly covering the distance between them.

As he caught her in his arms and swung her off her feet, she clung tightly to him. She was breathing deeply, her cheeks flushed, her eyes shining.

"Oh, I am so happy!" she said impulsively. "It has been such a lovely day, Charles!"

She made no demur as he bent his head and touched her lips with a featherlight kiss. As he set her down upon her feet, he kept his arm around her waist and she leaned against him as they turned in the direction of the house. Dusk was falling. Purple shadows hung beneath the trees. Rose must have lit the candles in the house, for faint orange glimmers shone from the casements.

Someone was coming through the French windows — a dark silhouette in the open doorway.

"I think your Mama is coming to search for us!" Charles said with an anxious glance at Tamarisk's thin gown and bare feet. "She will be angry with me for not taking better care of you!"

"She has somebody with her!" Tamarisk exclaimed. Suddenly she halted, a small cry escaping from her lips. "It is Grandpapa!" she gasped.

"But Sir John is . . . " Charles broke off, unwilling to remind Tamarisk of the death of her much loved relation. But Tamarisk had already realized her mistake. The shadowy figure walking toward them leaning on a cane, so closely resembled that of her grandfather that it was not surprising she had mistaken one for another.

"'Tis some stranger," she murmured, shivering involuntarily and longing suddenly for the warmth and light of the house. She was glad when Charles's arm tightened around her.

"Perhaps we should put on our footwear," he suggested. But the figures approaching them were now much nearer and he heard Tamarisk catch her breath at the same moment as he saw the color drain from her face. "What is it?" he asked. "What is wrong, Tamarisk?"

"I am seeing a ghost!" she whispered, the nails

of her fingers digging into his hand. She was trembling violently.

No! Tamarisk thought. It cannot be Perry — my Perry! I must be taking leave of my senses. Perry is dead. My tall, strong, handsome Perry. It cannot be! *It cannot be!*

She stood rooted to the spot, only Charles's support preventing her from falling to the ground as faintness overcame her. But as if she were living a nightmare, the two figures continued to come closer, her mother's now perfectly recognizable; her stooped, gray-haired companion a terrible parody of the man Tamarisk loved — a distortion of the memory — a lie. It had to be a lie!

"Hold me, Charles!" she whispered. "Hold me tightly!"

He did as she asked, remaining silent whilst he waited for this inexplicable drama to reach its conclusion. He could not know that this stranger approaching them was the man who had stood so long between him and the girl he loved; nor guess the depth of the shock she had received in mistaking him for her beloved grandfather. He had no way of knowing that her youth was denying the cruel advance of age. He could only sense her horror as her dreams shattered into fragments.

Desperately Tamarisk tried to steady her kaleidoscopic thoughts; to put them into some measure of order. Perry was alive! And with Mama! He would know of her journey to Italy to find him. He would know how deeply and faithfully she had loved him. At any moment he would approach her — he was moving as fast as his limp permitted — and with a grateful smile upon his deeply lined face he would hold out his arms to her and tell her how much he needed her; how blind he had been never before to recognize the magnitude of her love . . .

She thought of the strength of Charles's arms as he had lifted her down from the farm gate; the ripple of his back muscles when he swung her up into the saddle; of his slim thighs as he strode across fields that were yellow with buttercups, young John perched on his shoulders, laughing to be carried so effortlessly high above their heads. She remembered how youthful Charles had seemed as he turned somersaults in the hay for John's amusement. She recalled on the afternoon when he had worn, for the benefit of the farm children, his smart blue naval uniform, with its rows of gold buttons on the tailcoat, the gold lace on the cuffs and lapels glinting in the sun. She liked him so very much; respected and admired him. She had even felt regret that she could not love him as she had once loved Perry, realizing that he would make the gentlest of husbands, the kindest of fathers.

Now Perry was here, walking toward her, a ghost from a past which suddenly seemed a million years away — part of a half-forgotten childhood, the living substance of her dreams. He was near enough now for her to see the loving smile of greeting in his eyes.

But she felt no joy — only a frantic, unreasoning fear. She did not want to spend her life caring for a sick, old man. She wanted

664

to ride, to dance, to run barefoot on the wet grass the way she and Charles . . .

Her body tensed into rigid immobility as her mother and Perry covered the last few yards between them. Gideon held out one hand, the other grasping the cane supporting him.

"Hullo, my little Princess!" he said. "I hope my resurrection has not frightened you unduly. How young and pretty you look, my dear. I'll swear time has stood still these past few years, for they most certainly have not aged you!"

Tamarisk's eyes took in the wings of gray at Perry's temples, the lines of suffering about his mouth and eyes; her ears took in the sound of his deep, affectionate voice; her hand felt the unexpected strength of his even whilst she noticed the gnarls and veins that reminded her once more of her grandfather. Her heart melted with love for him. But it was a new love — a love heavy with pity. Slowly she turned to look at her mother whose gaze was centered upon the man beside her. In her eyes too was a look of love but with no sadness in it. There was only a radiance, an unmistakable joy.

Suddenly the tension was gone. Tamarisk took a step forward and with childish abandon flung her arms around Gideon and hugged him.

"It is so wonderful to have you home!" she cried. "I am so happy. 'Tis like a miracle, for now you can meet Charles. He and I . . . we are . . . we . . ."

Sudden understanding transfigured Charles's face.

"I have asked Tamarisk to marry me!" he said,

"and I think this time she will not refuse."

He drew her gently away from Gideon, taking her hand and holding it determinedly in his own.

Tamarisk let it lie there, like a small symbol of dawning hope, warm and safe at last.

THE END

BERLIN GAME
Len Deighton

Bernard Samson had been behind a desk in Whitehall for five years when his bosses decided that he was the right man to slip into East Berlin.

HARD TIMES
Charles Dickens

Conveys with realism the repulsive aspect of a Lancashire manufacturing town during the 1850s.

THE RICE DRAGON
Emma Drummond

The story of Rupert Torrington and his bride Harriet, against a background of Hong Kong and Canton during the 1850s.

FIREFOX DOWN
Craig Thomas

The stolen Firefox — Russia's most advanced and deadly aircraft is crippled, but Gant is determined not to abandon it.

CHINESE ALICE
Pat Barr

The story of Alice Greenwood gives a complete picture of late 19th century China.

UNCUT JADE
Pat Barr

In this sequel to CHINESE ALICE, Alice Greenwood finds herself widowed and alone in a turbulent China.

THE GRAND BABYLON HOTEL
Arnold Bennett

A romantic thriller set in an exclusive London Hotel at the turn of the century.

SINGING SPEARS
E. V. Thompson

Daniel Retallick, son of Josh and Miriam (from CHASE THE WIND) was growing up to manhood. This novel portrays his prime in Central Africa.

A HERITAGE OF SHADOWS
Madeleine Brent

This romantic novel, set in the 1890's, follows the fortunes of eighteen-year-old Hannah McLeod.

BARRINGTON'S WOMEN
Steven Cade

In order to prevent Norway's gold reserves falling into German hands in 1940, Charles Barrington was forced to hide them in Borgas, a remote mountain village.

THE PLAGUE
Albert Camus

The plague in question afflicted Oran in the 1940's.

THE RESTLESS SEA
E. V. Thompson

A tale of love and adventure set against a panorama of Cornwall in the early 1800's.

IN HIGH PLACES
Arthur Hailey

The theme of this novel is a projected Act of Union between Canada and the United States in order that both should survive the effect of a possible nuclear war.

RED DRAGON
Thomas Harris

A ritual murderer is on the loose. Only one man can get inside that twisted mind — forensic expert, Will Graham.

CATCH-22
Joseph Heller

Anti-war novels are legion; this is a war novel that is anti-death, a comic savage tribute to those who aren't interested in dying.

THE ADVENTURERS
Vivian Stuart

The fifth in 'The Australians' series, opens in 1815 when two of its principal characters take part in the Battle of Waterloo.

THE DOGS OF WAR
Frederic Forsyth

The discovery of the existence of a mountain of platinum in a remote African republic causes Sir James Manson to hire an army of trained mercenaries to topple the government of Zangaro.

THE DAYS OF WINTER
Cynthia Freeman

The story of a family caught between two world wars — a saga of pride and regret, of tears and joy.

REGENESIS
Alexander Fullerton

It's 1990. The crew of the US submarine ARKANSAS appear to be the only survivors of a nuclear holocaust.

SEA LEOPARD
Craig Thomas

HMS 'Proteus', the latest British nuclear submarine, is lured to a sinister rendezvous in the Barents Sea.

THE RIDDLE OF THE SANDS
Erskine Childers

First published in 1903 this thriller, deals with the discovery of a threatened invasion of England by a Continental power.

WHERE ARE THE CHILDREN?
Mary Higgins Clark

A novel of suspense set in peaceful Cape Cod.

KING RAT
James Clavell

Set in Changi, the most notorious Japanese POW camp in Asia.

THE BLACK VELVET GOWN
Catherine Cookson

There would be times when Riah Millican would regret that her late miner husband had learned to read and then shared his knowledge with his family.

THE WHIP
Catherine Cookson

Emma Molinero's dying father, a circus performer, sends her to live with an unknown English grandmother on a farm in Victorian Durham and to a life of misery.

SHANNON'S WAY
A. J. Cronin

Robert Shannon, a devoted scientist had no time for anything outside his laboratory. But Jean Law had other plans for him.

THE JADE ALLIANCE
Elizabeth Darrell

The story opens in 1905 in St. Petersburg with the Brusilov family swept up in the chaos of revolution.

THE DREAM TRADERS
E. V. Thompson

This saga, is set against the background of intrigue, greed and misery surrounding the Chinese opium trade in the late 1830s.

THE SUMMER OF THE SPANISH WOMAN
Catherine Gaskin

Clonmara — the wild, beautiful Irish estate in County Wicklow is a fitting home for the handsome, reckless Blodmore family.

THE TILSIT INHERITANCE
Catherine Gaskin

Ginny Tilsit had been raised on an island paradise in the Caribbean. She knew nothing of her family's bitter inheritance half the world away.

THE FINAL DIAGNOSIS
Arthur Hailey

Set in a busy American hospital, the story of a young pathologist and his efforts to restore the standards of a hospital controlled by an ageing, once brilliant doctor.

THE COLONISTS
Vivian Stuart

Sixth in 'The Australians' series, this novel opens in 1812 and covers the administration of General Sir Thomas Brisbane and General Ralph Darling.

THE TORCH BEARERS
Alexander Fullerton

1942: Captain Nicholas Everard has to escort a big, slow convoy . . . a sacrificial convoy.

DAUGHTER OF THE HOUSE
Catherine Gaskin

An account of the destroying impact of love which is set among the tidal creeks and scattered cottages of the Essex Marshes.

FAMILY AFFAIRS
Catherine Gaskin

Born in Ireland in the Great Depression, the illegitimate daughter of a servant, Kelly Anderson's birthright was poverty and shame.

THE EXPLORERS
Vivian Stuart

The fourth novel in 'The Australians' series which continues the story of Australia from 1809 to 1813.